Serena Davidson

About the Author

MYRLIN A. HERMES was "born in a trunk," as the saying goes. Her parents, eccentric world-travelers who had met in a 1960s San Francisco experimental theatre troupe, took their four-year-old daughter with them to live for a year on an ashram in India before settling on the island of Maui, Hawaii. Her father designed sets for the local children's theatre, and Myrlin grew up performing in its productions, cutting her teeth on Shakespeare's plays.

She graduated from Reed College with a double major in English literature and theatre, and her first novel, *Careful What You Wish For*, was published in 1999. In 2004, she moved to the UK to do historical research and study creative writing with poet laureate Andrew Motion, at the University of London (Royal Holloway). She has received grants and awards from the Institute for Humane Studies, the Arch and Bruce Brown Foundation, and the Arts Council England, and her poetry has appeared in the *Notre Dame Review*.

She lives in Portland, Oregon, where she is working on a novel based on the life of seventeenth-century playwright, spy, and proto-feminist rabble-rouser Aphra Behn.

The Lunatic,
the Lover,
and the Poet

ALSO BY MYRLIN A. HERMES

Careful What You Wish For

The Lunatic,
the Lover,
and the Poet

A NOVEL

Myrlin A. Hermes

HARPER ⬤ PERENNIAL

NEW YORK • LONDON • TORONTO • SYDNEY • NEW DELHI • AUCKLAND

HARPER ● PERENNIAL

THE LUNATIC, THE LOVER, AND THE POET. Copyright © 2010 by Myrlin A. Hermes. All rights reserved. Printed in the United States of America. No part of this book may be used or reproduced in any manner whatsoever without written permission except in the case of brief quotations embodied in critical articles and reviews. For information address HarperCollins Publishers, 10 East 53rd Street, New York, NY 10022.

HarperCollins books may be purchased for educational, business, or sales promotional use. For information please write: Special Markets Department, HarperCollins Publishers, 10 East 53rd Street, New York, NY 10022.

FIRST EDITION

Designed by Justin Dodd

Library of Congress Cataloging-in-Publication Data is available upon request.

ISBN 978-0-06-180519-6

10 11 12 13 14   OV/RRD   10 9 8 7 6 5 4 3 2 1

For my godfather, Herbert G. Miller (1939–1998),
and all my godfathers, lost and found.

The lunatic, the lover, and the poet
Are of imagination all compact:
One sees more devils than vast hell can hold;
That is the madman: the lover, all as frantic,
Sees Helen's beauty in a brow of Egypt:
The poet's eye, in a fine frenzy rolling
Doth glance from heaven to earth, from earth to heaven,
And, as imagination bodies forth
The form of things unknown, the poet's pen
Turns them to shapes, and gives to airy nothing
A local habitation, and a name.

A Midsummer Night's Dream, V.i.7—17

The Lunatic,
the Lover,
and the Poet

Prologue

Magicians and Messengers

Even the face you will remember is not her face at all, but only its reflection in the mirror: painted white, black lines inked in around her lowered eyes. She is not looking at you, because she is reading aloud from the book, which is open in her lap, as always, exactly halfway through.

The book is the key. You are certain of that. There are many books on her shelves, which in your childish memory seem to stretch forever up the walls—but this one she always grasps with a special tenderness, as if its leather binding were the skin of someone she loved.

"This one is your father's."

Your father: a myth, a mystery, a man who disappeared so long ago his story, too, might have begun with "Once upon a time . . ."

"If it was his, why didn't he take it with him, when he went away?" you ask her. Meaning "us."

She explains that the book had never belonged to your father that way. "Not his property, to own or keep, but still forever his, because he was the one who made it."

You consider this. "What did he make it out of?"

"Cheveril."

"What is cheveril?"

"A very stretchy kidskin—as stretchy as a man's wit, or a woman's conscience. As stretchy as the truth."

"And it is used for making books?"

She smiles. "For making gloves."

You smile, too, because you know this tale, your favorite fable: the one about the poor-but-clever lad, the glove maker's red-haired son. You can see him now: an affable familiar ghost who nightly gulls your gullible ear with strange intelligence. A feckless dreamer, blushing his freckles out, astonished by his great good luck—to be offered, for practically nothing (a skin stolen from his father's shop; his soul) a night with the courtesan, Lady Calliope, whom princes had traded their futures to seduce.

"But is that the true story?" you ask. "Was he really my father?"

She sets her stroking fingers now to soothe your tangled head. Sometimes she tells you no story is true. Sometimes she says they all are. Sometimes her eyes twinkle, and she spins a tale about an exiled scholar-spy, or an aristocrat's moonlit confessions—some fantastical romance of false fronts, misdirections, and conspiracies, true names concealed within cryptic encoded messages.

She is a magician, a messenger, conjuring her spirits out of breath, from air. "From thin air" comes the whisper in your ear. But it is not thin at all, but thick with words: rising around you, towers so tall they have no turrets but stretch ever into the sky; forests so dense and deep their pale inhabitants believe the sun to be a myth, and live their lives in a canopy of limelight, a world ever painted green.

"Our fathers are never what they are," she says, "but what we imagine them to be."

"Then where did he go?" Already half-asleep, you are still unwilling to leave your mother's voice, pouring you into dreams.

"He joined a troupe of traveling players and wandered the globe with them forever after." She snuffs the candle out, and with it the subject.

And something tells you: wherever your father has gone, it is not the sort of place where a person might ever be followed or found. He has disappeared into another world entirely—one infuriatingly near, and also impossibly far away.

What Is Carried Across

A translation. That is what the gentleman originally wanted, nothing more. The notice on the church door, if I recall it correctly (and you may trust me in that; though I may not have distinguished myself in Wittenberg as a brilliant philosopher, I am known to be a reliable and—some say excessively—accurate study) called for *"a man with some Latin and Poeticall Sensibilities, to translate a Romance into the Common tongue, as it is spoken in our Cittie."*

Calling on Baron de Maricourt at his offices in the Merchants' Guild, I carefully reframed my research for the University as "largely a matter of translation, actually—reworking antique Greek and Latin philosophies into modern languages." I was fluent, I explained, in German, English, French, Danish—even a little Norwegian. The baron waved away my translations of Ovid.

This irked me a little—I had spent threepence on parchment and new quills, and more than an hour copying them over in my best hand, in preparation for this interview.

As he passed me a parcel tied in twine, I noticed that his hands were harder than I had expected of a gentleman, his fingernails thick and yellowed, though clean. I was surprised as well to find the book an ordinary romance, such as any you might see sold for a sixpence at the church-door stalls alongside the quartos of yesterday's plays and sailors' "true" accounts of recently discovered New World islands. From his change of color I had expected political tracts; Papist propaganda; a bit of French pornography at least. Flipping through the first few pages, I was even more surprised to find the work already in our language.

"You wish this translated into . . . ?"

"Into the common tongue." The baron tugged at his lace ruff, which looked itchy.

Sweat had drawn a chalky line of starch across his freckled neck. "The spoken tongue, I mean—to be performed upon a stage."

"You mean—a play?" I had translated plays before—three summers ago, the manager of a company of foreign players had been so pleased with my quick revision of a couple of Plautus farces that he had given me a bonus: half a share from the comedy's third performance. But to make a romance *into* a play?

"You can do such a thing, can you not, in a translation?"

I considered the word—from the Latin *trans*, across, and *latum*, the past participle of *ferre*, to carry. Nowhere was it specified what must be carried, nor what might be crossed: form; genre; one's strict adherence to the truth?

The truth was, I needed the money. My fellowship paid for books, but not clothes, nor my tab at the college buttery, where they were threatening to cut off my rations of ale. The unexpected windfall from the Plautus translations was long gone; in a rare fugue of extravagance, I had used the gold to purchase an ingenious mechanical sundial, which now ticked confidently in my purse, otherwise empty.

"Of course, of course," I nodded like an idiot, assuring Lord Maricourt his romance might be translated in any manner he desired. "Exactly as you like it."

The letters began arriving the very next day, written in a surprisingly graceful and delicate hand that I, nevertheless, soon learned to despise:

"Could you contrive to add in early on in the first Act a Wrestling match or some similar Sport requiring the young men to undress?"

Sighing, I set this note atop the stack collecting on my writing-desk, covering yesterday's request for *"a melancholy Philosopher and his sober musings on the passage of Time."* The baron was hoping to win election to the City Council, and with each of these additions, he wished to curry some special favor with one or another of the noble electors, his guests at the Midsummer Ball, where the play was to be performed.

The problem was that there was, as yet, no play to perform, and this the morning on which it had been arranged that I should come to the baron's manor house to show him my scenes. Though I had sent Lord Maricourt glowing assurances of my progress, praising his suggestions and additions, in actuality, I had not even figured out how to introduce the love-story into which all of these troublesome complications would, in theory, eventually fall.

Yesterday, I had in desperation decided that the problem was the stiffness of my pen, and gone to the stationer to buy three new goose quills. I enjoy watching the slender apprentice prepare them, taking such precise care in trimming the nib, then shaving the feather from the barrel. He strips it entirely bare but for the slight tuft at the tip where he pinches the quill between his rosy lips to hold it firm, languidly running the razor up and down the length of the pen, first one side, then the other. More than once, his green eyes have caught me watching him at this task, and I have had to look away, feeling oddly ashamed. Nonetheless, the strange disturbance that this sight provokes in me has been known, at times, to inspire poetry; from childhood, I have kept a leather-bound diary (carefully locked at the bottom of my trunk) in which I gave flight to those fancies I would not have dared to speak aloud in the confessional.

But returning home from the stationer's shop I had felt no such inspiration. Instead, idly toying the quill between my fingers, I'd spent half an hour calculating the size of the shadow the remaining tuft of feather cast upon the page, and the corresponding waste in candlelight, and determined I could save three-eighths of a penny a term by shaving off this excess as well. Feeling quite pleased with myself for this discovery, I first tested that the blade of my penknife was sharp, then performed this surgery with a cheerful efficiency. I blew the tuft away, resisting the urge to make a wish, as if it were a dandelion. Then I set back to work, already feeling more hopeful about my prospects. Only I found the pen now balancing strangely in my hand, the naked quill tickling my knuckle in a manner that made it impossible to concentrate.

I ran my fingers through my thinning hair. My head ached with the lack of sleep, and I winced at the clatter of iron-shod wheels each time another ox-cart passed beneath my window on its way to market. The scholarship students' rooms are on the noisier side of the college, overlooking the alley and the river docks instead of the quiet, well-manicured fellows' garden. Some of my neighbors on the staircase actually prefer this arrangement, as it allows them to take advantage of their windows to sneak in and out of the college after the porter has gone to bed. I'd heard a group of them last night: laughing whispers and the smack of feet dropping onto the cobblestones; also, their return some hours later, clumsy with drunkenness. My page still sat before me, just as empty as before.

I picked up the romance again—an overwritten pastoral by someone who'd fancied himself a wit. The prose, freighted with Latin epigrams and odd forays into poetry, made me weary. Why all this trouble over a translation? But of course, this was not a translation—a matter of exchanging word for word, or even teasing out the best equivalent of some peculiar idiomatic phrase—but rather a remaking of the entire story!

For example, the narrative began with a long preamble about the hero's parentage and inheritance that revealed how he had come to his current, somewhat reduced, circumstances. But how to work this information into the plot of the play? I couldn't simply have a character appear on stage, say "As I remember..." and then conveniently recall those general circumstances of his history the audience should need to know before the action could begin. Or could I? At this point, I hardly had much choice; in desperation, I jotted down the hero's name and a brief synopsis of the chapter from his point of view. I could always change it later.

Scrambling frantically through old papers in search of something—anything—to show Lord Maricourt, I discovered a few pages of philosophy that had proved too fantastical for the Academy. These I tucked into my satchel, then unlocked my leather-bound journal from its trunk and flipped my way back through the varied notes I'd scribbled in it over the years—odd lines and jumbled fragments of poetry that on occasion came unbidden into my head, as if some Muse had been diverted on the way to someone else's pen. I found a few translations, and a sonnet that had never quite come together—an extended metaphor in which I compared men and women to players on a stage—and tore the pages carefully from the book. How these might fit into the rest, I would figure out later.

The halls were empty and my footsteps echoed off the stone as I slipped down the staircase past the porter's lodge, giving a nod to the old man, who scarcely acknowledged me.

I had spent half my life at Academia Leucorea. Arriving in Wittenberg at seventeen, I remember how I was entranced by it—nay, awed, freshly escaped from the monastery school for orphaned boys that had been my home for the length of my living memory. (There were fragments of my mother and my early life, but these were dreamlike, unreliable, and what I thought I could remember I distrusted, mostly on grounds of impossibility.) To my innocent eyes the small University town seemed as a glamorous city. The interview for my scholarship was held in the library, and I gaped openly, surrounded by more books than I had known existed in the world.

Well-read already in three languages, I spoke none fluently, including my own native tongue. I stammered out my desire to earn my doctorate, and then someday to teach as a fellow at the University.

The old dean nodded, asking what subject I intended to read—law, medicine, antique histories? Astronomy, alchemy, natural philosophy?

I answered him quite earnestly: "Why, everything."

He nodded happily at this reply, and put me down for the Divinity college; then, pushing up his sleeves, asked if I was willing to convert.

My world was yet so sheltered I had only ever heard the name of Martin Luther muttered by priests, in contexts that had led me to believe it was a euphemism for Lucifer. Still, I thought, I might as well doubt one church as another. In truth, though I had been raised to the priesthood, I did not entirely believe in anything; and if I did not even privately consider myself an atheist, it was only because I could not muster any more certainty in disproof of divine existence than in proof of it.

Through the years, I have wondered at times if this skepticism is the reason why, while I am known in the college as a dependable scholar, able to deliver a lecture on nearly any subject, I have never made my name in any particular philosophy. Though I always take great pains to ensure my written arguments are well-constructed and impeccably researched, I might have argued the opposite points just as easily, and been equally satisfied doing so. I am halted not for lack of study, but from too many contradicting truths, all competing for my belief. I cannot break my habit of hedging my statements with "so I have heard" and "it is said" and often have I been shamefully bested in debate by some cawing upstart flimsy in his facts but armed with deep convictions, and other cheap rhetorical tricks.

It has been so for as long as I could remember. Even as a boy at the monastery school, though I made great progress at Latin and Logic, I dug my heels in stubbornly at every leap of faith, questioning each catechism the frustrated priests tried to impart.

Instead, I turned my attentions to learning everything I could about the world that could be seen. Before I was nine years old, I could give the categories, names, and properties of every herb growing in the apothecary garden tended by kindly old Father Lawrence. When I, still very young, had first arrived at the orphanage, I had believed that Father Lawrence might be my own true long-lost father. Then I found out people, too, had categories, names, and properties, and learned this was a very wicked thing indeed to wish upon a man who had been so kind to me.

Whoreson, the other boys taunted me. *Witch's whelp*. They called one another out by the same curses, to be sure, but for me, the sting was sharper because they were true: my mother was a whore, and had been burned for sorcery. It was only the intervention of the abbot that spared my life, as he offered to raise the courtesan's orphaned bastard to the church—in an experiment, he said, of nature versus nurture.

A trunk of her possessions had arrived with me at the monastery school. But the only thing I asked for from the abbot was the book "this big" (I held my hands a folio apart) and bound in fine glove leather. It was the one, I explained, from which my mother had read me my favorite stories.

There was some argument among the priests about whether this grimoire was suitable for the innocent's possession. An impromptu council was convened around us in the abbot's office. Some argued that the volume should be burned, and anyone who had so much as touched it confess at once to a mortal sin. Others disagreed. If the book was indeed found to be of sacrilegious content, it should be studied, they said, by those who could learn to counter its danger. A lay brother was discharged to fetch the book, which arrived just as I'd remembered it, bound in fine mottled leather of, as one priest noted darkly, ". . . a most dissembling color."

A lengthy metaphysical debate ensued about the possibility of determining the moral value of a given text by the quality of the binding. Eventually, it was agreed by all that no, this was not a valid means of judgment. Nor, it was resolved, was the character of the one who owned the manuscript—nor even (this point incited the most heated controversy) that of the hand that authored it—but only the ideas themselves, the words as they were written on the page.

At this, the abbot (who had been, during this exchange, quietly examining the text under debate) looked up, his brown eyes twinkling with the beginning of a laugh. "Well, in that case, I do not think we need concern ourselves too much with its influence."

For—though the journal was clearly well-thumbed and its cover discolored with age—as he opened it to show them, the pages were blank.

The brothers came to view me likewise as a *tabula rasa,* upon whom they, with the pious diligence of the old illuminators laboring in their scriptoria, might eventually imprint their faith.

And I learned quick enough to keep my doubts and questions to myself, repeating my catechisms as they were repeated to me.

But sometimes, I would take the heavy journal from my trunk and flip my fingers through the vacant leaves, squinting at lines that I almost believed I could see. The apparition came to me when I let my eyes unfocus: a faint and backwards hand, as though I were reading the words from the wrong side of the page. If I could just believe in them a little more, I thought, they would appear and all would be revealed. I felt as though I were waiting for a religious calling; but my calling never came.

The same quarry as Michelangelo's *David*," the baron remarked to me proudly, as though the two pieces of stone might have known each other at school. "The whole thing carved from a single slab, unbroken." He nodded up at the statue of Diana in the fountain.

Through an innovation of clockwork, he had explained, she wept real tears—two thimblesful of water every minute. We had paused before the statue to watch them—dripping down her breasts like milk, skirting the contours of her stomach to pool in the delta that suggested her sex (demurely concealed by the sculptor) before trickling into the wishing-well below.

"Got another slab of it for the hearth inside. Cost a pretty penny, too." He patted her damp marble foot paternally. "Of course, the true worth of it is in the freight. Rather like myself, you know." He chuckled a little. "A self-made gentleman."

This claim, I realized, he had repeated several times, both on our walk up the drive and earlier, when I had met with him at his office. Did he mean it in encouragement, I wondered? Simple boast? Or was this a request—the "self-made gentleman" another character he was hoping I might fit into the comedy, already crammed fat as a capon? Again I tried to show him my pages, hoping with sufficient explanation I might mitigate somewhat their obvious roughness. Again he leaned back on his heels, grinning awkwardly, looking around at everything in the garden but my work.

He had met me at the gatehouse in muddied boots. "Walking the estate," he'd explained. "Always rise at dawn, you know, to check the property. Prefer to take my morning piss outdoors." He laughed so hard the laces on his jerkin strained.

All the way up the pebbled drive, I heard about the progress of the asparagus in the kitchen gardens; the place in the northeast corner of the wall where last winter's frost had left gaps between the stones wide enough for two men to pass abreast. I learned about the open courtyard plan of the manor house; the particular variety of clambering rosebush he had chosen for the balconies in back; the elaborate layout of the privet maze, at the center of which now we stood, admiring the statuary.

But not a word had been mentioned about the play, nor the romance from which it was to be translated. Nor had the baron showed the slightest interest in the pages I had tried at intervals to put before his eyes.

He nodded around the blooming garden as if to express a general and enthusiastic approval of his properties, broadly construed. "A self-made gentleman," he said again.

Perhaps he meant that I was not myself "self-made"—referring to my blatant plagiarism from the source material, obvious even at a glance? There was something oddly evasive in the baron's cheer. I had a queasy feeling that I was about to be sacked. This seemed particularly unfair, as I had not yet even had the chance to properly show my work.

"Please, your lordship." I fairly thrust the mismatched papers into his hands. "Only look upon these lines, and advise me how they might be bettered, before you render your final verdict on them."

Reluctantly, he took the pages. He frowned for a minute or so at my piece on the different Ages of Man, nodding solemnly but offering no comment. Finally, he tucked the papers into his vest, reddening. "Ah, my wife takes care of all those details." He cleared his throat. "I'm more of a thinking man, myself. Come up with the ideas."

His voice betrayed a hint of a country accent in the vowels, and with a shock, I understood at last the correct translation of *self-made gentleman*: the baron could not read.

"Beg pardon, sir," I said, feeling my own face grow hot. "Your wife?"

"Aye, Adriane. She'll look them over. She goes in for all that sort of thing. Poetry." He sniffed, dismissing the entirety of recorded literature with a broad, blunt-fingered wave. "Why, you should write a poem for her! You know, like to the kind they do at court for the fine ladies, comparing all her parts to lilies and cherries and the like."

"A *blason*?" There had been such a poem in the romance he had given to me. The trammels of the heroine's hair more golden than the metal; her eyes bright heavenly lamps, *et cetera*. I'd read it over wondering if the author had meant satire.

My stomach sank. I could picture the baroness now: a bourgeois middle-aged hausfrau with pretentions to Poetry, by which she meant the sort of treacly rhymes carved on the inside of wedding rings. She would be dressed as something greater than her station and lesser than her age, her graying hair bleached with sulfur and dyed weekly to the latest fashionable color. Doubtless, the romance had been hers, and also the careful handwriting I so despised upon the baron's letters.

"My lord!" We were interrupted by the baron's page, a tawny-freckled boy who stank of stables. He stopped short when he saw me with his master, obviously wondering whether our business was too important to disturb.

"What is it, lad? Is it Sofie?"

"Aye, sir," the boy was panting, still breathless from his navigations through the hedge-maze. "You said to fetch you when 'twas time."

"Of course, of course." Clearly, whoever "Sofie" was, her welfare held far greater interest to the baron than my comedy. He turned to me. "Forgive me, sir—I must attend to this. I'll not be long." He departed with the lad, leaving me to contemplate the fountain on my own.

I looked up to the tall brick manor house. On the balcony overlooking the garden, I could see a housemaid shaking out the linens, careful of the clambering roses. A grizzled gardener trundled past me on the path with a wheelbarrow heaped with branches and assorted rotting leaves. Taking them to burn in the bonfire, I supposed—I had smelled its smoke, acrid and faintly sulfuric, a counterpoint to the fragrant efflorescence of late spring.

I paced the bricks around the fountain, self-conscious that I loitered idly while all around me toiled at some useful occupation. Even the droning bees darted in and out of the flowering privet hedge, busily collecting nectar. I might at least work on the poem the baron had requested.

The *blason* was more of a courtly style than I was used to writing, but I had once tried my hand at the form—some lines composed to a famous beauty whose portrait I had seen hanging in a shop. I racked my brain to remember the comparisons I had used, hoping some of them might be applied. I gave a bow to the statue of Diana and spoke, addressing her as though she were the baroness:

My mistress' eyes are like the sun,

This was vague enough, I thought, to serve for a variety of colors. Clearing my throat, I continued on:

Her lips of coral red.

(They were likely to be painted thus, at least.)

Of silken golden wires spun
The hairs upon her head.

If she proved to be a redhead, I might change *golden* for *copper*; in the economy of iambs, both would scan as equal currency. I looked up, taking inspiration for my next verse from the goddess in the fountain.

My mistress' breast is like the moon:
Snow could not be more white,
And in her breath, such sweet perfume
As none could more delight.

I spoke more confidently now, drawing to the conclusion:

Her voice to me more pleasing sound
Than music's honeyed air.
A goddess goes she, o'er the ground—
By Heaven, beyond compare!

I was rather pleased with this fillip at the end: topping off my list of comparisons with the caveat "beyond compare," like those

Persian weavers who deliberately marred each carpet with a false stitch, so as not to offend God by seeming to aspire to perfection. I finished with another flourished bow to the statue of Diana. I had no coin to toss; my poem, I thought, would have to be both wish and payment for it.

A woman's laugh broke through the air; not a musical laugh, but a sharp repeating cackle, like the cry of a hyena. "That was terrible."

It was not the goddess speaking: she went on spilling her usual allotment of tears, indifferent to my praise. The voice had come from the other side of the privet hedge, where, after some investigation, I discovered an adjoining garden.

This was, I soon realized, the manor's apiary: half a dozen beehives sat on scattered wooden tables, tended by the sharp-tongued maid who had called out to mock me. In her long black beekeeper's smock and veil, she resembled a habited nun; though one attired as well in blacksmith's gauntlets. The leather gloves protected her not only from stings, but also from the heat of the ceramic smoker in her hand, in which some mix of coals and herbs belched out a foul gray vapor.

It was too early for the main harvest; she must be hefting the hives. I had assisted Father Lawrence in the same, and remember how he taught me to tell by tapping on the skeps of woven straw how fared the colony inside. If it made a solid thud, resounding with the contented hum of bees, the combs were well-stocked with honey. But if a hollow echo was accompanied by an angry buzz, or faint, or none, this meant the queen had failed to breed, and the hive must be harvested early, the remaining bees driven out and made to join another colony.

She nodded to me but did not cease her brisk, efficient motions, tilting up the side of the skep to direct the smoke underneath. Disoriented black bees stumbled out, heavy with honey.

"You do not think my poem will please the baroness?" I asked.

"No better than it describes her." Behind the thick black veil I could not see the maid's expression. Her voice was low and graveled, but not unmelodious. "For I can tell you, Lady Adriane's eyes are nothing like the sun. And coral is far more red than her lip's red." She sniffed and overturned the skep to draw the honeycomb, shaking from it the last few jealous bees before depositing the dripping amber wax into a bucket lined with muslin. "And even if she were that fair, nobody would believe it. Future generations will laugh and say, 'This poet lies—such heavenly touches never touched earthly faces.' Your verses will be scorned, like old men of less truth than tongue."

Truth? This was not a word I associated with poetry. Truth was the provenance of religion, natural philosophies, the sciences of the mind—not poetry. Poetry was fantasy, hyperbole, ideals; for this reason, in fact, had it always appealed to me as a far more satisfying channel for my passions than the messier romances of the flesh. A ritual visit to a brothel with a group of fellow-students in my first year at the University had left me feeling nauseated, shaken—and, above all, disappointed in the experience. How could the merely real hope to compete with the erotic world of the imagination? I had taken more satisfaction in translating Ovid's tale of Adonis and Venus.

" 'Tis a convention." I sighed, contemplating the prospect of having to explain the entire concept of poetic metaphor to an illiterate housemaid. "I grant I never saw a goddess either, and your mistress, I am certain you will tell me, does not float, but treads, as others do, upon the ground. It is not meant to be a literal description. When I see the lady, I shall alter certain lines, to fit the color of her eyes and hair to her particular beauty."

"Certain lines?" Her tone was skeptical. "And what if she were not beautiful? What would you tell me, if I were your mistress?" She removed her beekeeper's veil and bonnet and approached, allowing me to see that she was one whom Nature had made ill-featured and harsh. She was not deformed, nor toothless, nor scarred by the pox—merely dusky of complexion and thick and dark of brow, her upper lip revealing the faint shadow of a moustache.

She laughed to see my consternation. "Go ahead. Pretend I am your very, very baroness. Tell me my brows are black as ink, and my eyeballs bugle-beads. Tell me honest that you see in me no more than in the ordinary of Nature's sale-work. Then may your verses be believed, at least, in time to come."

"You would have me pay insult to you?"

"There are worse insults, than to be called unbeautiful." A grimace twisted her wide, ill-shapen mouth. "Of all the qualities that ever moved a man to love or a poet to praise, there is none more overrated than beauty."

For a moment, I pitied her. Though hardly handsome myself, I was at least a man, and might make my name in other ways. But to be a woman, and denied that essential quality of the feminine, the power to inspire passion and poetry? To be a woman, and to have no hope that your face might launch even a single ship to carry you across that terrible vast sea of history? To be homely for a man was unfortunate; for a woman it was a tragedy.

A glimmer of amusement appeared in her hard eyes, the crow's-foot lines around them deepening. "And it is not what you are thinking, either," she said. "The forgotten spinster's bitter jealousy. A poet who takes up the cause of beauty has no imagination. He would speak of 'honeyed airs' meaning only that they were sweet."

"But honey *is* sweet." I had seen the two concepts so often linked together in poetry as to substitute one for the other. In my experience, the word "honey" more clearly and frequently was ascribed to a metaphorical ideal of sweetness than to the actual, rather uncleanly, flux of a bee.

"Is it?" She fixed her eyes on me. They were, as she'd described them, narrow, black, and beady; but also unfathomably deep. She drew nearer. She was younger than I had thought before—perhaps late thirties, only a little older than myself. Reaching into her bucket, she broke off a piece of the fresh-harvested raw comb. "Taste and see."

Though normally I have but little appetite for sweetmeats and sticky confections (particularly on mornings such as this, when I had not yet breakfasted), once she offered it, I was left with little option but to put the dripping morsel in my mouth.

She was right. There was sweetness, but to describe it as the flavor of the honey would be to speak of the sunlight as the summer's day while ignoring all that it illuminated. Where the bee had sucked, there now was I the bee, darting in and out of cowslip bells. I heard the honeysuckle calling to me from the meadow, and, under it, the richer, deeper call of the hive, like the same note in a chord, but sounded an octave below. I tasted all the thousand honey secrets: stinging nettles and wildflowers, rosemary and rue, Nature's renewal and putrefaction, summer distilled to its perfume and prisoned in cells of wax. And I understood: the honey was a poem, and its theme that every growing thing holds in perfection but a little moment before it is consumed by devouring Time. I opened my eyes, unaware that I had closed them.

The wench was biting her own honeyed thumb, still watching me intently. She had a crooked gap between her teeth, and this detail, which a moment earlier I would have numbered among her flaws, I suddenly found inexplicably captivating. Her mismatched and ill-colored parts seemed joined together into a whole which—though it did not conform to any common standard—had its own peculiar fascination. It made me want to look at her. Nay, I *had* to look at her—and all because I could not understand why I wanted to look at her.

"So tell me, Poet," she said, licking her lips. "Can you distill the summer's taste as well as any bee?"

I swallowed, feeling slightly nauseated from the sweet; something more, as well. I would have blushed for shame, but all my blood had been diverted elsewhere.

"Dipping into the honey early, are we?" The baron appeared suddenly around the corner of the hedge. "If you think 'tis sweet now, wait until you try the mead Midsummer Night!" Bending over the wench's shoulder, he reached into her bucket for a fingerful of the amber sludge, which he slurped greedily. "I see you've met my wife, Adriane."

"Your wife!" I started back from the dark lady as if she'd given me the sting and not the honey. Now she removed her long beekeeper's smock and I saw that, underneath, she wore not a servant's hempen homespun kirtle but a gentlewoman's brocaded gown.

The baroness flashed me a mischievous wink, then turned to engage her husband in some business of the household, allowing me to make certain discreet and necessary adjustments to my clothes.

"Four pups!" the baron was saying. "One black, one roan, and two brindled white and chestnut, like their dam."

"All four whelped easily and healthy?"

"Aye—well," he added reluctantly. "There were five. The runt born dead." He grunted and spent several seconds smoothing his moustache. "Still—four hounds!" But this "four" did not sound quite so hearty as the one that had come before.

He turned to me, spreading out his arms in a gesture of good-will. "But I have not forgot the purpose of your visit, good sir. Come now, I shall show you to the upper lawn."

"The lawn, my lord?" I followed him out through the maze of hedges and clambering rose-vines.

"Where the thing is to be played, of course!"

"Your canvas, if you will," said the baroness.

"You'll want to have your actors in a day or two beforehand, I expect, for the rehearsals," the baron continued.

"My actors?" Mine? As in, players *I* was meant to find and or-ganize to some sort of rehearsal? "But my lord, I was only engaged to provide the translation—to turn the prose romance into a play."

"Exactly," Lady Adriane said, her low voice cool, amused. "A play—not a play-*script*. The lines are but the smallest part of what makes up a play." She took her husband's arm. "You must have players, scenery, musicians . . ."

"Oh, he need not worry about musicians," the baron inter-jected reassuringly. "He can make use of those I have hired for the dancing after."

"Very well." Absently, over her shoulder, she turned to me: "But make sure you have the songs finished in time that I may set them all to music."

"Songs?" I gasped. But the baron and his wife were already walking on ahead, discussing further plans.

"Perhaps it could also include some sort of mistaken identity," the baroness suggested. "Resulting in a comic love-triangle."

"Aye, like in that one—oh, what was it called, Adriane? That we saw played at court on the last day of Christmas?"

"What you will, my lord," I said, half-dazed, trailing along behind them on a path planted with primroses. "Whatever you will."

A Reckoning of Hours

The carillon bells were striking twelve as I passed through the city gates again, making my way towards the market square. My business with the baron had taken longer than expected, and yielded nothing but confusion. In town, the mood was festive—that is: drunken, rude, and clad in jangling bells and ribbons dyed in gaudy hues. I gave an inward groan as I saw a row of maids all dressed in white. I had forgotten about the Maypole. College Street from Market Square all the way up to the University would be crowded with the traffic of revelers and blocked by impromptu stages contrived of scaffolding and taffeta for the folk-dancing and crude mime shows. Someone would have dragged out the old much-abused bear for baiting with the hounds. I had seen it all too many summers before; now it struck me only as nuisance and spectacle.

I breathed a heavy sigh. The first of May already. Where had April gone? I realized with a mild shock that my own thirty-fifth birthday had passed unmarked the week before, forgotten by everyone, including myself. Then I was struck—or, rather, *wasn't* struck—by an even more disturbing lack of fanfare. I fumbled in my satchel for my small brass watch-dial, curiously quiet. Surely I had not forgotten to wind it? I hoped I had not in my sleepless state this morning been overhasty and turned the key too far. The man who had sold it to me warned that if I pushed the works beyond endurance, I would throw the entire mechanism out of joint.

His shop had been a cavernous room set deep into an alley and crammed with every imaginable personal effect. Daggers and swords hung from the walls, and crowns and jeweled carcanets sat high upon the shelves, pillowed in velvet. There were more mundane properties as well: silk handkerchiefs and rusted lanterns and intricate paintings done in miniature. I had paused for a long time before one of the framed portraits, but after engaging me in some trivial gossip, the shopkeeper had nodded, and, looking me over to take my measure, steered me towards a tray brimming with varied timepieces.

I am not normally a man enchanted by newfangled gadgetry; but the brass dial appealed to me for its practicality. I admired its complicated yet efficient machinery, economical in design as well as price compared to the other ornamental traveling clocks—most of which were more ornament than clock. Even the decorative toolwork pricked into the case of the plainest one had seemed too fussy for me until the merchant pointed out it served a functional purpose as well, allowing one to hear the hour strike when it was closed. As long as I kept it wound and free of tarnish, the old man vowed, it would provide me faithful and constant service.

I allowed him to put the device into my hand. It seemed to me an exceedingly fine and useful thing, to know the hour on cloudy days or fair, indoors or out, at any hour of the day or night. The money he'd asked (after another swift assessment of my person, cap-a-pie) turned out to be the exact amount in coin I carried in my purse.

The watch was my only possession of any tradable value—but my concern was more than the cost of it. Plain as it was, it kept excellent time, and I was affectionately proud of the little device, fretting over it as one might over the health of a small and faithful pet.

It ticked yet, and I breathed a sigh of relief. But how had it managed to fall so far behind its hour? I reached for the key on the end of its chain to reset the moving hand; then, thinking twice, changed my direction that I might pass by the old weigh-house, which had both weathervane and sundial built into its façade.

The creeping shadow on the dial confirmed my suspicions: the pastor of the church, eager, no doubt, to be done in his duties and start the festivities, had in his own holiday humor turned the clock ahead and rung the noon hour half an hour early. I chuckled, patting my pocket, and murmured a small apology to my watch for having doubted its fidelity.

The weathervane promised continued fair skies, and though I was in no spirits to join the Maying, the thought of returning again to my reckonings in my little room was enough to make me wish to be struck dead. Instead, I headed for the river—not down by the docks, where scholars sometimes venture for the rougher entertainments, but across the bridge, on the southern side of the Elbe, where the banks grow wild.

I walked along upstream awhile, following the donkey path though farmers' fields and pastureland. I was seeking out a place I knew. Just past the bend, the river slowed and fed into a pool all circled round with willow trees, whose weeping branches shielded its pleasant mossy banks from the view of those traveling the common road. The waters there I found possessed of a peculiar calm, smooth as a looking-glass, and just as suited to reflection. It had been my sanctuary in my undergraduate years, when, tormented by gentlemen's sons for my shabby clothes and monastery manners, I would sit for hours beneath a tree upon the bank. Sometimes I brought an inkhorn and my leather-bound journal, to write those sensual poetic fantasies I would not have dared to pen in the public scrutiny of the library scriptorium. But mostly I just sat, watching the reflected clouds draw strange images on the surface, until, like a curtain drawing closed, the wind blew wrinkles through the scene, wiping the slate again. The banks across were private property—the park-like grounds behind some foreign embassy—and in all the pilgrimages I had made there through the years, I had never seen another soul.

Until today.

The creature's face (for it did more suggest to me some angel or an airy sprite than either man or woman) was the most beautiful thing I had ever seen. I could not number in it all the graces I did note, and even if I could, such a *blason* never would have been believed. I would be scorned for ridiculous hyperbole, accused of spreading lies, just as the baroness had warned me earlier. But here were eyes bright as the sun, lips far more red than coral—the very embodiment, in fact, of my "mistress" as described in my poem. As if she had been conjured by my words.

To be just, I could not see her face itself, but only its reflection in the water. The maid was hidden from me by a drape of willow branches that trailed their leaves like fingers in the glassy stream. It must be an illusion of the sunlight on the water, I thought, that made the gold complexion seem to glow so bright. Seen truly, she would be fair, yes—fair as any mother's child born into the world—but not so incandescent as a candle, much less sun or moon.

The rosy lips fell open in a voiceless gasp, then let out a long and shuddering sob. The mournful sound did sorely touch my heart; I wondered at the cruel foe who could have been so churlish, to torment such loveliness to weeping.

Approaching the willow curtain, I drew back a branch to see a naked figure stretched like Narcissus on the bank, looking down into the water. Though her back was turned, still I could see the maid's misery in her shaking shoulders. Maid no longer, I should say—for I could well surmise the nature of attack that would leave her here, denuded and undone, to beweep her shame beneath a willow grown aslant a brook. (The other cause for which unmarried maids did drown themselves she was too slender for.)

I took a step nearer, intending to offer assistance—and saw to my shock that the maid was, in fact, a man, just as I realized what his actual employment had been, gasping and moaning there all by himself upon the bank. He was not weeping: his only torment was buried in the bud between his legs, and he held in his own hand his solution.

Feeling my face grow hot, I leapt back and hurriedly hid myself behind the tree trunk, hoping the youth had been too involved in his ministrations to notice my approach. My heart was beating like a frenzied bird flapping about in its cage, my ribs.

At the monastery school, the holy father who had blushingly explained to us the mechanics of sexual intercourse said self-abuse was forbidden because it was profitless; it unblessed the blessed mother. To "die" (as he had delicately put it) by one's own hand was the same sin as to kill oneself.

Of course, none of us boys put much stock in these warnings, and late at night the dormitory had been a chorus of rustling straw and adolescent groaning. But seeing this young man, I understood at once, down to my bones, what a sin it was, denying future generations copies of his beauty.

But why should he be having such traffic with himself alone? Surely such a well-formed youth—slender yet, but with shapely calves and thighs—might find a wench so moved by his beauty to desire to print a copy for her cradle. If I were a woman and had a womb to ache for such a seed, though I had before been chaste as ice, I would have offered myself to him right then and there, as wanton as a harlot. As it was, the ache I felt was something more diffuse, and with far less simple satisfaction.

From behind the tree, I heard his movements quicken; then he gave a final heaving sigh and fell silent—his youthful sap, no doubt, all spent upon himself. He passed a minute or two panting on the bank; then I heard a splash as he plunged into the water, making little rippling waves to break upon the pebbled shore.

I thought to take advantage of his preoccupation to make my retreat and was turning to leave when I heard a voice call out across the water:

"What hour now?"

I froze. Of course, I thought, he must be speaking to some friend or attendant on the shore, someone whom I could not see by virtue of where I was standing. I waited for the companion to answer, but he remained silent. Then the young man's voice called out again, this time tinged with impatience:

"Do you hear, forester?"

I had no choice now but to answer him. "Very well, sir. What would you?" I stepped out from behind the tree to see him standing waist-deep in the water, splashing it up to wash his chest and arms.

"What is it o'clock?" he said. With his head bent over so, I could yet see no more of the youth than the soft gold curls, brindled with streaks of wheat and honey shades; the slender waist and graceful limbs that had made me believe him a woman before. "You might say there's no clock in the forest, but I know you have a watch on you. I could hear it ticking earlier, while you were watching me at my soliloquy."

"Soliloquy?"

"The rank abusing of myself." He looked up, and I saw his face for the first time untranslated. "I make rather a habit of it, I'm afraid."

My immediate sensation, seeing him, was one of recognition. I felt as though he were an old dear friend I had not seen in years. Or perhaps it was only that I had conjured his face a thousand times for my poetry—imagining Adonis in my translations of Ovid: carving his dimple into Helen's cheek. But now that I saw my words made flesh, I understood as well that those lines I had written—comparing his cheek to roses, or his eyes to Jove's bright lightning—were not, as I had thought, exaggerations, but were in fact insufficient to describe the actual effect of his beauty. I could not think what to liken him to but all the world, and on just such a perfect day as this. He was May itself—nay, even lovelier, more temperate.

"Shall I compare you to a summer's day?" he interrupted my reveries.

My mouth fell open. It had been my very thought. Did the young man's gifts also include the power to read minds?

"Your face—'tis just long as one, and twice as hot!" he finished off the joke, then shrieked with laughter.

This only made my blush renew itself even more furiously. He was the naked one; why did I feel that I also had been revealed somehow, merely by witnessing his sins? My too-attentive eyes were now converted to the opposite extreme; they darted everywhere but where he now stood, clothed in nothing but his own, slightly rippling, reflection. I mumbled an apology—or would have, if my breath hadn't gone—and turned to make my exit.

"Well?" He was still looking at me expectantly. I felt like some poor actor on a stage who had forgotten his part. He rolled his eyes and gave the cue again: "What hour now?"

Did I report the church's time, or the sundial's? "I think . . . it lacks of twelve," I stammered back, hating my own lame uncertainty. I reached for the watch in my pocket, flipping it open just in time to see the hour hand click into place, transforming morning into afternoon. A dozen quick chimes hammered out in my hand, drowning for a moment the deafening staccato of my pulse. "Nay," I amended as the last chime faded in the air between us. "It is struck."

"Indeed?" he said sardonically. "I heard it not." He ran his tongue a lump along the inside of his cheek. "You come most carefully upon an hour, good Master Timekeeper." He returned to his ablutions.

I turned again to part. " 'Tis strange that you should call me that," I said, in afterthought. "My name means 'timekeeper.' My given name."

The young man's head shot up. "Horatio?"

Of course it was a guess—he had worked it out from the Latin: *horae*, the hours, and *ratio*, a measure or reckoning. But his inflection, as though he had suddenly recognized a dear childhood friend, gave me pause. His face was so familiar I might have believed the impossible—that I had met him before, and somehow managed to forget it. As if I might not sooner forget my own self. "Do you know me, sir?"

"No, no—of course not," he let out his breath, shaking his head bashfully, as though confessing to some minor quirk or foible. " 'Tis only that—nay, you will laugh and think me mad—but I have always dreamed that I should have a friend called Horatio. And here you have arrived, right upon your hour, as though delivered to me by Fate."

"I do not believe in Fate," I answered, automatically.

This caught the young man's interest. He looked at me quizzically. "You believe there is no divinity that shapes our ends, rough-hew them how we will?"

I hesitated. I was still technically a divinity student, even if the pursuit of my doctorate had long ago forgotten it once had any other purpose than the perpetuation of itself, and the dean given up hope that I might someday settle on a subject for my dissertation. Atheism, even agnosticism, was not a confession to be given lightly; if it were to get out that I had been speaking heresy, my scholarship might be revoked. "I cannot speak to the influence of the divine; but I believe our acts are undertaken of our own free will, and not fore-written in some heavenly book."

"Nor in the stars?"

"I have astronomy," I admitted, "but not to tell of good or evil luck. I do not believe in astrologers' prognostications, nor do I take my judgment from the stars." I gave a shrug and half a grin. "But who can say? Perhaps they are right, and the only reason I do not believe is that I was born on the feast day of St. George."

This made him laugh once again—a delightful noise, like gentle breezes rustling poplar leaves. "I do desire more love and knowledge of you, good sir," the young man said. "There is, I think, some small repast in my purse—a wineskin, a loaf of bread. Will you join me?"

I would have declined, for manners' sake, but that my stomach, like a forward child, answered for me, growling loudly its assent. I was too late now for dinner at the University halls, and had eaten no breakfast but the baroness's honey, which subtle taste lingered with me yet.

"Very well," I said, looking around for the promised picnic. The slender youth showed no signs of quitting the water—perhaps bashful about his nakedness?—so I guessed he meant for me to serve. "Where is it?"

"There." He turned to point across the river to the bank opposite, where indeed I saw a leather satchel slumped under a greenwood tree. "You do know how to swim, do you not?"

"Aye—I think." I had once perused a pamphlet on the subject. "I mean, I have the general idea."

The river was not wide; a man could skip a stone across it. Not a man such as myself, of course; I have always lacked in skill for that particular sport. Well, any sport, honestly. Whether billiards or bowls or darts, the problem was always the same: I could understand the principle, calculate the desired angle and velocity and spin, envision the problem and solve it in perfect geometry; I lacked only the arm to carry out my plan. I hoped swimming would not prove to have an equally wide gap between theory and practice. "Is it deep?"

"Not very." He was standing now in water to his chest and he proceeded in a few steps further, bobbing each time down a little deeper. He swam out to the center of the pool. "Why, even here, I think I could touch bottom, if I tried."

There was a challenge in his eyes, as though they were asking me something. I did not know the right answer. I did not even know the question; but I knew that I was less afraid of the water than of failing the young man's test. My mouth felt dry, but still my hand, like someone else's hand, rose to undo the points lacing my collar. "I'm willing."

Let me be clear, I am no Puritan; I have an anatomist's respect for the honorable machine of the human body, and have often voiced my praise for the ancients in their casual attitudes towards nudity, which seem to my mind more advanced than the false-seeming modesty found in our modern age.

Still, as I undressed, I could not help but be aware of how unattractive my body was, compared to the perfectly-formed youth's. Unrolled from my dark gray hose, an old man's shank: hairy, skinny, skin a bluish-white. The awkward phallus—I have always been self-conscious about its gangling, inelegant size, so unlike models of classic statuary. And surrounding it, as if in emphasis, a thatch of saffron-colored hair, far thicker and brighter than the auburn wisps upon my head. (My beard comes in the same ginger color, which is why I keep my face clean-shaven.)

Leaving my clothes folded together in the crook of a branch, I regarded the water with renewed trepidation. The young man was a bobbing head lost in the lime-colored light that filtered through the budding trees. He pitched his hands to his mouth and called out to me those nonsensical long vowels a falconer uses to summon his bird: "Hillo-ho-ho-boy! Come-bird-come."

I tested the water with my foot and found it biting cold, but eased my way in to the upper thighs. Clouds of silt rose from my footprints, muddying the clear pool, which my imagination filled with schools of slithering creatures, now invisible. A rough breeze blew across the water, shaking the budding trees and raising gooseflesh all over my body. It made me look even more scrawny, pale, and ill-prepared, like something plucked for Christmas dinner.

The bottom dropped away far more quickly than I had expected, and soon I found myself swimming, or at least treading enough water to keep my head afloat. The initial painful nip of the cold eventually faded into a sort of pleasant numbness on my skin. I had never before been submerged in enough water to float in it, like a ship, and the pamphlet had not mentioned what a strange sensation it was, to find oneself suddenly weightless. I could see my feet ungrounded, kicking along below me, haloed in green. By angling more to one side or the other, I found I could manage a crude navigation toward the young man. The pool was impossibly clear at the center, and seemed impossibly deep.

"How f-far is the b-bottom?" My teeth were chattering, though the sun still burned hot on my face and shoulders. "You said you c-could t-touch?"

He drew a deep breath and bounced upwards for momentum, then, holding his nose, dropped like a stone—down-down-down, his golden head disappearing into the darkness somewhere far below my feet. I felt my stomach sinking with him; I never would have agreed to this compact had I understood just how badly I should be out of my depth.

Whatever magic faith had kept me floating in the water now evaporated, suspending belief. I felt the pool bubble and give way beneath me, like something solid melting. I was falling, unable to draw breath, tumbling down after the fair young man into the bottomless deep.

I might have drowned, had he not shot up suddenly again beside me, so near I could feel the heat of his body. Desperately, I clung to him, both of us gasping for breath. With his assistance, I kicked my way to the far shore until I could at last touch ground again. Then he released me, and I pulled myself onto the grassy bank, wheezing. I stopped to sneeze and shake the water from my ears, feeling as though I had been new-baptized.

Meanwhile, he rose effortlessly from the water, glistening like polished ivory, and I was struck all over again by the fact that he was naked. I did not know if it made it better or worse that I was now naked as well. Did this make us equals, or merely highlight our vast inequality?

He took the satchel from underneath the greenwood tree, unpacking from it a wineskin and a bundle wrapped in a large linen handkerchief. The satchel was smooth tanned kidskin of the finest quality, like the cheveril that bound my private journal. It was marked with a patch that showed his coat of arms—a red field quartered in white, and on it his initials: a yellow *W* embroidered above the larger *H* in violet. Who was he, I wondered—this mysterious Master W.H.?

A student, that was clear—his scholar's gown and other assorted clothes were tossed carelessly over the lowest branch of the greenwood tree. From the sleeves of his robe, I could see that the young man was not an undergraduate, but, like myself, a tutor-fellow studying for a doctorate. He must be older than the eighteen or so that he appeared. And no scholarship student, clearly—

beside the gown hung a sleeveless Spanish doublet with knit-silk hose and a collar pleated into a stiff ruff by some servant skilled with the starch and ironing tongs.

Breaking the loaf in two, he offered me half. "Eat with me," he insisted. "I am dreadfully well-attended by dullards, fools, and spies, but ever lack for honest company."

His eyes met mine and I swallowed my tongue. Company, from *con pane*, "with bread." With crust and crumb are comrades sworn and sealed.

The bread was warm and whiter than any I'd ever had; the sack too sweet for me and strongly spiced, with just a hint of something bitter in the lees. In the linen bundle, we discovered also several slices of assorted cold baked meats (including the tenderest venison ever I tasted), a hunk of cheese, two ginger cakes, and an entire roasted pigeon, stuffed with leeks.

I could not help but express my amazement at this "small repast"—rather a banquet fit for royalty! But the young man only shrugged at it. "Cook believes I am too thin."

He drank freely from the wineskin but ate only sparingly, leaning on his elbow like an antique Roman—an image that caused the eerie sense of recognition to nag at me again, fluttering nervously at the back of my brain. Where had I seen him before? I dismissed the thought as foolishness. He might well make me think of Rome, from those days when Venus and Jupiter still visited men with some frequency and demigods were as common as any other mulatto breed.

He had taken an interest in some local vegetation: a low-creeping vine growing wild in the sandy soil. "Tell me, are you familiar with this vegetable?" He rubbed one of its hairy, dark green leaves, and it gave off a spicy, musky scent, not unlike that—I could not help but notice, in our nude proximity—of his own clean sweat.

"Only well enough to know it is a fruit," I said, pointing out a precocious yellow berry hanging in a cluster with several greener. I examined the specimen closer, noting its nettle-like leaves. "Though I have not seen this particular variety, I know its cousin. It is a very deadly poison, though when handled carefully, can be useful to the apothecary in the manufacture of certain sleeping draughts." All of us boys had been well-versed by Father Lawrence in the dangers of poisonous flora. Slow, painful paralysis, from the extremities inwards. Circular thoughts. Visions of spirits. Madness, raving. Impulsive acts. Painful bloody death. I shuddered. "As you value your life, I would not eat it."

"As I value my life?" He barked out a mirthless laugh. "Not a pin's worth, if you would know. I came down here this morning intending to drown myself in the Elbe. It was only the thought that the Almighty's canon had been set against self-slaughter that prevented me. I would not be damned, if I can help it."

Could he be serious? Looking closer, I saw the dark rings circling his eyes. Perhaps my first interpretation, that he had been weeping, had been the correct one after all.

The vine shook as he plucked the yellow berry, holding it up to the sunlight. It was large—nearly the size of a blacksmith's thumb—and the translucent golden skin revealed a network of sickly veins marbling the flesh.

"So let us perform a test," he said, rolling the fruit from hand to hand like a clown with a juggling-ball. "If I am meant for no particular future, I might take this poison and die today, and have it accounted no worser sin than gambling. But if heaven has another fate in store for me, as I have dreamed, then I must survive, to die another day—and you shall be my witness."

He rolled the fruit between his fingertips, then, peeling back the leafy crown, popped it entire into his mouth.

I tried to stop him, but it was too late—he had already swallowed. "Are you mad, sir? You could die!"

"And so I shall!" A high light danced in his startlingly blue eyes. "If it is not this day, it will be another. And if not another, then today. 'Tis all the same to me." Then he cocked his head up at me, cocked his brow, cocked a crooked little smile. "Nay, these I think I have eaten in Italy," he said, licking the last of the seedy pulp from the corner of his lips. "There they are called *pomi d'oro*—apples of gold. The French prefer to call them *pommes d'amour*; but here the fruit is known by a rather more prosaic name: the *tomato*."

I let out my breath in relief. Of course—it had all been another joke. He had never intended to kill himself—what a ridiculous idea. I shook my head, chuckling at my own gullibility.

"You know, a fortune-teller once foretold that I would die by poison." He shrugged. "Then again, he predicted the same forecast for most of my family. He was trying to sell us a set of goblets lined in unicorn's horn. But who can say?" Yawning contentedly, he stretched out on the grassy bank to await the verdict of the gods. "Perhaps I am dying even now."

"I told you," I said, arranging myself beside him on the grass. "I do not believe in fortune-tellers."

I blinked my eyes shut for what felt like no more than a moment, and when I opened them again I found the sun inexplicably low and amber in the sky.

I sat up, regretting this act almost immediately. My first thought was that I had been stung by a bee, but I could not tell where; a feverish throbbing pulsed all through my body. Rubbing my eyes elicited protestations of pain from both my eyelid and the back of my hand. My mouth was dry and my skin felt tight, an inch too small all over. I looked down at my arm, which even in the fading light glowed like a copper torch. I had been burnt to the color of my most furious blush.

The fair young man was standing over me. He wore a silken undershirt and stockings all unbraced, and nothing else.

"Your assistance, sir."

He needed me to tie the points of his doublet and garters of his hose. I scrambled up to help him, and he offered up each limb in turn with the casual brusqueness of one well-accustomed to being dressed by servants. But of course, I had known that he was a gentleman—and not only by his clothes, nor the seal upon his satchel-bag. In his fashionable Spanish-cut doublet and stiff lace ruff, he appeared the very picture of the gentleman-scholar, and I became suddenly self-conscious about my own nakedness.

"My clothes!" I gave a groan as I remembered: I had left them on the other side of the river. "I shall have to swim for them." I did not relish the prospect. An evening chill had come into the air, and the trees cast shadows across the surface of the pool, which rippled underneath with currents, ominous and dark.

"Nay, nay," the young man nodded up the bank as he pulled on his boots. "There is a little footbridge just past the turn, not a hundred paces yonder."

I gaped at him, wondering why he had not mentioned such earlier, before I had nearly drowned. But before I could say anything, he added: "I am engaged to entertain certain fellows of my acquaintance at supper at Father Jacques's public house tonight." He swung his satchel over his shoulder. "Come, let us go together."

I felt my outrage melting at the invitation. Still, I hesitated. "I can meet you there after evening prayers."

The young man raised his eyebrows in surprise. "A pious skeptic?"

"A reluctant truant, rather." Absence from religious services and meals was punishable by a half-penny fine, and I would have been marked down already for having missed dinner. Of course, most of those you would see at these "mandatories" were the scholarship students and impoverished junior faculty. The vast majority of the gentleman-scholars regularly skipped such tedious extracurriculars, duly accruing fines as a small and insignificant tax against their evening liberties; and the University, enriching its own coffers by this practice, tacitly endorsed it. "Besides," I grinned, "I have surpassed today my daily quota of transgressions— for I believe it is a violation of the University charter for students to bathe in the waters of the Elbe." Luther himself had said that devils lurked in the river, waiting to steal men's souls.

"Ah," the young man answered, with a twinkle in his eye, "but that law only applies in Wittenberg, on the other side of the river. On this side, we are on the grounds of the embassy—and the ambassador's residence is accounted property of state and his native territory, subject to its laws and customs." He spread his arms to either side and gave a bow, twisting his hands into a sweeping flourish. "Welcome to Denmark."

All at once, the pieces of my memory clicked into place, and I knew where I had seen the fair young man before.

His portrait, rather. It had been hanging for sale in the very shop where I purchased my watch. I had paused before it to scoff, actually, thinking the androgynous, angelic beauty was no more than the painter's fantasy made in oils. The lips, for example, had clearly been modeled from a woman's; they were too decadent for a man's mouth, or even a boy's. Still, as I browsed the shop, my gaze kept returning to the portrait in the mahogany frame. The pouting half-smile shifted from innocent to seductive to mischievous to sad. The piercing blue eyes followed me. They seemed to be asking me a question—but what could it be?

The shopkeeper had noticed my attentions. "Tragedy of Denmark, what it is," he sighed, shaking his head at the portrait. "Still a schoolboy, at his age! They say he refuses to marry—rails against the institution and abuses any woman who so much as speaks to him. No one knows what they are going to do about it." He gave a greasy wink, tapping his finger to the side of his nose. "You mark my words: he's more an antique Roman than a Dane."

I had not taken his meaning. "But who is the gentleman, that it should matter if he weds or not?"

As I recalled the shopkeeper's reply, I looked again at the seal on the young man's satchel, the embroidered letters: *WH*. Only this time, I saw the tiny line stitching shut the bottom of the *W*. Which, I realized, was not a *W*. Was not, in fact, a letter at all, but a crown, sewn in a thread of fine-spun gold. And underneath the crown, in faded royal purple silk, was the initial of Hamlet, Prince of Denmark.

The God in the Machine

Father Jacques's public house was near the river docks, set in a narrow alley populated by no enterprise more wholesome than alehouses. At present, it was called the Merry Fool, and I managed to locate it at last by the hastily painted caricature of a jester's cap and bells hanging with the holly above the door. The last time I had been in the establishment, nearly a decade before, it had been known as the Rose. In recent years it had also been called the Swan, the Royal Boar, the Upstart Crow, the Sacred Bull, and then the Swan again (an old license had been discovered, and with some careful revision, declared as good as new). It changed names with the seasons, I gathered, or roughly as often as the tax collectors came around.

Father Jacques was the proprietor and main attraction. His history—at least, as much of it as I ever was to learn—was mostly apocryphal, informed by colorful and often contradicting stories. Though his name suggested a Frenchman, his unplaceable accent did not, and theories about his origin and parentage abounded, and ranged from the merely implausible to the patently ridiculous. He wore a small gold earring in his ear, which some took to mean he had been a seafaring man, in his youth. Others said he was a spy, and still others that "Jacques" was not his name at all, but an alias, or else a bastardization of some unpronounceable foreign surname.

One persistent rumor maintained that he had taught with Luther at the University, and had put him up to that prank about the church door on a bet. (This part I never fully believed, but only because it would have put his age at well over a century.) But he might have had a century under his belt, or four. It was impossible to tell how old he was—you felt you would have to count the rings, like a tree. Every part of him that could be seen was brown and wrinkled as a nut.

His son, Jacques-*fils*, operated in a far more respectable neighborhood a far more respectable inn, frequented mostly by elderly academics and members of the upper crust seeking a predictable and quiet place to dine before the theatre. One came to the father's place for quite a different experience. Here there was no "upstairs," no private rooms to which the gentlefolk might repair with their retinues, but only common tables where, for the price of a mug of ale, any rude mechanical laborer might sit and argue his philosophy against renowned professors or the sons of noblemen.

As for the attraction to these nobles? Well, Jacques was most famous for allowing prodigal heirs to run up enormous bills on credit, which he delighted in presenting to their fathers at precisely that moment in the family affairs when a financial scandal would prove most embarrassing. His timing was impeccable; no matter how the *paterfamilias* would rant and rage (often hurling inventive insults, which Jacques would later ape for the crowd until everyone's sides were sore with laughing) inevitably the debt was paid.

The presence of so much profligate and susceptible youth naturally attracted a gaudy and diverse crowd of parasites and patron-seekers, prostitutes, actors, and spies. Any news to be known or rumor to be discovered could be heard at Father Jacques's. Like as not, it had been invented there. And slipping always through it all, fiddling and fussing, refreshing the drinks, and tapping his toe to the music, was the proprietor himself, the god in the machine—a smile surreptitious, in his eyes.

As I opened the door to the Merry Fool, I suddenly remembered why it had been so long since I had last frequented the public house. Holding my handkerchief against the humid stench of sweat and piss, smoke, civet, blood and boiled cabbage, I gingerly made my way across the sawdust-covered floor, through a swarm of vivid characters.

Circled together in a corner, a dozen or so musicians were playing a jaunty country dance in various keys; but this provided only a baseline of general cacophony, above which any actual communication was carried out at levels of shouting. Even in this din, my ear tuned at once to the unmistakable sound of Hamlet's laugh, a triple-pronged shriek rising above the other noises in the hall.

His cap was set atop his fair curls at a rakish angle, a cardinal's feather stuck into its band. Beneath it danced his dimples, in a face so beautiful it triggered a startle in me to catch sight of it again. The scant light from the smoking torches on the walls seemed to bend and brighten around him, so that, though he was not at the center of the room, he still appeared to be its center, the point into which all perspectives disappeared.

He was sitting at the head of a long table near the back, surrounded by all manner of onlookers soliciting his attention and attempting to impress. An armed and partly armored soldier stood guard behind Hamlet's shoulder. Beside him was a manservant in the red-and-white liveries of Denmark, who poured the prince's wine and took such gifts and tributes as certain of the supplicants made to present.

Because of this entourage, I could not immediately approach, but hung back, watching the prince while he selected out to greet and engage in conversation certain fortunates among the crowd that pressed in all around his table. Everything about him seemed larger than life, a little too much to be real. His gestures were broad, but graceful, and he made great use of his long and slender fingers, both singly—to pick out a point or indicate an aphorism—and unfurled, as though he held an invisible fan, which he would point skyward in emphasis, or flick to show his palm to those he had dismissed from conversation.

When this occurred, the guard would step forth, ushering away the visitor; then the prince would turn back to those at his table, where from every side courtiers, women and men alike, blatantly preened and flirted—casting expectant glances, laughing too loud at his every witticism—in bald attempt to attract the prince's attention.

Several of the gentlemen wore the gowns and caps of Academia Leucorea, like myself—but as unlike myself as possible within the confines of the uniform. In theory, our gowns render all fellow-scholars equals within the walls of the University; but I remember well from my own undergraduate years the various subtle signs and means of distinguishing grades of equality. As I approached the table, I watched a few of their glances drift casually upwards—taking in my faded hose, fretted with mending scars, my plain falling-band collar, worn unstarched—then slide away again, dismissing me as nobody worth notice before ever reaching my face. This must have been their function, as Hamlet's attendant lords; the prince himself had not even bothered to look.

I stood at his side for several minutes, almost close enough to touch him but dumbly ignored while Hamlet left no break in his animated conversation and the red-and-white-liveried servers elbowed past me in annoyance.

At last the prince's eyes flicked upwards and caught mine. "Horatio!" he said, greeting me warmly—as I had seen him greet many such this night—by rising to embrace me with a mime of kisses, cheek to cheek. The brush of his unshaven cheek against my sunburnt one was excruciating, and over far too soon.

He took his seat again and I thought for a moment this was to be the end of my audience. But instead, he turned to the gentleman at his right—a ruddy, round-cheeked undergraduate whose youthful portliness seemed to portend a truly magnificent obesity he was destined to attain in middle age with all his titles and inheritance.

"Gentle Rosencrantz—do move down a bit to give Horatio some room."

The young lord looked stricken by this request—though in fact it inconvenienced him no more than anyone else seated at the long table, as his displacement meant his neighbor—a gentleman as thin and sallow as he was rosy and plump—also had to move down, and so in turn all the way down the table. As they adjusted their positions, each face turned to note the new arrival with a mix of curiosity and resentment. I nodded both apology and thanks and took my place.

Though I had observed the way he attracted to himself every worshipful eye, the light itself seeming to fix and focus on the prince, I was unprepared for the sudden shift of these attentions onto myself when I was invited to sit at Hamlet's side. A goblet was procured from somewhere, and never half-emptied before a liveried serving-man rushed forth to fill it up again. The audience of admiring observers pressing in around the prince's table now ogled me as well, and openly.

Not all of the attention was so friendly. Several of Hamlet's lords still eyed me with suspicion, whispering together behind their hands, sometimes laughing. I imagined them comparing notes about my shabby clothes; my advanced age for a student; my spectacles and thinning, frizzy hair.

Then it struck me, like the punch line to a joke: these gentlemen were jealous. They were fair and rich and clever and titled and young, and jealous—of me! Of the scholarship boy, with moth holes in his hose! I felt as though someone were tickling my ribs from the inside. The warm fiction flowed over me, transforming me into someone with an identity. Prince Hamlet and I were bosom friends, had always been bosom friends. There was no one I held dearer, or was ever like to do.

But no sooner had I turned to speak to the prince than he leapt up again, this time to greet an old man who had slipped in through the crowd, moving with surprising spryness and agility, given his years.

"Father Jacques!" The prince's French was terrible; he pronounced the name roughly as it was spelled. But if the ancient publican minded the prince's murder of (presumably) his mother tongue, he did not show it. He placed his spotted brown hands in a vee on Hamlet's face, then kissed him on the brow and affectionately pinched the prince's cheek between his forefinger and thumb.

"Aye, this one," he said, looking into Hamlet's squashed face but speaking to the world in general. "This one is my favorite of 'em all."

Hamlet rolled his eyes skyward and answered sharp: "Aye, and so you said to Hal just yesterday." But underneath it, he was flushed with pleasure at the old man's words.

All evening, it was thus: I found Hamlet's attention only rarely—and then very briefly—turned in my direction. Instead he was engaged responding to the steady stream of visitors that paraded by to greet him: humble men and great ladies, lords, and blatant hucksters. Famous actors, whom to meet before this night would have been a story I repeated all my life, approached him humbly, falling to their knees to kiss his hand. A pair of merry courtesans in rustling taffeta gowns sat on his lap two at a time and put their arms around his neck, pressing him between some of the most extraordinary bosoms I'd ever seen. One even reached into her loose-laced bodice and offered up her nipple for the prince to nurse, which action he performed with relish.

I gaped uncomfortably at this display. Even at arm's length, it was closer than I had been in years to a woman's naked breast. But it was the hollow pucker of the prince's suckling cheek, the rhythmic motion of his mouth, that seemed to pull me sideways through a needle's eye.

I forced myself to look away and turned my head instead to peer down the long wooden table, which stretched on so far that I could not see the people sitting at its foot. The plump, ruddy young gentleman beside me—Rosencrantz, the prince had called him—was recounting a tale about a bet he had won last season, for which Hamlet had been in forfeit obliged to wear for a fortnight a grotesquely padded antique codpiece in the shape of a drainspout gargoyle.

"Did he wear it?" one of the ladies down the table asked, covering her shocked mouth with her hand.

"He practically *named* it!" Rosencrantz cried. "He would stroke it like a pet and hold long conversations with it in the street. He even had a little pocket fashioned into the snout. He kept comfits and cloves in it, and would offer them to anyone who stared."

"What happened?" I asked, thinking any man who was not a prince and behaved in such a manner would be taken for a madman and locked away.

Rosencrantz threw up his hands. "They asked him to pose for the fashion plate! Within a week the haberdasheries were overrun with copies in leather and velvet and cloth of gold."

"And what could we do then but send for a tailor to have our own copies made of the hideous thing?" the thin, sallow lord at his right added ruefully. "After all, it was the latest fashion."

Everyone laughed at this, myself included. The thin gentleman leaned forward, the better to see me around the fat one's bulk. He was older than Rosencrantz, or merely seemed so, with his gaunt and hollow face.

"Your name, sir?"

"Horatio," I answered, offering my hand. He stared at the ink-stained, quill-callused fingers in horrified fascination, but made no move to touch them.

"I think he means your surname," Rosencrantz supplied helpfully. "Who was your father?"

This I could not answer honestly. "I am . . . an orphan," I explained, "raised by the Church." This had not quite the sting of admitting outright to bastardy, but it carried well enough the implication. The gentlemen exchanged a look.

"I told you—he's nobody." The sallow, thin one squinted. He had a narrow, pointed beard that made his face look even more pinched, a size too small for the space allotted to it in his head. "Just another of the prince's *foundlings*. We'll never hear from him again." He turned away, to start a conversation with his neighbor on the other side.

"Do not mind Guildenstern," Rosencrantz said, rolling his eyes behind his fellow's back. "He is a good man—but you know," he leaned in to whisper to me conspiratorially, "he is no gentleman."

"I'd noticed," I muttered.

"No, no," Rosencrantz laughed at my misunderstanding, patting my arm in a manner I found rather condescending from one fifteen years my junior. His fair hair was oddly mottled and blotched in color—an attempt, I realized after a minute's perplexed reflection, to recreate with dye the natural variations in the prince's gold. "I mean, he is a younger son. Gen*try* but not gen*tle*. He shall inherit no title himself—that is why he is so concerned with everybody else's."

He briefly pointed round the table, giving the names and various holdings and estates of those assembled, most of which information I promptly forgot. I recall there was an exiled Italian duke with some eccentric entourage, including an albino catamite.

Another lord, whom Rosencrantz called a *thane* (I gathered it was some sort of earl) was engaged in argument with his wife over which of the two had spilled a jug of Burgundy all down her white silk gown. A turbaned gentleman, tall as a citadel and with skin the color of an aubergine, noticed our attention and salaamed. His hands were so large the thumb and forefinger could easily have circled someone's throat.

Rosencrantz did not give the names of the servants standing silently behind the prince; even when I asked, he did not seem to understand the question. He was, I realized, effectively color-blind to the shocking red-and-white of Denmark's liveries—he had simply ceased to see the arm that constantly refilled our goblets. I had to turn and introduce myself to learn the name of the prince's valet, Marcellus.

He would, I think, have said more; but now Hamlet was calling for Marcellus to produce for him his purse. He selected a coin for each of the prostitutes, which he slipped deep enough into their décolletages to make them squeal and giggle. He eased them off his lap with a slap to the rump and nodded to the guard to hustle them away.

Then he turned to me, and just as easily as he had commanded these servants, he demanded, "Good Master Horatio, what hour now?"

I reached for my satchel, where I had earlier put my watch, being self-conscious about the noise of it ticking. Naively, I now realized—as if anyone could have heard it strike in this din, much less its tick! The face it showed surprised me—how on earth was it past midnight?

Prince Hamlet was not fazed to learn the hour. He leapt atop the table, forcing me to grab my goblet up lest my wine be spilled upon the boards. "I declare that we shall keep our revels all this night, and none may rest until we see the dawn!" he shouted, to cheers all around.

He took his seat again, and I shut my watch-case and returned it to the pocket of my satchel. As I was opening the flap, Hamlet caught sight of the baron's sixpence romance beside my quills and inkhorn.

"Ho—what is this!" He picked my purse of the trifle. "Fit reading for a skeptic, sir? I thought you were a rational philosopher!" He flipped through the romance, beaming in delight at his discovery of this heretofore unsuspected facet of my personality. Hamlet read aloud from the first page: "*Sir John of Bordeaux, having passed the prime of his youth (as the date of time hath his course) grew aged: his hairs were silver-hued, and the map of age was figured on his forehead: Honor sat in the furrows of his face, and many years were portrayed in his wrinkled lineaments.*" He laughed. "What satirical rogue is this, to inform the reader that when the prime of youth is past, a man grows old; and also explain that this fact may be detected on his face by evidence of wrinkles and gray beard? Why, tell me 'tis not so! This is a slander all throughout, fit to entertain feeble-minded ladies, or such fools as . . ."

"Oh, that one is very good," interrupted Rosencrantz. He had just turned from his conversation with Guildenstern to recognize the volume in the prince's hand. "It has beautiful poetry." He extended his index finger, and in a high, affectedly "musical" voice that someone must have told him was to be used for recitations, he began to quote: "*Love in my bosom like a bee / Doth suck his sweet. / Now with his wings he plays with me, / Now with his feet . . .*" Rosencrantz was not as altogether unattractive as I had first supposed. His eyes were ringed with thick, long lashes, and the porcine face appeared near to cherubic, at certain angles. He frowned. "Oh, I cannot remember the rest, but there was something in it as well about a wanton boy being bound for his offense when he would play, and whipped with roses, then beaten with a rod." He gave a mournful sigh and cast his watery hazel eyes on the prince. "It made me think muchly on you, my lord."

Even Guildenstern was paying attention now to this lascivious book.

I blushed. "I am not reading the romance for pleasure, my lord," I explained, collecting the romance from Hamlet's hands. "I am turning it into a play." As briefly as I could, I explained about the baron's commission. "It is only a small private performance for Lord Maricourt's guests. A piece of propaganda, really, promoting the virtues of his barony."

"These virtues being . . . ?" Guildenstern asked, raising an eyebrow while he smoothed down his moustache—both of these features slim, well-arched, and glossy-black.

I sighed. "That is rather the trouble. His parcel is a hinterland deep in the Ardennes forest, peopled mostly by sheep. What of it is not boggy moor is thick wood—suitable, perhaps, to fugitives for hiding in, or to poachers for venison, but of little practical use to anyone else."

"Why, you must have as heroes fugitives and poachers, then!" Hamlet teased.

"Oh, what fun!" Rosencrantz clapped his hands together. "You know, Prince Hamlet is always talking about someday writing a play!"

"But he never gets more than a dozen or sixteen lines down," Guildenstern observed dryly, "before some new obsession comes along." He looked particularly at me when he spoke the words "new obsession."

Hamlet shook his head, a slight frown wrinkling his brow. "I have certain ideas of lines and parts in mind, 'tis all," he said bemusedly. "I cannot fit them to a story."

"My trouble is much the same, my lord," I said. "I lack not for ideas—for every day, the baron sends me three or four of them at least." I explained about the stack of letters on my desk, indicating with my thumb and finger how thick it had grown. "The Duke of Saxony would see an attack by a savage lion; while the Duchess requests that I add somewhere a fool in cap-and-bells—and asks also if he might fall in love." I did the baron terrible cruelties with my parody, but Hamlet's eyes were shining with delight. For the first time, my predicament struck me as funny, an absurd story to be repeated, embellished. All around the table, everyone was listening to my tale with rapt attention.

"With all these mismatched pieces, it should turn out to resemble a patchwork quilt rather than a drama!" Hamlet cried out.

"I fear Aristotle would not recognize it, my lord," I agreed, a trifle less merrily.

"Nor, I think, shall the author of the original," Rosencrantz bemoaned the travesty to his beloved book.

Hamlet's laugh rolled out of him again. "At this rate, you shall have to have a deity lowered *ex machina* at the end, as the Romans did, to set the plot to rights."

This spun him into a rhapsody about a recent production of *Dido and Aeneas* he had seen done by his favorite tragedians of the City, in which he recited from memory several passages about the Pyrrhic victories. The tales of ancient tragedies poured through him, of players whose faces were hidden behind masks and still, they moved the audience to tears. His voice rose and dipped with an incredible range and flexibility as he imitated one player after another. Then he gave a sigh.

"I have often thought I might yet make a go of it as an actor myself, should my fortunes turn." This last was spoken almost hopefully, as if life treading bare boards with a cry of players appealed to him more than a future in palaces.

I was struck by a sudden and wonderful idea. "Why, you should take a role in my play!" At once I saw my weeks transformed, tedious rehearsals turning into precious hours spent in the prince's company. "You may play whichever part you will, and I will write as many speeches for it as you like."

A mask of delight overtook Hamlet's face, only to be shadowed almost instantly by one of despair as Guildenstern and Rosencrantz, along with several other courtiers, began their protests, all speaking at once.

"My lord, the king your father . . ."

"He would be furious, my lord. He would surely call you home—perhaps for good."

"You know how he hates the theatre."

"Why, he will not even keep a Fool at court any more, not after—*ow!*" Rosencrantz abruptly fell silent, shooting an affronted look at Guildenstern.

"His majesty thinks play-actors are no better than any other sort of liar," Guildenstern explained succinctly.

Hamlet rolled his eyes. "Ah, yes, *the-king-my-father*. He would never hear of it." He sighed and slumped back down into his chair.

My stomach sank. I would not have caused him any distress or trouble for the world. I was embarrassed even to have mentioned it among these courtiers, all of whom, it seemed, knew the king—the very King of Denmark!—so intimately that they had understood as one, instinctively, why such suggestion would be a *faux pas.*

"I saw him once," I blurted out, desperate for some connection to this rarefied world. "Your father."

Hamlet's head snapped up. "Saw him! When?" he demanded suspiciously, as if he supposed I had come directly from this meeting, with instructions.

"In a parade, my lord," I answered honestly, taken aback by the fierceness of his gaze. "When the Danish army marched the streets after the victory against the Poles."

It was among my earliest memories, one of few from before I was sent away to the monastery school. I had watched the procession from my mother's window, where she liked to sit in the evenings brushing out her hair. She pointed out to me the king on his decorated charger, his banners snapping in the winter wind. A dense sable beard, all silvered over in hoar-frost, still could not disguise his sneer. The conquered prince of Poland was pulled on a sled behind, bound and on display, his miserable captive.

Hamlet laughed indulgently at this jejune confession, convinced at least that I was not a spy. "You must have been a babe in arms," he said, "for I was born the year my father smote the Polacks."

My eyes widened in disbelief as I silently performed the calculations. One might count the years back to the Polish wars and know the prince must be near thirty now; but I knew as well that this fact must be forever forgotten and constantly under debate, even among those who knew him well.

The conversation turned to other topics then, and all eyes, thankfully, were drawn away from me. I excused myself from the table to the alley behind the alehouse to relieve myself into the gutter. The cool night air blowing in across the river felt soothing against my sunburnt skin, and I breathed deep despite the stench of urine. The heady drug of royal attention was a stimulant to which my feeble heart was ill-accustomed.

I was about to enter the alehouse again when the door flew open and a blond whirlwind in a scholar's cap spun out, catching me in half a tackle.

"Hurry!" Hamlet said in an urgent whisper. "We haven't much time."

"Time for what, my lord?"

"Our escape! I said I was going for a piss, but they'll come looking for me soon. I told you I was most dreadfully attended."

He caught my hand and pulled me along and we ran together through the nearly deserted moonlit streets. It was a thrilling feeling, like flying, sprinting across the stones hand in hand, both of us panting and trying not to laugh.

Finally, when we were well away from the pub and any potential followers, I called out to him, "Where are we going?"

"I have no idea." He stopped dead in his tracks, leaving me to overrun him and have to double back, gasping for breath. "I did not think it through so far." He frowned for a moment, then he let out a cry of triumph. "Ha! I know—we'll go home! To my house, I mean. They'll never think to look for me there. They'll be all night scouring the city in search of me while I am asleep in my own bed."

•　　•　　•

Home" proved to be a wing of the Danish embassy, where Hamlet led me upstairs from the dark official chambers and reception halls to a luxurious but sparsely decorated sitting room. The walls were wainscoted with elaborately carved oaken panels, but hung with neither portraits nor tapestries.

"We needn't wake the servants," he whispered, opening a cupboard to remove a pot of brandywine and a pair of silver goblets. "They'll just breed gossip. If you stoke the fires, I shall pour."

I nodded, glad for the occupation. The hearth coals were still smoldering, buried in the ash, and quickly I kindled them back to life. From this flame, he lit candles and set them in their stands. We pulled a pair of armchairs near the fire, and Hamlet served up the wine.

"Now that we are alone—" He dragged his chair a bit nearer to mine, his eyes glimmering mischievously. "We must discuss which role I am to have in your play."

I gaped in confusion. "My lord, I thought you said your father . . ."

"Aha!" He held his index finger up, stopping my tongue with a gesture. "I said my father would not hear of it. And so he shall not, if we are careful. I must adopt a new name—play the role, in fact, of a player playing a role." He made it sound like some delightful game, not a conspiracy to deceive the king. Treason, of course, to think of it that way.

But he continued unabated: "The only trouble, as I see it, is that the Duke of Saxony has often been with the Duchess to my father's court: they would know my face . . ." This plan was starting to sound more untenable by the minute. Hamlet pursed his lips; I could not feel my own. "So I shall have to assume some disguise."

"Of course, a disguise," I babbled, as if this were the simplest matter in the world. Frantically, I tried to imagine a costume in which the prince would not be recognized. No other man in the world had a face so delicate and finely crafted. A wig could hide his fair hair, I supposed, and his gold complexion might be dimmed with paint. "Perhaps some character role?" He could play the melancholy philosopher, I thought—I might dress him all in black, perhaps even give him a skull or some such *vanitas* prop to carry as he ruminated about the Ages of Man. I shook my head. Nay, this would be no disguise—he should still be Prince Hamlet, and unmistakable. Perhaps a cap-and-bells then? He might play the antic fool, whose sophisticated wit seduced and bewildered the innocent country maid.

"A character role!" Hamlet said, much affronted. "Why, I thought you said I would play the hero!"

I shook my head. "The hero of the romance is a love-struck naïf," I said. "A perfectly typical youngest son, composer of bad poetry to his mistress's eyebrow; you would be something too much in the part." I sipped at my brandywine, chuckling to think of it. At least he would show himself well in the wrestling match. "Nay, the best role in the play is . . ." I looked at the prince again: his high cheekbones and fine features, eyes like the lamps of heaven indeed, and hair more gold than gold. His voice, with its youthful flexibility and range—I had heard him this evening, performing his imitations, swing abruptly from Jupiter's basso thunder to Ganymede's lilting counter-tenor. I hesitated, hardly daring to propose it: "You could play the heroine."

Hamlet gave a start, and for a terrible instant, I thought I had offended him unspeakably. Then a grin began to wrinkle the corners of his eyes, hovering there for a long time before ever reaching his mouth.

"Do you think I could?" he asked me in a titillated whisper, looking much younger than his years and most convincingly girlish. Then, lowering his lashes bashfully: "But I can hardly walk in skirts."

I smothered a smile, making a mental note to ask someday about the circumstances under which he had discovered this. But I had another reason to smile as well: "Then the role is perfect—for she spends the better part of the romance in disguise as a fair young shepherd boy."

He laughed at this—his merry laugh, like sleigh bells, not the sharp one that I found so unsettling—and poured more wine to toast our endeavor. He was near enough that I could breathe his breath in, perfumed with wine and rosewater. Conspire, I thought, from *spirare*, breathe, and *con*, together. To draw breath as one.

We stayed a while longer by the fire, talking. He told me of the traveling troupes he had seen of English boy-actors, famous worldwide for their skill at playing women's roles as well as men's.

It was one of these, we decided, that he should undertake to imitate. For a while we tossed around potential names and histories for our "famous foreign player," sometimes crossing the line from the merely implausible to the ridiculous and collapsing into hysterics again. While I listened to the prince, I felt my pulse begin to flutter. My breathing shallowed and the palpitation took my chest. And as my heart galloped faster and faster, so came Hamlet's words into my ear: faster and more pointed, and falling naturally as he spoke to the rhythm of my heartbeat—which is to say, blank verse.

Finally, he stood and yawned, saying, "I must to bed."

I stood abruptly, embarrassed to have overstayed my welcome. But he caught me by the wrist and said, "Nay, do not go."

My heart was still pounding. "Do you need assistance to undress, my lord?"

"Aye," he said, leading me by the hand into the adjoining bedchamber.

My fingers shook as I undid the points I had tied earlier. I slipped the doublet off his shoulders and then the silken shirt over his head. He did not seem self-conscious at all about his nakedness— but of course, he was often seen thus, by his servants. I lowered my eyes. He was no more naked now than he had been when we had met and lain together on the riverbanks. Had it really been only this afternoon? Never in my life, I thought, should I experience another night and day so wondrous strange.

I helped him into bed, pulling up over his chest the fine soft linens scented with sandalwood and lavender, smoothing down his coverlet. He settled his head on the bolster. Again I rose to leave, but he said, "Only stay a little while longer and talk with me until I am asleep—for I have bad dreams."

"Of course, my lord." I pulled up a chair and sat beside the bed.

" 'Tis the reason I cannot abide draperies." Here, as in the sitting-room, the walls were bare, his windows shuttered but curtainless, with generous wide window-seats. "I am like a child, frightened of a painted cloth. There is a tapestry in my mother's chamber that yet shows in my nightmares." He shuddered. "I run my sword through it and it bleeds hot blood."

He closed his eyes, but still he went on speaking. He told me about his childhood, how the capital of Denmark was built upon a cliff at the very tip of a narrow peninsula. Isolated thus by the sea the young prince grew up believing his father's country to be rather the largest and most interesting part of the entire world, which he did not imagine extended much beyond what he himself could see. Sweden, which existed only when the weather was fine, he believed to be an island much the size of his own palace; and he thought all trees in the world were plum trees, for those were the sort that grew in his father's orchard.

I could not tell exactly when he dropped off, for even in sleep he continued on talking. Sometimes he would toss and thrash the bedclothes fitfully, until he was uncovered to the waist; sometimes he was so still I could barely see his lips move, forming soundless monologues. Once, in the prince's sleepy murmurings, I heard my own name. At first, it startled me awake from my own dozing, and I answered, "Your servant, my lord."

"Nay, my good friend," he mumbled, then rolled over in bed, turning his back to me, his eyes half-closed and glazed in dreams. It made me feel honored to know some shadow of myself was with him still. I wondered what it would be like to climb inside his mind, to dream with him.

His back was freckled. This was a surprise—in all of my philosophies, ancient and modern alike, I had always read that perfection was the state of being unblemished. Yet here before me was a perfect skin, and just as spotted as the sky with stars. I have read astronomy, as I had told the prince. Indeed, many a night have I spent peering at ancient charts of the heavens, deciphering their geometries. But never had I seen a map drawn with such precise hand, on such exquisite parchment.

I let my eyes drift over him in the flickering candlelight, studying him as I might a text of some rare antique philosophy. I found a row of faint brown spots along his shoulder blade and these I called Orion's belt. With these as my guide, I easily spotted Castor and Pollux, the Pleiades, the Northern Star. I had told him I did not believe in the stars' foretelling, nor did I pluck my judgment from their signs. But following with studious eyes these imagined heavens on his skin, I could not help but think: had I a pot of sepia ink and a brush three hairs across, I might paint in the constellations, set sail by these charts, and discover a new world.

A Little Key

If you were to ask me, "What is beautiful?" I might recite for you the history of philosophy. Every culture known to man has had its own preferred aesthetics, of course— the Greeks, for example, with their sculptures of Apollo depicted as a soft and beardless boy; or the Egyptians, who so preferred darker complexions that their great beauty, Cleopatra, was praised as being burnt even to black with the amorous pinches of the sun. In France, the current fashionable color for a woman's eyes was green; while in our country, blue was yet considered preferable. The Italian courts had made rather a cottage industry of the science, releasing every few years some new treatise or manual detailing which parts on a woman should be long, short, narrow, wide, fair, dark, high, or low—often mathematical in their precision, and containing as many as thirty-three specific requirements.

Baroness de Maricourt would have fallen short in each of these. Why, then, did she incite in me such an inexplicable excitement? I tried silently arguing aesthetics point by point with my rebellious flesh; but it responded only with its own point, which it made insistently. I felt just as absurdly bested as by any cocky sophomore I had ever met in chambers to debate. I shifted nervously from foot to foot, hoping my billowed scholars' gown disguised my state from the lady's perspicacious gaze.

At the moment, fortunately, her attentions were focused elsewhere. When I had first been shown into the grand entry hall, Lady Adriane approached me, holding out her hand—which I, bowing, then bent to kiss. Abruptly—almost rudely—she had snatched her hand away, presenting it to me again, this time with the palm turned pointedly up.

"The scenes?" she said impatiently.

I'd opened for her my writing-book. No longer kept locked in its trunk under my bed, it now resided full-time on my desk, shoving aside those philosophies and books of religious scholarship I was meant to have been reading. "I did not have time to copy over the parts, but . . ."

"Hush!" she interrupted, taking the book out of my hands. Without its now-familiar heft, I felt weightless, disembodied.

She read quickly, but, I did not doubt, with perfect comprehension. Her concentration was so absolute that I could almost feel her dark eyes moving hungrily over my words, as though the parchment were my own bare skin. At the same time, she appeared to have forgotten my actual physical presence in the room; and it was only then that I began to notice my peculiar condition. Even Medusa's face still had the power to turn a man to stone.

She might have been called handsome, I allowed. In a young man, such features would turn heads; it was only for a woman's face that her nose appeared too large, her jaw too strong and angular. One might even go so far as to call her looks "striking"—or some similarly violent adjective. Her wiry black hair was pulled back from her face in an elaborate style of intertwining twists and coils, over which she wore no hat but only a netted caul. With the strong slant of her brow and her decidedly Roman profile, it gave her a look both opulent and severe, like a falcon: fierce, alert, and bold.

The past three weeks had gone by in a blur. Nearly every day had been spent in Hamlet's company, and my nights in the flickering radius of candlelight upon my writing desk. When I ran low on candles, I had taken my inkhorn and pages and gone to the public house to continue writing there. Finding myself short on coin to pay for my fare, I begged a jug of wine off the proprietor by promising to name a role after him in my play; then, when that jug was gone and the work not yet completed, promised him another. (So now, in addition to all the other confusions in the plot, I had to work in not just one but two characters called "Jacques.")

I was oblivious, those hours, to any other world; nothing was more real than the green wood on my page—an eternal summer, a forest where anything was possible. Where the saucy, androgynous shepherd boy Ganymede might seduce the hero (a stammering auburn-haired poet) on the pretext of teaching the tongue-tied lad to woo his lady-love. Where the hero might fall in love, and even pledge troth to the bewitching youth—who at last (in one of those twists that turned tragedy in a heartbeat to comedy) revealed himself to have been the very lady all along, disguised. I had even, as a private joke with Hamlet, included the Roman god of marriage, who was to descend via a contraption to be hired from the theatre.

I would not have written such a taxing role for any ordinary boy actor, for fear of overexerting his voice and hastening its change; but I had heard Hamlet speak twice as many lines in an evening without pausing for breath. Besides, I thought, the longer the prince's scenes, the more time I might spend with him in rehearsals. In these, at least, I thought, we should be undisturbed by Hamlet's courtiers and attendants, from whom our endeavor must be concealed.

"Come." Without looking up from her reading, Lady Adriane abruptly spun around and began a brisk pace up the marble staircase. "We need to set the songs to a tune, so I can teach them to the musicians."

I followed her, less concerned for the musicians than my book, which she showed no signs of releasing. I had not gotten back those scenes the baron had taken before and had been forced to recall the speech about the ages of man and the others as best as I could from memory. This exercise had, I must admit, much improved the juvenile poetry; but I could not bear to lose the entirety of my book.

After climbing the stairs, we traversed a gallery so thickly hung with paintings that I could not tell the color of the walls. I wondered if these were heirloom portraits of the Maricourt family, or if the baron had himself been patron to such a multitude of artists.

At the end of a long corridor, she turned without warning into a room. Blindly following her, I was halfway through the door before I realized: this was the lady's own bedchamber. A curtained bed was set upon a dais, with a slanted writing-desk to one side and a mirrored dressing-table to the other. A small warp-weighted loom was set up in the corner, with a colorful tapestry partly begun on the wooden frame. More tapestries were hung from every wall, depicting all manner of strange—and yet, strangely familiar—scenes.

Without ever taking her eyes from my pages, she crossed the room to sit before an instrument resembling a small harpsichord. It was set against the wall between two doors that opened out onto a narrow balcony so overgrown with rose vines that all the light cast through was tinged in mottled shades of lime. Lady Adriane set the book on a convenient music stand and turned over her shoulder, seeing me still standing frozen in the doorway.

"It is all right, Master Horatio. As long as my husband hears the virginals playing, he will know I have not been seduced."

It was a long moment before I realized that she was joking. She shook her head, showing me the gap between her teeth, then turned back to the music.

"Come," she said, "you can stand beside me here and turn the pages."

She began with *"Blow, blow, thou summer breeze,"* playing a variation on a popular jig, which I thought well-suited to the syncopated rhymes I had incorporated into the verse. (*Thou dost not my heart please / So well as a true friend to meet. / His sunny smile doth warm me more / Than all thy honeybees could store, / Although thy breath be sweet . . .*). The virginals had a complex, nasal sound, much darker than a normal harpsichord, and its wiry, droning harmonies soon sent me into a hypnotic reverie.

While she played, I watched the ebony keys of the instrument leap up to kiss her crooked fingertips. Why had she snatched those hands away from my respectful kiss? Had she taken note before my peculiar physiological reaction and thought I'd meant to initiate some impertinent advance? Or was she, like Hamlet's courtiers, merely disgusted that a man as lowly as I should attempt to kiss her gentle hand? I nursed this grudge for a little while. Turn her pages, indeed.

Standing at her shoulder, I was in an ideal position to see into the inner workings of the spinet. I watched with interest as she moved her hands over the keys and the corresponding jacks, her eager lackeys, jumped to pluck their strings.

But this vantage point was also well-placed for other distracting views. Her gown was cut in the Italian style, low in front, with a stiff collar that stood up to frame her clavicles. Leading me to muse for an uncomfortably long time upon that bone: its linguistic history (*clavis cula*, the Romans had called it: the little key); its dusky hollows; its likely similarity in slope and splay to her pelvis, hidden somewhere underneath the forbidding bones of her corsetry.

"Have you a nib on you now?"

"Madam?" I squeaked.

"A sharpened quill?" Over her shoulder, she ran her tongue across her lips seductively and smiled at me as if she knew my mind.

I jerked back from the music bench and her revealing bodice. "I assure you, Madam, 'tis entirely involunt—"

Lady Adriane sighed at my incompetence. "A pen, Master Horatio? You are a poet, are you not? Never mind—you can take one from my table." She pointed to indicate a little desk beside the bed.

I obeyed, glad to put the distance between us. Taking her words at face value, they suggested nothing improper. Was it her interpretation, or my own, that insinuated hidden meanings into our innocent conversation? Even the act of sending me to fetch a pen I wondered at, given the writing-desk's uncomfortable intimacy to the lady's bed. Though the curtains were closed around it, still I caught—or else merely imagined?—a whiff of an intimate scent rising from her sheets, female and exotic. The angle of the desk suggested that the bed itself was used more often as her writing-chair than the forlorn wooden bench intended for the purpose. This had been pressed into service as a second table, I guessed, noting the stains of rings and drips from many cups and oily marks from spattered candle-wax.

I found an enviable swan quill waiting in the pen stand, nearly new and with a freshly sharpened nib. The ink in her inkwell had gone sluggish, and I thinned it with a little vinegar from the cruet.

"Your heroine is quite compelling in these new scenes," she said, her fingers still picking out the same droning refrain. "Far more so than the ingénue in the original."

"Thank you, Madam," I answered, stirring the ink.

The music stopped, and I heard pages turning. "Tell me—is she the same fair mistress who inspired these poems?"

I laughed a little, nervously. "I am afraid you are mistaken, Madam—I have no mistress."

"*Beauty's Rose*, you call her here." She read aloud: "*From fairest creatures we desire increase; and thereby Beauty's Rose might never die.*"

It took me a moment to place the words; and when I did, I nearly spilled the ink in my haste to intercept her from my private sonnets. Why had she been moved to turn so far ahead in the book? "Those are not part of the play, Madam."

"Another commission then?" she asked. "Something you are writing for a patron?" She slowly thumbed her way through the pages.

"Nay, they are . . . How could I explain those poems I had composed in the prince's honor? "For a friend."

"A friend?" She raised an eyebrow, then looked back to the poem at hand with a dubious expression. *"Oh, let me true in love, but truly write,"* she read aloud. *"My love is as fair as any mother's child . . ."*

"A very dear friend," I amended, before she could finish speaking the line.

"Rather a passionate one, it seems." She flipped back through the verses again, picking out lines here and there as she went. *"You are my all-the-world . . . Thou hast all the all of me."*

Those were my thoughts. Hearing them reinvented in her voice irritated me like a deep itch, too far beneath the skin to scratch.

She turned the page. *"Time shall never cut from memory, my sweet love's beauty, though my lover's life. His beauty shall in these black lines . . ."* Her voice trailed off. *"His* beauty? Oh—I see. Your mistress is a master." She pushed back from the bench and stood facing me, my writing held open between us in her hands. "You are in love with a man."

"Nay!" I lunged at her and grabbed her roughly by the wrist, tearing the book from her grasp. I wanted, desperately, to strike her. I wanted to stop her questioning lips with mine, bend her back over the keyboard and raise her farthingale and prove my manhood to us both. I imagined the droning instrument collapsing, tangling us together in the wires like Venus and Mars caught in her jealous husband's chains.

But I did not strike her, nor enact any of these other wild fantasies so uncharacteristic to myself. As soon as I wrenched my book out of her grasp, the strange spell passed, and I looked in horror at my hand grasping her wrist, our bodies pressed intimately against the music bench, and both of us breathing hard. I released her arm and backed away, mortified.

"My apologies, Madam—I assure you, you have misunderstood the lines." I offered an awkward bow without ever pausing in my retreat. "I will copy the songs and send them to you by messenger tomorrow morning, which should be sufficient time for music. Our business here is concluded, I think." I stumbled my way blindly into the doorframe, then turned tail and ran. It was not until I was halfway to the gatehouse that I realized I still held clutched in my hand her new swan quill.

I could not bring myself to turn back to return it, though I knew I should. It was an expensive pen; if she wished, she might bring me up on charges for stealing. As well as any number of other illegal or unsavory activities for which—on the basis of a few ambiguous lines, removed from proper context—she now imagined she had some evidence! All the way back into town, I argued in my head as before a court of law, dismantling her claims with all the impassioned rhetoric my imagination could muster in my defense. I explained that "lover" was meant only in the Platonic sense, and that my seeming obsession with this young man's beauty was in no more than its philosophic implications, of youth and the passage of time.

But still, I could not leave her words behind me. My own words, rather—those same that I now carried, bound in cheveril. My book; my hand. And no matter how impeccable nor watertight my explanation of my innocence, her eyes—two droplets of the blackest ink that I had ever seen—moved knowingly across my lines, silently questioning. It was this quality, I realized, and not beauty, that made those most forgotten parts of me come springing into life at her attention. More than anything, I wished there were some way to tell what she was thinking.

※

*B*e careful what you wish for ...

    If you were to ask me "What is beautiful?" I might answer you thus: a diamond in a sea of diamonds is invisible. Is not the source of its beauty, then, discovered only in its contrast with the Ethiop's ear? And is not the ear, by that same contrast, rendered equally rare and beautiful?

    Or to put it another way: 'tis a good thing that I came along. Such a sweet tale as this would soon begin to cloy without some bitter sauce to season it.

    My mother used to say that any man who would marry a woman for her beauty was too much of a fool to take on as a husband. My husband may be illiterate, but he is no fool. He married me for the land, before he learned the land was valueless: unarable, remote. Its honest tenants were all shepherds—poor woolgatherers who could be taxed for nothing more than colorful homespun yarns.

    A decorated soldier of fortune and fortunate investor in his youth, he had already built his manor house in Wittenberg and outfitted it to the standards of a gentleman, and he was anxious to adopt at last the final decoration of a title. But it was the green expanse of Ardennes forest that kept the orchardman's son from sleeping. He had looked over the map rolled out upon his desk, thinking of early mornings with his father, gathering windfall apples and walnuts from the walk. Though text perplexed him, dancing before his eyes illegibly, he had a head enough for figures, and all night paced back and forth working rough calculations. Perhaps a million trees. Perhaps even more. A man could walk from dawn to dusk without ever coming to the end of them—and himself baron over them all.

The difference between "forest" and "orchard" he accounted as a negligible technicality; much like the detail of his marriage to a coarse-featured and well-tanned country spinster with a mannish taste for breeches, books and the smoking of a pipe.

My father, Baron Ambrose Peregrine de Maricourt, with his disappointment of daughters (I was thirteen before I learned this was not the proper plural, like "murder of crows") had raised me as a son, educating me in Latin, history, and rhetoric. The womanly arts were handled by my mother—music, penmanship, and the weaving of elaborate ornamented tapestries.

Well, we had to do something with all that yarn. Besides, they helped to hold the scanty heat. Our castle, ever more fortress than chateau, was by now more ruin than either. Built atop the highest peak by some ancient potentate as a bluff of force to his neighbor, it had never been intended for year-round habitation. In the wintertime, the fires might be stoked to blazing, and still you had to break ice to sip the wine from your goblet at the table. Of its roof, the best that could be said of it was that it offered from every room an excellent view of the stars.

If the orchardman's son believed my foulness was at least an assurance of virtue, he was disabused of this notion right away. True, I bled on the wedding night, but with miscarriage, cursing the star-crossed apothecary, whose potions always worked exactly as promised—but a little too late.

The physician, believing the bridegroom had come before the priest, winked as he assured us my womb was undamaged, and the seed sown in the marriage-bed would root. My husband went pale; he had never touched me. But he did not say a word. Nor did he ever ask my lover's name.

You will not, I expect, be satisfied with the same discretion. After my father died, I had tailored down his doublet and hose, well-saved from his youth, and disguised myself as a young man when I traveled into town. That vulnerable gap between my legs I sealed with a roll of wool knotted into the toe of an old stocking and stuck into my codpiece, believing this talisman protected my virginity better than the sword swinging at my hip. I was too innocent to know that cocksure, effeminate youths attracted their own nature of seducer.

Mine was a well-known libertine. He had charmed so many such innocents in his time, he called himself "Merlin," and I half-believed him. On discovering the dark-eyed hayseed lad he'd bedded was, in fact, a lady, he was not fazed at all, but only laughed and flipped me over to the other side. He met his end soon after in a tavern brawl, but not before introducing me to the love of tobacco and beautiful boys: a pair of dangerous addictions for which there is no known remedy.

But this is not his story; our Master Horatio is, I think, some humbler bird than hawk. For the hero of a tale, his profile is, I will admit, something less than heroic. He is precisely average: neither tall nor short, handsome nor un-. His hair is reddish, but more brown than red. He is absolutely unremarkable to see—so much so that if you watch him long enough, this in itself becomes a remarkable characteristic—his transparency absolute; he is all men and every man.

And I have been watching him for a very long time. Far longer than he knows, and far closer than he could ever imagine possible. After all, have I not been here beside you, all this while?

Oh, yes—though I may not be able to see you, I know you are there. Well, who did you think I was talking to?

A distant ancestor of mine, medieval alchemist and magister experimentorem *Petrus Peregrinus*, was much celebrated for his epistle on the magnetic powers of the celestial spheres. He invented a pivoted compass, by the use of which man might direct his course towards cities or islands and all parts of the world, either on land or sea. But this was only one of his inventions. In his time, he was even more famous for his curved mirrors, now lost, by which he could throw fire and make small objects to float in the air, as well as certain other magicks, such as the power to make faraway lands seem near enough to touch.

As I sit before my dressing-table, looking into my own eyes, I might almost believe that this, too, was a magic mirror: that I could see you, watching through this dark imperfect glass that shows only in black and white, warping what it reflects.

But every loom must be warped before the tapestry can be woven. And, as our scholar might attest, "text" and "textile" share a common root. Which suggest that no story told is ever cut new from whole cloth, but instead woven together from ends and scraps: found yarn and loose threads.

So call this tale a "found yarn" if you will; I always did prefer to leave my tapestries a little unraveled around the edges.

Odin's Wound

Elsinore, seen from the sea, at first looks like nothing so much as a smudge on the face of the water, a trick of the light. The light plays the sort of tricks here that send shudders down sailors' spines—particularly in these last and coldest hours of the night. In summer, in these northern lands, the gray shadow of dawn begins to creep into the sky long before the sun stirs.

But it is not only the eye that is tricked here; and it is not the thought of pirates or sea-serpents that makes sailors whisper a prayer to themselves as they find their ships approaching the castle. It is the sound of a low moaning that rises off of the cliffs, like the ghostly noise of sailors, lost in the flotsam of ancient wrecks. Or you might think it was a baby's cry, carried in fragments over the sea by a chance of wind, or the voice of a despairing young girl, singing to herself broken bits of old love songs. These voices draw you in with their despair, their bottomless need for assistance, understanding.

vengeance. Everyone hears something different in the cliffs of Elsinore, and even those skeptics who claim it is merely the breeze playing panpipes at the mouths of sea caves and underground tunnels will turn pale and admit it is an eerie music. No one who has heard the sound ever forgets it, and everyone arriving in Elsinore over the sea spends his first few nights tossing and turning with nightmares of the approach.

The gods of a land are born out of its horizon—its marriage of earth and sky, of water and sunrise. The gods of the North Sea are gods of thunder, gods of revenge. They are elemental gods and tricksters, weary warriors. They bear scars of ancient wounds; they are missing hands and eyes. They understand that Heaven is another battlefield, and know no wisdom worth having ever comes without a price.

The King of Denmark understands this deeper than he knows. In his blood and bone, his body bears witness to the history of his land. Descended from Vikings, he is great in both stature and girth, with a thick black beard that once would have been the making of his name. A gray mist hangs low over the water, grazing the masts of the ships gathered and ready to sail at dawn for the disputed colonies.

Two sailors lead between them to the beach a sleepy-looking ewe, the sacrifice to consecrate their endeavor. Each of the men has made his confessions to his church, entrusting his soul to Heaven should he die in the conflict, but summoning the winds for the journey requires an older magic—transmutations more complex than wine from water, or blood from wine. The king's ancestors nod in recognition as he prepares the ritual, which, though the name of Saint Michael has replaced that of the pagan god, has remained otherwise unaltered for thousands of years.

And, though the king supports the church, the paradise he anticipates resembles in all but name the great palace Valhalla, where those who died heroically, in battle, were carried by the Valkyries to fight and feast. His forefathers did not fear death, except a coward's death—succumbing to the ravages of illness or old age. A warrior who returned triumphant from every battlefield was cursed as much as blessed, to witness in comfort his own decline. For such a hero who found himself on his deathbed and wished to join at the immortals' table, it was no shame to seek his own remedy with a small incision by spear point, called Odin's wound.

But that was long ago; these days, the church's views on suicide are clear. Though the king has been assured many times by his confessor that it is no less heroic to die in one's bed than one's boots, still this morning he is awake before the sun, in full armor, pacing the cliffs by the beach. In the tender light, he might yet pass for a man half his age, the silver in his famous sable beard mistaken for sea-salt.

The king's advisors made valiant attempts to dissuade him from leading the fleet himself. At his age, they protested, surely he had earned a respite from the battlefield—for, though this campaign has been referred to always as a "royal visit" from the monarch, anyone with an eye left in his head can see these are armed ships of war.

But he insisted. It was nearly thirty years ago that, leading a similar convoy, he first took the territories from Fortinbras, himself delivering on that lord the fatal blow. Now the king has had word of the son gathering an army, rising to take back the land his father lost. Another Fortinbras, like those ancient monsters who grew another head as soon as the hero had cut off the first. To whom besides himself (the king demanded of his men) could it be more sweet and fitting for the task to fall of sending Fortinbras, son of Fortinbras, to his father's fate?

His advisors wisely resisted the obvious answer. The king's only legitimate son is rather a sore subject with the monarch. Though intended, like his father, to commence in a military career as soon as his education is completed, the prince has lingered so long in school he might be accused of malingering—or else, it is joked, he must surely have earned his professorship by now. And the reports and rumors arriving from Wittenberg of the prodigal son's antics there—while impressing the duly impressionable young ladies of the court—serve in the soldiers' barracks only to make the prince even more of a laughingstock. Not that young Hamlet is ever called a coward. Treason, of course, to think of it that way.

They are gathering now on the shore, the king's soldiers, standing in twos and threes together smoking, not speaking, stamping their feet in the cold. They practice the feints and parries they have learned, or check their armor; archers test their strings in the damp air. Some have served beside the king for many years, in many wars; others are scarcely half the age of his delinquent son. Those too young to grow a beard wear their helmets with the fur-lined beavers down to disguise this fact. The king nods his head to these boys as he passes. They would return from this combat men, or not at all. This strikes him as meet, a fitting trial to test who deserved the privileges of manhood.

Early this morning, stirred by dreams of battle and blood, he visited the queen's bedchamber to perform upon her his conjugal duties. A similar leave-taking just over thirty years before had conceived his son, the perpetual scholar, and though it is too late now to hope for another heir, still his superstition honors the ritual. A private passageway was constructed for this purpose between the king's bed-closet and the queen's, concealed at either end by heavy French tapestries. He likes to slip in after she has fallen asleep, to take her by surprise. He likes to feel her struggle against the crush of his body, though her strength is nothing to his and easily he subdues her.

When he was done, he pulled away and threw the bed curtains back, examining her naked body in the candlelight. The bruises he left had been deliberately placed; nothing about his handiwork is sloppy, in love or war. He noted the positioning of each of them, the little red berry-marks raised by his signet ring on her white breasts. On the voyage to Norway, he will remember each and every mark, imagining the bruises fading, their edges yellowing, taking a greenish tint beneath the skin; and in this way will he be able to imagine his influence upon her even when he is gone. He ran his hand over her bare white body as if looking at a map of a battlefield laid out, on a territory belonging to himself alone. Then he kissed her once on the lips and dressed, his mind already gone ahead to his preparations.

He gives the signal. The horn is sounded. The sun is beginning to rise. The ewe bleats as a dim suspicion of her destiny begins to cross the vast untended pasture of her mind. Finally, she struggles and tries to run—far too late. The purpose of the knife is unmistakable. The soldiers gather around as the king prepares the rites of war.

From her bed, the queen hears far away, as in another world, the sheep's fatal scream. She has been since he left neither awake nor asleep, unwilling to trust her own senses. At the second sounding of the horn, she gets up and pulls a dressing-gown around her shoulders, moving with a somnambulist's care. Creeping slowly enough not to alert the guards outside her door, the queen slips past the Arras tapestry and through the passageway to her husband's chamber. The lamp left for the king to find his way by has gone out, and so she makes her way by touch, light as a ghost, or a girl.

She was a girl, the first time, more than thirty years ago; and though it has been more than a decade since her husband has last gone away to war, still she finds herself compelled to repeat this old ritual. Nor would she mention it to her confessor. God knows what He knows, she trusts, and He will judge accordingly. Besides, as any footman in the castle can tell you, the chapel echoes badly, and is rife with eavesdroppers.

The king's bedchamber is deserted, and the faint light of dawn reveals scattered evidence of finality and haste. For weeks—perhaps months, even—these rooms will be unused, unvisited even by the servants. The coals have already been allowed to go out in his fireplace. The queen shivers in her flimsy dressing-gown, taking in the room. She is alone. Steeling herself, she pulls back his bed-curtains to reveal a rumpled, empty bed. Its emptiness stares at her, challenging her to admit an emotion. Crawling into the darkness, she cocoons herself in heavy blankets that smell of the king.

"He is not here," she murmurs. Even now, after more than three decades, she could not tell you whether it is fear or sorrow or relief that brings the flood of tears into her eyes.

The queen was once the belle of Elsinore, but hers is that fair and rosy sort of beauty that is at its very peak in the ingénue; and loses something priceless and intangible when it ceases to be purely effortless. Her full cheeks have begun to hint at jowls, as her husband loves to remind her, pinching at a fingerful of the offending flesh. In subtler ways he reminds her as well, *silently, with his roving eye: never again will she be the most interesting woman in any room.*

And as for Himself? The queen looks at her husband sometimes and wonders how he can have remained so completely unchanged, after all these years. Broader in the belly, yes, and grayer in the beard, but still the same man she married. She can see in him sometimes the young war hero destined to be king, returning triumphant from battle after battle, beaming, his goodwill casting a genial glow over everything. And he is still that person, when everything goes his way. When his armies are winning, his sleep undisturbed, his soup hot, his ale cold, and his will unquestioningly and swiftly obeyed, the king is as sunny and charming a man as one could hope to meet. It is merely when anything at all goes wrong that he swiftly becomes awful to everyone. A lost battle, a lost key, a saucy letter from the prince, even a bout of indigestion is enough to cast the cloud over him: a silent rage hanging about his head, ready to strike out at whatever is careless enough to catch his attention.

Mostly, everyone at court tries always to ensure that nothing ever goes wrong. Misplaced possessions are swiftly found and replaced, errors are corrected or covered up. A whispered word of warning is passed on days when his mood is foul, and instantly everyone becomes as invisible as possible.

She herself has done this for many years, tiptoeing around the bad moods, rewarding the good with extravagant displays of affection. She dotes on him, like a precocious child at her father's knee, habitually babbling endearments at a pitch that might equally well convey either adoration or terror.

In a book she had found once in his library about a wise and ruthless prince, the author had taken up the question of whether it was better to be loved by one's people, or feared. His answer was that, if a monarch could not manage both, it was safer (a nice distinction) to be feared. But King Hamlet, she thinks, has done that Italian prince one better: he inspires a love that is itself a form of fear; a fear she clings to as stubbornly as love.

"Gertrude?"

For more than thirty years, she has been addressed as "Your Majesty" and "Madam." Even her husband, who might have spoken more intimately, never uses her given name. Instead he calls her by the affectionate generic "Wife"; or else he refers obliquely to her relationship as queen of his country, mother to his son—parties by whom his own perception of her is always triangulated. There is only one man to whom she has always been Gertrude, only Gertrude. His face appears in a wedge of dawning light as he pulls back the curtains of the bed.

"You were not here," she says. She dries her cheeks, leaving her tears behind on the sheets still rank with her husband's sweat. "I did not think you would come."

"I did not know if you would want me, after so many years." The bed-clothes pull away under his weight and un-cocoon her as he kneels atop the coverlet.

Gertrude shivers, though not at the draft. When the truce with Norway had been declared, she thought she should never be alone with him again—and here he is near enough to touch her. Why is he not touching her? There is a reserve and formality to his manner, and she wishes he would cast it off.

"I have seen you with him, hanging with your arms about his neck. I thought perhaps you had come to love him in earnest, after all this

time. Every day I have waited for a sign that you had not forgotten me."

"To give such a sign would have been to murder us both." After all these years, still he can astonish her with his transparency. "He knows how you love me." How could he not? It had been obvious—the eyes entreating her across every room, his clumsy schemes to speak with her alone. "The only thing that has kept you breathing is that I have never revealed—with a careless glance, a word, even a blush—how every minute I burned for you as well."

She sinks her hands into the fine cloth of his undershirt, rubbing it against the coarser weave of hairy chest beneath. "Now give me less of your tongue's art, more of its matter."

His kisses taste of smoke and earth, and they layer like autumn leaves atop the memories of his kisses tasting of smoke and earth that have sustained her all these years.

With the king, she has learned the arts of a whore. A practical woman, she knows if she does what pleases him, it will be over more quickly; and so she wraps her legs around his back, moaning and hissing out hysterical confessions of lust.

But with the king's brother, she does not make a sound. She does not make a sound, and he does not make a sound. His mouth moves like a pat of butter melting to salve fresh bruises, and the older, yellowed ones, and still he does not say a word, not even with his eyes. His fingers paddling in her neck to soothe the knots away that she had not known until then were there. His hands are everywhere, and then not just his hands, and him still half-dressed, and they do not make a sound. He moves slowly—then quickly—then, for an instant, not at all. And still he does not make a sound, and she opens her mouth and thinks she is screaming, but finds all that her breath can manage is the faintest squeak.

He smiles at this, rolling onto the bolster beside her. "My mouse," he says, caressing her cheek between his thumb and forefinger.

She laughs, and finds the tears rising again. "I had forgotten why you used to call me that."

At twenty, the brothers had been as alike as two acorns; but thirty years have given each his own distinctive face. Claudius is unmistakable in the lines run through his forehead, ringed under his eyes. Heavy, it is said, is the head that wears the crown; but, she thinks, the lack of it sometimes wears heavier.

"You are my wife, Gertrude, not his."

Not this old argument again. "It was only a promise."

"A consummated promise." He is sitting up now, gearing up his anger. "A handfasting is a marriage, if it is consummated. And after that, to marry with my brother!"

She closes her eyes and sighs. After so many years, she could almost give his lines as well as her own. "You know I could not refuse. I was not even seventeen. My father wanted..."

"Your father!" he cries. "You wanted! You wanted to be queen."

"Very well. I wanted to be queen." At first, her father had encouraged her engagement to Prince Claudius. Then, through his spies, he discovered that the ailing king's voice for the succession was to go not to the elder of his twin sons, but to the younger by nineteen minutes: Horwendil, Lord Hamlet, the hero lately returned from the wars. Her father had laughed at her objection to the switch: "Why, I cannot see a hair's difference between them, except that one is to be king!"

She had convinced herself it was the truth—if she had come to love a face, she could learn to love it, she thought, on whichever gentleman it might appear. Two men could not be closer than sharing the same womb. So she had returned Claudius's letters and turned all her charms instead upon his brother.

"And within two months—two little months!—I lost my wife, my father, and my crown."

"I could have refused to marry him and angered my father and been shut up behind the convent walls, and now I would be a nun instead of queen. I could have taken poison—I had the vial in my hand—and I would be dead. But instead, I am queen. These were my choices. This way, I thought, I could at least be near you. We have had a life together, even in pieces. And I have had the worser time of it, I think, than you—for I have had to be his wife."

Her voice is shaking. What is it with these men, these Hamlets? Her husband, her lover, her son—each of them looks at the world through the same eyes, orates over the same neurotic, self-absorbed obsessions, seals his letters with the same signet-ring. Each one more proud, ruthless, and stubborn than the last. And to each of them she is bound less by her own desires than by the inexorable, painful pull of destiny.

Her son had been a frail child; born too soon, he had not been expected to live out his first day. The midwife took one look at the bluish creature she had whelped and sent word to hire a gravedigger. "A pity too," she sighed. "It would have been a boy."

For days the young prince had vacillated between life and death, his tiny body seeming to choose one, then the other. Gertrude hovered, too, between sleep and wakefulness, as if by constant vigilance she could hold his life in place. She did not consult the stars to see whether the hour of his birth had been a lucky one for the country or inauspicious. She visited no oracle to hear whispers of what the future might bring. Blindly, she held him to her breast, whispering, "Live." And blindly, he obeyed.

Claudius puts his lips to her bare shoulder. She cannot see the bruise, but she knows it must be there by the tenderness of his kiss.

"It is madness," she tells him, "even to risk what I have risked for you."

"We have been lucky so far." His words are breath and tongue against her neck. "Perhaps Heaven is smiling on our love."

"We have been lucky," she agrees, folding herself into his familiar warm embrace. "Thank the gods young Hamlet was born early."

Forever in a Playhouse

Guildenstern and Rosencrantz had arrived before me. I groaned, clutching the small paper-wrapped parcel in my hand, hoping it would not attract their notice. Framed in Hamlet's doorway, they made a peculiar silhouette, like the number 10: the one long and lean and immaculately tailored, the other round as an O, with fussy Venice lace at every straining seam. Even before I drew near enough to make out the subject of their squabbling, I could see their heads turning like to one another at intervals, like some sort of mechanical toy, which, regularly wound, would continue repeating the same argument until doomsday.

When I saw that they were not arriving at the prince's apartments but leaving, my mood brightened considerably. I considered hiding behind the willow tree in the yard until they had gone, but it was too late—they had already spotted me.

Abandoning their conversation, Guildenstern bared his bottom teeth as I approached, not quite a smile. I gave a neutral nod.

"I wouldn't bother visiting," he sighed. "Hamlet's in one of his swoons. He must have them regularly, you know."

"He's very ill, poor dear—he should be bled!" said Rosencrantz. His face was even ruddier than usual, and glossed with perspiration.

"Aye—monthly, like a woman." Guildenstern's sallow lip curled under in a pursed smirk, and with a thumb and forefinger he delicately smoothed his anemic moustache.

Fishing through his pockets, Rosencrantz eventually located his handkerchief and mopped the sweat from his brow. "What did he mean—had we been sent for? Sent from where? By whom?"

"He had no idea who we were," snapped Guildenstern. "He was soused off his head on Hippocras. I swear, that apothecary is the devil himself."

"Hippocras?" I was taken aback by the mention of medicinal wine. "Is my lord Hamlet ill?"

Guildenstern merely rolled his eyes.

"Now remember," Rosencrantz chided him, "dear Horatio has not been acquainted with the prince so long as you or I. How could he know?"

This statement came off as at once generous and patronizing, not unlike the fleshy arm draped heavily across my back. Instinctively, I recoiled from it, only to find myself flanked on the other side by Guildenstern's far bonier embrace.

"Let me advise you—friendly, in your ear." Even Guilden-stern's voice was pointed: an edge sharp as honed steel hiding beneath a courtier's honeyed tones. "If it is advancement you are seeking—a wealthy patron? a friend at court?—you had best look elsewhere. Even if you managed to hold his interest for more than a month or two . . ."

"—which you shan't, mind you," piped Rosencrantz, sniffling now into his handkerchief.

"Of course not," Guildenstern agreed. "But the point, you see, is that Prince Hamlet is a fool's bet. A lost cause. He will never be King of Denmark, unless his father grants him the right of suc-cession."

I shrugged, as much as to say this news meant nothing to me.

Guildenstern sighed and explained: "Without the king's de-cree, the prince will not inherit automatically. It goes to a vote of the council, who may elect any male relative to the throne. A formality, really, when there is only one son. But, if it were to be done, it should have been done years ago—as soon as the prince came of age. I daresay he was rather expecting the decree to come down today, in his father's birthday letter."

"But it has not?" I gathered.

"And alas, he has gone mad!" wailed Rosencrantz. He blew his nose with a loud honk, only inches from my ear.

"He is not mad," Guildenstern contradicted him at once. "After all—he kept our birthday gifts." He shrugged. "The prince is spoilt, as princes are wont to be. He pouts and sulks and rages like a child when he does not get his way."

I tore myself from their clutches, sputtering with outrage. "I have seen him lofty at times, and sour to those who love him not!" I allowed my tone to implicate the pair of fanged adders before my eyes. "But to those who serve him honestly, he is as sweet as summer!"

Guildenstern appeared unimpressed with this. "And many a summer's day is fine, until a storm rolls in. Beware: Prince Hamlet's mind changes with the winds."

He pushed past me and through the gate, Rosencrantz tumbling after.

"I thought it was when Mercury went into retrograde," the young lord said, *click-clack, click-clack* upon his rosary.

The scene I found in Hamlet's sitting-room was one of violent disarray. His writing-desk, and quite a large radius around, was a disaster of torn and crumpled pages, like some deciduous tree that shed leaves of parchment. A table was laid out with a supper of cold meats (untouched, I noted, except by the gathering flies) and a Venetian wine decanter (empty). The furniture had been shoved rudely against the wall, all but a cushioned footstool, which lay on its side in the center of the room.

It was the scattered books that struck me most chillingly, however. A king's fortune had been unshelved and lay about piled in towers, or toppled towers spread across the floor. Some volumes were splayed on their stomachs on tables or over the backs of chairs, while one had been abandoned with an empty goblet left propping open its pages, leaving ringed purple stains.

The prince's favorite large armchair had been pulled to face the hearth, so dangerously close that soot darkened the upholstery. Worried about the leaping coals, I approached the chair, intending to return it to its customary place—then saw a pair of legs draped over the arm.

"My lord?"

The prince was sitting sideways in the wide seat, a thick volume open in his lap. However, he was not reading, as I had first surmised, but only turning the pages as he tore them one by one from the book and discarded them into the fire.

"Ah, Horatio, there you are," he said casually, as though I had merely stepped for a moment into another room. He held up the folio for my perusal. "Have you studied anatomy?"

I had, and admitted as much—though something of the gleam in his eyes caused me to stumble over the words.

"So tell me this," he said, continuing to rifle through the pages. "Of what substance is it made—the soul, I mean?"

"The soul, my lord?" This had not been covered in my studies of medicine. I tried to recall the teachings from my readings in divinity.

"I will tell you the answer: Words."

"Words?"

"Words!" he crowed. "They are all that will remain, when we

are gone." He tore another page from the anatomy—the figure of a man—and sent it fluttering into the flames, pausing to watch it curl to ash and smoke. "We are no more than the page upon which our souls are written. And where does the tale go, when the book is burned? It may be remembered, and put down again. You and I are made up of our words."

Casting down the dissected anatomy book, he picked up another from the floor. I knew it by its cover as Gruter's *Roman Histories*. Every student at the University has, or has had, a copy. Along with Ovid's *Metamorphoses*, it is used for practicing translation in the introductory Latin class.

"Thirty," Hamlet groaned. "Nero died at thirty." He stressed the phrase rather oddly, I thought—not on *died*, but *Nero*. "He went mad, you know." Again: not *mad*, but *he*. It made all the difference. There was something to him still of his usual charm, though it seemed strained, as though requiring something of a performance to maintain. This, from the man whose salient quality was effortlessness, worried me more than the tantrums and burned books.

"Nero was too young to become Emperor," I suggested mildly, hoping to turn the subject to the source of his distress, "given power he did not know how to wield."

"He was a tyrant, a traitor, and a murderer!" the prince burst out. "Do not make his excuses. An unnatural murderer, for he killed his own mother. But I have done as much and worse in my nightmares."

I fetched the footstool, righting it to sit beside his chair. "Those are but dreams, my lord."

"It was real, as real as you or I, here now." He clutched my arm, and, in spite of myself, I felt my face go warm with pleasure. "Nay, more. A hundred thousand times more real. I have seen myself in my mother's bedchamber. A tapestry stained with hot blood still beating from the wound. I have heard her scream, in my dreams, felt the dagger's hilt in my hand as flesh gave way to gore." He shook his head. "But why should I do such a thing, even in dreams?"

"You have had a letter from the king, your father?" A bit abrupt, but I was losing patience with this talk of dreams and souls. Fortunately, it seemed to work; the prince barked out a laugh.

"So was it Rosencrantz, or the other one? Never mind—they are fanged adders both, but I shall have my revenge on them; I have seen that in my dreams as well. But your spies have given you false coin in this: the letter was my mother's doing." He pulled a rolled sheet of parchment from his doublet and read aloud from it in a mocking falsetto: "*O Hamlet, why do you consume yourself in single life? Grant, if you will, that you are beloved of many; but that you love none is most evident by your improvidence for your own future! If you die issueless, the world will weep that you have left no copy. For, just as you are said to be my glass, recalling the lovely April of my prime, your sweet issue shall bear your own sweet form. For love of me, make me another little boy just like yourself. Or else, for shame, Hamlet, deny that you bear love to me or anyone! Oh, change your thought, that I may change my mind! Dear my love, you know that you shall have a father when you let your son say so.*"

He began to put the letter back into his pocket, then in a sudden defiance, tossed it, too, into the fire. "As if a grandchild should be enough to satisfy *the-king-my-father*! Nay, he will not be content until he has my very life. Did they tell you what he sent me, for a birthday gift?"

"No, my lord." I chose my wording carefully. "Just—what he failed to send."

He gave a grimace, then gestured over his shoulder to the far end of the room, to which he had turned the back of his chair. "I cannot bear to look upon it. Even when I close my eyes, I can see it still."

Turning my head, I was startled to see a huge and bearded man standing silent in the shadowy corner behind the door, watching us. My stomach dropped out of me and my heart thundered up in my chest before I realized it was only the figure of a man: a suit of armor set up on a stand. What I had taken for a beard was the sable lining of the helmet's faceplate.

"But—what is it for?" I asked. He could not be meant to wear such a thing. For one thing, the suit was far too large; the gauntlet-arms alone would nearly circle Hamlet's waist.

"A message. Such was the very armor he had on when he struck down old Fortinbras of Norway," he answered with a sigh. "A fool so ambitious as to wish to keep his father's land. He would not flee with his wife in exile, though she carried his son. He claimed his gods were buried there." He gave a shrug. "So he was buried with them. This was thirty years ago, and now the son has gathered up a band of ruffians and malcontents from the skirts of Norway, who have various grudges and claims against my father, from the war. They would have their lands returned, and to this end commit violence against our citizens and acts of piracy upon our fleets. I say return the land to them, as it is worth nothing to me. But young Fortinbras and I are of an age, and the king wishes me to fight a duel with him for the territory. A duel to the death."

"A duel!" It occurred to me that I had never seen the prince wielding a sword, even for practice. "And have you met this Fortinbras?"

"Once, at his uncle's court. A decent enough fellow, earnest, but totally obsessed with avenging his father's death. Morbidly so. It makes him a bit of a bore, actually." He swung his legs around and pushed against the marble hearth to scoot his chair back from the fire. "Still, I have no desire to kill him, or be killed, over a strip of land worth nothing but obstinate pride."

He tossed the history book whole into the fire. Bound vellum, it smoked and gave off a stink like a tanner's shop, but Hamlet only collapsed back, chin in his hand, watching it burn. As a child, he had told me, he loved better than anything the coals buried at night in the ashes of the hearth. His first toddling steps were taken in pursuit of these glowing jewels, and when his careful mother prevented him from reaching this goal, he would rail at her and scream, trying to wrestle himself from her tyrannical embrace. He showed me scars he still bore on his hands from those times she caught him too late, and it seemed he never learned despite his countless "accidents." I had laughed with him at this tale, but now I could see in him some of this willfully self-destructive child still.

"Thirty!" He kicked his legs out from the chair, folding his arms across his chest in a gesture almost hopelessly adolescent. "You know, a fortune-teller once predicted I would die at thirty."

I nodded, refusing to allow my digestion to be affected by this prophecy. "Was this the same goblet-salesman who warned your family would all be poisoned?"

"Nay, this one said it would be in a duel!" He looked at me, and his eyes were ringed with worry. "The blind witch read my palm, and swore it!"

"Well, if she was *blind* . . ." I could no longer conceal my skeptic's smirk.

Hamlet smiled at this. "Horatio, I can always count on you to do my doubting for me." He rose and went to the window, looking out at the sky. "But if it is not this year, it will be another. I am dying, Horatio. And of the commonest illness affecting man—mortality." He laughed a shrill cackle. To hear him laugh, I did not wonder there were those who thought my friend a little mad.

"A merry birthday celebration, this," I said dryly.

"And what do those two traitors, my false friends, present me with?" From his pocket, Hamlet procured a pair of gaudy ornaments, one silver and one gold. "From Rosencrantz—" He showed me a pocket looking-glass, engraved on the reverse: *Thy glass will show thee how thy beauties wear* . . . "And from Guildenstern," he opened the gaudy pomander to reveal a pocket clock, far grander than my own. "*Thy dial, how thy precious minutes waste . . .*" he read from the inscription.

I could not help but feel this last was meant as a slight against me as well; I took particular pride in keeping the hours for the prince, who never knew the time. Holding out my hand for the gilded dial, I compared it to my own plain brass before concluding: "It runs rather fast."

I thought this a good time to offer my own birthday gift— though none so rich as that which he had already received. For some reason unable to look in his eyes, I dumbly handed him the parcel tied in a scrap of ribbon. To add another to the jumbled heaps of books about Hamlet struck me as ridiculous, and yet I gamely offered forth the little volume.

Eagerly, he unwrapped the parcel. Finding no title-page on the quarto, he began to turn the pages in confusion. "But—the leaves are all vacant."

I felt my cheeks grow hot. "They await the imprint of your mind, my lord. It is a diary, to commit your thoughts."

He appeared vaguely puzzled as to the purpose of such an office.

"That you may later reacquaint yourself with what your memory cannot contain." I had made the little journal myself, out of pages taken from my own writing-book. With my penknife, I carefully cut out the bottoms of half-pages and those partly marred by blots. Then, assembling these waste-blanks together, I cut diamond-shaped holes at the top and bottom of each page, securing these with twin laces of leather cut from an old winter glove, and knotted into tiny roses. It was tedious work, more physically intricate than study, and more than once had I drawn blood from my cuticles with a slip of the blade. But it would be worth it, I had told myself, for the look on the prince's face.

This was not quite the look I had pictured.

"This is only part of the gift," I extemporized. "I will take down what thoughts you visit here, as often as you will, and use these passages to enrich your book—that is, a sort of tale, or, ah—*history* of your life, which I have already begun to compile." I had not intended to mention the sonnets I had composed, either to the prince's portrait, or more recently—but there it was, out.

Hamlet's eyes lit up, and with them the entire room. "Do you mean to write another play, and about me?" He examined the blank book with new respect. "A play about its hero's thoughts—what a novel idea!"

I had intended poems, but he seemed so pleased with the idea I could not bear to disappoint him. "Naturally, a play. Statues crumble, portraits fade, but a play may be performed again and again *ad infinitum*, and its paint and marble is the blood and breath of life. The tongues of generations yet unborn will think your thoughts—learning to be your being, long after every soul now breathing in the world is dead." I thought this speech particularly moving, and was pleased to see Hamlet's cheeks taking on their customary color.

"To live for-ever in a playhouse," he sighed. "Now that would be felicity indeed." He clasped my arm, newly invigorated. "It is a brave gift, and deserves much thanks. Yes, a play is the very thing. What hour now?"

I felt for my watch. "Twenty past one," I said, guiltily pleased that he had not thought to consult his own pocket for the answer.

"My favorite tragedians in the city are recently returned from their tour of the provinces and play at two. If we hurry, we can yet catch the prologue."

I hesitated. "I have an appointment at the Academia this afternoon." I had been called to meet with the dean to discuss my recent frequent absences, as well as my plan to pay off my burgeoning debt in petty fines.

Hamlet pouted. "You are never truant from your studies, even for a holiday? A royal birthday is a holiday." His hot hand enclosed my own suddenly cold one. "There is more to be learned in this world than is found in books of philosophy." He ran his tongue across his rosy lips. "More of earth, and heaven."

My breath caught in me. At the best of times, the full force of his gaze had that effect on a person; it was profoundly disconcerting. I wondered how much of the prince's reputation as a great philosopher was merely his ability to reduce his debating opponents to gibbering fools, just by meeting their eyes.

At last I relented, reasoning that it would be unwise to leave the prince alone in such a labile state. Besides, I told myself, I still had to engage a cast of players for the baron's comedy, and where better to find them than at the theatre?

The place the coachman dropped us was not, as I had been secretly hoping, the same playhouse where my translations had been so well received, and where I returned with some regularity to hear a play (rarely ever to see much of it, bruised by errant elbows and fondled by pickpockets among the groundlings). This theatre was much smaller, and also seemed older, dingier; the wood was splintering in places and there was a faint but pervasive damp smell, like moldering mushrooms.

Still, it gave me a thrill when the manager (a lanky, long-haired man with circles under his eyes) recognized Hamlet at once. Saying he had saved for us "the Royal Box," he led us up a creaking staircase to a rather cramped compartment at the top.

From this dizzying height, we could see the stage quite clearly, as well as look down into the other boxes. Disappointingly, they were empty, or else their occupants had drawn the muslin curtains for privacy. Hamlet motioned for the man to pull ours shut as well.

For seating, there was only a single long couch, laid with cushions. The prince waved me toward it while he bought a bag of chestnuts from an orange-girl. I perched myself on the edge at the far end. He slumped into the seat, giving a yawn, then turned to me.

"May I lie in your lap?"

"My lord?" I stammered. A witty retort, I know.

"With my head in your lap, I mean." His wide eyes blinked in perfect innocence. "It is how I have always taken in a play."

"Of course, my lord."

As he arranged himself, I wondered if this should be taken as an intimacy, or mere royal entitlement. A prince was trained from birth to see every attendant as his property, to use as he saw fit. He might indeed lie thus with anybody—heavy head pillowed just so between his companion's thighs, and hotly breathing. I tried not to think too much of it.

Instead, I craned my neck to look down on the groundlings. How strange and small their pointed caps appeared! The play had not attracted much of an audience; I counted only a few dozen standing around waiting for the actors to begin. A selection of bored, heavily painted prostitutes reclined against the stage. It was not until an unexpected moustache sharpened my gaze on one of them that I realized these were not women, but unemployed boy-actors hanging about, advertising their talents in tattered gowns of gaily colored taffeta. It was one of these underfed anonymous foreign players the prince would have to impersonate, when we began rehearsals for the baron's comedy.

Now that I gave notice to it, there did not appear to be any actual women present, apart from the pair of wenches selling oranges. I hoped today's performance did not have too martial of a theme; I once saw played a tragedy about the war between the Romans and the Goths that disturbed my digestion for a full month afterwards. I have always been particularly affected by the sight, not of blood itself (a surgeon's incision incites no such revulsion), but of violent bloodletting.

Hamlet finished peeling a chestnut and popped it in his mouth. I could feel the mastication of his jaw through my hose, and I was ashamed that he might notice their threadbare condition.

"What is the play?" I asked as the trumpets were sounded.

"A classic tale," he whispered back. "*The Passionate Friendship of Damon and Pythias*."

I was familiar with the story, of course, of the two philosophers of Syracuse so famously devoted to one another. It had been several years since I had read it, however, and I could not immediately recall which of the two men was condemned to death, and which the one that took his place, pledging his own life against his friend's return.

As the prologue began, I soon became engrossed in an intricate backstory involving the drunken tyrant Dionysius, whose recent overthrow of his brother had led to the arrest of that deposed king's most faithful sergeant at arms, Pythias.

The actor playing Pythias was too old for the role by half, his gray hair dyed a garish yellow. He had an annoying habit of drilling into his lengthy speeches an unnatural rhythm, quite removed from the meaning of the lines, accompanied by broad gestures—as if his hand were a hacksaw with which he hoped to fell the audience. I frowned, trying to cast him in my comedy—perhaps he could play the courtly Fool?

Damon was a well-built youth with chestnut hair cut blunt across his jaw, and a face that could only ever play a younger brother. He did well enough in his role, I thought—you might believe, as he embraced his friend through iron bars of painted wood, that he actually thought the old ham was beautiful. I made a note to speak to him about the lover's part.

Then Pythias began another endless monologue comparing the deposed and Jove-like king to the tyrant who had so recently dismantled him. The prince shifted his weight on my lap, rolling on his back to look up at me.

"Have we such perfect amity?" he asked. "Would you be such a friend as Damon dear, and pledge your life for mine, and keep my place, if I had such a need?"

"I would." Even as I spoke, I shocked myself. Not with the answer, but by how quickly it had been decided—without a moment's hesitation, or even conscious thought. It rattled me, as a scientist, to know something so absolutely, instinctively, without examination or trials in proof.

"Swear it!" Hamlet's eyes stared wells into mine. I put my hand to my heart, having naught else to swear by.

"Hic et Ubique." I made the oath, as is the custom, in the scholars' tongue. Here and Everywhere.

At once, I felt my universe shift. My heart leaped from my chest, and when it returned again, it beat at odds. I had become an instrument, and tuned to Hamlet's key. My mind was trued to Hamlet's truth, aligned with Hamlet's mind in such a perfect marriage, it seemed the most natural conclusion in the world when he rose up to seal the vow with a kiss.

But I see now, the word *kiss* is insufficient for the fatal impact of his lips on mine. Rather, it has too many meanings—diverse contexts, dense sensual and spiritual connotations. Lovers kiss, but so do brothers. A father may kiss his son; the sun, the meadow; the wind, the sails of a ship; the sea, the shore; and some there be that shadows kiss. A supplicant may kiss the mantle of his king; a pilgrim, his holy relic; a ball, its neighbor on a billiards table. A kiss may seal an indenture, bless a child, bid greeting or farewell, reveal, deceive. It may be public, private, holy, unholy, righteous, unauthorized. And all of these were here invoked. It was not because Hamlet's kiss was specific to any of these meanings, but precisely because it was so ambiguous, that I found myself utterly gobsmacked by it.

In fact, it was not until much later—after the devoted friends had been reunited and pardoned and the players were gathering to take their bows—that it even occurred to me to ask: "Would you return for me, as Pythias?"

But in my lap, Hamlet had gone to sleep.

Sub Rosa

Concerned about thieves, he said—but doubtless after our wedding night, harboring as well a newfound fear of cuckoldry—my husband planted rosebushes. Not for any lack: there were Damascus roses in the garden, both red and white, kept for their attar; and bushes he had brought in a cart home from Provence with pale-pink blooms as fat as cabbages. He'd dug the holes himself, as if to prove to some ghost scowling over his shoulder that, though a gentleman now, he was not afraid of honest work.

(There was a ghost, of course. Not over his shoulder, but inside his head: his father, who had left the world owning no more than when he came into it, cursing his only son, who had turned his back on the emperor's orchards to join his armies instead. By the time he returned, a wealthy man, his father was already buried and the sapling planted at his grave grown taller than the son who stood embracing it and wept.)

But beneath my windows, he set common dog-roses—a clambering variety, better known for their thick foliage and vicious thorns than for their blossoms, which were odorless, and pale as winter butter. These he set to climb the walls of the house, where my bedchamber overlooks the upper lawn and gardens. An ambitious climber himself, he admired their tenacity, and envied their speed. When my husband returned from his travels to court, or to meet his ships at port in Lisbon or Venice, he instead judged the passage of time by how tall his roses had grown in his absence. In five years, they had already reached the second-story windows, and the maids complained that they could not shake out the linens in the morning without catching them on brambles. (The chamber-pots suffered no such injury; and doubtless their contents contributed to the luxuriance of the foliage.) Now, after nearly a decade, they have grown to cover my balcony entirely in a canopy of briars.

You may think me a caged bird; but this arrangement suits me well enough. This city thrives on innuendo. Everyone has heard the tale about the maid of spotless reputation, ruined on her wedding day on the mere rumor alone that she had been seen at her window talking with a man. Abandoned and humiliated, she was so overcome by the accusation that she fell down dead from shock and grief. A tragedy, they call it now—but only because the maid was later proved innocent. If she had truly been talking with a man, they'd call it a cautionary tale against wantonness.

But the shade from my rosebushes allows me to sit unobserved on my balcony at any time of day. The sunlight filtered through the leaves is just strong enough for reading, but not quite bright enough for embroidery, which I loathe. The rose hips make a tasty jam and a healthful brandy toddy, and

the dried petals, when added to my pipe, both scent my tobacco and pro-
voke vivid dreams. Lastly, while maintaining for my husband a façade of
impenetrable chastity, my roses also provide a convenient curtain, shielding
me from any spy to those activities I should wish to carry out underneath.
You see, my husband had forgotten two important things. First, that rose-
bushes, like all living creatures, obey the will of those who tend them, not
who planted them.

Also: some of us are bred for briars, not blooms.

✀

I was crossing under the shadow of the baron's clambering rosebushes when I heard the voice, so low and velvet it might have
been a shadow itself.

"Good Master Poet."

Arrested in my tracks, I sought the source of this address. Nobody was about that I could see, either in the courtyard or the
upper gardens.

"He is the one, is he not? The young man." In the bright summer's day, the baroness, in a blackberry-colored gown, was near
invisible in the shadows of the brambled canopy overgrowing the
balcony.

I followed her gaze to the lawn, where the players were gathered up for the rehearsal. The eye was drawn at once, of course, to
Hamlet, deep in conversation with one of the actors—the one who
had played Damon (his real name has escaped me, for all in our
company were ever called by the names of the parts they acted).

"Which young man, my lady?" I stalled for time, panic tuning my voice a step too sharp.

She answered dryly: "Your *master-mistress*, Master Poet. The heroine." The baroness was yet staring down at me with those disconcerting dark eyes. "He is the inspiration for your sonnets, is he not?"

A blush crept up my face. How could I ever have believed a prince might be passed off as a common traveling player?

"Oh—do you mean Little Willie Hughes?" I cringed speaking the name; it had been Hamlet's own suggestion, but like many points of the history concocted deep in our cups, it seemed in sober daylight spotty and implausible. "A very fine boy actor from abroad, exceptionally skilled in his portrayal of young ladies. *A man in hue, all hues in his control*, they say—a sort of pun, you see, on the lad's name."

I was babbling now, my cheeks growing hotter and hotter under her patient gaze. She listened as though dissecting every word I tossed into the air, until the weight of such diligent and careful attention smothered me at last into silence.

"Your poems do not do him justice." This simple and withering critique was delivered in the same dispassionate tone with which she might comment on the weather.

"I know it," I sighed. It was nothing more than I had told myself a hundred times before. "My skill is not worthy of its subject. As a poet, I am but a rank amateur, unseasoned . . ."

"Your skills as a poet are fine," she snapped. " 'Tis your heart that wants seasoning. I think you had better look at the scene from up here. A new perspective."

She bent down, out of sight but for a rustling behind the floral canopy; then a braided ladder uncoiled from the balcony, falling with a soft thud in the dust at my feet. I gaped at this incongruous jute rope.

"I find it convenient sometimes to be able to leave the house without alerting my husband," she offered as her only explanation. She bent over the balcony to look down at me, and I caught a glimpse of her full face in the light: biting her thumbnail, a long black tendril escaped from her coif. "Do not worry. It is perfectly safe."

I did not know whether she meant that my ascent would be unobserved by her husband, or that the braided rope was like to bear my weight and not send me crashing into rose brambles. The woody canes were thick as a child's arm and brandished fearsome sharp thorns, curved like the claws of a cat. Still, with some difficulty and only a touch of vertigo, I scrabbled up the swaying hammock-ladder, where I found at the top a gap in the brambles just wide enough for a man to pass unharmed.

Awkwardly, I threw my leg over the ledge and pulled myself onto the balcony. I was panting with the exertion from the climb; I could not imagine how the baroness ever managed it in skirts.

I found myself for a moment half-blind in the shade and dappled light, which illuminated the balcony and the baroness in finger-widths at a time. She turned to me, and for a moving instant, the hollows of her cheeks were filled, her lashes bright with sunlight. Then she drew closer and the shadows reappeared in half-moons underneath her eyes.

I turned away, busying myself with pulling the ladder up after me, refolding it into well-worn creases. Though this removed my only means of escape from the narrow balcony, I dared not leave evidence of my ascent. It would not do, for Hamlet's inquisitive head to come popping over the ledge, allowing the baroness to interrogate "Little Willie" directly.

I squinted through the brambles. Hamlet was still engaged in the task of perfecting the unperfect actor. He sawed the air with his hand, demonstrating a habit of the boy's; then performed for him a more measured and elegant gesture, flawlessly. Thank goodness he was occupied, at least; I had that much to be grateful for.

The sound of the prince's laughter pierced the air. I knew that peculiar triple-pronged shriek; doubtless, he had made some joke, probably at young Damon's expense. The boy flushed crimson, and a frown furrowed his unlined brow, but his eyes still shone with adoration.

The baroness followed my gaze. "Look at him, flirting with that poor child."

She was right; the chestnut-haired youth was hardly more than a child, no older than the schoolboys who arrived at University each autumn in freshly pressed black robes. Last year, he might have played the heroine himself; now he had been reduced to the smaller role of her poor-but-honest suitor, the youngest son. At first the young man had complained to me, resenting sight unseen this "famous foreign player" who had stolen the choicest part without audition—as if she had been his mistress and the interloper had seduced her. But on meeting Hamlet, all such thoughts had been of course forgotten instantly. The cherub-faced boy instead now mooned about the stage after his "lady," utterly unable to remember his lines. "I think the lad has taken too well to his lover's part," I said, chuckling indulgently.

"It is easy to watch and laugh while beauty makes fools of others." She looked at me, and her dark eyes were now filled with pity. "And so hard to see when you yourself are the one playing the fool."

Suddenly, the young actor's gestures seemed sickeningly familiar. But still I did not know whether this was shame at recognizing my own foolishness in the lovesick boy, or jealousy at seeing my role so easily recast. Heartburn rose in my chest; I felt as though I carried a weight of hot coals in my belly.

Hamlet had moved on from the chestnut-haired youth to another of the players. This boy, even younger than the other, was playing the second ingénue, the heroine's sister-cousin, and Hamlet made a great show of bowing and kissing his hand, calling him "milady," while the first young lover looked on jealously.

I was by this time used to the prince's effect on people. I had witnessed it a thousand times. When he addressed them, men's gestures became as broad as those of players on a stage; women listened to his witticisms with their faces already bent towards laughter.

But, now this admirable quality irritated me, ever so slightly, like an itch. How blithely Hamlet could stride through a room, unaware of the turmoil he left in his wake! How many people were thinking of him right now? How many men's souls had he stolen, how many women's eyes amazed? How many were speaking, dreaming, arguing, reading, writing about Prince Hamlet right at this very moment? And he, meanwhile, would never give any of them so much as a thought!

At the small of my back, Lady Adriane's touch was as firm and cool as the blade of a knife. Her hot breath tickled the nape of my neck as she whispered low, in my ear:

"Fool. Did you think you could run around night and day with the Prince of Denmark without anybody's putting two and two together? Or perhaps you believed we would all be so easily deceived as the shepherds in your comedy?"

My soul leapt out of my skin. *Of course, of course we have been caught*, raced my heart. The rest of me had turned to a pillar of salt.

I forced myself to breathe. It meant nothing that the baroness knew of the prince's activities—unless she decided to inform Hamlet's father. Perhaps she could be bribed, persuaded that any scandal in the production would reflect poorly on her husband's reputation as well. The key was to proceed in the negotiations rationally, and remain calm, indicating strength.

"What do you want?" My trembling voice came out in a crack-and-stutter. So much for calm. I was sure she could see how the pulse at the base of my Adam's apple was throbbing. Hamlet would never forgive me, and I would never forgive myself.

Her laugh was surprisingly light. "This is not blackmail, Master Horatio," she said. "After all, I may have discovered one of your secrets—but, in fairness, I have also revealed one of mine."

She indicated the ladder coiled in my frozen hands. The ends of the rope attached to iron hooks in the wall, hidden under the vines. When coiled up tight, the ladder fit neatly into place, invisible to anyone who didn't know exactly where to look, but ready to unroll in an instant, in case a quick escape became suddenly expedient. What did it mean, that she had chosen to share this piece of information with me? I felt as though I were playing a game of chess, but in a dream, where I had forgotten all the rules and did not recognize the pieces.

"But there is one thing I still do not understand." Her hand was steady at my back, her voice strangely soothing in my ear. "You are no Dane yourself, and owe no particular allegiance to their prince. Still, he expects your attendance at a moment's notice, at all hours of the night—and you go to him. He sends away his servants and desires you to attend him alone."

I nodded. I had not to that point considered it a hardship. Rather, it was a thrill to me anew each time I received the knock at my door, his messenger bearing an invitation for me to come away.

"But still, you do not wear the liveries of Denmark, nor live with him at the embassy. Have you not accepted his patronage?"

Against my will, I felt my body stiffen.

"Oh, I see," she said. "He has not offered it."

I blushed all my answer. Though it may seem shamefully naive to admit it, I had honestly not considered such a thing as seeking employment in the prince's retinue, preferring instead to pretend, against all evidence, that I too was a gentleman. It rattled me to realize it; as pragmatic and circumspect as I considered myself to be, I had taken terrible risks with my future at the University without even a thought to my own reward. My devotions, made for friendship, expected no other recompense; but her tone insinuated sinister meanings into the prince's silence.

"I am his friend," I countered, "not his attendant."

"Nor his poet?" she countered. "His biographer? The sonnets you write for him—they are no formal commission? He has not paid you for them?"

I drew myself up indignantly. "I would not seek payment from him for those private letters he has inspired me, in friendship, to write! Else, he should think my honest feelings naught but rank flattery, designed to shake another coin from his purse!"

She pursed her lips, considering carefully. "So . . . you would be free, then, to accept payment from another patron, for the poems—one whose interest in them was only truth?"

I stared at her, understanding her meaning at last. "You wish to read my poetry?"

"To publish it, in fact. A cycle of sonnets about your love."

A curious sensation came over me at the idea: something like hunger; something like lust.

"I would pay for the privilege, of course," she continued in the same casual, theoretical tone. "Not a prince's ransom, perhaps—but enough to keep you in bread and ink." She ran her eyes over me again and smiled, not unkindly. "Perhaps some new clothes."

How often had I wished for some means to rescue me from the shabby poverty that set me apart from the prince's other favorites! Guildenstern was not the only one to remind me that, if *companion* at its root dined at another's side, likewise did *parasite*. I swallowed hard, wondering what Hamlet would think to see our friendship laid bare for the world.

"I do not have enough yet to make a collection," I protested weakly. "And those I have are rough."

"Then I will help you write them. We will work together." She flashed me a look both seductive and businesslike. "Line by line. One each day, perhaps? There are only fourteen lines in a sonnet. You might finish them in the first hour of the night, and have the other twenty-three to spend, if you liked, with your beloved Hamlet."

I did not like the sound of the prince's hallowed name in her mouth.

"And what if he does not approve?" I challenged her. "My poems belong to him. Perhaps he will not wish for me to share them with the world."

"They are addressed to him, perhaps—but they are the children of your brain, and so your property, to copy and distribute as you will." She gave a pragmatic shrug. "If he returns to Elsinore and wishes to invite you to join his retinue, he may negotiate with me to obtain your contract. And I will set a dear price for you, too. Men never value what is too cheaply won." She shook her head at me like a schoolmaster with a disappointing pupil. "But at this rate of sale, you are like to lose everything. Waiting on him night and day, waiting for him to make up his mind. And of course, some rival may yet pluck the treasured post of Favorite Poet right out from under your nose. After all, such extraordinary beauty must attract many admirers."

I followed her gaze down to the garden. Hamlet was still flitting from player to player, scene to scene, never looking back at those he left behind. Always moving forward, donning another disguise, adopting yet another persona to add to his repertoire.

I shut my eyes. He was still the prince, and as perfect as ever he had been. Only now, the pleasure I felt at the sight of him was dogged by doubt. In my heart was now the hard core of a cruel fear—the fear of losing Hamlet, not to death, or madness, or the seas of time, but to some other, more prosaic betrayal.

I turned back to the baroness, suddenly angry. "I thought you despised poems about beauty." My tone was dangerously insubordinate, I knew, but this entire conversation was unauthorized. "Why do you take such interest in reading mine?"

"Why do you take such care in writing them?" Lady Adriane returned. "The perfumier preserves the essence of the rose, but to no benefit of the flower itself. Rather, the bloom is struck down in its prime, its scent stolen to sweeten the courtier's gloves. So tell me—is your desire to preserve him in your poems, like a fly in amber?" This was drawn out mockingly. "Or to possess him?"

A cold breeze traveled up and down the fine hairs on my arms. Right and wrong had somehow been confused. Her eyes were black, but they did not lack beauty, even so. They might convince me beauty all was black.

"You need not tell me your decision now," she said. "After all, I understand you shall be quite busy enough with the play until Midsummer Night. But after the performance, when my husband is impressing all his guests with his imported fireworks on the lawn, I will fake a headache and retire early to my bed.

"I will lower the ladder at the strike of midnight; the party will be all night keeping the wake around the bonfire, and our business will not be discovered. Come to me then, if you would be my poet, and have me to your mistress."

She licked her lips and that word, *mistress*, forked upon her tongue. Midnight. Mistress. Midsummer Night. It was clear to me from the way her eyes drank hungrily of mine that her offer was for more than mere collaboration, and I must admit some certain parts of me in particular were sorely tempted.

I bit my lip just a little, not enough to draw blood. The pain steadied me, gave me focus; elsewhere I was aware in every inch of me of her proximity. My head slumped forward in a weak and miserable nod. I told myself I was promising nothing but to consider her offer.

She was not beautiful. And yet she stood before me, tyrannous and proud as if she had been beautiful. Her voice was nearly inaudible, nearly nothing more than hot breath whispering into my ear: *"Make me your diary, and I will grant you immortality."*

L ay out my suit of sabel," Hamlet said as he undressed for bed on Midsummer's Eve. "I want to wear it tomorrow night."

Sabel was the yellowish one, I remembered after a moment—halfway between parchment and candle-flame. My study of the prince, like any new philosophy, had necessitated the learning of arcane languages and specialized vocabularies. I found the courtiers' tongue, with its circumlocutions and declensions of rank and lineage, more complicated than either Greek or Latin.

The latest fashionable shade from Paris, *couleur d'Isabel* derived its name, so I had heard, from the eldest daughter of the King of Spain. When her father laid siege to Ostend, she vowed never to change her underclothes until that city fell. Goaded by this promise, the citizens resisted occupation another three years—by which time the lady's "whites" were decidedly not.

For a time, I had misheard the word as "sables" (Hamlet's French, as I have mentioned, was terrible; else, he'd have gone to the Sorbonne, which offered better entertainments) and wondered why fashion demanded one to wear dark furs in June. I still marvel at the ingenuity of the French dye-master who managed, with nothing more than a salacious story and a famous name, to clothe the courts of Europe in the color of dirty linens.

"I thought you meant to stay home tomorrow night," I said, fetching the suede doublet and brocaded satin sleeves from the prince's clothespress.

Hamlet scowled, tugging off his collar. "A friendly thought! I should be kept at home like a beggar the night of my debut!"

"The night of Willie Hughes's debut, you mean," I reminded him. "If someone were to recognize you . . . to send word to your father . . ." I faltered. My tongue felt like the tongue of a shoe, so much insensible red leather.

I had still not been able to bring myself to speak to him about my conversation with the baroness. Whenever I meant to mention it, somehow the words ended up melting in my mouth; or else I would be overcome by too much feeling, my heart raging like a wild beast.

The trouble was that I did not know what I hoped he would say to the news. In my most joyous fantasies, would he laugh at my concerns, revealing a hidden suit of Denmark's livery-cloth, already cut and tailored to my size? Might he make more specific promises—for what was a mere baroness's patronage, after all, compared to a position in a royal court? I might be made a gentleman, granted a coat of arms—even knighted, in my service to the crown. Perhaps, when Hamlet was king, I might even be given a title of special honor, such as "Groom of the Bedchamber."

Then I would catch myself in these daydreams. Horatio, the courtier! How laughable the image appeared to me—in a dandy's heeled shoes and peacock-feather hat, coating my tongue with flattery. Wagering my love on the fortunes of noblemen, as one might bet on a cock in a fight—as if I were (I cringed even to think it) *Guildenstern*? Still, it chilled me to know how quickly my own idle thoughts could learn to run up crooked and ambitious paths.

There was another problem; surely the prince would ask to see the poems that had attracted such interest. But I was yet too bashful to show them, afraid to be thought merely another of those sycophants and flatterers every prince is heir to. When I described him as in every way superior to myself, it was the plain truth of my senses and my science, nothing more. But might this be mistaken for a courtier's obsequiousness? Was this the fear that kept me from broaching the subject of my future in his service? Or was it the fear that plagues all lovers—that my plea might be denied?

Hamlet—though pleased by the promise that he might achieve immortality through the written word—had yet shown little interest in the content of the work itself. To the labor of its creation, he was indifferent, as though the play I was meant to write were the natural product of himself, his beauty casting off lines into the air, for general collection.

My mind flashed on the Lady Adriane's eyes, devouring the contents of my pages, hungry for my words. Another, more troubling possibility occurred to me: perhaps I had not told the prince about her proposition because I did not want to refuse it.

"Not that shirt with it," Hamlet snapped me away from my thoughts. "The scarlet silk."

I went to help the prince untie his codpiece at the back, where it laced to the jerkin. The points, I found, were not the neat bows I had tied that morning, but tangled knots, all clumsily redone, as though in haste.

"I am thinking only of you," I told him. "I could not bear to witness any wound to your good name."

"Well, I've given my cook the day off, and must go out for supper, at least. Unless you would have me starve my stomach, to fatten my good name?"

I did not answer, busy picking at the knot at the small of the prince's back. My frustration grew as it stubbornly resisted.

The "dress" rehearsal, which wasn't, had been terrible, and no amount of reassurance from the players that such ever presaged a successful opening had assuaged my fears. Hamlet had arrived more than an hour late, and in a foul humor that manifested itself in a cutting and sarcastic wit, both on and off the stage. The heroine's teasing manipulations took on a cruel, sadistic edge; her young lover had, in fear, been put out of his part entirely, and everyone's delivery thrown off.

"Besides," the prince sighed, pulling his undershirt over his head and pressing the clutch of warm silk into my hands. "I am promised tomorrow night to my lords Rosencrantz and Guildenstern. I dined with them this afternoon, and invited them to attend our performance."

I could not believe my ears. Why did he always have to tempt fate with these unnecessary risks? "I thought you did not trust them," I said, swallowing my anger.

A cloud passed over Hamlet's face. "I never said any such thing!"

I was so surprised to hear him lie, I did not heed the note of warning sounded in his voice.

"But you did, my lord," I protested. "Have you forgotten? On your birthday, you called them traitors. You said you would soon take your revenge . . ."

"Well, I was mad that day." A terrible hard look came over his face. His eyes were cold and colorless. "A man may say many things in his dreams that, upon waking, he would never endorse nor believe." He knelt before the chamber-pot, and in a moment came the sing of Hamlet's piss on hammered brass.

Parts and Pieces

The hottest day of the year began with an unexpected snow. I arrived at Lord Maricourt's house to find white feathers rising in great clouds from a trio of kitchen-wenches gathered in the garden, plucking geese. Carried on the breeze, the down was everywhere: tumbling in tufts across the lawn, caught in hedges and soaking in the fountains, clinging to the potted topiaries meant to represent the role of the "green wood" on the stage.

The scullery maids refused my invitations to remove. An hour after dawn, it was already hot as noon, and in the kitchens, they said, the birds were roasting before they could get them plucked. I ran for my master and they for theirs and a quarrel ensued between the baron and his cook over what should be done with the mess they had left behind (for by the time I managed to rouse the baron, the pluckers had finished their task and dispersed, though the feathers had not). The cook, with all these wildfowl yet to truss and stuff, denied the outsides of the birds were any of her concern and stormed off in a huff. I sent a housemaid to fetch a broom, but moving the feathers from the set proved impossible, except one at a time, by hand—which task the baron (still in his dressing-gown and cap) steadfastly began to perform.

Finally, the baroness called down from her balcony to suggest I "alter certain lines" to change the setting of the play from a summer scene to winter, and explain the snow thusly; and the baron, grateful for a solution requiring no more of his efforts, voiced his effusive agreement.

Struck dumb by the thought of revising several speeches and nearly all the songs in three hours' time, I missed my cue to protest, and so I spent the rest of the morning hunched over a desk in the baron's study, muttering, "Who ever heard of a wintertime pastoral?" and tearing fingers through my hair as though I could pull the rhymes out of my head. A play is not written, after all, but wrought, like a piece of iron: hammered and worked until it reaches the desired shape. By the time I finished copying the new parts, I was damp with sweat, and my shoulders ached as though I had been working before a forge.

By then it was afternoon in earnest, and the servants were beginning to carry the chairs down to the lawn. On stage, a half-dressed jester crossed in a panic, asking, "Has anyone seen my motley?" while our painted canvas azure sky was unrolled against the backdrop of a cloudless azure sky.

The actors accepted the changes with good humor, and the senior among the men—in the role of the heroine's father, the banished Duke—even recalled an old speech about the "icy fang and churlish chiding of the winter wind" he might insert into the second act. Only the musicians, receiving the revised parts to "*Blow, Blow, Thou Winter Wind,*"complained that "most friendship is feigning, most loving mere folly" was hardly a fitting refrain for a romance. I checked my watch. The longest day of the year and already we were nearly out of time.

I borrowed a small pocket glass in our little "tiring-house" behind a hedge of evergreens. It had been a good while since I had last looked into a looking-glass. The face it revealed was, I must admit, a bit of a shock. How plain it appeared to me, after so many months of looking every day at Hamlet's! And how brown I had grown, walking every morning in the sun to his door—or home from it, on those nights when his dreams kept him from sleeping.

My sleepless sunken eyes were ringed in blue; my beard, a week or more neglected, had broken out in uneven ginger patches that only served to make my hollow cheeks look leaner. And to think, I had been walking around with him all this time as if I were beautiful as well! More than beautiful.

Sighing, I took up powder and a comb and began to grizzle my beard. I had not originally intended to act in the play myself; but finally despairing of any other way to get young Damon to remember his lines, I had written in the role of the hero's ancient and faithful servant, in whose person I might be called upon to assist the boy with a whispered cue.

For the lover's later scenes, alone with his lady-in-disguise, Hamlet had offered (with an enthusiasm I must admit I did not entirely like) to rehearse the lines with him in private while he dressed. Together they disappeared into the makeshift closet curtained-off behind the stage for the heroine's quick change in the second act.

They had been in there for more than an hour, and whenever I passed the little closet, my jealous ear strained to make words from the murmurings within. Were those endearments my own, from the scene in Act Four, or improvised? And what might be causing the curtains to billow so? Most maddening of all, I thought, what if, in spite of these tutorials, the boy still managed to forget his lines?

I frowned, the expression exaggerated in the mirror by the lines drawn between my brows. One of the players had shown me the proper way to apply the paint, but out of habit I took up the paintbrush like a pen. It was heavier, my pen being as light as a feather, while the brush was made of horsehair and ebony. The paint, too, was thicker than my ink; thicker even than what I would think to call "paint"—more like grease, or wax. Still, the task before me was a familiar one: creating history from nothing, drawing the soul of a character out of a few simple lines.

Following the player's instructions, I painted a perfect semicircle underneath each eye for the perfect servant, pledged to follow his master "to the last gasp of truth and loyalty." A thumb dragged across my cheeks to simulate an old man's toothless hollow. "I have lost my teeth in your service," I rehearsed my line from the opening scene. I thought of him: this man of fourscore, indentured from seventeen, and with no thought but his master's comfort, no wish except to die out of his master's debt. The speech in which I offered up my thriftily saved gold to the penniless younger son was sure to bring tears in the house. But I was thinking more of Hamlet, who, entering directly after, from the right, could not help but hear the scene, and be moved by the promise of such fidelity.

Finally satisfied with the creases, I set the paint with a dusting of fine powder. I pulled on the horsehair wig, then the mud-colored hat, frayed at the brim. Looking into the glass was like looking forty years into the future: I recognized my eyes, in a weary, impossibly haunted face. The wizened lips fell open in an expression of surprise. I had the eerie feeling the old man in the mirror was looking back at me, and just as shocked to see himself so young and innocent.

I hesitated outside the oilcloth "door" to Hamlet's makeshift dressing-room; there was no place to knock. Clearing my throat earned me no reply, so I raised my voice. "Ten minutes, Master Hughes."

The curtain drew back. A young lady stood before me. She was uncommonly fair, uncommonly tall. Beautiful the way a paradox is beautiful, the way something impossible and true is beautiful.

His body had been painted and shaved, molded by some corsetry to imitate the swell of a female breast at the top of a gown, the gathering—no wider than my circled hands—at her waist. The players had shown the prince what to pluck and draw and shade and hide to create a perfect mask of femininity. "What a piece of work is woman!" I had heard Hamlet shriek from behind the curtain, while he made another face upon his face.

And, though I knew this was deception—or perhaps because of this—I found myself unwilling to disbelieve it. Before me stood the answer to a prayer I had not dared to speak aloud, had scarcely dared to write in the silent confessional of my poetry. The master-mistress of my passions, as if by magic and all the pagan gods rendered unto me: a female Hamlet.

"Oh, my sweet lord," I breathed.

The lady's cupid-bow lips drew back in a sly, amused smile. Sliding a graceful hand around my arm, she spoke in a tender voice made rich with laughter: "Nay, you must call me Rosalind."

They were fascinated by him. That was the only word for it. When Hamlet was on the stage, no one could hope to look away. Even the plain black gown in which the melancholy princess first appeared, in mourning for her banished father, set off Hamlet's fair so well I thought, were it to me, I should never have him appear in any other color. He was eaten by their eyes, licked and tasted by them, and when he went offstage, they all held breath and waited, patient as spaniels, for his return.

But the root of their fascination (as I learned by eavesdropping on passing conversations at the interval) was more than charm or beauty but that titillatingly unanswered question of what lay between the actor's legs. Was it, they wanted to know, a man, at the heart of it, playing a woman disguised as a man? Or else a woman in earnest, disguised as a man, then forced to imitate herself?

It was not, I must say, that Hamlet was so skillful in his portrayal—an actual trained boy actor might have noted a number of flaws in his technique. The heroine's stride, for example, was longer than might be called strictly maidenly, causing her farthingale to swing ungracefully about her ankles; and her voice came out neither lisping nor small, but in an unrestrained and melodious alto.

But when the play called for this wit-cracking girl to disguise herself in breeches, neither was she quite convincingly masculine. To assist in obscuring his identity, Hamlet had agreed to keep his face painted as a woman's throughout; and this effect, in the shepherd-boy costume, was particularly striking. Striking, as well, was his hourglass silhouette—for in the frantic scramble between acts, he had not had time to remove his corset, and the open collar of his peasant's chemise seemed to reveal the swell of a nubile breast.

And in the scene where this disguised "boy" agreed to act the part of the hero's lady-love, his imitation, in the outward appearance of a man, seemed more genuinely womanly than the coltish adolescent girl had been in skirts.

Standing with my promptbook at the side of the stage, I watched it all. The play, I knew, was flawed: the plot implausible, characters contrived, the ending utterly ridiculous. The hero, as expected, made a muddle of his lines, and the meter lagged or overlapped itself running ahead on too many feet. But even as I cringed, marking the notes into my book, I knew no one had noticed the heroine's lover: they were all looking through his besotted eyes.

Smoke in the air from midsummer bonfires and dust from midsummer drought made for a glorious sunset: layers of vermilion, saffron, violet. Any mortal thing of beauty would have been ashamed to play against such a spectacle. But the audience, facing east, saw only the reflection in Hamlet's eyes, which were all the colors of the sky at once, changeable and yet ever-perfect, as if he kept Heaven inside his head.

Consulting a compass and an almanac, I had arranged for the stage to be angled in such a way that the afternoon sun, setting between the manor house and a nearby grove of poplars, might cast its longest and most rosy rays without impediment upon the mock-wedding scene. In a forest of feathers, in an onion of disguise, the two youths knelt to one another on the stage and pledged their souls, marrying themselves as surely as if they had gone before the priest.

Watching the scene played, I realized what I had not while writing it: that I had conjured up a portrait of my own deepest desires. I was in love with Hamlet—not as I had told myself, merely as devoted friend, nor faithful servant, but ardently, passionately. I would court him as a lover, marry him if I could, if such a thing were not unspeakable. Unthinkable, even—yet here it was, before me on the stage, the two men kissing and embracing, openly. I was surprised to find tears springing to my eyes. I had shown my love before the world, and all the world had fallen in love.

In epilogue, I will note only a few strange effects, reported to me afterwards by sources of varying reliability. The Duke was said to have been driven nearly to distraction by the piece. For weeks after, he would summon his musicians from their beds at every hour of the night to play sweet tunes to soothe the savage longing in his breast. Still, he swore to all who would listen that he was sure in his heart that an actress had played the role.

Hamlet's performance, I am certain, also helped to spur the subsequent craze in the City for boy actors, with the youngest and fairest and most delicate among them valued best. Like nests of birds, entire companies of children hatched overnight. Barely decked in gaudy satins and silks, they cried out bawdy fables cribbed from heathen poets—even on Sundays. Demand was extraordinary, as everyone flocked to them in hopes of seeing the mysterious "Mr. W.H." once again—or else discovering the next just-like. Any player over the age of twenty-one was ruined as a result, and companies of experienced tragedians long established in the City were forced to go traveling once again to the provinces and courts of Europe.

•   •   •

After the play, I was consumed for an hour or two in the business of collecting and dividing the shares to distribute among the players. In the end, however, I found I must have made some error in my calculations, for I was left with only a single share, and Hamlet and myself both yet unpaid. I was tempted to pocket the money—it was precious little silver in any case, not a whit of difference in the weight of a prince's purse. But it would be enough to spare me, at least for a little while, from having to accept the baroness's offer.

I was to meet her at midnight with my answer. The minutes until then seemed as rungs in a hammock ladder that had already been released, and now uncoiled irrevocably toward the ground. And still I had not spoken of my dilemma to the prince. The guilt from this betrayal weighed down the matter of the money in my mind, until at last, with a sigh, I divided the silver into two equal shares, knotting them into two squares of sackcloth. Leaving the baron's offices, I felt lighter for this decision. I would not turn against the prince; I would find him and confess all, soliciting his mercy and advice.

But Hamlet was lost to me by then in the crowd of star-eyed courtiers, all debating hotly about his identity, his gender, the general state of his character, and whether he had ever played in the City before. Unrecognized without my paint and costume, I moved anonymously through the partygoers. For a dizzying moment, I was caught up in a circle of dancers—spirited young ladies whose skirts opened like poppies underneath them. But though they cajoled me to join them, I pressed through these yards and yards of silk and scent and sweat, with no desire but to find the prince.

It was twilight by then, and the upper lawn was near to deserted. The majority of the party had begun to gather on the lower lawn, where the baron was shouting instructions to his footmen, preparing the fireworks. The curtained dressing-room was empty.

I rounded the corner of the stage, where I found myself nearly overrun by a trio of drunken clowns wearing masks and Carnival attire. They jostled past with much laughter and boisterous roughhousing. Caught by an errant elbow, I turned to utter a scold and found myself staring into Hamlet's eyes.

We gaped at one another. Then the prince began to laugh, wildly. "Horatio!" he cried. His breath was sherry sack and roses—heavy on the former.

I looked again at his companions. Venetian masks could not disguise their shapes; I knew them at once as Rosencrantz and Guildenstern.

"A word in your ear, my lord," I pleaded, setting off a flurry of whispers between the two courtiers.

"Horatio! You know I keep no secrets in this company," Hamlet insisted, embracing an arm about the neck of each. "For as I have told you—I trust these gentlemen as well as I do my own kin; and love them just as truly now as I have ever done."

This declaration was filled with a drunken exuberance,

and even moved the prince to shed a tear. He broke for a moment from his followers to wipe it away, as though he were ashamed of his womanly emotion. Though his expression was difficult to read behind the half-mask, I saw—or thought I saw—a wink. But this was in all likelihood nothing more than my hopes playing tricks with the moving shadow of Hamlet's handkerchief.

"My lord," I said, "I have come to deliver your salary, for the performance."

"Salary?" The prince laughed at this idea.

"Half a share." I handed him the little bundle of coins.

"Nay!" He cried out in a parody of outrage. "I'll have a whole one, I!"

"You were the star," said Rosencrantz.

"Indeed," said Guildenstern. " 'Tis only fair." His drunkenness did not make him sloppy, like his fellows, but only slowed everything he said or did to half its normal speed.

Reluctantly, I handed over the second bundle of silver. This left me with nothing, and no more time to postpone my confession. "My lord, I have been offered a . . . situation here by Lady Maricourt." I blurted out ungracefully. "A commission, rather."

"Another play?" Hamlet asked delightedly. "Why, this is most excellent!"

Like a small avalanche, Rosencrantz tumbled into me in a jovial heap, sloshing a half-empty bottle in his hand. "Why, you should come along with us, in celer—celebration!"

Guildenstern's smirk nearly eclipsed his razor-thin moustache. "Oh, indeed," he agreed, with the air of one who had just been proposed the most delicious amusement imaginable. "By all means, come."

I could not trust these two; instead, my eyes sought out the prince's. "Are you going now to eat, my lord?"

A beat. Then, simultaneously unable to contain their laughter, the gentlemen exploded into hysteria. All three were in particularly high spirits; even Guildenstern wore spots of color in his ashen cheeks.

"Of course, a man must have his daily meat!" Hamlet cried.

"Unless it be a Friday," added Rosencrantz, "for then he must have fish."

"Oh, I fear dear Horatio has no stomach for fish—unless the prince can tempt him with a piece of cod, which as you know, is the rarest dish at this *country-house*," said Guildenstern, pointedly stressing the primary syllable. He plucked at his undershirt, puffing it up through the slashes in his sleeves.

"I cannot make any sense of this," I said in annoyance. "Are you going to an inn?"

"Aye, and out again," said Guildenstern.

"Let us to the nunnery!" Hamlet supplied, and Rosencrantz paddled his fingers nervously in his rosary beads.

It was this familiar childhood sound, the *click-clack, click-clack* of the rosary, that made their meaning finally clear to me. "You mean to visit a brothel?" I shuddered to think of the prince in one of those filthy shacks clustered by the river docks, bubbling stews of taffeta and mud and human flesh.

"Never fret, churchmouse." Guildenstern bared his teeth at me. "I'm sure, if you reach in his pockets for the coin, your prince will buy you a tart of your very own."

"Or else share one!" cried Rosencrantz.

Hamlet shot him a fearsome glare. The young lord's long-lashed eyes went very round, and he gave a helpless shrug and coy giggle in apology.

Guildenstern rolled his eyes at this, and tried to interest the prince in exchanging his long-suffering look. "Will you go, my lord?"

Behind the velvet mask, Hamlet's expression was unreadable. "Ready the horses," he told them. "I will follow presently."

Guildenstern's glance drifted briefly in my general direction, as though I were worthy of no more than the most careless and peripheral attention. "With all haste to your will, my lord."

He gathered Rosencrantz, and, drunken as they were, still the courtiers fell into elegant sweeping bows, practiced as dancers.

Hamlet watched them disappear towards the stables. "Hypocrites," he muttered under his breath. "They make a great show of picking and fondling the fairest of whores, but always end up in bed together when we go upstairs."

When he turned back to me again, his drunkenness had all but evaporated. "Forgive me," he said. "I must put on a show before these gentlemen a little while longer, at least."

I was amazed, and knew not what to say. I looked in confusion from the prince to the courtiers' departing forms and back again. "But—why, my lord?"

"Why? Because they are my father's spies!" He sighed in exasperation. "They'll spy for anyone who will pay them, actually. They heard about the play yesterday, and came to blackmail me—or, as they put it, allow me the opportunity, as a friend, to make them a better offer. Luckily, the matter was happily quelled: we struck a bargain that they should return to Denmark remembering no sins that should dishonor me, and full of praise for my virtuous conduct and most gentle manners."

In a low voice, like the breath of a ghost, I heard the words between his words. "You bribed them to perjure themselves before the king?"

Treason, of course, to think of it that way. If the messengers' omissions were discovered, they might be exiled, tortured—even put to death. I was suddenly filled with a morbid curiosity to know what price the gentlemen had set on their own heads. What kind of money did it take to purchase a man away from his peace of mind?

"How much?" I whispered. My mouth felt very dry.

He did me the decency, at least, of lowering his eyes. "They were persuaded."

Of course: Hamlet possessed far rarer currencies than gold. He might make grown men greedy for things they had never imagined desiring, or discover things about themselves they would wish they had never learned.

"Of course." I chuckled a little, mirthlessly. "But why did you stop there, in your persuasions? I am sure, if you had tried, you might have persuaded them, as well, that hot was cold. You might have said the North Wind blew with gentle, sultry breath, and sent them traveling without their cloaks into a blizzard. I am certain they might have been persuaded to believe in a great many fictions, my lord, besides your virtue."

"Do not be jealous of them," he cajoled.

"Of that pair?" I winced at the thought. "Or of your next *dearest and truest friend*? Or else of the . . ." I hesitated, having heard the word *whoreson* too many times in taunts throughout my youth. ". . . the woman you will love tonight?"

"The use of love is not the same as love." He loosed his mask, pushing it up onto his brow like a maiden's cap. It was tied with a quantity of ribbons in crimson and gold, which spilled in a confusion down his back. When he tossed his head, they made a whispering sound against one another, pages turning in a book. "An actor in a play may give every outward sign of affection, and still his own heart remains unmoved."

I crossed my arms before me. "You speak of the stage, my lord."

"We princes are set on stages," he answered, "in the sight and view of all the world. Duly observed of all observers—the expectancy of our bright state."

He spoke as though he were on a stage, the way Hamlet always spoke—as though he were quoting something famous. I was suddenly sick of it.

"Forgive me, sir," I said bitterly. "I am a scholar, not a courtier. I cannot understand how visiting a house of ill-repute may improve one's reputation."

A hard look came into the prince's eyes. "You would rather my father's court was filled with vile whispers about you?" He turned away in frustration. "Already, there are those who call me a misogynist. They say I will never marry; that I cannot produce an heir. And if these rumors were to find some proof, my enemies could move to block my advancement to the throne. And my name—which you have promised to preserve with your pen for the world—would be spoken with a leer and a lisp, remembered only as an amusing footnote to history."

"Princess Isabella," I murmured sorrowfully, thinking of dirty linens.

He took my hand in his, fondling the callus my pen makes on my finger as I write.

"My body is the property of Denmark," Hamlet said. "My signet is my father's, like my name. But my soul is mistress of her own choice, and she has marked you with her seal, where it can never be erased." He kissed my hand and pulled me close against him, whispering, "I would not have you wear my colors on your sleeve, but in your heart's core, in your heart of hearts, as I do thine."

He put our still-joined hands to his chest, where beneath the sabel suede I felt a faint but steady beat. "This is your heart," he said. "I gave you mine, not to give back again."

A sudden cry went up from the lawn as the first of the fireworks burst out, the sky lit bright as day, but only for a moment. For an instant, he stood before me in perfect illumination. His eyes were fierce and dark, the indigo of the midsummer-midnight sky; and like the sky, fretted with golden fire. The ribbons spilling down over his shoulders might have been a maiden's curls; the golden silk as soft as lovelocks, titillatingly feminine. Then the picture faded, leaving only its afterimage, pale and green, to haunt me all my life thereafter, whenever I close my eyes.

"Come with us," he offered in my ear. "I'll buy you a girl."

The thought of this transaction left me fairly queasy. I thought of Lady Adriane waiting at the top of her balcony, the rope all coiled up like my insides. "I cannot, my lord."

He made a low, amused growl in his throat, not quite a laugh. His mouth grazed my ear on its slow tour across my cheek. "I'll share one with you," he offered, *sotto voce.*

This thought was very nearly worse.

You have a female soul, I thought. *A woman's heart, as well as a woman's face. It never needed painting for the stage—it was painted original and perfect by Nature's hand. You must have been intended as a woman: how could any hand, coloring those lips, that translucent rosy cheek, have had any subject in mind but Venus, emerging naked from the open shell?* I thought this, and yet I said nothing, afraid to break the spell.

Then he kissed me, and this time his kiss was unmistakable: a lover's kiss, eager and hungry, his probing tongue proving itself nimble at more than wit. I found myself responding just as eagerly, caressing him from the nape to the small of his back. It seemed almost impossible that it should not be female, this hot, lithe length of slender body pressed against my own.

Something too much in this. Some thing too much. Against my stomach a rigid knot of flesh poked willfully. It was the joke played on my hopes by Nature—that meretricious whore, who must have, like Pygmalion, fallen in love with her masterpiece and desired it for her own use. And so she added the stroke of the pen that turned comedy in an instant to tragedy: the prick of my fair Rose.

I tried to pull away, but found myself wedged against a dark wooden bulk: the machine by which the pagan god of marriage had entered to right all wrongs at the end of the play. I felt the crank and iron gears against my back. For the first time, it struck me with the cold, hard certainty of truth that I could not expect a similar miracle.

He made like he would kiss me again, but this time I pulled away from his embrace. My throat cramped, "If I may have your love, it is enough, and more than I deserve," I said. "But . . ." I swallowed hard, "the *use* of love must remain to women's pleasure."

He began some protest to this, but I shook my head. I clamped my lips together and said nothing, though I was full to bursting everywhere with words. They stung at my eyes, which I squeezed shut lest they overflow in verses. They rose in my stomach, tasting of bile, rushed hot to fill my loins.

Tenderly, I kissed the prince's cheek. "Good night. Be blessed."

Then I went away from him through the dark, to meet the baroness.

Midsummer Night

In my dream, she was lying back in bed, her black hair all undone, and wherever her hair was not, her nakedness. And I could not tell you which of these affected me more: the hair, or the nakedness. Or the way her lips closed around the stem of her hammered silver pipe.

Her pipe was a curiosity, worked by a fine and nimble hand to resemble the scales of a snake, the shallow bowl set with two gemstones for the serpent's eyes. It curved upwards and the tip was tapered, so the slimmer end rested neatly in the gap between her teeth. I liked the fit of it there—the way it kept her lips apart, inviting the eye into her very mouth.

Her breath was sour with wine and sweet with the black tobacco she preferred, which she kept in a sandalwood box. Imported not from the New World but the far reaches of the Old, its smoke was permeated with the scent of the exotic spices and perfumes that shared its long journey from the Orient.

And as her ravenous mouth spread my own, I tasted in the pungent odor of her breath the exotic dust of their journey, ten thousand miles or more, in slow gypsy caravans. And I was traveling with them, along paths more ancient than my most antique philosophers', on roadways never built by man, but cleft by his feet into the earth.

I marveled at her body under mine—how small and slight it was, this creature called Woman! I might gather it entire up into his arms, the way I gathered tendrils of her hair up to kiss her neck, then let it spill down over her shoulders, again and again. So small, and yet possessed of depths that enclosed me, though I had closed myself around the prince as fingers clasped in prayer.

Still, he was always there, Hamlet—the third, invisible, embraced in the space between us. Even when there was no space between us at all; not enough to dance on the head of a pin. Even when something inside me broke—like a looking-glass breaks, or a wave—and I clenched my teeth to keep from shouting. As my eyes fluttered shut, I called on Heaven, and saw Prince Hamlet's face.

For a long time afterwards, I lay in her lap, weeping. And with each salt-tear rolling down my cheek, another piece of the story slipped out. It came in a frantic jumble, peppered with fragments of poetry, half-misquoted lines Hamlet had said to me, divorced from their original contexts. I made no attempt to censor or edit the tale, but repeated his cruel words, and his crazy words, and sweet; and she received them all with the same silent, intense interest.

The only light came from a taper burning on a little writing-table near the bed, and its reflection burning in the mirror. She took up the candle to light her pipe. In its flickering bronze radius, her face looked old, then very young. I would learn that whenever she reached for the little silver pipe, she was about to lie to me. Or else, done lying, and about to tell the truth.

She spoke at last, exhaling smoke. "You think he is ashamed of you."

As if a shade had been lifted, it became clear to me: Hamlet *was* ashamed of me. How could it be otherwise? The evening repeated in my head—I saw myself, grotesquely caricatured, through the prince's eyes: a lame, uncouth peasant, mocked and despised by his friends of noble birth and gentle breeding. His words of love were just another of his cruel practical jokes—no doubt he was repeating them now, in some put-on voice, for Rosencrantz and Guildenstern!

"If he is ashamed, I cannot fault his judgment," I forced myself to answer. "I know I am not his equal—not in beauty, or birth, wealth or wit. I am nothing but what he makes of me, and he is everything."

She was smiling at this. It infuriated me.

"And now you mean to mock me for it, as well?"

"Not at all," she said. "I only find it amusing, how blind you are to your own talents. It is not the young man, but your love for him, that is extraordinary."

"Whatever my love may be, my talent is too poor to express it." In anticipation of this meeting, I had looked over my early sonnets, hoping to find in them something salvageable. But those attempts composed to a beauty painted in oils now only embarrassed me. How gaudy they seemed, layering comparison upon compare, likening the prince to the sun and moon, earth and sea, and every beautiful thing in all the world.

"Your talent could wring poetry from the vilest creature." She bent to kiss my cheek, and her dark hair fell down around my head like tentacles. "You simply cannot read your own work. It is fresh and passionate, refreshingly free of any religion but what you have divined in your lover's eyes. There is no good or evil—only beauty and ugliness, love and despair. They are more like the works of the antique Romans—Catullus, Theocritus—than anything produced by our modern pens." She chuckled. "You may well be the last of the world's great pagan poets."

I must admit, it pleased me to hear her flattery, though I did not believe it. "You mean they are filled with old clichés and superstitions," I answered stubbornly. "I am a common man. I do not have the courtier's wit."

"Is that what you want? Any man with a little Latin grammar can learn a passable imitation of the courtier's wit." Rising from the bed, she tossed a velvet dressing-gown around her shoulders.

Open at the front, it only served to accentuate her nakedness. " 'Tis easier, I swear, than teaching a bear to dance. It is no great trick to bury a needle's-worth of matter in a haystack of art."

Her breasts swung down pendulously as she relit her pipe, and I found I could have had her once again.

"Negotiating as a courtier is more difficult. You must learn to ask for what you want without saying what you mean." She looked up at me. "You have your writing things with you." Again, it was not a question.

"In my bag." After some stumbling in the dark, I located my satchel on the floor. Tangled in the shoulder strap was my crumpled undershirt, which I pulled over my head.

"A poet is by nature observant, and careful with his words," she said. "Such a person may indeed prove useful to the prince at Elsinore—but he must be made to recognize your worth."

I readied my pen and ink and sat down at her dressing-table, my book open before me. "What am I to write?"

She considered for a moment before replying: "A sonnet—in the style of a courtier. Address it as a letter."

I was unsure precisely how a courtier might address his letters. "My Lord," I wrote across the top.

She interrupted. "That is not quite correct, is it? He is not particularly *your* lord—not until you wear his livery."

I took up the small silver scraper to scratch out the "My" before the ink set in the parchment. I was breathing deep. "Lord of my Love," I penned into its place, defiantly.

To my surprise, she smiled. "That is it," she whispered over my shoulder. "Now go on with the introduction. Tell him his merit has compelled you strongly to—a *duty*, say, in his service, and you are sending him a letter with purpose to speak of this."

"Why not simply come to the point?" This was what irritated me most about the language of courtiers. "Obviously, I have sent him the sonnet, if he is reading it. And he may well assume it has some purpose—otherwise, I would not have written it."

"Nonsense," Adriane said. "At court, sonnets are sent back and forth all day long with no purpose at all but to show off the sender's wit."

She bid me again to write, and against my will, my pen rose to the well at her command. Four lines of a fourteen-line letter gone, to explain that I had, in fact, written a letter. Four more in which she directed me to apologize if my talents proved too poor to express all my feelings, and beg that the letter, nevertheless, be read with kindly eyes. I sighed out through my teeth. How did princes ever manage to get anything done at all, with everyone ever spouting these circumlocutions at them?

Looking over the first quatrain, I bent again with the remover to remove the word *letter*, substituting the more sophisticated-sounding *embassage*. This allowed me to change that tired line about being the prince's *debtor* for one instead mentioning my *vassalage*. Thanks to Heaven all those French nouns rhymed.

"Now you may begin to allude, in veiled terms, to your own desire," Adriane said. "Do not mention livery specifically—

only say you hope your fortunes will change, and clothe you in some . . . *apparel*, say, to show you worthy of his respect."

I imagined myself all naked under Hamlet's eyes. I might cast my horoscope, I thought, by those bright stars, and divine my future as well as by the heavens. For what other pleasure could give me joy, if I were out of Hamlet's favor? On the other hand, were I assured of Hamlet's love, what trial or torture would I then be unable to bear? His esteem was the measure of my fortune, good or ill. I counted up my lines.

"That leaves only the final couplet remaining."

"Perfect," she said, "for now you play your hand. Until that day when you are shown so worthy, you will neither trouble him with words of love, nor come into his sight."

"What?" I threw the pen down as though it had bitten me. "You mean I cannot see him at all?"

"Not much to bargain with, I'll grant, but it is all you have." Her arms were crossed beneath her breasts, her nipples hard and dark, like beads of polished glass. "Absence makes true hearts grow fonder. He will respond, if he values you."

I did not speak. Nor could I look at her. She put her arms around me, raked her fingers through my hair. "Surely you do not believe such a short separation will alter your love."

"Nothing will alter it." I said this simply, as one might comment on some obvious fact of the weather, or say that day was likely to follow night.

She shrugged at this. "Then you have nothing to fear." Yawning, she turned back towards the curtained shadows of the bed. "But send the sonnet or not, as you will. It matters to me only that you write it."

In spite of myself, I was yawning as well. I knew the difference between the call of the nightingale and the lark. The shortest night of the year was nearly over, much too soon. The sky outside was already half-light.

"Oh—I nearly forgot." From her hand, she took a silver ring set with an onyx stone. This she placed into my palm, saying: "Your livery."

The craftsmanship was doubtless that of the same dexterous silversmith who had worked the delicate filigree of her pipe. But the ring was molded in a single seamless piece, burnished so smooth my thumb would never, in its thousand-and-one attempts, determine where the setting ended and the stone began. It was made to a woman's proportions, so small it fit none but the narrowest finger on my weaker hand. But on that finger, it fit perfectly.

A night spent in tears, I have found, hangs over a body as profoundly as a night devoted to strong drink. As I marched home under the glaring eye of the rising sun, my head throbbed guilty iambs with each footstep. What had seemed in the darkness the source of every delight was now my chiefest torment. I could not put the baroness behind me. Her body—which only an hour before, I had desired savagely—now disgusted me, and just as savagely. I detested it—its blatant nakedness, and, paradoxically, its infuriating furtiveness: secreting itself away in folds, secreting piquant liquids, pungent scents. Her smell, clinging everywhere, obsessed me: overripe fruit and musk, decay and bonfire.

How could I have believed her beautiful? She was downright ugly, once I considered the image in my right mind. The spill of her breasts (which I had held like water in cupped hands, and suckled as a man dying of thirst) struck me now as displeasingly—nay, *damningly*—asymmetrical. I remembered the black wires crawling out from the pits of her arms, from the foul pit between her legs: cavernous, sulfuric, hot as hell. I winced at the vivid memory of its taste. Lingering, internal, and slightly metallic, distressingly like the bile rising now to tickle the back of my throat.

And worse, how eagerly I had made its acquaintance, exploring its cunning and intricate folds, as if it were some devious device—a quaint piece of clockwork, perhaps: something rare, and curiously wrought. But inside, it had revealed itself to be a trap, deliberately laid. Aye, a trap—and I the rat who took her rotten bait.

No, I was worse than a rat. I had been made that thing I most despised: a spy. For what did it matter, really, if I made my report to the world in sonnets or court documents or gossip around the inn? To be a poet is to be made procurer of another's private soul. For the basest part of myself, I had betrayed the best part of myself. I had introduced into our love a witness, and it had changed everything.

·　　　·　　　·

Returning to my room, I sat immediately at the writing-desk and read over the sonnet she had guided me to write. The power of the poem still seduced me. It was a study in politics: part supplication, part subtle threat. How much richer and deeper the language seemed, under her influence!

And as I read the lines, I understood a simple truth about the world for which they had been written. A prince might, for amusement's sake, keep company with a plainspoken pauper; a king could not. When Hamlet was at home, he must be surrounded everywhere by courtiers; because wherever the king was, was the court. He had spoken of Elsinore as a prison—but what he could not escape there was himself, his destiny. My destiny.

I filled the inkwell and swiftly copied the poem onto a sheet of my fine letter paper. My hand shook only slightly at the final lines. I would have to apprentice myself to the baroness a while, to learn to be worthy of Hamlet's world, that I might serve him anywhere. Until that time, it would be better that I did not show myself before him, lest my insufficiency in this regard be proved.

I signed the letter *He that thou knowest thine*, blowing on the ink to dry it, though I knew this haste would be revealed to Hamlet's eagle-eye by the faint blurring in the serifs. I sealed the note with candle-wax, then hurried down the stairs, calling for a messenger to deliver it quickly, before I could change my mind.

● ● ●

I might tell you I became her lover only because she was my patroness. That is what I myself believed at first; and what I stubbornly continued to believe long after hard evidence might have
convinced a skeptic otherwise. It would be dangerous to refuse
her, I told myself—knowing full well how much more dangerous
it was to accept.

I might tell you I became her lover for the prince's sake: for
Hamlet's safety, and at his behest. For had not he implied that I
should have a mistress, to avert the dangerous conjectures of ill-
breeding minds? This, I thought, was the sacrifice I must make for
my love. I liked this thought, and entertained it often. It gave an
air of poignancy and romance to this commonest of habits, midnight fornication.

I might even tell you (as I myself was half certain, by daylight)
that I was never her lover at all. Our affair, I might explain, was
only a dream in earnest: an invention of my fantasy, to liven up my
story. I could try to convince you this conjugation described here
is intended merely as a metaphor for what she took from me, and
transformed, and returned again; and that entirely another sort of
intimate exchange took place between us, between the sheets of
poetry alone.

But my body would tell another tale. If these excuses were all
my thoughts whenever I returned to Adriane's rooms, her touch
chased all my thoughts away. Even her voice, beckoning across the
darkened chamber, embraced me palpably, like the tingle of her
fingernails raked down my spine brainstem to testicle.

Nor was it her money, nor anything money might buy, that made the minutes drag across me, inch by agonizing inch, on those evenings when I had been summoned to her. As night fell, I began to feel the ticking of my watch as an itch all through my skin, sending me into a frenzy of petty discontents. I could not eat or drink. I could not think or read or write. I was filled with murderous, bloody rage. As the hour hand crept upwards, muscles in my arms and legs began to twitch and quiver, aching for their customary exercise. Waiting for the hour to strike when I might climb her ladder, as helpless on its ropes as a marionette.

Just before dawn, I would return again to my own comfortless straw mattress, exhausted, and too full of dreams to sleep. For—just as sinners make more zealous pilgrims than men of easy conscience—my thoughts, having strayed, returned to Hamlet even more intensely than before. His face those days was like a bright torch burning in the little room. Nor could I shut my eyes to it, for that only confined the sight to even closer quarters in my head. I tossed and turned but could not find a quiet spot in my own mind in which to rest.

Each footstep in the hall distracted me with hope of a messenger from Hamlet—or perhaps the prince himself. My attention would seize on the sound, my heart racing until I heard the visitor continue unabated past my door, freshening a dozen times a day the sting of my disappointment.

Even on those nights I did not go to her, I rested no more than a few hours at a time. In my fragile insomniac state, the prince's continuing silence weighed on me, magnifying the memory of every loss I had suffered in my life. I lay awake revisiting old memories of childhood sorrows and slights, weeping at scars as if they were fresh wounds. To each man I passed in the street, I compared myself ruthlessly, desiring the best qualities of each. If only I had the delicate features of that fine-boned gypsy lad—or the company of friends, like that fat knight in the laughing crowd—then might I have his love. And yet, it seemed that if I might just regain Hamlet's favor, all these old losses would be restored to me again.

But days and nights passed into weeks, and still no word. A dozen times a day I imagined going to him, confessing everything, begging his forgiveness. Several times I even started up his street, only to catch in a window some reflection of myself—unshaven, underslept, and guilty as the night is long—and turn back again, cursing my fate.

Underneath it all, the feeling remained that Hamlet was ashamed of me, and that if he knew about my habit with the baroness, he would be even more ashamed. I did not dare show my head before the prince in this state of disgrace. In spite of everything, I was too proud for that. Then I heard a rumor that he had gone traveling for the summer holidays, and even this small hope was lost to me.

My only comfort came from my book. Reading through the poems, I could discover some shadow of him faithfully recorded there. And the memory of his sweet love had the power to raise my soul from its deepest despair—inspiring it, like the lark, to dare to sing at the gates of paradise.

I took up my pen again. Only by my song might I yet hope to coax my angel to unlock those pearly gates; to allow me pleasures I had only imagined when I closed my eyes and dreamed I held my true-love in my arms.

A h, yes," Adriane said impatiently. "Yet another sonnet on the theme of his boundless restorative powers—as though he were a tonic you hoped to sell."

Her thick black lashes were stiff and also soft, like the tuft of feather at the tip of my pen. They brushed my cheek, raising gooseflesh, as she bent down over my shoulder and spoke into my ear. "Tell me—have you written nothing else?"

I shut my book abruptly. "You wanted to know what it is to love him. Even a poet can sell no soul but his own." I hoped the tension gripping me would be taken for indignation.

The truth is, I had been writing other poems. But these pages I could not bear to show her, because they were about her: my mysterious dark mistress, deceitful and cruel and irresistible. They were about my constant torment and misery: lust, driving me to madness in pursuit of her; madness in possession of her; madness in regret. I wanted to leave her. I wanted to take her coldly, brutally—to penetrate her, as she had penetrated me: down to the bones, through whatever in me was a son of Adam and made of mud.

Instead, I summoned Hamlet's image to my mind, all fire and air. "The other half of myself—my thought, my desire—is with him always, wherever I may abide."

"And this is love?" That mocking tone of hers—the one that crawled under my skin and slumbered there, breaking free to taunt me at unexpected hours. "A melancholy obsession with your own fantasy?"

But then she lay back in bed, her anger disappearing like her curls into the blanket folds. "Read me that last one again."

If the poem was particularly to her liking, she might have me read it to her three or four times, while she reclined, lips parted slightly, a flushed and blissful expression on her face. When I came to the final couplet, she would let out a long and contented sigh; and only then did it seem she had achieved the pinnacle of her pleasure.

And, truly, it was only then that I achieved the pinnacle of mine. In those darkest hours between midnight and dawn, I found access to a vast imagination, a wit of which my daylight self was hardly aware.

For her amusement, I transformed myself into characters of my fancy: traitors and jesters and monsters and kings. When she pressed me for too many personal details about my history, I reported to her only as much as I could invent, telling stranger and wilder stories, impossible tales.

I surprised myself with this talent for lying. For as long as I could remember, my life's work had been the discovery and catalogue of the truth. If you asked me what I knew, I could reply with a list of proven facts, unadorned by speculation or emotion. Even my poetry reflected this, each sonnet presenting an argument to its logical conclusion, neatly as a geometric proof.

But she listened to my stories, finding the meaning in my words—often more than I myself had meant in telling them. It surprised me to discover how seemingly disparate things were linked together in my mind. Sometimes she would be reminded of an image in a sonnet, or some similar turn of phrase in a seemingly unrelated poem. Or she would marvel at my knowledge of some obscure source, only to find the correlation pure coincidence. These odd juxtapositions had a certain poetry of their own, convincing me nothing in human memory was ever lost, but recurred again in unexpected ways, to astonish the world anew.

So I wrote, guided by her attention, encouraged by her praise, fearing always her scorn—or, worse, her indifference to my words. Physically, she drew me, as a magnet draws base metal; but out of me, she drew my poetry. For her, I performed miracles, impossible alchemies. For her, I spun the straw of my life into gold.

The Prince's Fool

Day followed night followed day with a sameness that left behind no sense of the passage of time. My hours were spent like the spokes of a spinning-wheel, turning and turning, never traveling except to return to the place where they began. So it was not until I woke one day to gray skies and a decided chill in the air that I realized summer was nearly over. Only a few weeks remained until Michaelmas, and the beginning of the term. I had spent the time removed, in dreams.

The overcast sky gave no clue to the hour, but a quick glance at my watch confirmed that I had missed noon dinner at the schol-ars' hall. I would have to go out, or go without until suppertime. My stomach rumbled. At least I had a few coins in my purse. I still thought of it as *her* money, my payment for selling my soul in poetry. It weighed heavy on my heart to spend it, but not so heavy as the grumbling plummet in my belly.

Wrapping my new long wool cloak around me, I braved the rain and went to the tavern where I had passed so many happy hours with the prince. I chose this place not because I hoped to see him there (though of course this hope ran ahead of my eyes always everywhere) but only wishing to rekindle some memory of the feeling I had had in his presence, like anything at all was possible. That is what it was, to be with Hamlet—to feel that at any moment, something wonderful and strange beyond all imaginings might happen, setting into motion a chain of events to which you would discover you had been bound—irretrievably, always—by fate.

His absence from the tavern (now called the Drunken Savage) was depressingly apparent even before I made my obligatory scan of the customers. The weather had kept all but the most devoted drunkards at home. At the back, a rude crew of mechanical laborers was engaged in dramatic and passionate debate about some minor flaw in the construction of a wall. The only other noise was the clatter of dice from scattered tables, where a few degenerate truants in scholars' caps sat gathered listlessly at games of chance.

"Master Horatio!" A handkerchief was dancing in the corner; attached to it a plump, pink, well-ringed hand. "Master Horatio, over here!" Rosencrantz leapt up, motioning for me to sit at their table.

Guildenstern, engaged in keeping score on a piece of slate, looked up too late to object. The ruff of his collar was starched so stiff and fashionably large that he had to turn his head to look at anything in his periphery. He did not turn his head to look at me. Still, he greeted me with an absent pat to the arm, nearly cordial.

They began to exchange the conventional inquiries about my welfare, but I cared for just one subject: "How fares my lord, Prince Hamlet?"

At the sound of the name, Rosencrantz started violently, upsetting his goblet—which was fortunately empty. He looked to Guildenstern. "What say you?" he whispered, as though I could not hear, sitting beside them.

I looked from one to the other, trying to make sense of this peculiar behavior. "Is Hamlet well?" I asked. "Is he returning soon from his holidays?"

For the first time, Guildenstern expressed an interest in me. He swiveled his head in my direction, lips pursed like a fish testing a suspicious bait. "Do you mean you did not know?"

"Clearly not." I fought to keep my voice expressionless. I refused to give them the satisfaction of guessing my anxiety.

Guildenstern frowned, weighing his mistrust of me against the pleasure of watching me receive unpleasant news. He picked some invisible mote of lint from his indigo coat, on which marched rows of smooth stars, cast in gold.

Actually, they were probably brass. For some reason, this small epiphany gave me undue pleasure. I did not know why it should be so; I myself could not afford even brass buttons for my faded black doublet (a poor-man's gray by daylight). And dirty, now, as well—somehow, I had gotten a chalky white smudge on the sleeve.

"Well, why should the poor be deprived?" Guildenstern decided after no more than a minute's deliberation. He craned his long neck, side to side. No one was listening, but still he lowered his voice to a dramatic whisper before confessing, with great significance: "He has gone to . . . *take the waters . . .*"

I searched this phrase for meaning, but found none.

"He has been sent away, to the *Nunnery*." Again Guildenstern insinuated an air of disgrace into the words. I felt like a foreigner who has learned the vocabulary of the local tongue, but can make no sense of its idioms.

"The prince is visiting a . . . brothel?"

"Nay, a convent!" Rosencrantz interjected. Under the table, he fondled the rosary for comfort in his lap. "He has taken sanctuary at a healthful seething bath in a remote wooded valley, tended by votaries. *Chaste* votaries," he hastened to add. "Devoted to Our Lady of the Spring. The waters are said to be a sovereign cure against any distemper."

"They must be healthful," Guildenstern muttered. "The odor is terrible."

"I do not understand. Is it some sort of spa?" I looked from one lord to the other, while they exchanged between them a glance pregnant with significance.

"Well, to be blunt—" Guildenstern's lips curled in distaste. "It is where families of note send the relatives they want to forget about. When a guilty Duke starts seeing the brother he murdered for his title sitting at his banquet table . . . or the king's cast-off mistress cracks, and tries to drown her own daughter for spite . . ."

Rosencrantz nodded vigorously, ". . . then they are sent to the Nunnery to take the waters, and be cured."

"Cured? Cured of what?"

"Madness!" wailed Rosencrantz. He dabbed at his eyes, then patted his ruddy forehead with the same damp handkerchief.

"He is not mad," Guildenstern snapped, "but incorrigibly wicked. He has poisoned his blood, drinking, gambling, drabbing about with low sorts." His eyebrows implicated me in this. "Chief among his faults are reckless youth, and wantonness."

"Nay, those qualities are his graces!" Rosencrantz chided. "Hamlet's youthfulness is remarked on everywhere with delight, not scorn. And what you call wantonness is but a gentleman's sporting—anyone at court will tell you so."

Guildenstern rolled his eyes. "And the queen wears in her wedding-ring a jewel any eye can see is glass. But still it is praised as a diamond—the rank of the hand lends to the item in appraisal what it lacks in worth."

"But Hamlet *is* a diamond," argued Rosencrantz, still steward of the prince's excellence. "For, moving all those around him to temptation, he himself remains unmoved, as cold as any stone. One falls into such shameful thoughts at the sight of him." He gave a sigh. "How lovely he makes every mortal sin appear! What wickedness, to be sheathed in such sweet flesh!" He wiped his eyes, confessing to me shyly across the table: "He loved me, once."

"Indeed," drawled his companion bitterly. "And I shudder to think what might have happened had I not been there to rescue you."

"How fair, the skin that all his sins enclosed!" Rosencrantz closed his eyes, wet black lashes sticking thickly together. "As perfect as—as a church full of lilies at Easter!"

"Lilies that fester smell far worse than weeds," said Guildenstern. But the specter of Hamlet had been invoked. A tremor shook his lip, which his lascivious-speaking tongue darted furtively from the corner of his mouth to moisten.

Then I understood: even this constant obloquy was a form of praise, a tender obsession with the prince's flaws. Guildenstern's seething resentment was his love for the prince, turned traitor on itself; his daggers would find their target in his own heart. I felt for him, shockingly, a moment of pity. Then I shuddered, seeing another possible destiny for myself in his carefully drawn face, its dust of powder going to paste in the damp air. Is this what Adriane's tutelage would make me into? A spy and petty gossip, despising the one I had once desired?

"The hardest knife, ill-used, will lose its edge," Rosencrantz countered with his own truism. "And he has been ill-used, in Elsinore. His father still refuses to speak to Hamlet, nor let him come within his sight. His own father! No wonder he has gone mad."

Madness. It was just what Hamlet had feared. He had begged me to stay with him, to keep at bay those tormenting demons of his dreams, visions he was sure were prophecies. And the prince's noble mind had been overthrown as soon as I had thrown him over.

Then an even more terrible thought occurred to me: "What happens to those who are not cured?"

Guildenstern shrugged. "They never return," he said.

"'Tis terrible," Rosencrantz shuddered. "It is as if they were dead. Worse than dead—as if they had never been. No one ever mentions them again."

Guilt burned through me like an acid, hot and cold. Hamlet would be forgotten entirely. And it was I who had forgotten him, neglecting the hero of my poems to write instead about the baroness. I had promised to make him immortal, all his virtues understood through all the world; but I had failed, and he had disappeared. I could not bear it another minute. "I must go to him at once."

"Well, you are in luck," Guildenstern replied. "The valley is only sixty miles away. Less than a day's ride from the city, if your stallion be swift." And though he said this with a smile of perfect innocence, I saw his eyes, sharp stars, dancing with glee. An impossibly long journey through the forest, and impossibly dangerous, for a man without a horse.

The distance between myself and Hamlet felt like a physical injury. If only the dull substance of my flesh were as nimble as my thoughts, already at his side! Aye, "if only." I shook my head. And if wishes were horses.

Well, my wishes were all the poems I had sold for Adriane's silver; and with this I might hire a ride, if I had enough.

Fumbling for my purse with shaking hands, I summoned the proprietor. He did not receive me nearly so warmly in this company as he had when I had been with Hamlet; but I did not wait for niceties.

"I need a horse," I said. "The swiftest one you have."

If he was surprised by the request, the old man did not show it. He nodded, taking his time as he leisurely looked me over, clocking my worth. I winced, knowing the price had doubled the moment I began the bargaining with "I need" and not "How much . . ."

"Quickly, please." My attempt at a commanding tone came out instead as moaning. "The matter is urgent."

"Fourpence a mile," Father Jacques finally settled on. "Plus a groat fer yer guide."

"A guide? Why do I need a guide?"

"To keep yeh from gettin' lost!" he stated the obvious. "Plus he'll bring yer horse back when yeh get there. Unless yeh wanted to pay for the return as well?" Gold glittered in his hopeful eyes.

I blanched at this.

The old man scratched his beard and shrugged. "I was yeh, I'd take yer guide. Highwaymen."

"I shan't have anything left to steal," I grumbled, fishing in my purse.

Father Jacques looked offended by this. "My horse!"

I paid him what he asked. The lion's share of my quarter's wages gone, to be with Hamlet. If I'd had kingdoms, I would have traded them.

As soon as he saw the money, his demeanor instantly changed. "Thank yeh, sir." He gave a very deep bow, proving far more flexible than I would have guessed for a man of his advanced years. "Yer horse'll be ready in an hour. Two at the very most."

"An hour!?"

The old man's shoulders hunched. "I'll have to wake yer guide."

"Sleeping! At this hour!"

Father Jacques shrugged again. "He's drunk."

At the bottom of my purse, only one lonely coin remained, and that a penny. I offered it to the old man. "Hurry, please." I hoped the prince could lend me a horse to return on; else I faced a long, miserable trudge on foot.

Rosencrantz sighed. "He may not even receive you when you arrive, you know," he sniffed. "He wouldn't us."

He signaled the serving girl to bring another round. A glass was pressed into my hand. The wine was weak and cloying sweet, but still, I gave my thanks. I had nothing but my good graces to feed me now.

"'Tis all his mother's fault, you know," Guildenstern said. "Everyone knows they have slept together."

I smacked the table with my palm; wine goblets leapt up in surprise. "That is a filthy lie!"

Guildenstern gave a feline smirk at my discomfort. "I swear it is true—every year since the prince was born, his filial goodnight kiss to her in her private closet has grown longer. And the queen younger!"

Rosencrantz chortled at this, turning to me to explain that her royal highness's birth date was a notoriously movable feast.

"Moreover, I overheard her laundry-maid repeat that she was worn out with washing the seamy sheets of her mistress's incestuous affair. *Incestuous*," Guildenstern repeated. "The queen has no male relative living but her son. *Quod erat demonstratum*." His left eyebrow twitched upwards in triumph.

Watching him, I made note of the Latin word for eyebrow, *supercilium*; as well as certain apt derivatives now proved upon his haughty face. "Nothing has been demonstrated," I scoffed. "It is but rumor, conjecture, and fantasy, and I'll not believe a word of it."

"You've never been to Elsinore," Guildenstern drawled. "Dull as a mausoleum, mostly. The same painted-up faces day after day, mouthing the same conversations over again importantly, as though they were chiseled in stone. After a few million endless runs of dark and stormy nights, everyone in any decent company has slept with everyone."

"Unless they found sufficient entertainment starting vicious rumors." My tone just toed the line of accusation.

Rosencrantz poured more wine and tried to make the peace between us. "Whether 'tis true or not matters little, as long as it is believed. At court, it is better to be vile, than vile-esteemed. Is not what people think of you, ultimately, what you are? History is kept alive in the minds and mouths of men."

"And gossip even more so," added Guildenstern, through a line of neat sharp teeth stained gold with sherry. "Why, remember the terrible scandal over Hamlet's first love?"

"Surely you do not believe those rumors." The rosary *click-clacked*. "He was an innocent young boy!"

"Young as he was, that boy was never innocent." Guildenstern snorted.

I had not heard from Hamlet any tales of first or last or any loves at all, and against my better judgment, I was curious.

"He was a basta—er, a man of no station, like yourself, dear Master Horatio." Rosencrantz blushed. "And terribly clever, as well, like yourself. A great wit. He could read your fortune in the dregs left at the bottom of your wine."

"A crude prankster, who entertained the court at dinnertime," said Guildenstern. "And dull, as well, from what I have heard tell—his jokes went on incessantly, rambling from subject to subject until the table roared to have him silenced."

"He was the king's Fool," Rosencrantz explained.

"He was the prince's Fool," snapped Guildenstern. "Lascivious as a changeling child, the prince would leap into the poor buffoon's lap, begging to suck kisses from his lips."

"That was only because he painted them with cherry juice," Rosencrantz said, "to redden them. He painted his cheeks as well, and lined his eyes with kohl."

"Just like a *lady*," said Guildenstern.

"Like a clown!" insisted Rosencrantz. "He had a fine motley cockscomb cap, with bells on either end."

"Ah—the cap!" Guildenstern clapped his bony hands together. "I had forgotten. The little prince loved to spread his hands up under it while he rode the poor man's back, caressing and fondling the prickled skull as if committing its shape to memory."

"He was bald, you see," Rosencrantz interjected.

"Fools carry lice," Guildenstern sniffed, "and are obliged by law to shave their heads once a fortnight. Their heads and all the rest as well, if young Hamlet's report can be believed." He smirked, allowing the significance of this last to penetrate.

"The prince swore to me their affection was innocent," Rosencrantz cried. "He only sought out the warmth of the jester's bed, when troubled thoughts kept him from sleeping."

They could have continued in this argument, but we were interrupted with the news that my horse was saddled and the guide awaiting me outside.

I shouldered up my satchel and doffed my cap for their hospitality—no better fed, but warmer for the wine. But something turned me back: the fatal curiosity that is the heart of all my scholarship. I could not bring myself to part their company without asking one final question:

"What happened to him? The Fool?"

"To Yorick?" Rosencrantz's brow corrugated as he murmured vaguely, "I think the prince said he was sent away . . ."

"Of course they would have told him that," scoffed Guilden-stern. "Prince Hamlet is so *sensitive*, you know." He turned his narrow smirk on me. "Naturally, the slave was put to death."

"To death?" All at once, I felt the effect of the alcohol. I stead-ied myself on the table's planks, determined not to swoon before these gentlemen.

"Beheaded, probably." Guildenstern's nose twitched, as though suppressing a sneeze—or more likely a laugh at the queasy look on my face. "Well, what did you expect? That's what happens to clever bastards who are caught in bed with the *dauphin*. Even if he is the one on top."

What Dreams May Come

I was guided through labyrinths of corridors by a little wimpled nun in white. Room after room, she cut a swath through dense-packed clouds of steam, making me grateful (though it had incited no small protest at the time) that I had put on the flimsy linen robe and wooden sandals offered by the sisters in place of my dusty traveling clothes. They would not answer my questions about the prince—nor, in fact, anything else—but remained silent and white as sheets of paper, rustling as they moved.

A vow, I supposed, though faintly through the walls I could hear the rising notes of women's voices singing hymns with the lilting refrains of country ballads.

Then I remembered where I was, and wondered if this sound might, rather, be madwomen's wailing. Everything was softened by the continuous musical gurgle and drip of water on water, echoing everywhere.

"Where is the spring?" I called ahead to the little nun.

She did not speak, of course, nor break her stride, but swept back the long sleeve of her habit, pointing straight down, to the floor. No, the gesture was stronger than that; she pointed down *into* the floor.

I squinted at the tiles underfoot, and for the first time saw that the intricate design repeated at certain intervals (which I had dismissed as decorative) was not, in fact, inlaid in the stone, but latticed out of it. Through these holes, I could make out the dark suggestion of water beneath our feet.

"The sanctuary is built atop the stream?"

The wimple nodded.

I willed myself not to feel the floor beneath my sandals sink and sway, like the deck of a ship. We were sloping gradually downward. The heat grew more intense, as did the stench of sulfur. At last, we arrived at an arched doorway, where she left me, disappearing back into the fog.

The archway opened into a large atrium, ringed by fluted columns of impressive scale. From this perimeter, wide marble steps terraced down to a great bath at the centre. Vapor was rising from the surface of the pool in rippling sheets, curling into clouds as it escaped the open roof. The sun had set some time before, and the few lingering clouds parted to show their silver to the moon.

Then my eye seized upon another sight, even more beautiful.

Framed in the arch of pillars at the far end of the bath, he was standing on a wide stone platform thrust out over the water, as if readying himself to take a dive.

Though I had taught my inward eye to reproduce his image every day, always the mind misremembered some detail: the way the curve of his eyebrow, for example, precisely mirrored the angle of his jaw. The tiny, teardrop mole: was it on the right cheek, or the left? And even if my memory had been perfect in these minutiae, still it could not capture the quality of the whole in movement, that quintessence of Hamlet that made him impossible to pin down or define.

Adriane had been right in one respect: absence did make the heart grow fonder, the appetite more keen. I understood why a miser might choose to keep his most precious jewel locked up in a cupboard, examining it only rarely, so custom never had the chance to dull his fresh delight.

Still—I had to admit it—he looked terrible. His hair, uncombed, hung down in knotted locks, and a fawn-colored beard was stippled in unevenly on sunken, sallow cheeks. Across the high stone platform, he was pacing back and forth, muttering something under his breath.

"Hail to your lordship," I called out to him.

Hamlet stopped his pacing. "Ere I can make a prologue to my brains, they have begun the play," he muttered, half unto himself. Then he raised his voice: "But what is your affair in hell, sinner?"

This is, at least, what I thought I heard, clattering on my

wooden shoes. I was uncertain how to react to this strange greet-ing: had he mistaken me for a fellow inmate of this odd asylum? "Do you know me, my lord?"

"Horatio," he chided me at once. "I could as soon forget my-self. My eye, my tongue, my heart—you are no less to me than any part of this wretched unstoppable machine called Hamlet, Prince of Denmark."

I very nearly rushed forth to embrace him, but remembering Adriane's teachings, stopped and gave instead an awkward bow.

"Your servant, sir."

"Nay, I'll change that name with you." He hurried up the steps into a small adjoining room, returning after a moment with a flagon on a serving tray, flanked by a pair of Italian goblets.

"Were you expecting company, my lord?" I asked, noting the second cup. He did not seem surprised to see me here, though he had not sent for me.

Hamlet pressed a smile between his lips while he thumbed open the beak of the pewter lid. "Do you remember the day we met?"

"Remember it, my lord?" Did he think it a day I was ever likely to forget?

"To think—you had never seen a tomato," he mused, "and feared it like death itself. You believed it would poison. But now I'll teach you to drink deep, ere you depart."

The wine was dark as ink and poured all dregs. He pressed a goblet in my hand. "Nay, come, let's go together." Raising his glass in a toast, he grinned, running his tongue into his cheek. "I would call it my blood—but you, Horatio, would remind me that it was truly Rhenish hippocras, spiced by my own apothecary."

The wine was indeed heavily spiced with gingerroot and cloves, as well as some unidentifiable medicinal herbs, which left behind a musty, bitter aftertaste. Still, in this present heat, and after my long journey, I was grown quite thirsty, and downed the draught. The prince also lay down an empty cup before he spoke again.

"But what make you from Wittenberg?"

"To see you, my lord," I answered. I did not wish to credit too much the influence of Rosencrantz and Guildenstern.

He affected a cheery, formal tone. "And I am glad to see you well, Horatio. Now we will shake hands and part, each to his business and desire—" Despite his words, his hand showed no signs of quitting mine. Rather, it pulled me closer, crawling hotly up my sleeve until he held me by the bare crook of my elbow, staring in my eyes. "For every man has business and desire."

The way he knit these two together made me wonder if he had found out somehow about the truth of my relationship with my patroness. He was watching me intently, a peculiar narrowness to his cloud-ringed eyes. "I pray, do not mock me, fellow-student—they told you I was mad?"

I swallowed. "So I have heard, my lord."

He was pleased to hear me admit it so freely. "And did in part believe it?"

"I did not know, sir," I said. "I have come to judge on the evidence of my own eyes."

"A very good answer!" He released me. "For what can a man trust, if not the report of his own eyes?" Cackling as though he had made a joke, he paced to the edge of the platform, looking down into the bath. "But your worries are misplaced. I may at times put on an antic disposition, but I assure you I am perfectly sane."

Which was, of course, exactly what a madman would have said. I knew I could not judge on this report.

"Tell me what has troubled you, my lord."

He shrugged me off. "No—you will reveal it."

I stopped, ashamed. It was true, I had already been framing this moment into a story for Adriane, as always I was framing every moment of my life into a story for her.

"Not I, my lord, I swear it." I resolved that it should be the truth; but still, I could not meet his eyes.

"Nay, though you swear by my sword, you shall be the one to tell the tale," Hamlet predicted, waggling a long thin finger at me, then crooking it to his own head. "I know it, as I came with a caul."

I did not believe in the powers accorded to cauls, nor in prophecies, nor second sight; nor did I believe those astrologers who told me I did not believe because I was born in April. But the prince was born in May. And if the heart of one man did think something, though the whole world disagreed, I was pledged to believe it—if the one man was Prince Hamlet.

"I swear by what you will, my lord. I shall not reveal a word—unless you yourself should bid me otherwise." I crossed down to stand at the prince's shoulder, half a step behind. "Have you been troubled once again by bad dreams? By your . . . your prophetic soul?" It was the term he had used for his spells of melancholy.

His pallor confirmed it, and the wild expression in his sleepless eyes. "Horatio—I have seen such things to make me wish I had never been born. My oldest friends conspire to deceive me. The most innocent-seeming maid looks in my face and lies."

Tearing away from me, he paced, gesturing wildly, as though he meant to convince someone at the far end of the hall. "My enemies are behind every curtain. I feel hot blood upon my sword and sink it even deeper, to the hilt." He mimed the thrust, but then his hand curled upwards, as if afflicted by a sudden palsy. "Then it becomes a skull-bone in my hand, grinning at me as if we were old friends!"

The prince recoiled from the platform's edge. "My father!" he cried. "Methinks I see my father."

"Where, my lord?" I leaned forwards to follow his eyes, squinting down into the steaming water. The height as well as heat made me light-headed; I might almost have believed I saw a shadow swimming beneath the glassy surface, in the roiled dark.

"In my mind's eye." Hamlet shuddered. "Every time I catch my own reflection." He pulled his fingers through the dark artichoke fuzz on his cheeks. "I must be shaved," he laughed. "Will you to it?"

"Of course, my lord." He looked almost to normal then, as he left the platform and began to climb the terrace.

"The time is not yet," he said. "This visitation is but to whet my almost-blunted purpose. We have some history left to rewrite."

I followed, wheezing slightly; it took concentrated effort to draw serviceable breath from the damp air. "History is past, my lord. It cannot be rewritten."

He turned to look at me over his shoulder. "So it is for most, Horatio, but not for us. We go backwards, like crabs." He demonstrated this for me a while, leaping up the stairs, while I held breath, seeing in each misstep a fatal fall. "You see, I have discovered the secret." He came and put his arm around me confidentially, whispering unnaturally fast: "Our past is ever being rewritten. In fact, it is the only thing about us that can be, you see? Our future is already set in stone, forever to be our present. We can only be truly alive now—in the past."

For the first time, I put some credit in Guildenstern's account. Hamlet, I thought, might well have lost his mind.

I trailed, a pace behind the prince, into a hotter but less humid room that stank of the perfumes of Araby. These, I thought, must be contained in the great variety of ewers and painted urns that lined the wooden shelves along the walls, along with varied switches and other strange implements such as one might use to curry horses.

I had read of such a room in Seneca's descriptions of the Roman baths. A weathered sandstone table on a dais at the back was laid with layers of linens. This, I thought, must be where the bather would lie, while the attendant massaged his body with olive oil, then scraped this slick unwholesome skin away with the strigil, like peeling back an orange. I spotted the instrument, hanging from an iron hook set between two torches lit upon the wall. Translating the innocuous word *strigilis*, I had not pictured such a fearsome-looking scythe; no wonder there was screaming.

The sisters had prepared for us more modern instruments of barbering. At one end of the table, a cloth had been laid out with a brass basin, a lump of castile soap, and an open razor with an ivory handle. Its blade was black with age—all but the edge, which had been sharpened to reflecting.

My thought must have been written on my face; or else Prince Hamlet read my mind.

"Terribly irresponsible of them," he agreed. "Leaving such a thing alone with a lunatic." He vaulted himself onto the table and perched on its edge, his legs swinging like church-bells. "They are all afraid to do it, you know. They are hoping I'll save them the trouble."

"To do . . . ?"

He drew his index finger across his throat. "How clear, how simple it would be. A few passes of the blade, and it would be done: the royal house of Denmark razed. My noble mind overthrown, and all the expectancies—of fashion, form, of family, our fair state—forgotten. Blasted, for a moment's ecstasy." He leered at me cockeyed, then laughed to see my face. "But do not fret, Horatio! How-strange-or-odd-soever I bear myself, I am perfectly well. I can tell a hawk from a handsaw, when the wind is southerly."

"A hawk from a what?" I had never heard a madder phrase in all my life. Slowly, I moved to place myself between Prince Hamlet and the razor's edge.

"A *hernsew*," the prince enunciated, rolling his eyes at me. "A heron-fowl?" He sighed in exasperation. "One hunts them for sport." He always forgot I was not of a class to have practiced falconry. "When the wind is north-northwest, they fly sou'easterly, and may be taken in the sunrise for the hunting-bird."

I nodded. Was it possible, then, to understand him, in another tongue? Perhaps the prince was sane after all, if after his own fashion. Still, I discreetly slid the razor into my hand, even taking it with me when I went to fill the basin from the spring.

While Hamlet arranged himself to his comfort upon the table, I took the shapeless lump of soap and began to work it between my hands into a lather, thick and white as clotted cream. It was not unlike my daily ritual of mixing up my ink: calculating the proportions, measuring out my pigments carefully, whisking in just enough water to give it a dense but fluid consistency, like blood.

Soon the prince had the suggestion of a snowy beard all down his neck and to his collarbone. The sight provoked in me a feeling of intense tenderness—a precocious nostalgia—to think, I might still be his faithful servant when his fair was so silvered in earnest.

Still, it was a relief when my first tentative strokes began to peel back the illusion, showing him again young and bare-faced.

I had an intuition as I worked of a more ancient and solemn ritual. Looking up through the arched doorway, I understood the reason why. Those trunkless pillars at the fore, now overgrown with moss, had once held that cracked granite pediment, now used as a paving-stone. In its first life, this bath had been a temple.

The walls flickered with torchlight, showing the ruined remains of antique tile mosaics. They were well-picked by time and thieves, so that what legends they had once depicted (a man bearded in snakes; a pair of gladiators wrestling to the death) now had to be puzzled from tattered clues and half-invented. Some chipped and broken tablets remained as well, but I found I could not focus my eyes upon them long enough to read the words. They seemed to have been written in some foreign alphabet—like Latin, but backwards. They swam before my eyes, and I felt my stomach cramp with a sudden wave of nausea.

"Who made this place?"

He thumbed the foam from his lower lip to answer, leaving a stamp of bare red mouth. "The Church."

I shook my head. "The outer abbey, perhaps even the sanctuary. But this bath was built by no Christian architect."

"Why say you so?"

I pointed to the capstone on the nearest column, carved in simple spirals, modeled on the mathematical perfection of the nautilus. "Because that cross is more ancient than Christ."

"I know nothing of its history," Hamlet admitted, "but a fable I have heard about how the spring came to have its heat. A simple tale, but it is worth repeating."

"Then you should tell it twice," I made the old joke. "But do not clench your jaw so much." The shaving soap smelled of olive oil and ashes, and gave the prince's skin a liquid slickness and a peculiar pliancy as I pulled it taut across the bone.

He closed his eyes, the better to remember his tale. "The little Love-god, lying once asleep," he began, "laid by his side his heart-inflaming brand."

I felt my own heart swell with heat. I did not need to close my eyes to picture a young god lying beside the spring. "So . . ." I prompted the prince for more, only because I was so happy to hear him speak. "Cupid laid by his brand and fell asleep . . . ?"

He squinted, his recollection of the next part vague. "Many . . . nymphs? . . . that vowed chaste life came tripping by . . . ?"

"Maids of Diana," I surmised, noting the crescent pattern repeated in the stone. They had come here for their devotions, then, and the lustiest of gods had doubtless stopped to spy. No wonder he'd had to lay down his brand. I remembered when I had first discovered the prince, in similar ministrations.

"And in her maiden hand, the fairest votary took up that fire," he put his hand on my hand, holding the razor, and guided it a few slow, heavy strokes. The shave he would have had was closer than I was entirely comfortable with, but I did my best to satisfy. The rhythmic friction of the razor echoing in the small chamber sounded harsh, like it should hurt, but he did not protest. "—which had warmed many legions of true hearts."

I laughed. So the general of hot desire was, sleeping, by a virgin hand disarmed. "And, this advantage found, did steep, to quench it?" I guessed at the end of the tale. The world would thus have been much remedied, freed of the tyranny of love.

"In a cool well by . . ." Hamlet gestured to the spring.

"A cold valley-fountain," the scientist in me could not resist correcting him. A subtle distinction, but one is dug by man, while the other grows naturally, of the ground.

"Which, from Love's fire, took heat perpetual . . ."

Nothing was perpetual, so I had read in some philosophy. Not the sun, the firmament, even the great globe itself. These had had beginning, and would end at doomsday—so (the author had argued) they must be properly cited as origin: dateless, and still to endure.

". . . growing a bath and helpful remedy for men . . . diseased." Hamlet's voice faltered at this last, and for the first time he seemed truly ill at ease with his predicament.

Perhaps, I thought, the waters here could even cure me of my passion for the baroness. Even still she held me in her thrall, infecting my imagination. Even now, she was lurking in my head as I heard the prince's tale: her face grinning at me from the thievish votary of the moon; her dark eye winking as she made off with the prize.

"A fable must end with a moral," I reminded him. "What by this does your story prove?"

He bared a sad, ironic smile. "Love's fire heats water; water cools not love."

This I could not deny. Adriane had tried to steal my heart; but she had merely succeeded in dividing it, afflicting me with love for her as well. And now was I twice sick at heart: in helpless love with a married woman and an unmarriable man. I took my time gingerly shaving around the Adam's apple.

By now, I was sweating so freely my skin felt strange with it: itchy, or perhaps just ticklish, crawling with tiny rivulets. I felt an inordinate gratitude towards the breeze rising to caress and cool my cheek; it seemed a friendly air, eagerly nipping at his salt.

But Hamlet flinched at the same air as if he had been bitten by some creature shrewd to its intent. I felt each individual thorn of the prince's beard spring erect in my palm, like the quills of a frightened porcupine.

His eyes flicked open. They were vast and black as the night sky, and just as starred. Staring up into mine, they seemed to see something beyond sight, beyond surface—something only shadowed and deferred by everything around us now. They peered into my guilty soul, and seemed to seize there on the one impediment to the perfect marriage of our minds.

"Something yet remains untold—"

I was struck by a sudden terror: what if the prince indeed had such strange powers as he claimed, and could read the truth already in my thoughts? What if this were all some test of loyalty, to see whether I would confess?

"What is it, my lord?"

"Where Cupid got new fire."

It took me a moment to understand what he meant. The fable now seemed something long ago, inconsequential. But the answer weighed upon me: Adriane's gaze, burning through my mind like a coal. "In my mistress's eyes," I finally confessed.

"What's that?" A sharp turn of his head turned the razor at his throat into a pen, drawing out a line of scarlet ink. I gasped as the color welled in drops across his throat, like garnets in a jeweled carcanet. Had Hamlet's movement been deliberate? Rather than slitting his own throat, was he hoping I would do the deed for him? My soul, condemned for murder; his for suicide gone free. But though I had pledged to be Damon to his Pythias, I could not perform the act.

"Forgive me, my lord." I moved to staunch the blood with the linen towel. It was only a scratch; for this I whispered a prayer of thanks to any power willing to receive it.

Ignoring this wound, he continued his trial for the other, his finger needling my chest through the damp linen robe. "What mistress? Is there some lady fair enough to have at last captured your heart, that all your poetry is now of her, and you have none left for my praises? Her eyes so like the sun that they'd return the fire to Cupid's brand—and to your cheek, as well, for by your blush I can tell I have not hit far of my mark."

I hardly needed him to tell me I was blushing. I felt faint and dizzy, and I wished I might sit down. "Her eyes are nothing like the sun," I replied, a bit defensively.

"But who is this mysterious mistress?" There was an undeniable strain of jealousy in his voice, and against my conscience, I savored it, like the taste of some rich meat I knew could only cause me indigestion.

"Lady Adriane, my lord," I whispered at last. "My mistress is the baron's wife."

He stared at me for a moment, shocked. Then the prince howled out a tart, frangible noise, which broke and echoed off the bare stone walls, and still did not sound quite like laughter.

"Oh, Horatio! For a moment, I thought you were serious! I take your meaning now. Of course, the lady is your mistress, as your master's wife." Catching his breath, he leaned back again on the table, conversing upside-down. "You always jest in such sober countenance—I was quite nearly fooled. But I have seen your baroness: a face such as hers might indeed move a man to groan, but not with love."

This stung a bit. Adriane had always behaved before me as if she were beautiful; and in truth, I had forgotten she was not. Beauty was a rare quality, to be sure—but why should it be the only virtue that might move a man to love? Adriane was as proud as if she had been beautiful, her power over me as absolute. The face the prince mocked and dismissed as undesirable had made me moan in lust a thousand times. Even when I had been lying in her lap, already duly spent, that face had snaked down under me, sucking the marrow out until I groaned another on her neck, as much in pain as pleasure.

But none of this did I confess aloud. Instead, I ran my thumb under his new-reaped chin and gently turned the other cheek.

"In faith, I cannot trust my own eye to judge," I demurred. The truth, and a deception. "Since I left you, you are in my mind every moment. Those eyes that see the world around me do so only well enough to govern me about—but still, I am half-blind. I might find myself lying beside the most hideous, malformed monster, and call it beautiful, for my inward eye is ever turned on you."

I finished the shave and hastily exited the close quarters to empty the basin into an aqueduct. The sudden rush of cool air on my face made me feel dizzy.

From this awkward angle under the roof, I could not see the moon, but only its reflection in the bath. Nor, I found, could I bear to look on the reflected image for too long, as the steam upon the water caused the moist stars caught in it to writhe and dance and take on tails of fire. I felt as though we had been carried back in time, before the fall of Caesar.

Hamlet joined me after a minute, looking out over the dense gray mist. The simple robe hung from his shoulders in a timeless drape, giving him a classical air, like a young emperor.

Of what strange substance was he made, that so many different tales could be read in his face? Millions of them, hanging about him like ghosts, shadows of himself. But no man casts more than one shadow. Everyone has but one soul. What was so special, then, about this Prince of Denmark, that he took on so many different shades?

For he had always been my mind's model: whether describing Adonis's brow, or Helen's cheek, or the bloom of full-blown Spring. Even before I met the prince, my mind had been ever seeking him: the pinnacle of Art, the masterpiece of the Creator's artwork. He was noble in reason—nearly infinite in his faculties. In form and motion—well, I have sufficiently expressed how admirable I found him in these. At that moment, he seemed to me all the beauty in the world: in proportion perfect, in hue, containing within him every hue, like light. The paragon of all that was mortal, and immortal; angel and animal, his mind divine. All this I apprehended in a flash, intuitively. I tried to convey it to him, but the words came out in stunted phrases, fragments. I hadn't the slightest idea whether I was making any sense at all.

But Hamlet only shook his head at all this praise. "I am a man; take me for all in all." His face was mottled, bronze and gold and black; but even this did nothing to diminish his beauty. If anything, he seemed to be becoming more and more himself.

As if opening a wardrobe to disclose a rare and gorgeous ceremonial robe, he opened up his robe to show himself. His naked skin was glowing with a smooth, translucent sheen, like wax. In ancient times, wax had been used by sculptors to hide chips and defects in inferior stone; and so, an unadulterated statue was lauded as being *sine cera*—"unwaxed."

But the chiseled god unveiled before me now was totally sincere, and waxing desperate with imagination:

"To you alone will I speak the truth," he said. "But you must swear to trust in me, no matter how strange my behavior. You must believe me—no matter how incredible the tale."

I was thrumming all over, as if the sea-change tearing through my soul were remaking and remolding my body as well. I looked down at my hands, and they, too seemed to shimmer—stardust-glazed, and radiating light.

The torchlight flickered, but the shadows dared not to distort the prince's face. Rather, the world around began to flicker and grow dim, while Hamlet, embracing me, grew clearer and brighter, the only true thing to be seen.

"To die . . ." he was muttering. "To sleep . . . no more . . ." He was paler now even than he had appeared before, and would have swooned were I not there to steady him. "In my dreams, yours is the last voice I hear." His fevered brow was pressed into my brow, his hand cupping the base of my head, his eyes half-closed. "The rest is silence."

I drew a shaky breath and my eye fell upon the empty goblets. "The drink . . ." My tongue felt sluggish. "The drink."

Do you remember the day we met?

The thoughts crawled through my mind, taking some wrong turns in what seemed to be particularly complicated corridors.

You had never seen a tomato.

Eventually, my understanding arrived at its destination: some poison in the wine. The razor had been nothing more than misdirection. Hamlet had wanted to die after all—but not alone.

I could see each individual droplet of steam, rising upwards in a curtain, separating our world from another, like, and unalike. The scene went up around us, at first indistinct and green—like the phantoms lingering when one has looked into very bright light—but coming closer and becoming clearer with every breath. A vivid memory of a place where I had never been: a great and lavish hall, and I was at its center, kneeling.

I was both myself and watching myself, as sometimes occurs in dreams; and I was both myself and not myself, as we may recognize a friend within a dream, though he takes the person of another. As I knew at once the man there dying in my arms, though his face kept shifting with the light.

The stone beneath us was slick, not with steam and seething water, it seemed, but hot blood. Blood was everywhere—not all of it, surely, from that narrow rapier scratch; but Danish blood—I could tell by the smell of herring, and the sea. And I heard myself, the famous skeptic, whispering a prayer as I bowed to kiss the most beautiful corpse in the world.

It was not a dream, but a vision of my future. For a terrible instant I knew as if it had already happened, as if remembering with an eidetic clarity what it would be, to be that other Horatio. To watch, helpless, as cold marble leeched the last of the prince's heat. To touch those blue and lifeless lips against my own, astonished to discover in such anguish how the gesture might still send a fist of desire coursing through me: groin, chest, throat.

"No," I pleaded with him. "No, not yet." I pulled him to me, kissing him in earnest then, until his lips stood blushing to their normal rosy shade. I kissed his eyes: the left, the right, until they opened into mine. I kissed the hollow nautilus of his ear, my rough unshaven jaw against the prince's tenderly abused one. The nape of his neck smelled like marjoram, and from his hair rose a scent like rosemary, the aroma of memories.

I kissed his brow, furrowed into horns. I was born under the sign of the bull, and stubbornly I breathed my own life into Hamlet until I felt hot breath returned. The throat is ruled by Taurus, I remembered, and the voice. I followed the rhythm of his pulse. It was faint at first, but gained in strength as I listened, until I could feel it echoing through me. My body was beating with it, my entire self a heart, his heart, his heart of heart.

The heart is ruled by Leo, the lion. The lion is king of the beasts. I fell to my knees, my breath coming in pieces.

Magdalene knelt thus, I thought, before her lord. With her saltwater tears did she wash his feet—which are governed by Pisces, the fish. She anointed him with perfumed oil, and with her own long hair she wiped it away. And, more even than the waste of it, how such flagrant sensuality must have inflamed the betrayer, ashamed to see his own unspeakable desires expressed with such a wordless eloquence.

And I remembered those untranslated gospels, lost to history, which seemed to suggest that Magdalene's story was only a metaphor, and that it was another kind of sensual worship the prostitute had offered, prostrated before her lord.

"Do not condemn her," the god-in-man had said. "This is her prayer."

Hamlet's eyes, the left, the right, were closed; but he was pulling me even closer, between his thighs. The thighs are ruled by Sagittarius, the centaur—who is a swift archer, but not so swift as Love. Virgo the virgin blushed now and discreetly turned away.

I fit my cheek to the delicious hollow of the prince's pelvis. It is ruled by Libra, and the elegant triangle between his hips hung there like perfectly balanced scales. At their crux, his penis rose, an unanswered question. Ruled by Scorpio, it stood between us like the scorpion's sting, but I closed my eyes and took it in my mouth as if it were the key by which I might hope to unlock myself.

A beatific sigh broke through the prince's lips, and his hand came to rest upon my head as he drove the action to its climax. And when the question was answered at last in a shuddering hot rush of essence (from the verb *esse*, "to be"), it was salty, and bitter, and sweet as the Passover feast.

The prince slept on unbroken through the night and day and night, and did not wake again until the following morning, by which time I (having been kept quite well by the nuns for food and drink, if not for company) was itching to return to the City.

And of course, by "the City" what I meant was the baroness. The past few days, I had been granted respite in my duties by the coming of her monthly cycle; but she would surely summon me again, now that the moon was on the wane. To Hamlet, however, I was vague about the nature of my obligations.

He gave no sign of suspecting anything amiss, and even had his own horse saddled for my journey—though not, I noted, liveried in the colors of Denmark. Instead, the palfrey was outfitted in common drab, with no visible insignia at all. Though before, I never would have noticed such a slight, now I marked it ruefully; was he even now ashamed of me?

We embraced for eternities, counted in those elongated seconds of bliss, two souls touching without reserve. Then, separating at last, we stood together in an awkward silence.

"Be good," I bid him, helplessly.

"And what if I am not?" He teased me. "What if I am an ass? A rogue and peasant slave? What if I go about after midnight, and do not come home 'til dawn? Seduce virgins with promises, and then cast them aside? What if I should talk back to my elders, lie, steal, make my mother cry? If I do bloody murder?" he said. "Will you love me still?"

I smiled at his hyperbole. "Of course," I answered, unfazed, and was rewarded for this loyalty with one last kiss from the lips of my sweet prince.

"But do not so," I added—imagining for a moment the sort of damage that might ensue were this fair young man given leave to loose his charms in force upon the world. "As you are mine—"

"For term of life." With a flourish, he mimed signing a document printed on the air.

"Then your good report is also mine. Take pity on your poor biographer," I begged, setting my foot into the stirrup. "My book can be only as worthy as its hero, after all."

"Sometimes I think you love the hero of your book, and never me at all." A shadow of his former troubles played across his brow; still, Hamlet hid a laugh behind his hand to see me try to mount his prized Barbarian.

My seat did not improve at all along the long, uncomfortable journey back to the City. Nor did my mood. On the approach, each milepost had seemed to me a happy sentinel; but now I counted them as the distance separating me from my love.

The Barbary stallion hardly paid me any mind. He plodded along dully, as if he knew I sighed to see the miles pass, and was obliging me by making each one come more slowly still. An hour or two I whittled down composing poems to the thud of hoofbeats; but call for lines about mule-stubborn nags is low, so I had no high hopes for them.

I knew this poverty of speed was willful; for once, when our course was shadowed by a pair of rough unsavories, dark hoods pulled low over their faces on the sunny August day, he kicked up his thoroughbred heels and soon lost them in dust. But once the danger was past, the stallion fell again into a heavy tread, even straying into the gutters to graze on wildflowers and herbs.

No invective I could hurl at the creature had any effect. The horse merely blew out his lips and turns his black and mournful eyes on me in accusation. He was right—what was my hurry? My greatest grief still lay ahead.

It was decided: I would break it off with Adriane. I could no longer live with my heart like a peach, cleft and twisted from its stone. But still, I dreaded the scene. I wished it might be done already. I wished it might never be done. I wished I could think of the words to speak, my last ever to her.

I remembered my spurs then and gave the beast a swift kick to the sides. But the creature responded with such a mournful groan, I was instantly sorry for it. Seeing the spot of blood on the spur worsened my guilt still. I felt in the saddlebags for a bit of carrot to soothe the beast, and found instead a bag of brownish lumps. Though they looked rather unappetizing to me, the Barbary enthusiastically nipped one from my stiffened palm. So eager was the creature, I was moved to taste one of the lumps myself.

My tongue was instantly candied, so sweet my palate could not tolerate it for more than a moment before I spit it out. Wastrel prince, I thought, feeding imported sugar to his horse.

I imagined Adriane's reaction when I told her, then remembered I should have more serious matters to discuss with her when I saw her next. Already my not-yet-a-week apart from her seemed like a year.

I realized with some shame I could not recall the particulars of our last lovemaking. In the countless fevered nights I had spent clutched in her, the circumstances of that one night had been lost to me. Had she lowered herself upon me that night, or was I the one atop? Perhaps we had done it more than once? It troubled me that I could not remember; it was the sort of thing I thought one ought to keep in one's memories of a love affair.

Perhaps the thing to do, I thought, would be to make love to her one last time. She would likely throw herself upon me as soon as she saw me again, covering me with kisses. It would be cruel to turn her affections away. I might break it off afterwards—after I had dressed, of course. The sleeping household and the threat of discovery would keep her from making too much of a scene. She would weep—she was a woman, after all—but silently, I was sure of that. She was that sort of woman. Even her hysterics would be strictly calculated.

Once I had decided this, I felt the muscles in my lower back relax a bit. My hips settled into the steed's pace, which even seemed to pick up a bit. I would have one last night with her, to set apart from the rest in my memory. Once more would I collapse and shudder into her open lap. Or else breechward would I direct the travails of my tongue, making myself that most delicious and ridiculous thing: a man with the head of an ass.

I could not decide which to prefer. Perhaps we would have time to repeat the act—for always she could coax me into willingness again. But then we should be rushed, and I had hoped to take my time.

Another milepost gone.

Of course, I thought, it would likely take the prince several days to settle his affairs at the sanctuary, write to his father, and return to the City. It might be a week, even, before he sent for me. There was no reason I should not remain with Adriane all those nights, considering the time as but a single long night of farewell.

This seemed to me as unequivocally the best solution. When Hamlet returned and summoned me, then might I bid the baroness a bittersweet *adieu*. Yet, I should never need to trouble the already troubled prince with the truth of our affair—which was as good as ended, in my head.

The Rival Poet

My visit with the prince was food to my imagination, rain to the summer-parched earth, sending up shoots of new green everywhere. For several days I was kept busy writing all that had happened between us into new sonnets. I found these ruminations so pleasurable, I even penned another poem weighing the question of which was better—the pleasure of being with him, or of writing the works by which my pleasure would be shared with the world. I wished I could split myself into two people: one to be with Hamlet every moment, and the other to distill this precious time into words.

But no matter how a man gorges himself in one feast, it cannot satisfy him forever, and soon enough he will find himself hungering again to break his fast. As a week passed without word from him, then two, I soon felt pangs of anxiety and boredom creeping over me again, and my work suffered for it. I was starved for the sight of him, for some new inspiration, some metaphor I had not used before. Thus did I pine and surfeit, day by day, either gluttoning on all, or all away.

D idn't you already write one on that theme?" Adriane asked. *"The appetite of love, today allayed, tomorrow sharpened in its former might?* Something like that . . ."

I shrugged and reached for her pipe, inhaling the sweet hot-cold haze of her tobacco. Blowing smoke, I gestured to the east, where, through the tangled rose briars, showed patches of a hazy purple sky. "For as the sun is daily new and old, so is my love in telling what is told."

She did not seem duly convinced by this. Since I had returned, she had grown day by day more distant and impatient with me. I feared she was losing interest in my poetry.

I could hardly blame her—I was losing interest in it myself. Barren of any new interest or variation in the plot of my romance, I was left with endless repetitions of old arguments and themes. How could it be any other way, when my imagination was drawing on the same much-reviewed encounters? More and more I relied on Adriane's sweet weed, noted for its stimulation of all the appetites, to pique my inspiration.

"I heard Prince Hamlet has returned to the City," she said to me. "You have not spoken to him?"

I shrugged again. Ten nights running the lamps had been lit

at dusk in the prince's windows, and still no word from him. Ten fingernails had been, one by one, bitten down to blood.

She drew on the pipe and looked at me. "What if he has taken another lover?"

I folded my arms across my chest, staring up into the dark folds of her canopy. I wanted to ask her if she had heard something of this; I didn't want to know.

"So what if he has?" I answered defiantly. "It would not affect my esteem for him—I can see no rational reason he ever loved me in the first place."

"Come, now—" she challenged me. "You are saying it would not affect your love for him at all, to know he no longer loved you?"

I gave her the only logical answer. "It does not affect his worth at all, that he should find another worthier than I. I know I am not his equal—why should I count it among his flaws that a man of his intellect should also be aware of such an obvious fact?"

Still, her words stuck with me. At my desk the next day, I drew up a legal contract, swearing the fidelity of my heart, even if Hamlet should frown on me, or look upon me strange, or not at all. I would own the prince's judgment as my own, even if it turned me against myself.

I raised my hand to the oath and read it. Adriane acted as witness, of course. And judge. And, later, executioner, blindfolding and undressing me.

But when she had me read the poem to her over again, in her wide black eyes I detected a shade of sorrow. She had grown jealous of him at last, I thought, because my tongue like every tongue said: "This is Beauty." And, because of this, the world could not see her for beautiful.

The world, or me? Had she some womanly sense that I intended soon to leave her? I knew, despite all her protestations, that she was jealous of Hamlet. Was it only for his beauty? If I could only make her see how those dark eyes became her cheeks, pale gray in the early dawn—as well as the bright sun becomes the morning, the evening star the dusk. It seemed correct and fitting that Woman should be made so: opaque and inscrutable.

She turned to face me in the bed. "I only wonder," she mused, "if you would make the same promise for me. If I were to betray you, throw you over for another—would you still love me? Would you remember me in your poems?"

I looked at her beside me on the pillow, the shadows dramatic on her face. Jealousy surged through me as I realized her eyes were mournful not because she pitied her own state, but because she pitied me! She was the one who had taken another lover! And, though I had been planning to break it off with her for weeks, the thought of her leaving me was another matter altogether. Desperately, I took her roughly in my arms, desiring her again.

But birdsong interrupted us; the lark and not the nightingale.

"It will be light soon," she told me. "You will be seen by the guard."

Frustrated, I withdrew from her unsatisfied. "Bid me come again tonight," I begged her.

But she put me off with a shake of her head, blushing as though ashamed. "I cannot."

"Why not?" Worry led to suspicion to certainty: she had made a date with another lover.

She lowered her eyes. "My husband is returning from his business abroad. He has sent word that he will visit my bed tonight."

She was an excellent liar. No one who was not so close as to be practically inside her could have noticed her muscles clenching with tension, the quickening of her heartbeat.

But I was that close.

"It is his right," she said nervously. "He is my husband."

The lady protested too much, confirming my suspicions. I did not know who else my mistress loved, but I could narrow the field to every man in the world but the one she had named.

Still, I did not press the issue. I pretended to believe her. I am not sure why—was it so she would think me naive and gullible, perhaps letting slip more information inadvertently? Or perhaps it was a selfish blindness—as long as I turned my eye away, allowing myself to be deceived, I might continue to have her. After all, on the nights I spent with her, she would be no less mine, though I shared my prize with every greedy lover in the world.

"Does he come to your bed often, still? I hate to think of you having to endure relations with him," I said. Playing the role of the innocent, deceived—though we both knew I was too old to be so naive. Had I convinced her? Or was she acting as well, pretending to believe my feigned belief?

"On rare occasion," she said, stroking my hair as if I were truly that young, and could be soothed by such easy manipulations. "And a good thing, too, in case—" she paused, reluctant to continue, or else feigning reluctance.

Of course. A good thing, in case I should discover some sign of her infidelity—see the love-bites, smell the odor of another man on her. She might claim the baron had come for his bedright.

"In case I should become pregnant," she answered at last, watching for my reaction from the corner of her eye. "The cuckold would believe the child his."

All day I sat at my desk trying to write, preparing my daily recitation of the prince's virtues, like a monk repeating his paternoster. But I was bored, unable to concentrate on the task at hand for arguing circles with Adriane inside my head. Of course she had grown bored with me, as with my poetry. I was tortured with self-doubt. Should I keep writing about Hamlet, though he avoided me? Did I have anything left to say?

I flipped back through the book of sonnets. Page after page of musings about the passage of time, the ticking clock consuming life and youth repeated in new metaphors. Again and again, I vowed my love would live forever in my words—but where was he? Captured in a line here and there, in pieces; I had left behind a portrait not of him, but of myself.

At dinner at the high table in the college dining hall, one of my old professors tried to engage me in conversation. But, though I had once admired the man greatly, and would have attempted to make a decent showing of my wit, I now found myself growing impatient. To his questions about my current research, I replied vaguely that I was writing about ". . . aesthetics—the relationship between Beauty and Love," and he recommended a great many ancient texts on the same subject.

For some reason, this irritated me exceedingly. If, as the professor seemed to indicate, there was nothing new for me to say about the subject, then why should I bother with the labor of inventing it? Why, I wanted to ask him, should my brain have been so twisted and deceived, to put me through this agony of mental childbirth, if all my answers might be found in some antique book? I envied his naive belief in the wisdom of the library. I wished it were so simple—if I might only open some five-hundred-year-old manuscript and see the prince's image, find a character with his mind! Then might I find some guidance on how to proceed with my poetry. But Hamlet was greater and nobler and fairer than all those subjects immortalized by the great ancient poets. If only he might be served by a talent as rare as himself!

Weary with worrying, I went to bed, but even sleep gave me no respite. I was instead consumed with a complicated dream, in which I was aboard a ship, trying to save the prince from a series of increasingly improbable misadventures, including pirates. Finally I jerked awake and sat bolt upright in bed, certain beyond all certainty that Hamlet was in danger.

I forced my heavy eyelids open. Awake, but dreaming still, I saw his image hanging in the air: Hamlet's spirit, sent through the streets all this way to summon me, his will that had shaken me from sleep. I knew this was impossible, but still, I was certain of it in my heart of hearts: Hamlet needed me—nay, he was *expecting* me—tonight.

I rose in the dark and did up my clothes, then checked my watch by the sputtering torch in the hall. Just after twelve. Now was the hour when I customarily arrived to Adriane's balcony.

But tonight, I turned up the road, not down, negotiating the eerily deserted square by starlight. I crossed over to the fashionable side of the City, where tall stone townhouses faced one another like sleeping giants, all dark and locked up tight. There was no moon, and it was so dark I could not see my own body moving beneath me. I floated through the night, invisible, uncertain this was not a dream.

Hamlet's front gate stood unlocked; in fact, ajar, just wide enough to allow a man exactly my size to pass. It would have been an excessive gap for a thinner visitor, while one significantly stouter would have found it a bit of a squeeze. This I took as further sign that Hamlet was expecting me. It was his insomniac heart, still enclosed within my chest, that leaped and raced and would not let me rest.

In an entire world asleep, one window was a burning square of light, and it was Hamlet's. One shadow stood, framed there in silhouette, and it was his. He was looking out the window, watching for me—I was certain of it. I willed him to look down and see me waiting below.

But of course he could not, in his well-lit sitting-room, see anyone lurking in the yard below. It was, after all, so dark I could not see my own hand before me.

I did not wish to knock the household all awake. Guards gossiped, and from such reports were nasty rumors bred. Instead, I knelt on the grass in the tree-lined yard and felt the ground for something I might use to rattle the shutters. Seizing on a likely pebble, I drew my wrist back, and was just about to let this missive loose when—

"O, no!" I gasped, but soundlessly, for all my breath had gone. My fingers forgot the stone and it slipped to the ground.

A second shadow had joined the first in the window. Hamlet was awake, but not alone. It was not his desire but my own blind hope that had brought me here tonight. His thoughts were far from me; to another, they were all too near.

If my rival were a building, he would have been a steeple: tall, long-legged, lean. He was nearly of a height with the prince. Taller, if you counted his hat—a fashionable tricorner, turned up at the back and sides. Against the window, it cast a shadow in the shape of a ship, the ostrich plume adorning the pointed brim unfurling like a sail. He approached the prince with a proud, stiff-legged swagger.

I was suddenly in a terror of being seen, realizing what it

would look like if I were discovered spying at this hour. I pulled back from the patch of light cast by the window, into the weeping embrace of the willow tree at Hamlet's gate. Leaning against its trunk, I wiped my own hot tears away.

From this sheltering cabin, I played the watchman to the pair revealed above—ashamed, but unable to tear myself away. My mind had seized upon a reckless hope that this was not what it appeared to be.

The shadow-lover took the prince's hand, and their heads bowed together—kissing, or exchanging whispered intimacies, I could not tell which by the way their shadows merged on the shade. I did not know which of these circumstances would have been the silver lining, which the cloud. I did not wish to witness this. But I remained, still rooted to the spot.

"Master Horatio?"

I started, hearing my name spoken. The voice had come from quite nearby—perhaps a few steps to the other side of the willow trunk where I now crouched. I retrieved my breath and was about to call "Who's there?" when a second voice gave answer to the first.

"Can't be—too tall."

"His poems described him as an aged, unlettered clerk: friendless, lame, possessed of nothing." This tally was accompanied by a familiar sound, like calculations on an abacus: *clack-clack-clack*. I knew the noise an instant before I placed the voice: Rosencrantz. "Naturally I thought of—"

Guildenstern answered with a snort. "As I explained, that was a mere poetic convention: a metaphor, you see, designed to heighten the contrast between the imperfect lover and his ideal beloved."

"I suppose," Rosencrantz answered meekly, sounding unconvinced.

"Well think about it—if he were literally *unlettered* he could never have written the lines in the first place. Honestly, Rosy— you'd think any two-penny hack with a little Latin grammar could confect immortal verses, if only he were inspired by *true love*."

"Well, Horatio always carries around that great book of his, and he is always spying and making notes. And the prince seems to care particularly about what he thinks. Almost as if he were Hamlet's . . . Hamlet's . . ."

I held my breath. Did he know that we had embraced as lovers? My heartbeat pounded in my ears as I wondered how he would finish the sentence.

". . . aged father!" Rosencrantz decided at last.

I felt my face grow hot. Never had being likened to a king wounded a man more deeply.

"Pay attention, for heaven's sake, or else we shall have no report to give," said Guildenstern.

Rosencrantz gave a mournful whine. "And we've already spent nearly all the Lord Chamberlain's money."

I frowned. I would have to warn the prince that they were not to be trusted, these fanged friends, spying for hire. At least I spied for love.

Then I remembered—Hamlet had thrown me over for another. What was he to me, or I to him, that I should offer help? He would think I was trying to buy his favors back by playing politics.

I heard digestive rumbles in the dark. Then Rosencrantz: "Did you bring along anything to eat?"

Guildenstern sucked his teeth. "Shall I call the orange-girl 'round for a packet of roast chestnuts? Idiot—this isn't a box at the theatre!"

Above them, the careless exhibitionists were embracing openly before the window. Hamlet caressed his lover's cheek with his cupped hand and exchanged with him some words. The rest was a flurry of elbows parrying as clothing was swiftly undone.

At least, Hamlet's clothing was shucked; the anonymous rival took command in this, but did not move to unhook his own doublet. Nor did he doff his hat, its ridiculous feather billowing like a sail before his face. He led Hamlet to the window-seat, his back against the shade, and knelt before him. The ship upon his head set a swift course south, in search of Hamlet's buried treasures.

"So *that's* what a professional poet does for his patron," sniffed Guildenstern.

Another poet. Of course—the feather displayed on his hat was his quill, his tool of trade. I do not like ostrich, personally, even had I the means to afford such an ostentatious feather for my pen. It leaves behind a thicker stroke, forcing the hand to write much larger, less precisely—and besides, all that bedraggling nonsense to make a mess of the ink. The third or fourth flight feather of a gander is more my style: a true-plain pen for true-plain poetry.

"Hush!" answered Rosencrantz. "You know that is not what he has hired him for. He plans to commission the author to write his story, for the stage. *The Historie of Hamlet, King of Denmark.*"

I swallowed. I had heard a version of this tale before. The ocean is vast, I told myself. It supports many boats, both great and small alike. The prince's bounty was as boundless and his love as deep. Why could he not have more than one, to sing his praises each in different form?

"Do you suppose we shall have parts in it?" Rosencrantz continued with his star-struck babbling. "I wish a great poet would take an interest in me." He sighed. "Those sample poems he sent the prince were simply beautiful."

Faint hope remained. A modern poet might wish to promote some new contemporary style, or focus on his own ideas, merely amending the particulars of his phrases to reflect his subject. The prince might yet prove prouder of the classical odes I compiled, whose influence was nothing but himself.

"I can't say I much care for his sonnets, personally," Guildenstern confessed archly. "Their rhetoric, in my opinion, touches on the strained. He is likened to be the pinnacle of Beauty, Goodness, Truth—even *constancy*, if you can believe that one!"

I gasped. The situation was worse than I had feared. Those very qualities I had perceived in the prince, the other poet had also noted, and even chosen the same poetic form! Furthermore, his golden quill had made its argument already, leaving nothing for my pen to offer but echoes of the same.

Rosencrantz let out a soft giggle, which faded to a wistful sigh. "Yes, he spends all his art in the prince's praise, comparing his breath to the violet, his cheek the deep vermilion of the rose. His hands are lilies, his eyes the sun and stars . . ."

"An abuse of clichés," sniffed Guildenstern.

"But—it is so," I mouthed, dumbfounded. "It is true." Even as I thought it, I knew it was a witless defense—even Rosencrantz could argue as much, and indeed, he did:

"But Prince Hamlet truly *is* that fair."

"Exactly," Guildenstern drawled. "One should always save one's grossest flattery for when one is lying. What is it, to a beautiful youth, to be told he is young and beautiful? That is robbing him of that which he possesses, in order to pay it back to him again! Paint roses in the bloodless cheeks of ancient dowagers; such efforts are abused when they are wasted on an honest beauty."

"Ah—pearls before swine," said Rosencrantz, as though the adage recommended this. They were silent for a moment, watching the figures moving above.

"What about that magnificent clever actor the prince would flirt with all the time?" Rosencrantz suggested brightly. "Oh, dear me—what was his name again? Kid?"

"Kit," said Guildenstern. "Kid was his roommate. Can't be him—he's dead."

"Dead! Well, there's a pity," sighed Rosencrantz. "Such a good-looking young man."

"He was a shoemaker's son," sniffed Guildenstern.

This seemed to close the subject, at least for a short while. Then Rosencrantz started up again: "But it would have been just his style, would it not—to leave his true identity a mystery, and sign the poems with such a *nom de plume*?"

"*Nom de plume!*" Guildenstern mimicked. "Nay, you dignify too much the name he sent the poems under, to call it that. A cheap pun, more like—juvenile, obscene."

"But that sounds very like Master Kit, as I recall," Rosencrantz pointed out. "Remember, when he'd had too much to drink, and he would stand upon the table, waving about his—ahem—*part.*" I heard the rosary beads *click-clack* and could tell that he was blushing. "You know, the one *belonging to a man*. Perhaps it was a sign from him."

"Nonsense!" Guildenstern said sternly. "The name means nothing. It was merely a tactic to get the prince's attention. You know Hamlet's weakness: he can never resist a mystery."

I was forced to agree. An anonymous collection signed with a bawdy sobriquet—exactly the sort of coy detail to best intrigue the sonnets' recipient, who was curious as a cat, and just as impossible to deflect from whatever puzzle had captured his attention. If I had been a courtier in earnest, I might have thought of such a trick myself.

There was another long silence, while we watched the lovers' shadows—Hamlet lying back helplessly against the window, groaning while the poet's head bobbed in and out of view.

"What about bacon?" said Rosencrantz suddenly.

I groaned with Guildenstern. By now I was just as annoyed as he with his companion's constant talk of food. I feared my stomach should start rumbling at any moment, and wondered if such a noise might reasonably be passed off to each of them as having been produced by the other.

But they had moved on to discussion of another candidate. I did not catch his name, but as a viscount and a baron, he was determined pedigreed enough to love the prince.

"But such poetry is not his style," protested Guildenstern. "Acrostics in Latin, perhaps. But romantic odes? Precious phrases of poesy comparing to nosegays his lover's breath? He hasn't got it in him," he declared, snapping the subject shut like a tinderbox.

Rosencrantz sighed. "Well, who do you think he is, then?"

"Well," said Guildenstern, "if you must know, I'd set my wagers on—" He lowered the tone of his voice, and whispered, dramatically slow: "Evie."

"You cannot mean the Earl of—Oh, that old dandy! But it is true, he has fallen out of favor with the court."

" 'Tis the truth: *vere est*," Guildenstern swore it in the scholar's tongue: "Every word of it almost tells his name. And heaven knows he should be bored by now with moping over that Italian boy."

I did not run in such lofty social circles to know the players named, but still I got the message clear enough: these were the type of men who properly served princes. Lordlings famous for their learning; University wits; gentleman dilettantes known casually to all at the court by ridiculous pet-names. Common men could not be poets; nor could poor men; nor could I.

"Goodness!" Rosencrantz interrupted any further evidence for the candidate in question with a squeak. "Whoever he is, the gentleman's got on top!"

It was true: the poet now stood and took control, mounting the prince. Hamlet bucked up his hips, spreading his knees. Against my will, I watched my rival rise over my love, thrusting into him, pelvis against pelvis.

"What—without even any butter! Cheeky fellow!" Guildenstern exclaimed admiringly.

They moved in syncopated rhythm, legs tangled together at angles: a broken cross, intersected at its crux. *Crux.* I seized upon the word. Derived from *cruciare*, "torture." From this prolific root springs crucial and crucify, cruise and crusade, crooked, crook, crotch, crutch, crouch, crochet. I watched the history of language played upon the shade in an excruciating dumb show.

My rival rode his lover even to those nameless depths which I had never dared to penetrate. The point of his ship-shaped hat dipped fore and aft with the roll of his hips, as though cutting a cleft through choppy seas. Hamlet stiffened and groaned, clutching to the poet like a drowning man to flotsam.

I wanted to cry in pain, and I wanted to cry a warning, and also to cry out in anger at the prince's flagrancy. How dare he have such reckless disregard for his own reputation when I had written and worried and fretted and thought of nothing else. But I did not cry. I bit my tongue until I tasted hot blood, and I swallowed it.

Meanwhile, Rosencrantz and Guildenstern had begun a whispered catalogue of the prince's flaws. He was not young enough to behave as he did, they said; he was too young for all the thoughts that filled his troubled head. He was overly cruel. He was overly kind. He was rash, impetuous. He was lugubrious and slow to act.

"And the worst of his faults?" said Guildenstern: "He is too fond of hearing his own praise."

"Which only makes his praisers praise the worse," Rosencrantz sighed.

I stifled a bitter laugh. What compliment could any poet pay the prince, but that he was himself? There was no greater praise to be offered in any tongue. Rosencrantz and Guildenstern could disguise their jealousy with scorn, but we all knew the truth: we were all in love with Hamlet. And Hamlet, for his part, had but one fault, which turned all his sweet graces bitter: he loved us not.

Or if he loved a little, still he always would prefer another. My fury was irrational, disorderly, unjust. I scolded myself. Why should this injury enrage me so? The other poet had stolen nothing of mine. I had never been married to my Muse, and therefore could not claim I had been cuckolded. Still, my heart (the prince's heart, so he had sworn, so long ago) cried out for vengeance.

But I did not heed it. Instead, I turned away, bowing a silent farewell to the gentlemen, and to their lord as well. He was too dear for my possession, and like enough he knew his estimate. The greater poet could take his prize. I would be grateful to know Hamlet would live immortal, even in another's words. I should be glad for this, even if it were to be another poet's name and not my own, living alongside Hamlet's on the page, when I myself had long been buried and forgotten in a common grave.

Then I remembered: it would not even be the rival poet's actual name, but his bawdy *nom de plume*. This, more than anything, enraged me. My poetry was the only gift I had to offer a prince, my single chance to leave some tiny mark on history. But my rival must be a famous lord already, for whom such endeavors were no more than a lark. A hobby—the bastard child of his intellect, tossed off under an alias. Not something you would admit to, in company. A bit of an embarrassment, perhaps, his poetry—like his midnight habit of fucking boys!

I knew that I should walk away. Still, a self-destructive curiosity compelled me, tugging at my heart (his twitterpating heart). What might the poet's chosen name be? An obscene pun, Guildenstern had said—a sophomoric joke. Careful not to make a sound, I moved to stand just steps behind the gentlemen and whispered voicelessly into the dark, willing each of them to believe it was the other who spoke.

"What was the poet's name, again?"

Even as I spoke the words, I knew it was a grave mistake, the one question I should never have asked. Not because of the risk they might discover me (by the time their argument over which of the two had spoken finally turned its suspicions upon a third party, I would be long gone). It was not even the moral burden of complicity it implied with their treachery. No—it was a much more selfish and insidious regret that seized me as soon as the question escaped my mouth.

For, once I knew my rival's name, it would belong to me intimately. I would never forget it, no matter how I tried. It would muzzle my Muse; I would take up my quill to write and sit for hours scrawling it into my margins, trying to puzzle out how it was spelled. I would choke on my supper in the dining hall, thinking I had heard somebody speaking the name aloud. If I passed a man wearing a feathered cap, I would check his fingers for ink, immediately suspicious of anyone eloquent and tall.

I understood this in an instant, and as the two men turned to answer each other in astonished unison, already I was wishing it were possible for a man to stop his ears as he shuts his eyes, so as never to hear the name of my now forever-rival poet: "Master Will Shake-spear."

The Rival Poet (Encore)

I am, as I have told you, long-accustomed to dressing as a boy. As I have grown older, my face has cooperated with this deception, growing more masculine in its features. My skin has slackened at my jaw into a suggestion of jowls. My voice, too, has lowered from a boyish alto to a not-quite baritone, like an apprentice's on the verge of breaking. So my male self has grown older, as well—more slowly, as befits the occasional use I make of him. He has perhaps aged five years to my twenty. And so, through him, I can experience my own lives passed—the brash optimism of seventeen, the recklessness of twenty-one. I can still pass for a youth, by candlelight.

He has proved useful, allowing me to slip into places no woman would be allowed, and few gentlemen of any name. No one ever notices an extra page on the scene, swelling the ranks of anonymous servants. My dark tunic and breeches are the color of no one's livery; and so, I am always assumed to belong to someone else. It is as good as truth, the old stagehand's saw: anything painted black is invisible.

But tonight I cannot remain in the shadows. I must negotiate. And so I exchange my servant's cap for the three-corner hat worn by minor gentlemen. Its wide felt brim, turned up at the back, comes to a point over the brow, to shade my face from scrutiny. And rising from the crown—to distract the eye away from any inconsistencies in my disguise—I pin the brilliant white furl of a curling ostrich plume.

You are William Shakespeare?" are his first words to me. "You?"

"No," I answer the prince. "You are."

He frowns. Even his frown is beautiful. "I was told Shakespeare would be here tonight."

"So he is. All the immortal part of you is in his words, so you should change that name with him, and give him yours."

For a riddler, he is impatient with those who turn the riddling back on him. "You are a saucy lackey."

I laugh, knowing where he stole the phrase. Or do I? Perhaps the playwright had borrowed it from him to fill Rosalind's lips; or the actor, forgetting his lines, spoke extempore, and the copyists, hunched down furtively scribbling for the cheap overnight quartos, wrote it into the official record. We do not know anything for certain in this world. "I cannot help myself," I say, "for I speak for my master."

"Your master?" Hamlet takes interest in this. "Then you are Shakespeare's page?"

"I might be called so, for I bear his text."

"He has sent more poems, then?" Hamlet searches my hands for the papers. "Well, where are they?"

"In me. I have conned the lines from him," I say, knowing he will take it to mean "memorized," not "tricked," though both of these are true.

How careful Horatio was, when he left his dormitory room, to secure every dear possession he owned in the padlocked trunk beneath his bed. There he had placed his books, his winter woolens—even the china basin and chipped water-jug. Trifles to a man of any worth, but all his treasures still.

But my only desire, his most priceless possession, he could not lock up in his chest. It lay upon the desk untended—open to a poem that had been left there, most likely, with the ink still wet.

Horatio would be furious to know I had circulated even those few sonnets I had released to fan his reputation. He thinks of these still as unfinished drafts. But writers always see their lines as unfinished: each work is perpetually one more revision away from perfection, every book always halfway through. He is ashamed, and does not want the prince to see the seams and rough edges. He will present only his best and most rational face to Hamlet; but he shows every facet to me.

He trusts me to see his imperfections because he feels superior to me. I am a woman, and therefore to be pitied. A woman and worse, unbeautiful.

But a woman, no matter how beautiful, understands: everything in life has rough edges, hidden flaws. A woman knows which jeweled brooch hides the hole in the threadbare bodice, and how its casually crooked slant is in fact calculated with geometric precision to direct the eye to the less pockmarked side of her face.

"I am his reader," I tell the prince. He is my poet's hero—my object, and my rival as well. I stand a little prouder, though this must reveal more of my face. "His music. I give voice to his poems."

He makes it sound like a mystical transaction, some special power I hold over him. But this is not so. I want, that is all. I want what everyone has to give. So he gives me everything, and feels like he is taking something from me for it.

Hamlet is laughing at this. "You, his reader? But you are only a boy."

"I am not a boy!" I insist, adopting the belligerent whine of an adolescent in protest—but, in fact, I speak nothing but truth. "I am older than I look."

"You must be," he says. That famous profile: sharp as a blade to the lips, then melting into sensuality. "One would think your mother's milk was scarce pissed out of you."

"I have heard the same rumored of you, Prince of Denmark—though not on account of your youth."

He raises his eyebrow as if he were scandalized, but he is not scandalized. He is nearly preening. This is what it means, to be immortal. It is to be forever subject of spectators, and speculation. It is to be everything anyone can imagine of you, now and forevermore.

"Why choose a youth of breaking voice to read his poems? I would sooner the town crier spoke the lines!"

"Why address them to a man of breaking mind?" I retort haughtily.

His jaw falls wide. "How dare you speak so to me? Do you not know who I am?"

"I know everything about you." I answer him. "And I have everything

yet to discover. It is prophesied by some that you will be the fall of your fa-
ther's house."

"Is this what your Shakespeare writes?"

I shake my head. "He cannot see himself what he is writing. But the
reader sees a narrator made progressively more unreliable by love. The
wanton female boy he praises as fair, kind, and true is proven by his own
report to be, in fact, unfair, unkind, and false—no matter how belied by
false comparisons."

The prince's expression darkens. "Tell me who this 'Shakespeare' is, and
what knowledge he has of me—for I would have him hanged for treason!"

"No!" I cry out, womanish for an instant in spite of my intentions. I
calm myself. "That is only one interpretation. Of course, it all depends on
how you read the poet's lines."

Now he is scandalized. The words impede him like a slap. "Why do you
tell me this?" he demands. "What is Shakespeare to you, or you to he, that
you should speak so freely—nay, impertinently—of your master?"

I lower my eyes. I choose my words carefully. "My father had a daugh-
ter loved him more than he loves you, and never had his heart, for it was
yours."

He is moved by my unexpectedly tender confession. "Your sister has my
sympathies," he says. "She is the poet's mistress?"

"Aye, my lord."

"And you think he should be writing poems to her rather than me? You
would have me give up my biography to verses instead about crying babes,
housewives chasing chickens in the yard? That is not an occupation worthy
of his talent."

I bristle, though I must not reveal myself yet. "Is there nothing in a woman's life worth writing?"

He shrugs. "Perhaps, if she be fair. Is this mistress fair?"

"No, my lord," I must admit.

He laughs low, like music playing far away. "A callous youth, to speak so of your own sister."

"Perhaps, my lord, but true. Truth is a rarer quality than beauty."

He considers this. "Her hair is black, like yours?"

"Just like, my lord."

"And her eyes," he says. "I expect they are black, as well—like yours."

"Just like."

"So what would he write?" he laughs. "My mistress' eyes are nothing like the sun?" His humor dissipates as he hears the words, somehow familiar. He curls his knuckles to his teeth as though summoning a memory, something caught on the tip of his tongue.

"An honest poem about an honest love would be more rare than another anonymous ode to another anonymous beauty."

In plays, great beauties are seduced by those who treat them cruelly, in comedies and tragedies alike. Still it flusters me to see the spark of interest my abuse has produced in his eyes.

"So what if you were to take his place, and write my imperfections?"

"I am a reader," I demur, "not a writer."

"What do you read?"

"Anything," I boast. "Poems. Palms. The future." Every input of my senses I reduce to the fact of his beauty, repeating it to myself until it becomes nothing but words, so much meaningless noise. These words I carry are all

that will remain of this boy in forty years' time, in four hundred. How could I be seduced by words?

How could I be seduced by anything else, but words?

"So read me," Hamlet says. He offers his hand, open, to mine. "Read my palm, and tell me what you see." He puts his hand in mine. Fingers like pods of vanilla, like ripe string beans. I draw in sharp breath at his touch.

"What is it?" He is earnest, looking down into his open palm. "Tell me—I must know the truth, however terrible."

"You should quell that habit, Prince of Denmark," I advise. "It will get you into trouble someday."

"But will I die?"

"Everything dies," I tell him. "It is not a fate particular to heroes, nor to you." I bend over his palm. Traversed with faint pink scars from his childhood pyrotechnical experiments, it is impossible to decipher: the head-, heart-, life-lines all commingled, cracked and split and sent off into different directions, his palm as partile as a spiderweb. It is stunningly beautiful: a lotus-flower made of pain. But a hand can reveal more than the lines on it.

"You have an especially fleshy Mound of Venus," I tell him, caressing the swell with my thumb. "You should practice your fencing more."

He pales, and I feel his fingers grow cold in mine. "Why?" he demands. "Does it indicate I am like to die in a duel?"

"It indicates you have soft hands, young prince!" He will belong, body and soul, to the one who sees his fate, presents to him his quest—that much is clear. "Most like, you will die fat and scant of breath."

He is the coal, I tell myself. To hold him is to embrace suffering. I release his arm, remove myself from his vicinity. I put on my best bravado. I swagger a little, as I must in my elevated shoes.

"But you are not the one to whom the sonnets are addressed. I see my poet was the more deceived. For he has sworn blank verse you were a hero of heroes, a miracle of talents: the courtier's eye, the scholar's tongue, the soldier's sword. But I see you have the hands of none of these."

True, his hands are lily-white, and tender as the devil's playground, but to my surprise, I am the one whose breathing comes up short. He had seen where my eyes dropped when I mentioned "soldier's sword." There, they had lost my tongue; for my speech stuttered, stopping and starting again distractedly.

His body eases: here, he is on familiar territory. His walk is unhurried, closing the distance between us. When we are nearly touching, he says: "Now show me your hands." *A command, unmistakable, though he whispers it.*

I drop my head and will not look at him. If he sees my face this close, I cannot hope to maintain my disguise. I worry about my wrinkled, freckled hands, which will never be compared to lilies—do they betray my age?

But if these, for a gentle lady's hands, are neither smooth nor fair, they are for a servant-boy's both fair and smooth.

"You play?" *He has noticed the calluses on the tips of my fretting fingers.*

I nod, afraid even by my breathing I might give myself away.

"What?"

"Viola."

"Da gamba?"

"*Di fagotto.*"

He gives me a sharp, questioning look, as if I might have accused him of something, but I swear, I only named the basson viol.

"It vibrates through the body as it sings, playing the arm who plays it, happy to hum and buzz the harmonies." I wrest my wrist out of his grip. "But I am not what I play."

"I see," he taunts. "You play at manhood, but you are yet a boy."

"I play at manhood," I confess. "But I am not a boy."

He laughs. "Why, even your precocious height, I now see, is but the altitude of your raised shoes."

It is true, I had worn my ingenious Italian gutter-stilts, which (designed to protect the rich gowns of Venetian courtesans from the common filth of the canals) raised my feet near to a full foot off the ground. I had wanted to be able to look him in the eye.

Yet I do not look him in the eye. He is like the sun. I cannot look at him directly. For reasons I cannot understand, I am shy. Instead, I look down at my feet, where his gaze and mine meet at an angle.

"Do you admire my chopines?" I ask, turning my foot this way and that. The pointed toes are tipped with fat white roses of twisted silk, which attract the eye across the length of white silk hose. "Not an hour after I first wore them, I was stopped by a cry of traveling players and offered half a share in the company. Everyone wants boy-actors these days, so long as they be well-shaped and tall."

Men's minds are made of water, and flow primarily downhill. I follow his gaze in its travels up my leg. A curious fact, but true: everyone, male or female, desires a boy with a woman's luxurious calves. And so I take my advantages where I can, and wear my hose gartered above the knee. Fashions have assisted me as well. My onion-shaped Venetian breeches disguise my female hips and thighs, creating the illusion of illusion, as they suggest that I am not, in fact, increasingly shaped so myself. For a moment, I am caught up in the deception, imagining the leg I turn to him is, in truth, the leg of a voluptuous, well-turned youth. I am fed by his wanting; I want him to desire me, the way everyone in the world desires him.

His eyes come to rest on the codpiece of my breeches, but the flood of heat this attention calls into my sex does not produce the expected evidence. "You are yet an unripe peasecod!" he teases, reaching out his hand to brush my hair from my face.

But before he can caress my cheek, I turn my head quick to catch his thumb between my teeth and suck on it, hard. I run my tongue into his fingerprints, advertising my talents until his thumb shudders and jerks in my mouth and I see his cock straining the cloth of his codpiece in jealousy.

I reach around the back, under his doublet, to undo the cloth. It is tied with a neat double-knotted bow, and I silently thank Horatio for his thorough intelligence about the prince's habits as it comes undone with a single tug. The codpiece comes away, and there it is: slender and delicate in color as an orchid, long and purple, trembling in the breeze.

A glittering drop of royal jelly—prince-seed, worth its weight in diamonds—dances at its tip, anticipating the same succulent mouth. I fret it with my callused finger, kneeling down to tease the length of his sex with the tickle of the feather from my hat.

"I cannot," he protests weakly. "You are just a boy!" But the hand hooked expertly around the back of my head belies his words. Parting his legs, he lies back against the window frame, resting a hand behind him, at the nape of his neck; and the other behind me, at the nape of mine, urging me on. "Why—you haven't even a beard!"

"I have." I stand and unbuckle my belt. I take down my onion-breeches, and show him my beard. It is not a boy's at all. I raise one knee to mount him, and a mouth opens between my legs, as large and wet as something newly born.

He goes red with surprise, then white. His erection falters, then stands again while his eye rolls from my face to the face between my forked legs.

I bend over him, lowering myself onto the indecisive little point of his pleasure. One leg of mine thrown around his waist, one of his raised in the air. We rock back and forth together at odds until a rhythm is at last negotiated between our sweaty bodies. Then I reach my hand down into the soft udder of his testicles, milking the swollen ridge between them.

"Who are you?" he pants, desperately, as though his pleasure might only be found on the precipice of a mystery.

"Your future," I answer.

His flesh grows too too solid, and then, shuddering, it melts, like suet thrown in a hot pan. Moaning, he presents me with the treasure of his beauty bared, clinging to me as if it hurt to give it.

Then I understand: I had planned it this way all along. To come to him. To take the poet's place. It was no longer enough, to love him through a go-between. I came here tonight not to see him, but to be seen.

Many a Glorious Morning

Insomnia had softened for me the distinction between dreams and waking life. Sometimes, dozing over a half-finished poem in the afternoon, I would think I heard Hamlet's voice and hurry to the door, heart hanging by a thread, to find myself welcoming empty air. And full many a summer morning, as the rising sun sent fingers early through my window grate, I imagined the warmth beside me in the bedclothes to be his, only to wake alone and twice as miserable, the butt of my own joke.

So when a late September breeze came through my window one early morning, rustling the rushes strewn for carpet on the floor, I took this for the sound of a scholar's cap and fresh-starched robe being cast off, and his stockinged feet shucked from their boots.

Humid with dew and carrying the scent of violets, the warm breeze breathed gently upon my face. I kept my eyes shut tight, imagining it was his breath, knowing it a deception, yet wanting still to hold fast to the dream.

But dreams are like water: the tighter you try to grasp at them, the faster they seep away through our fingers, losing the illusions they had once reflected. I fought to stay asleep, knitting my lashes shut, but my eyes refused to remain closed against the morning light.

They opened into Hamlet's eyes. I blinked, but the dream refused to disperse.

He grinned at me. His eyes were blue as robins' eggs, and bright as Robin Goodfellow's. I did not have to look outside to know the sky was clear today: cloudless and infinite.

He was wearing a sky-colored satin doublet, above which his bare head floated like a tousled golden sun. It was a new suit, not one I would have dreamed him in. Still, I reached, disbelieving, to rub the salt from my eyes.

He intercepted my hand, intertwining it with his own. It was almost too much, to touch him, to know for certain he was real.

"Ink on your fingers. You have been writing. But why have you not written me?"

"I have written you, my lord," I answered. "I have written you every day." My laugh was rough with sleep, and this made me sound as if I had been weeping. Clearing my throat, I said, "I never promised to send my letters."

"But why did you not?" He visited kisses on each of my stained fingertips in turn. "You know I would have paid the postage due."

I felt the apples of my cheeks ripen. "It was not for want of the money, my lord." I was grateful Adriane's ring was on the other hand. Under the woolen blanket, my thumb fondled circles around the sinister jewelry; while on the other side the prince undertook a similar test of my dexterity.

I pulled my hand away. "I would have sent the verses, my lord—but other poets have since proved better suited to the style."

A smirk distorted his face—a theatrical expression, too large for so intimate a stage. "So I'll read better poets for their style," he scoffed. But the sting of this insult had scarcely landed before it was followed by a soothing balm: "Yours I would have for love."

He looked around the room. "So where are they—these promised tables of my qualities?"

I could not lie to him. But how could I confess that I had been bold enough to give his verses to another? "Within my brain," I answered at last. "And perfect there, though all I have on parchment are rough scribblings."

"Well, tell me them aloud, then," he persisted. "Just a line or two."

My mind was empty. I struggled to remember the best of my comparisons. "I chide the violets, for stealing your breath. The lily has stolen the color of your hands; the rose, your cheek."

"The red, or white?" the prince asked, coyly. But I was too fond of him to answer in kind.

"Both—one for your blush, and the other when you grow pale. And I could not walk through the kitchen gardens without the darling buds of marjoram so tightly curled making me think on your hair."

Hamlet ran his fingers over his tousled bare head. "It is not so curly as that!"

I lowered my eyes, flashing a bashful underbite. "Not there."

Whatever further might have passed between us, Hamlet murdered with a kiss. And at that same moment, the most precocious ray of early morning sunlight slipped through the grate, flattering every color. I was held suspended in perfect joy between these two events, not knowing which had suddenly filled my room with the promise of a glorious day.

My mattress was too narrow for us two to lie abreast, so Hamlet straddled me, his hair catching the sunlight behind in a bright corona of gold.

Like the sun traversing mountain-tops, his humid kisses moved down the slope of my brow. My night-shirt soon was scarfed about my neck, a cloud of cotton, as his celestial face strayed lower, sending golden fingers scouting down into the valley-lands.

In my fantasies, I had played my rival Shake-spear's role with the prince, mounting him, to penetrate him deeply, from above. But I never had the chance, nor agency, to take control and play the bugger's part. It took naught but the shallowest assistance from the prince to hold me floating, weightless. His mouth closed hot around me and he guided with his hands as the landscape of my body began to tremor and quake. At last, the earth cracked open, loosing its geysers in pale streams that spread across my belly, all shimmering in the light as though the prince's touch had learned the alchemy of Midas.

Hamlet smiled heavenly magic down upon me, and I felt my pleasure a second time, gilded by the prince's pleasure in me. But he was already setting his feet to the floor, bowing to grasp his cast-off mantle.

"I must away."

"So soon? But you've been here . . ." I felt for my watch on the table beside the bed. "An hour. Not even an hour. Fifty minutes."

He chuckled at this. "Horatio—when you do not have the time to the minute exact, then shall time itself be fallen out of joint and doomsday nigh."

I did not know quite what to make of this odd compliment. "Your lordship flatters me."

"Do not think it." He revealed a dimple deep enough to lose an eye in. "Why should I waste my flattery on the poor? Nay, I should candy up my tongue and crook my knee to lick where some reward may follow from my fawning."

Fawning indeed. Not five minutes before, he had grazed my body like a hungry young deer, his mouth all velvet. I knew what he meant to say was that his feelings for me were unmotivated by desire for profit or advancement. But, like everything that rolled casually from the prince's tongue, it could be split infinitely into multiple meanings, many of them cruel.

I could not help but think my over-quick performance had disappointed him. Even now he was leaving to find another lover. His other poet, most like, would be the next to ride his face, masking him from the world with over-painted flattery. Or else those base contagions, Rosencrantz and Guildenstern, spreading malicious gossip like a sickness.

"What is your haste?" I asked bitterly, though I knew the question and the bitterness were both beyond my rights. "You are expected your friends?"

The mattress dipped down as he sat next to me, tugging on his boots. He rolled his eyes around the little room, and through his eyes, I saw how bleak and anonymous it was, how temporary. Though I had inhabited it for years, I had never fully occupied it.

"Hullo!" Hamlet pulled a straw out from his hose. "Horatio, I've never known a less comfortable bed. You must allow me to send you my own second-best. The mattress is stuffed with eiderdown. Three hundred and fifty geese!"

It was a very generous offer, but still that "second-best" stuck in my craw. I knew I would never rest in the bed, no matter with how many geese, for wondering which of my rivals was resting that evening in the best.

I pulled my night-shirt down over my belly, suddenly ashamed that he should see my nakedness. "I would not have you pay more than my work was worth, to purchase something else."

He turned his hands up, crying in frustration, "On my life I swear you are the most exacting judge ever I coped withal."

Courtiers used "cope" (from *coepit*, taken) to mean "met." But among the greasy apple-boys who prowled the docks, uniting easy women with hard men, it was used as quick slang for "copulate." Hamlet's diction slipped from high to low even swifter than his tongue could turn the words.

"I meant in conversation," he protested, catching my face.

Another innocent remark; another pun on copulation.

"And what of the—others?" I could not bring myself to speak the poet's name, even to acknowledge his individual existence. I turned my jealous fury instead upon every base, anonymous wrack the prince had ever permitted to ride his celestial face. "How many poets has such *conversation* coped withal? For whose advancement have you crooked your knee, candied your tongue?"

A deaf priest could have taken the prince's confession, writ so plain across his guilty face.

"How many?" he cried. "How much? More, Less, Most, Best! I am sick to death of numbers. Love cannot be weighed and measured like wheat. When I am with someone, I love him totally, as much as I can love or imagine loving anyone. Then, when I find myself directed to love another, I love her, and just as truly and completely."

"O, my dear lord," I breathed.

He sighed so plaintively I felt my own throat tightening in sympathy. "Do I offend you so, with these buffets of fate, these sins of my corpse? It is true—I act without thinking; or else I think until I cannot act at all. I may argue a decision for hours, examine it from all sides—and still, in the end, I am ruled by instinct and base impulses. Afterwards, I am ashamed."

"A man's shame does not cancel the effect of his actions," I said. "He may be sorry, but still the damage has been done, and the disgrace remains."

"Alas, it is my curse," said Hamlet, "to be the flute of Fortune. One day she wakes me with a merry jig and I must dance and make jest, though I be presented with the gravest of matters. Then I am overcome with such melancholy, it is as if all my mirth had been mislaid somewhere, and I might never find it again. How I wish I were a man such as you—never his passion's slave!"

"Oh, my dear lord"—my voice caught in the break between laughter and tears. If he only knew how I had been enslaved! How I was still enslaved. I felt the burden of my guilt redoubled.

"I cannot help my fate," he said. "But you must be the witness to my conscience. Your book keeps the tables of my soul. Good or ill, your words are my eternity. And if you should hate me . . ." With this, his eyes welled sweet large tears. "Hate me now," he pleaded. "Do not leave me last, when all my other friends have already abandoned me." The tears hovered on his eyelashes, pearlescent in the morning light; and each of them as precious to me as if they had been pearls in earnest. "Do it now, so I may have the worst blow first, and all my other losses may seem mild, in comparison."

I touched his cheek, turning wet tears to faint gray ink. It seemed a miracle on the order of water into wine. What more proof could I wish of the depth of his esteem? This simple, spontaneous outburst of emotion convinced me where any rational argument would have failed.

"No more," I begged him. Like a father who suffers his child's injuries more deeply than his own, I could not bear to see my love in pain. "Please, my lord, no more be grieved by"—I could not even bring myself to name the transgression—"by that which you have done. It is but a fleeting, sensual fault, no more. You must not grieve."

Instantly, my request was obeyed. The sun shone again in Hamlet's face, the rain dried on his cheeks, and roses returned to bloom in his complexion. With cheerful abandon, he threw his arms around my neck.

"I knew you would forgive, Horatio! You always suffer nothing, though you suffer everything, accepting the blows and blessings of Fortune with equal thanks." He laughed. "Would that my own blood were so well watered with good judgment."

And I was wracked by a terrible schism, like the same aged father, watching his child's reckless deeds of youth with delight and fear commingled. Surely, I thought, it would be no breach of love to wish him just a *little* hurt—if only to teach him more caution for the next time.

The prince lowered himself to peck my cheek, a kiss more sound than substance. He did not even meet my eyes as he made vague promises to send word soon, his mind already wandering ahead, to the next affair.

He was like a child, I realized, completely natural. Flirtatious one moment, petulant the next. Sometimes shockingly wise; sometimes shockingly cruel. Innocent.

Then he was gone, like a candle—out!—more quickly than your eye can leap across the gap left on the page. A Lack of Hamlet came at once to fill the space that he had occupied, rushing in like darkness, modifying everything. My room was emptier at that moment than it had ever been.

I stood upon my desk and peeked through the window, hoping to catch some last glimpse of his progress in the street, but he was gone. I looked up to the sky to see the sun, but there was no sun there to see. An ugly rack of clouds had smothered up its beauty from the world, and what light seeped through now cast everything in shades of gray. I sat back at my desk, holding my head in my hands as though the heavens themselves had betrayed me.

What I needed, desperately, was rest; but I was not so optimistic as to entertain any hopes of sleeping now. So I took out my notebook and pen and wrote an account, as faithful as my memory allowed, of the sweet, scant hour he was mine alone.

But I found I was unable to recall the scene with the same innocent pleasure I had first experienced in it. Hamlet's quick departure cast a shadow over the whole, turning his words of affection into hollow flatteries, his golden touch to gilt. Parsing the prince's sentences, I found nowhere in all his proclamations of remorse any promise to reform. Doubtless he had already gone, to kneel likewise before his precious Shake-spear, or some even baser rogue. And I for pity had even excused him from any guilt he might suffer on my behalf.

Rage burnt in my chest like a foreign object, separate from myself. But I could not direct this anger toward Hamlet without remembering the tears he had shed for my love. A pair of those rare pearls might buy a barrelful of my own common, saltwater variety. They had ransomed all his ill deeds away.

I turned the page in my notebook and started another poem. "Roses have thorns, and silver fountains mud," I wrote. The sun might be masked temporarily by clouds, even eclipse—but those did not change its essential nature. It might still stain the skin with its burn. "And loathsome canker lives in sweetest bud."

A voice came in my ear: "Look—you cannot even describe his flaws without comparing him to something beautiful." It was Adriane's voice, so clear I had to turn my head to prove to myself I was still alone in the room.

Shaking my head in disbelief, I returned to the poem. "All men make faults," I wrote.

"And yours is this," she laughed. "This argument, excusing his erratic behavior with rational excuse, making sense of his so-called *sensual fault*."

I leapt up in a rage. This could not be my imagination. She

must have followed me! She had been hiding somewhere, watching the entire time, voyeur to my most intimate engagements.

Furious, I searched my room—which, I discovered to my surprise, was much larger than I had ever previously known, and filled with countless nooks and closets where a spy might lurk, unseen.

"Where are you?" I shouted. My question echoed back at me from the empty walls, a frightened, foolish cry.

Still she taunted me, and her voice seemed to come from every direction at once: "You feed his fatal pride, and so make yourself accessory to the thief who will steal him away."

Then I realized: the voice speaking was my own. She had squirmed under my skin and into me and become me. She had taken possession of my body, and now she had my mind as well.

I jerked awake. I was slumped over my writing-desk, my cheek on the open book. I looked around, still disoriented, while the room reconciled itself into its familiar dimensions and shapes. Then I realized what I had been muttering under my breath. It was my own argument, taunting me from the page—the other half of the same poem. This battle was a civil war, between my love and hate.

The dismal light might have served for any dreary time of day. I had no idea how long I had been sleeping. I reached for my watch, but in the excitement of Hamlet's unexpected visit, I had forgotten to wind it, and it had stopped.

Then it occurred to me that I had no idea how long I had been dreaming, either. Was it possible I had imagined the entire thing? The morning had had the surreal beauty of my most vivid fantasies, coupled with a nightmarish intensity.

I hesitated, licking my cracked lips before picking up my book. With some trepidation, I flipped back a page, to the notes I had written—or thought I had written—after the prince had gone. There I found, in my own broken-hearted hand, the proof of our hour together.

I was a bit taken aback by the sharpness of my relief. In the first shock of his departure, I would have preferred the prince had never visited at all, than to abandon me so rudely, and so soon. But I was wiser now, and knew even a bittersweet and brief reunion was better than none at all. Brushing my fingers over my own lament, inkstain to ink, I read:

Alack, he was but one hour mine!

But, for that hour, I thought, he was mine.

I had to see Adriane. I did not even think to satisfy my lust, but only that my priapic tongue might spill its news. Only she could hear my confession, and until I had confessed, I would remain in a torture of indecision. My heart (the prince's frustratingly impulsive heart) beat in elevens. At times like this I nearly regretted making the exchange.

But the same heart that wavered in indecision and knew no logic but the absurd was exceedingly clever at concocting complicated plans and schemes. If Adriane's husband were at home, I decided, I would say I had brought more song lyrics—ballads she had commissioned. That was good—it sounded like the sort of thing the baron might have once approved, and since forgotten.

I would act as if this had been planned ages ago. "But they must be set to music," I would say. "I cannot hope to finish them in time, otherwise." Surely Adriane would play along.

Even if the baron were suspicious, even if he would not let us a moment out of his sight, we might, I thought, have a means of communication. I would write out what had happened in the guise of the verses. She might offer her interpretations and advice by penning in the chords, or in those Italian directions—*forte*, *glissando*—which indicated the emotion of a piece. Without a word between us, without even our eyes meeting in a glance that might damn by revealing too much—we could conduct our affair, right under his illiterate eyes.

I cut a brisk pace through the near-deserted streets, navigating my surroundings without noting them. So total was my concentration, I did not notice until I was at the City gates how dark the sky had grown.

My skin was tense from every follicle standing at arms, like a regiment at fencing practice. Consciously unclenching my jaw, I was surprised to find my teeth chattering. I realized, almost as an afterthought, that I was freezing.

Black storm clouds hung low, heavy, and irregularly mottled, like fat buttocks, all flatulent with thunder. Then the sky began to piss down rain. One stinging drop slapped at my face, then another.

Some empiricist I! I had trusted the prince's clear blue eyes at dawn to forecast a fair day, and though I knew the quality of the light had dulled, still I had not thought to bring my cloak. At least my satchel, kept well-waxed, held watertight. Raindrops beaded and ran down its seams to squelch into my shoe with every step. At first, the asymmetrical *fwap* of one heavy damp woolen stocking-toe annoyed me; but then I stepped into a wheel-rut-*cum*-mud-puddle, and my other foot took on its share of cold wet misery.

So proud had I been to show off the prince's cast-off undershirt, I had left my doublet unsleeved near to October. But the fine silk was not so thick as the coarse-spun hempen weave it had replaced. Wet, it plastered a transparent second skin upon my skin, offering little protection to either body-heat or body-modesty.

The closer I got to Adriane's—imagining there a blazing fire, sweetened hot wine to drink, and her more delicious sympathy—the more I began to anticipate her point of view, and the clearer it became that all my distress was Hamlet's fault. Hamlet had promised a summery day, and made me travel forth without my cloak. Hamlet had allowed dark clouds to overtake me. Even the anonymous coach-for-hire that splattered me with mud as it passed in a swift trot for the City, I fancied to contain the prince, traveling on some covert affair, the curtains pulled to hide his face from the world. I added the rude-looking stain on my breeches to my already groaning list of resentments.

But as Adriane's house came into view, I forgot all these concerns, worrying instead about how I would be received. I did not think I could bear to be turned away, to walk the cold, wet distance back to my own cheerless, lonely room.

Come in, come in! I expected you sooner." The baron elbowed past the downstairs maid, greeting me without a hint of surprise. He shook his head, clucking. "Red skies this morning, you know—but I expect you didn't learn that in your philosophies."

"Expected me sooner?" For a moment I wondered if there *had* been an appointment. Meanwhile the housemaid attended to my dripping clothes with a brusqueness that suggested her concern was less for my health than the condition of her floors.

"I should say!" the baron laughed. "Why, your colleague has already come and gone!"

"Ah, yes," I nodded, automatically feigning recognition. "My . . . colleague, did you say?"

"The other writer?" The baron stood with me before the fire. "You missed him by a minute. You two will be working together on the project, I assume?"

"Other writer?" I repeated stupidly. The feeling had just returned in a rush to my fingers and toes and I could not think on my feet.

So it was true: the suspicion I had dismissed as just another dark moment, my jealousy fueling mad delusions. I had imagined it vividly, but never honestly believed it. It was true. She had another lover. A sob rose unexpectedly in my throat. I stifled it, but at the price of my placid expression.

"Master Horatio?" the baron muttered. His broad face wobbled for a moment, with the suspended intelligence of one who has just begun to be aware that he has committed a *faux pas*. "Oh, dear. A professional competitor?"

I swallowed salt. "Something of the sort."

The baron clapped me heartily on the back—eliciting a squelch from my waterlogged doublet. "Well, as I am lord and master of my wife, I say the play shall be yours."

I gave the baron a weak smile, ill-comforted by such odds.

"Tell you the truth," he flattened his tone to take me into confidence. "The other gentleman was not the sort a canny man would want to have around his wife, if you take my meaning."

My heart skipped rope. I did not know if it was worse that I myself was not, apparently, considered worthy of the baron's suspicions, or that the man who had replaced me as her lover was. "What sort is that, my lord?"

"You know—poets," the baron snorted, toggling his broad nose with the back of his balled fist. "Lot of fancy-men."

"So he was . . . fair? Good-looking?"

Above his curly beard, the baron's freckled cheeks grew ripe. "Well, I'd not be the one to say, of course," he answered, quickening his pace. "He was tall. Well-built, I suppose. Carried himself with goodly pride. Fresh, really, stamping his boots upon the floor. He did not doff his hat to me." He glanced over his shoulder to test my reaction. "I do not think he would have doffed it, even, to a prince."

Something in this was too familiar. "Did he give his name?"

"At the door, he did." The baron scratched at his temples as if testing for the nubs of horns. "I remember it was unusual. Something to do with a weapon. Fall-staff, perhaps? Touch-stone?"

I tried to swallow, but my mouth had gone dry. I could not feel my own heart beating.

"Shake-spear." It was not a question, and I did not inflect the phrase as such. I spoke it coldly, as it was: an imperative to war.

"That was it! Master William Shake-spear." The baron paused in the hallway, nodding. "Funny name for a poet, I remember thinking. Sounds more like a sergeant at arms."

The Aftereffects of Belladonna

I dip my fingers into a pot of what looks like clotted cream, but is in fact ceruse: white lead, mixed into white vinegar. Toxic, of course, but it gives a sheen to the skin like nothing else—not asses' milk, nor the albumen of an egg, nor even the old country remedy: ashes from the burnt jawbone of a hog, sifted for three nights under the waxing moon and laid on in layers with oil of white poppy. These all produce a lightness to the skin, but cannot create light: the illusion of translucency, natural radiance. For this deception, more venomous potions must be used. To stain my lips and cheeks a sulfur paste, which burns. There are those who practice this dark magic daily, and pay for their beauty with their lives, losing teeth and hair, wizening into crones in a matter of years.

But pain is always part of the bargain, in spells of transformation. I drop into my pupils a perfume distilled from a rare and poisonous flower. It is so bitter I can taste it even with my eyes. Blinking, I gradually watch my own face come into focus again, so beautiful, it hurts to look on it. It is as flawless as the moon, smooth as a pearl appears before it is tested against the teeth.

True, my belladonna tincture taints my breath with venom and leaves my eyes weak and watery by day. At dawn this morning, the sunlight through my windows was so bright it made my teeth ache. But, in addition to its cosmetic uses, this distilled Italian lily allows me to see like a cat in the dark—invaluable for reading late by fickle firelight.

Horatio would correct my taxonomy: "Belladonna is a nightshade, not a lily, which is, in fact, a relative of the onion." But what else would you call a bloom of perfect beauty, which, festering down to its essence, becomes something rank and vile, to make you weep?

*H*e bows as he enters, but does not remove his hat. Of course, a prince would not be accustomed to doing so, having so few occasions apart from religious services where his authority would be outranked. Still, he might have played his part better, as he had come to me under a common man's name. An uncommon common man's name, at that.

I had left strict orders that I was not to be disturbed, so when the servant tapped open the study door, I turned to scold her. But my voice was stopped by the fact that I hardly recognized her. Normally the face of the downstairs maid is set in a perpetual scowl, especially when she has been sent to answer the door—a duty she feels is the proper provenance of my husband's valet. But her cheeks were spread wide as a fool's moon, and her eyes shone as if she had been using my belladonna drops. I guessed my visitor's true identity even before she gave his pseudonym.

But as he enters, I take advantage of the darkness in the hall to play innocent. "You are Will Shakespeare?" I modulate my voice to keep it light, devoid of all suspicion.

Prince Hamlet takes my hand as if to kiss it, but instead twists my wrist roughly out of my control. He holds my fingers to the light. By the pricking of my thumbs, I am revealed: the horn-sharp calluses from my viola.

"No," he answers triumphantly. "You are."

I struggle to pull away from him. I fight to catch my breath, my balance, and my tongue, like butterflies in a net. "Do you know me, sir?"

"Aye, madam," he answers. "Better than I would. You are my dear friend's mistress, more than just his master's wife. And—would it were not so—you were my lover."

He releases me so violently I have to find my feet, then he turns away, his brow clutched in his hand. Theatrical, that one. Well, two can play.

I lower my eyes in cool dismissal and sigh. "Well then, keep speaking, as you know so much." A woman's trick: men are proud, and will often reveal in vanity more than they'd intended, if only given opportunity. And Hamlet is a body of undirected energy, eager to spill his conclusions. He paces as if he had not paused one minute in his calculations since I left him a fortnight ago, slipping homeward through the moonless night with my breeches still damp.

"You came to me under the name of Shakespeare, having sent words of such sweet splendor none would ever guess they were as false and stolen as the name."

"Stolen!" I am incensed by his audacity, and also awed. Aroused, as well, though to what I cannot say. The truth is women, too, will reveal them-

selves for pride and vanity. "Have you not guessed the truth? It is by my will all this has been done."

"Your Will Shakespeare," he sneers.

"Aye, mine." I go to the chest where I keep my greatest treasure. I need no key to open the drawer. I do not fear a thief; all of my husband's servants are illiterate. I take out the pieces my poet has given me in our sleepless nights together. Mismatched, odd-sized scraps of sonnets: unnumbered, incomplete, and out of sequence.

When he sees the pages in my hand, Hamlet stops pacing, and his cheeks grow taut. "Give my letters here," he demands.

"Your letters? I own the rights to this poet's work."

"But they were written for me!"

"They may have been addressed to you," I correct him. "But they were written for me. He says quite clearly he intends his lines for the world. I am, for want of a better word, the world." I rifle through the pages, though there is no need; I know the words by heart.

Still this action inflames the prince's curiosity. He is like a cat; it is his fatal flaw. In an instant, he is breathing hot over my shoulder. But I am jealous of my property. I hold it to my bosom as though the verses might learn to nurse, so close to the chest that you would have to be inside me to read the words.

"I must learn what is in these lines!" he hisses at me, and his air of sweaty panic is familiar. Then it claps me on the head, so obvious, I cannot believe I never realized it before: the secret of Hamlet's love for Horatio.

"Now I understand! All this time, I thought you wanted him for your biographer. I saw him with his book in hand and thought he was there to take down your glorious deeds. But now I see the true purpose and use of Horatio—the constant, quiet friend whom you might consult at any moment in private aside. He is the one holding your promptbook!" I laugh out loud at this epiphany. "You are known for the quality of your wit, your noble mind—but you are just his character, imitating what he imagines of you, repeating his lines as your own. Without him, you are just another actor! Full of a lot of sound and fury, yes, but with nothing significant to say." I gather up my armful of poems and walk them to the hearth. "So do you want to be?" I ask, "Or not?"

"What sort of a question is that?" the prince demands, covering his fear with belligerence. He has gone so queasy in the face, I half-believe my bluff: were I to discharge the pages now into the fire, he would disintegrate, as clean as ashes.

"When I am with Horatio, I feel I cannot die—or even if I were to die, it would not matter, for he would remember me so perfectly I should be again, just as I am." He glances at the poems in my hands. "Better than I am—you are right in that."

He studies his reflection in the polished mantelpiece, his skin the self-same bluish-white of the Carrara marble. It is not a heroic complexion—just the ordinary pallor of a terrified armorless boy, alone against terrible odds.

"'Tis true enough, I know my own estimate. His love is worth more to me than my high birth, or wealth, or any talent I possess. It is me, and I am it." The prince shrugs. "I will pay his debt to you, whatever it is he owes."

In my pickpocketing days, when I would clock a gentleman's worth by the swing of his purse on his belt, I would hunt long hours before I found such a promising pendulum. But that is not my desire now.

"Your money is worthless to me, Prince of Denmark. I must have my Will. My Shakespeare."

He meets my eyes. He knows what I want of him. It is the same thing everyone wants of him: to wear his skin on mine. To play him and be played by him. To take away some piece of him immortal and my own.

"If you would have Horatio," I explain slowly, "then you must take his place."

He licks his lips, but in this shadow, I cannot see whether this be a lascivious gesture, or nervous.

"I am not a poet," the prince protests. "I haven't the art to reckon my sighs and groans into rhyme."

"So write in blank verse."

"In faith, I have tried, in the book of blanks Horatio gave to keep my thoughts, but my pen cannot keep pace with my head. I write a phrase, and think I have heard these lines somewhere before, and then I feel ill here, all about my heart." He puts a hand to his solar plexus, as in times of stress, old soldiers will reveal their scars, flinching to prevent an ancient wound. "It is but foolery, as would perhaps trouble a woman."

"So trouble a woman with it," I implore. I stroke his arm with my horned thumb, as though plucking out a tune in pizzicato. "Speak, and I will write it down for you."

He shakes his head no, but he shakes it to my rhythm.

"Tell me those dreams Horatio would call fantastical, and I will break with him, and bar him from my bed."

"And yourself from his heart, as well?" he asks. "Create an argument from air, from nothing?" He glares at me, suddenly vicious, and tears his arm from my beseeching grasp. "As you are a woman, I know you can do it."

I cannot help but smile. He is no stranger to this skill himself, to accuse my entire sex. "I believe I can contrive a dramatic enough scene to turn a poet's heart."

His feet traverse the floorboards until I fear he might worry a groove in the wood. "If it must be done, best it were done quickly. Even tonight."

"It cannot be tonight. The moon is full."

For all his wicked punning with the wenches in the tavern, he is so innocent of women's ways, he does not understand what I mean. But it serves my purposes to keep him ignorant in this, for now at least.

"I would not have you seen by the guard," I explain. "My husband does not love me, but he takes a jealous pride in his possessions, of which I am among his rarest and most valuable. Though he does not value me as much as his title, his holdings, his hawks and horses, nor his hunting-hounds, still he will defend his honor."

"I am not afraid," the prince insists, cradling his thumb around the hilt of his sword in a show of bravado. But I can see from its gilding the rapier is a lightweight prop: a piece of jewelry for a gadabout's belt, and not a proper weapon at all.

"You should be," I tell him plain. "My husband is no learned man, but he earned his fortune in the wars. It would take him longer to choose which blade to run through you than to do it, once he'd made the choice."

Hamlet pales, and leaves off playing with his jeweled toy. "When is the moon next new?" He winces as he speaks. "Horatio would know."

So he does feel some remorse towards those he betrays.

"Michaelmas night is near enough," I calculate. "The guards will be drunk on their quarter's wages, and my husband sleeping off roast goose and harvest cakes. After curfew is sounded, I will leave a candle burning in my window. Come to me then, and we may reckon our accounts."

In the shadow, Hamlet's azure suit looks black, his eyes some color darker even than black. But I know this very danger, the possibility of death, is part of what will make him come.

"And after, I may have Horatio?"

"I do not trade in slaves, Your Majesty," I answer, drawing up as if offended. "I will release him from his contract, that is all. If he wishes to follow you, he is free to do so, of course. But I can offer no guarantee that this will be his choice."

Hamlet does not need to answer; his smirk speaks loud enough. If anything is certain in this world, it fairly cries, it is Horatio's devotion to his royal self.

*B*ut when, not half an hour later a furious drenched Horatio stands in the self-same spot before me, he is consumed by another obsession entirely.

"Is there nowhere I can rest my pen, but William the Conqueror has come before?"

He tears his cap roughly from his head. Then, finding this gesture insufficient to express his outrage, he throws it to the floor, where it lands with a dull splat, bleeding rainwater. His overall appearance, however, is too miserable to suggest much threat. His hair is slicked onto his head, and he is shivering, wearing neither cloak nor buskins, nor even his woolen scholar's *togs. Only one man could addle him so deeply, for the ever-vigilant to travel forth so unprepared, and I test an earlier suspicion.*

"You saw Prince Hamlet this morning?"

He looks up, startled. "Why, how did you . . . ? Ah, of course—Shakespeare must have told you."

"He did," I confirm. Just now, in fact.

He runs his hands back through his hair (where it is thinning, he is the one thinning it) and paces, retracing his lover's footsteps without knowing it.

"I knew it! The prince must have gone to him directly from seeing me."

The prince must have come to me directly from seeing him. I guessed as much earlier; Hamlet had been in such a hurry to find me he'd hired the carriage, after all. Once you have spent your energy in assembling a puzzle, you do not hesitate to fit the last piece into place. Unless, of course, it be the puzzling, and not the finishing, that is your true desire.

"Come stand by the fire," I bid Horatio. "If your fingers stiffen with the cold, you will be unable to write tonight."

For a moment, I think, he is tempted to refuse, out of pure obstinacy. But he is too practical to suffer rheumatism just for spite and grudgingly comes to stand beside me, warming his hands over the coals. His silken shirtsleeves drip onto the andirons, causing hiss and sputter enough to cover the sound of our whispered conversation.

"What do you care if I write, tonight or ever?" he asks. "I thought Shakespeare was your spy on Hamlet now. Or did you not offer to him the same bargain you offered me?"

"Just the same," I answer. How can a man be compared against him-

self? *"But how can you upbraid me for my fascination with him, when you introduced us?"* I show the stack of poems, still sitting on the mantel, those brought lately on top. Page after jealous page about a rival poet who does not even exist. *"'Twas your pen wrote about his grace and majesty, his learning, his tall build."*

I finger through the sonnets, handing some to him directly, alluding to others. His eye flicks over the words as I describe them, then turns from what is written on the pages to see, as if for the first time, the pages themselves.

"But—why are these letters here? Surely you did not show them to Shakespeare?" His face falls blank with horror. *"They are mine!"*

"They may have been written by you," I correct him, *"but they belong to me. I may do with them whatever I please."*

"But he is a great poet, an immortal, and I—" Horatio bows his head. He is both of these: a legend, a god, untouchable, unreal, tall as a tale; and a lowly jealous hack struck speechless with self-doubt. *"Tell me—does Shakespeare laugh at my poor efforts? Does he insult me?"*

"At times," I admit—for it is true, my poor poet does abuse himself so in his sonnets. It amazes me, reading them, to see him describe his own designs as crude, unpolished. If one such as he does not see his own greatness, I wonder, how can any of us hope to know our worth? We are all castaways, casting messages in bottles into the sea.

"But what did he say?"

I search the stores of my memory. *"He has called you friendless, feeble, poor, despised. He likens you to an ancient sad slave, and says your poems are unworthy of their argument."*

He cannot deny these accusations; he was their inventor, after all.

"And still, you love him, Shakespeare?"

I am sorely tempted to comfort him. I want to wrap his hunched shoulders in my arms, to kiss his broad forehead and tell him he is the greatest poet who has ever lived, the greatest who will be produced by our world. But I must provoke his jealousy if my plan is to succeed.

"I love him." Will Horatio understand, when all has been unraveled, what I am confessing to him now? Or will he remember only the deception? "And at times he has even admitted he loved me. But if he loves a little, there is another he always prefers."

"Prince Hamlet."

I nod.

He takes this in without surprise. "And the prince returns his love, and wishes to keep the poet for his own?"

I nod.

Horatio closes his eyes as if praying, or working out a complicated philosophical proof. There is only one logical conclusion to this argument. Resigned, he gives half a nod and sighs.

"Then let him have Hamlet, and the prince his poet, as they are so well-matched in their mutual perfection." He reaches his hand out for mine. "You and I may rightly comfort one another, as we are alike in our wretchedness."

But love will never by logic be dictated. "I cannot, unless one heart were split in two." I do not tell him it must be his heart so divided. "I will wait to see if Shakespeare comes to me Michaelmas night."

"You would be pitied by him—pity me instead," he pleads. "Tell me you love me, even if it be a falsehood."

Horatio is not one to reveal his sorrows on his face. This stoicism has led many to believe he does not suffer the blows of fate as deeply as other men. But I know better. And though he only blinks a little more rapidly than before, I hide my face between my booked hands, unable to witness his suffering when I shake my head.

Through chinked fingers, I watch him bow, reshape his flat-brimmed cap from the damp rag left crumpled on the floor. This he affixes squarely to his head, and casts at me a final, damning glare, as if daring me to call him back again.

But I am mute.

Past grief already, he is white with anger.

"Then I hope you catch him, your Michaelmas goose—and grow sick and bloated from it, too!"

Love, and Other Feathered Creatures

But inside, I was thinking, "I hope you catch your Shake-spear, and grow sick of him, and return to me."

It could be no other way. I was the cooked goose, and would have willingly been devoured whole, if only her lips would do the devouring. Shake-spear was a fowl of no such common feather—rather, a proud, serene swan of the Elbe. Or whatever river it turned out the dastard had come from.

Well, Adriane would test his mettle, all right. I was almost sorry for the gentleman. How many poets could resist her siren song? She promised bottomless adoration, always held just one more revision out of reach. In such pursuits lay madness.

If my rival could spend a month of nights with her without forgetting entirely about the prince, then might I grudgingly con-

cede that this Shake-spear deserved to have his name promiscu-
ous with Hamlet's in the annals of History.

The loss of my mistress, I accounted as my own fault. Adriane
was right—I had been the one to introduce her to all of my rival's
better qualities. For a week or more, all my writing had been nothing but Shake-spear. Addressed to the prince, of course, but written in such jealous admiration of the other poet as could not help
but pique the reader's curiosity about him. I had painted in her
mind the picture of myself as a dejected cuckold, poor in talent,
and at last she had come to believe it. I gave a sigh. I had written
myself right out of my own romance.

Even this I was certain the clever Master Shake-spear had
somehow arranged, with his devastating and acute critique of my
work. If I could only see his face! It maddened me that I would not
even recognize the man who had done me such injury.

For weeks I was haunted by moments of irrational fear, suddenly certain the poet was walking beside me in the crowded
street, or dining at the same long table in the scholars' hall. I even
made such discreet inquiries about the author as might be passed
off as idle curiosity. But, while certain of my fellows thought they
had heard the name before, no one could be found who claimed to
know the poet personally.

Hamlet did not send for me at all during this time; nor did
I make attempt to contact the prince. In a way, I preferred to be
without him, for then my mind could not be muddled by such
new discoveries as might dishonor Hamlet's character. I preferred

to love, willingly deceived by an illusion of my own invention.

But when I sat before my desk to lose myself in this world, even my Muse eluded me. My mind and its subject were magnets of like charge, and could not be made to meet. Without Adriane's expectation spurring me to write, I could not summon the will to muddle through, line after sour line, as if working a tiresome puzzle, until the moment the correct solution leapt out at me, suddenly obvious.

I sat instead and listened to the ticking of my watch, each hour it struck another of Hamlet's heartbreakingly finite life that would never be committed to my page. The open book loomed before me, menacing: a whitewashed brick wall. My ink dried to dust in the inkwell. I fetched water, mixed it up, and watched it all evaporate again. I did not write.

I tried to reassure myself this lack of matter did not translate to a waning in my feelings for the prince. But this argument was halfhearted. I tried to turn instead to those studies I had once embraced with such devotion. Now they seemed cold and colorless, Latin as dead as its native sons.

In my first years at the University, I had gorged myself on learning, but as soon as I mastered a subject, I quickly grew bored with it and moved on. After a month or two, my former passion for the details of historical battles, or foreign legal briefs, or travel diaries from Italy, would seem to me a childish fad, far removed from new obsessions. Was it possible my love for Hamlet had been as ephemeral as any of these?

But in this, there was one difference: I had not yet mastered my study of the prince, nor captured his excellent mind to satisfaction in print. I still did not understand what Hamlet meant to me, what he ever had meant.

I had never failed a subject, not since I was a child at the monastery school. Perhaps this is what kept me from closing the book entirely on the affair—though the journal haunted me every night and morning from my desk, its empty leaves spread open, white as wings.

Michaelmas night, I went to the evening services just long enough for my presence to be taken down by the steward, sneaking out before my refusal to take sacraments could be remarked upon.

It was curious, I thought. Love, so I had been told, was the holiest of all heavenly blessings; but both my loves, the better and the worse, were counted sins. My love for one was called adultery; for the other my sin was in adulterating pure Platonic admiration with the awkward intrusion of my clumsy earthbound self.

It seemed fitting, then, that both those who had tempted me rewarded me for it with naught but suffering. I did not know if the church, even the Catholics, would call the pain of loving Adriane fitting penance for the sin of loving her; but I understood at last Saint Augustine's epiphany: we are punished not for our sins, but by them.

Still, I held out hope that Shake-spear might refuse Adriane's invitation tonight, and by this rejection she might yet be swayed to return to me. There was nothing to be done for it but wait; still I was gripped by restlessness.

I left the chapel by the deacon's door, intending to return to the dormitory. I thought perhaps with all the pious theologians at their prayers, I might be able to snatch a line or two of poetry out of the air. I had no other potential destination in mind, until I felt the night air on my cheeks. It was cold enough to see my breath before me, were it not too dark to see anything before me, even breath. My mind was as clear and starry as the moonless night.

Nor did the darkness slow my pace. I knew the way so well, my shoes could have walked it without my feet inside. Making the sign of the cross upon myself, I whispered another of Augustine's prayers: "Lord, make me chaste—but not yet."

Arriving shortly at the baron's house, I insinuated myself through the familiar gap in the wall. The only lantern lit was at the gatehouse watch-station, where two guards lay slumped one against the other, drunk, or victim to some stronger soporific.

The house was a charcoal sketch done on an oilcloth canvas: simply a more perfect darkness outlined against the sky. I navigated the hedge-maze from memory, counting my steps. I could see the flicker of a candle burning in Adriane's window. So she yet expected him, her visitor? Drawing nearer, I saw the hammock ladder was indeed hanging in its place, between the stone wall and the bramble bush.

A surge of hope liquored my blood. The poet had not yet arrived. Probably lingering over some late assignation with Hamlet, more happy he.

I had intended (insofar as I had intended any of this at all) only to see whether my rival had indeed come to her, and perhaps to catch a glimpse of his face. But now that I had come all this way—and found the ladder so encouragingly waiting—the need overtook me for some stronger satisfaction.

I considered the problem from another angle. Whoever had his wish in this, the baroness or the prince, would have his (or her) Will. Shake-spear, that is.

Therefore, I thought, this most unruly Will, whom both my loves desired, should be my mirror and my guide in this. If I were Shake-spear, I considered, and came upon such a scene, of my mistress awaiting my rival, what would I do?

Why, pull a bed-trick, of course.

I would come to her by the name of Will, and in the darkness press my will upon her, as the rogue and talented seducer she desired would have done. I would play the role of immortal poet, not of timid scholar, until she was fulfilled by another kind of will-fullness.

I laughed at the thought. If, in the treasured peak of love, she were to cry the name of *Will*, would my name not, in that instant's reckoning, in fact be Shake-spear's? What's in a name, I thought, but the intention with which it is spoken and the manner understood? When the dawn uncovered all deception, even she would be forced to admit I was her very, very *Will*, whom she had called her own.

I hoisted myself onto her balcony, turning automatically to retract the rope. Always, no matter how severe my lust, I stopped to secure the ladder from the view of any spy, coiling it carefully, knot to knot, so that it would unroll in an instant, should the need arise to make a hasty exit. This by now had become such a habit, it did not even occur to me that a less cautious suitor might not have thought to stay his pleasure long enough to do the same.

The taper burned low in its fat brass candlestick. On the table, wine was poured: two silver goblets, one near full, the other drained until more air remained in it than wine.

So—Adriane had grown impatient for her lover, cheered her spirit with spirits, and gone to bed. The deception would prove easier than I had anticipated. I might wake her with caresses, and thus avoid the problem of my height, which could not be made to match the gentleman's. Behind her bed-curtains, she might swear that I was her Will.

But as I neared the bed, I saw that the hanging velvet curtains had been parted strangely at one side, pulled back and tied to the bedposts, like the proscenium of a puppet theatre. And featured on this stage, ill-met, well-lit by firelight: a golden ass.

The bare male buttocks stared at me like a pair of close-set eyes. Bent thus, only his rump and a faint geography of spine was visible, but still the scene before me was self-evident. Heedless of the quilts, the lovers had fallen asleep together, kept warm enough by their passionate embrace.

Now I noted the cloak tossed over a chair; a pair of gentleman's riding boots, lying discarded before the fire. Upended on the floor—doubtless thrown carelessly in the throes of some love-game—lay a tricorner hat; stuck into its brim, a great white plume.

Shake-spear. So the trickster had beaten me once again. Anger rose in me, buoyed by a wave of humiliation. Would it ever be possible for me to have an idea in my head that had not been thought of first by Shake-spear?

I was in a terror of being discovered. I knew I should make retreat, but my feet were held immobile by a more obstinate will. Awe of celebrity forestalled my better judgment: I was in the presence of *Shake-spear*!

This was the poet who had stolen my Muse and all my loves, whose authority had left my art tongue-tied. He had even begun to replace the prince in my most private fantasies: a god whose vast weight crushed me underneath him—tall as a mountain, tall as a myth, his true identity always obscured. Sometimes I had imagined him a beast, sometimes the comeliest of men.

Curiosity maddened me. Never again was I like to have such opportunity to see the illustrious author stripped bare—to behold his shape; whether he be fair or dark; a youth of flourishing years, or gone half-gray. I took up the taper in the window. The molded brass candlestick was warm and surprisingly heavy, and its weight helped to steady my nerves. Trembling with trepidation, I brought the candle near to the sleeping figure, directing the light with the cup of my hand, to see my dearest enemy in heaven.

Love personified could not have rewarded the thief of his sight with a more beautiful betrayal. Cupid couched thus could not have seemed a meeker or sweeter beast: his hair of gold, hanging comely behind and before and indeed all about his head, the sweet ambrosial savor of it unmistakable. His neck and brow more white than milk, his cheeks flushed violet with the late exertions of their lust. They were tangled together limbs and limbs, blissful adulterers—both of them as stark as a bald head. But she did not look naked; only Hamlet.

I gaped at them, unable to translate the evidence of my eyes into sense. At last, kneeling there over his sleeping form, I made the classical error, neglecting the candle still clutched in my trembling hand. Uncut, the wick burned up too quickly, and a translucent bead of impatient hot wax over-spilled the rim of the candlestick.

Too late! I saw it fall. Time slowed, too late to do anything for it but moan in anticipation as the hot teardrop spattered on the prince's naked shoulder, hardening white.

With a jerk, the knavish lad came suddenly awake, while I, coming just as suddenly out of my reverie, hurried to smother the treacherous candle-flame. The sweet scent of snuffed beeswax, and (less sweet) of singed hair, lingered in the air, accusingly.

"You?" I gasped, breathless with disbelief. "You are Will Shake-spear?"

He shook his head. "No." His voice was pitted with regret. "You are."

At last I understood. There was no rival. There had never been. My own poetry had led to this. It had introduced to each of my loves the other, and they had both abandoned me.

"Then take her!" I shouted, heedless of the baron or the guards. "You are my love, and so take all my loves! What more have you now than you had before? I wooed her with your beauty, and had you but asked, I could not have refused you whatever rights I might have had to her. But to do me this injury of deceit?"

Even in this darkness I could see the tears on Hamlet's cheeks. Before, this show had moved me to forgive outright; but I knew now that I could not judge the prince by his outward display. My purest, simplest faith had been, in Hamlet, shamefully misplaced. Those claims I had made for him in my poems had been belied by the evidence of my eyes.

Then I fled like a coward, down the rope, pushing through the hedges, tearing the branches apart as though I were emerging at last from a dense evergreen wood. The air was shocking cold and pained my lungs; I wondered how long I had forgotten to breathe.

I thought back on the scene, perceiving the set of the stage: the early assignation, the wine tainted with sedative. The fire stoked to cast its light; the bed-curtains carefully tied back to frame the scene. She had plotted all this.

It was her fault, then. Hamlet was right and perfect, and had been wrongfully disgraced. I repeated this, but found no comfort in it.

At the bridge, I stopped and peered over the side of the low stone wall, sorely tempted by the pull of the current below. I was suddenly bone-tired of the world. My muscles ached with weariness, as if I had been pounded by a mallet. The split, syncopated beat of my heart (never my own heart) cried out for the soothing rest of death.

But I was saved by one consideration: dying, I would leave Hamlet alone, and slave forever to her whim and will. Though he should kill me with his spites, still we must not be foes, lest Adriane win the argument.

It was that hour of night when even the barman was going to bed, and only the musicians were left in their clutch in the corner. Scarce few even of these remained, circled knee to knee on low wooden stools, each keeping time in quarter-beats or whole. The lutenist tapped his toe to the music; the fiddler his heel, which gave the impression of a pair of synchronized bellows producing the melody. The piper marked the measures with his brambled brows, and the tabors player could not keep to anyone's time.

"Better he should play the skin with a penknife than beat it to death with that stick!" somebody called out, though the joke was as old as knives and skins.

Dipping my pen, I went back to my writing—having, after all, chosen this particular seat near the fire for its light. The unbroken view it offered to the tavern's entrance was, I told myself, mere happenstance.

Still, whenever the door opened, my heart swelled in anticipation, only to contract painfully back to its ordinary size as Not Hamlet appeared. Not Hamlet caroused with a troupe of actors in celebration after a show. Not Hamlet played at dice with gentlemen. Not Hamlet drank and fought and spat and laughed and fiddled and danced in every corner of the world, except under my pen.

Hours before, I had prayed for inspiration; now my head was so filled with matter I could not keep my pen long enough in ink to write it all. A day earlier, had I been granted but a single wish, it would have been to have the talents of my most exalted rival poet. Now, to discover myself Will Shake-spear, and no happier than before—this irony stung worst of all my disappointments.

"Another'un sir?" the publican was standing over me, a dishrag in his hand.

I shook the small pouch on my belt, then shook my head. Someone should coin a phrase: as quiet as an empty purse.

But instead of going away, or else telling me to get out, Father Jacques tilted his chin to indicate my book. "What have yeh, there?"

"Poetry," I answered curtly, in no spirit to be questioned.

"I kin see that," the old man said, a trifle impatiently. "Looks to me like a cycle of sonnets in the English style, modeled after Sidney's *Astrophel and Stella*. But what's yer Theme?"

"Despair," I growled. In truth, I had long given up hope of seeing the prince appear, and had remained at the pub nursing my pence of ale only because I could not spare the candlelight at home.

"Not much of a Theme," he said. "What's yer Plot?"

I sighed, wondering where I might begin. "Two loves have I . . ."

The old man blew air out his nose. "A comfortable despair!"

"I have them not," I amended, "but yet they have me still. Like spirits, they suggest to me these lines of verse."

He conjured himself a three-legged stool from somewhere and sat beside me. "And of these spirits?" he asked. "Which love yeh the better?"

"An angel . . ." I answered, then bit my lip, uncertain just how much I might safely confess in this company.

But Father Jacques had raised his brows in recognition. "A young man," he guessed, "right fair . . . ?"

I admitted it with a nod. I could not have been the first of Hamlet's dejected lovers (from *de jactare*, I winced automatically, "to throw away") to seek the barman's counsel.

"And the worse?"

"A woman—foul, ill-colored, false, and filled with evil pride in all her faults. This . . . *female evil* . . ." (good taste censored the first word that came to my mind for her, and the second as well) "has tempted the p— —that is, my better angel—from my side. She would use him for her own purpose, encouraging his madness and licentiousness, corrupting him to be a villain, a devil, as wicked as she!"

"And has she, now?!" The wrinkles on the old man's brow magnified his expression of surprise.

I shrugged. "It has not been three hours since I discovered them together. As neither is here with me, I must conclude they are yet together, in bed, and one in the other's . . ." Closing my eyes, I cursed hellfire and damnation, picturing how the two might yet be joined, and where. I would have summoned the force of cannon-fire to part them, had I any to my command.

The tavern-keeper clapped me on the back in sympathy, then disappeared briefly into the cellar, returning with a good-sized jug of strong, sweet sherry-sack and a couple of yesterday's hard loaves. These he deposited on the table, winking at me. "On the house."

Virtuous Lies

Swallows fly south for the winter, and the scholars return to Wittenberg. First-years flocked behind their masters, their crisp, black robes pressed glossy, while sophomores wore their worldliness upon their faded sleeves. The upper classes left servants to the unpacking, flitting at once down to the taverns and clubs to trade tales of grand tours in Italy and France.

For the fortnight after Michaelmas, it was impossible to take any public thoroughfare to or from the University without digressing a dozen times to navigate around some dusty cart or carriage stopped dead in the street, swarmed by harried footmen unloading trunks; or else the piled leavings of their horses—easily mistaken, in these earlier evenings, for piled leaves.

I found my world once again defined by Academia Leucorea, the University my entire universe. I received a summons to meet with my research advisor, and went with misgivings, half expecting to be sent down for my sins. But the dean accepted without question my excuse that I had been consumed in research towards a work of philosophy, which unfortunately I had been unable to complete as planned.

"My argument was flawed," I admitted. "It all fell apart in the proofs."

The professor murmured some clichéd encouraging words about learning more from failure than success, and saying I clearly wanted for more responsibility, assigned me to teach the introductory astronomy course.

"A fascinating series of eclipses this season," he assured me, passing off his lecture notes. "I am certain you will take close observations of the effects, and interpret in them something of significance."

Though I did not share this certainty, having half-expected expulsion, I could not with grace withhold my gratitude.

So I found myself three mornings a week before a hall of wiggling, sniggering schoolboys, droning through lessons on the concurrence of Neptune's tides to the fluid star, the moon; on sextiles, quintiles, and trines; on which planets were ruled by air and which by fire.

Meeting Hamlet for the first time, I had guessed him to be still in the dewy springtime of youth, estimating his years at eighteen, or thereabouts. Now I realized I had only misjudged a man of thirty so badly because I myself was nearer now to forty than the twenty-five I flattered myself. Actual boys of eighteen looked twelve; and the dewiness of blooming youth, I soon discovered, was far more romantic an image when confined to the poet's page.

Sometimes on the floor of the lecture hall I pretended I had been engaged to play a character role on the stage. A common stock figure in any *commedia*: the pedantic, humorless schoolmaster of indeterminate middle age. However, my cagey parody went right over their heads; and the term closed in around us all like a bright, familiar jail.

I was in the library one early morning, just after the matins bell, taking notes from an ancient ephemeris on the upcoming lunar eclipse, when an unanticipated shadow fell across my page.

His hair wanted cutting. More than wanted: it pined and pleaded for it, as did his beard. The hooks down the front of his doublet were done one out of every eight or ten, and many of these cockeyed. His black silk hose were fouled with mud, laddered with bramble-snags. Unbraced, one had slipped its garter to expose his knobbed pale knee. Any gentleman's valet who sent his charge out so disheveled would be whipped, if not discharged outright; Hamlet had not been to bed tonight. Not to his own bed, at least.

"Do you still provide assistance with translations, and the like?" he asked me circumspectly, casting his eye over the handful of scholars scattered at the slanted wooden desks. Only the most dedicated or most desperate were at their studies at this hour, and none took note of him.

He was carrying with him the little diary I had made for his birthday gift. It had been splayed open in so many places it fanned out from its makeshift shoelace binding like a pleated ruff, showing lines crabbed in a scribbling secretary hand. These darkened the pages inconsistently, so that some showed only a couplet, or even a single exclamation, while others were densely blobbed with ink: long, formless speeches unbroken by any punctuation more definite than a colon. I thought I caught sight of my own name two or three times as he flipped the pages. Finally, he extracted a sheet of letter paper, folded twice, with a quatrain written with flourish across the top third. This he set against my ephemeris.

> *Doubt thou the stars are fire,*
> *Doubt thou the sun doth move,*
> *Doubt truth, to be a liar,*
> *But never doubt I love.*

I stared at this doggerel. "A bit long for an engraving on a ring," I said.

"It was meant to be the beginning of a sonnet," pouted the prince.

"Well, in that case, the meter does not scan." I moistened my lips with my tongue, not wanting to ask what I wanted to ask; but the stronger desire won out. "For whom was it written?"

Hamlet's pout curled up at the corners, already celebrating his triumphant homecoming through the welcoming gates of my good graces. "Come now—how many famous doubters have I professed to wear in my heart of hearts?"

I stifled a bitter laugh. "My mathematics goes only to geometry, my lord." I returned to the half-drawn chart, noting the malefic aspect of the eclipse to retrograding Jupiter, opposite Mars.

"Ass." He slapped his book down on the desk beside mine and straddled a stool. "Just for that, I'll send the poem to an ingénue in my father's court, who never doubted a thing anyone told her in all her life."

Producing a pen and penknife, Hamlet meticulously shaved fingernail-like curls from the tip of the quill, humming a tune about bonny sweet Robin Hood. With the feathered tip of the pen, he chased the parings down the slanted board into the gutter, then tested his leg against that of the table. Both proved wobbly.

Then, leaning across the divide between the desks, the prince casually dipped his pen into my inkwell.

I seethed at this familiarity, but allowed nothing to show on my face. I simply dipped my own quill and went back to my copying, keeping my eyes fixed upon my tables.

Beside me, the prince scrawled half a line, then sighed dramatically. "How do you spell 'Ophelia'?"

I refused to be ruffled. "In Latin, my lord, or Greek?" I asked, as cold as any stone.

"How should I know?" His hatless head showed a hairline more dramatically peaked than I remembered, and darker: it could hardly be called blond. "In Danish, I suppose."

"I have forgotten all I ever knew of the Danish tongue." My voice, louder than I'd intended, echoed through the hall. A few heads popped up from their studies, and the Librarian even turned from his business at the shelves to scowl at us.

Hamlet smirked and bent across my lap to dip his pen again. I turned my head away, trying to ignore the spice of Hamlet's sweat, the flood of memories it called to mind. I could not concentrate; the scratch of his quill against the page seduced my wandering eye.

That I love thee best, most best, he wrote, *believe it.*

He glanced up just in time to catch me looking. I dropped my eyes in embarrassment.

"A very clever ruse," I noted, careful to keep my voice low, both for privacy's sake, and to keep it from shaking. "You do not actually say you love her, but only that she must believe it. I am certain she will be taken in—and when you tell her you never loved her at all, she will be forced to admit she was the more deceived by the trick. And then there will be one more fallen nymph, reciting your moment's sins forever in her prayers."

He laid down his pen. "Forgive my trespass," he said.

I did not speak.

"You were the one who told me I should take a wife."

"I never meant another man's, my lord."

"You had her first!"

Indeed, I had. I remembered vividly the parched, raw quality of mornings after nights with Adriane—as if my senses had all been flayed to the quick—and for a moment, I almost pitied him. But I had learned well from her to dissemble, and allowed no shadow of my thought to cross my face.

He persisted: "If you would share her with her husband, then why not with me, who has shared with you everything else?"

Our conversation had by now become heated enough to interest all but the most obtuse scholars; and even those still hunched over their copies I suspected were only feigning attention while in fact transcribing each salacious word their ears could catch.

I angled a sheet of paper so he could read it as I wrote, and motioned for the prince to do the same. The remainder of our conversation was conducted in a puzzle of hastily jotted lines, whispered explanations, gestures, and heavily pregnant looks.

"That you have her is not my overriding grief—although I must admit I loved her dearly. My chief concern is that she now has you," I wrote.

"She was willing, that is all." He hooked his foot into the cross-rung of my stool, reaching over to write on my page, "When a woman woos, what woman's son will sourly leave her?"

"So she coveted you for your beauty, and you were too kind to refuse?" I scribbled back, in shorthand.

Hamlet graced this assessment with a nod. Even now the only faults he admitted to were an excess of beauty and of kindness.

I sighed. I had deceived myself to think there might have been some other explanation. He might have been with her only for my sake, I believed; and perhaps she had, likewise, merely hoped to drive my heart from him. I had even daydreamed scenes between them, bargaining for my love. But I needed to reread another *Will*—William of Occam, for the true answer was much simpler. Leaning over to his page, I wrote: "So—young men will do it, if they come to it. By cock, they are to blame."

Hamlet held his head in hand, and, turning his book to a fresh page, he took another angle: "It was a foolish rashness. In my heart there was a fighting. I tossed and turned over this until my sheets were shackled around my ankles and I dreamt myself a slave, chained to my body, chained to every other mortal man since time began. So I rose up in a mutinous fury and went to her—still intending no such trespass as would dishonor you."

I parsed this paragraph. "So you mean you were not yet *quite* naked when you entered her closet, but had your undershirt still partway scarfed about your neck? I shall make note of it."

"You ran away and left me all alone, with no one to consult whom I could trust." He gave a helpless shrug. "So in the dark I groped her out, and had my desire of her, under cover of night. But our indiscretions sometimes serve us well, for I fingered her packet before I withdrew."

"Fingered her what?!" Some misguided chivalry buried deep in my breast yet leapt to defend her virtue.

He reached into his doublet and unfolded a stack of mismatched papers onto my desk. With a shock, I recognized my own handwriting. It was not just the first few finished sonnets she had shown him then, but all of them—to the last miserable, self-abusing verb.

Looking over the scribbled lines, he slowly shook his head. "My poor soul . . ."

His pity was the worst of all. More sharp than the cold sting of rejection was to have the one who had done the rejecting know exactly how sharp it had stung. But soon I realized he was speaking not of my "poor soul" but of his own:

"These center on my sinful earth," the prince complained. "And not the better qualities of my mind."

I had been wrong, I discovered: selfish indifference did sting worse than pity after all.

"The test of the portrait is in how truly it captures, my lord," I answered him coldly. "The worth of these can be no more than that of their subject."

"And that is this," he gestured with one hand upon the pages and the other over his heart, as if swearing before a court of law. "And with you it remains." He passed me the stack of poems. "Remember the parts of me consecrate to you," he said, sighing broadly, dramatically. "And promise me you will not mourn too long, when I am dead. I cannot abide a surly funereal humor. Do not weep any longer than the sullen church-bell tolls."

Of course Adriane had been encouraging his ridiculous morbid fantasies, the voice of his "prophetic soul," which spun dire warnings and pronouncements out of everyday nightmares. I rolled my eyes. Even now, I loved Hamlet absolutely, but following Hamlet meant existing in an entirely different universe, believing in things the rational world had rejected for good reason as absurd.

"You are not about to die," I said, "unless by your own reckless act you call your end upon yourself."

He looked down, and it occurred to me that this might be exactly what he intended. A deep foreboding set into my bones.

"And remember," I warned sternly, "should you be tempted in that direction, the church has set the canon against self-slaughter. If you pursue your own destruction, you will be damned for it."

"I thought you did not believe . . ."

"No, my lord," I squinted at him over my spectacles, "but you do."

He shook his head. "It is not the being dead I fear, but having to die; and that problem is solved quick enough. Once I am dead, there's no more dying then."

"Speculation," I reminded him. "You cannot know what may be or not in a land from which no traveler has ever carried tale. Perhaps death is nothing but dying, over and over again, as in your dreams."

He shuddered. "Then I would believe in Hell. I should hate to have to do it more than once."

His breath smelled like rot and roses; something more familiar, too. Something sweet and foul, almost metallic, that drew the marrow of my bones even as it turned my stomach. Then I understood two truths at once: Hamlet was drugged; and I myself had also been drugged when I had forsaken him, addicted to the fantasies produced by Adriane's notorious silver pipe.

"But be contented," he continued. "You may proceed with your literary work. When I am dead, there will be some interest in an accounting of my deeds. When I am fallen to the wretch's blade, sentenced by that final judge, who never grants bail to any who come before his court, if anyone should task you to recite my merits, I beg you to say nothing of these peccadilloes. Say nothing of me at all, in fact." He tilted his head at me coyly. "Unless . . . you could devise some virtuous lie?"

"Virtuous lie?" It took me a moment to realize the prince meant to assign me some common work of maudlin propaganda, such as any monarch's hacks churned out to stoke the frenzied crowd at festivals. "You mean a book extolling you as a hero, noble in your reasoning? Expressing admiration for your acts?" I tried to stop myself, but it was as if I had swallowed poison. The words kept vomiting themselves in spasms from my mouth. "Describing you as the expectancy and rose of the fair state?"

He paused, taken aback. "I suppose, something like . . ."

I blew a heavy sigh. "Be a model for a fashion plate, or mold for a sculptor's form. Go before one of these if you desire immortality. Marry your ingénue; breed fair children with your face. What philosophy have you to offer a poet's pen? When have you done anything heroic—made a difficult choice, put into practice any great plan? You are a prince, yet you have done nothing to prove yourself nobler in the mind than any other man, woman, or child!"

For the first time that I could remember, he was struck silent. When he spoke again at last, his voice was softer, chastened.

"Then teach me what to consider," he begged, "and warn me when my considerations become too curious. Be my eyes for me, my judgment, when I cannot trust my own."

I shook my head. "Already, I have been too often truant from my own studies, for love of you. Truly, I haven't the disposition for it."

"For truancy?" he asked, "or love?"

I could not answer him. I looked down at the stack of poems, unwilling to decipher the lines. I told myself I would burn the pages, each one, straightaway; I knew I could never bring myself to do so. I made myself count one hundred in a moderate time, and when I at last allowed myself to look, Hamlet was gone, and his absence everywhere again.

Wise Children

He wore his beaver up. That was his flaw, his fatal flaw. He wanted the son of Fortinbras to see the beard of the man who reunited him with his father, in death. And it is this detail that haunts the king long after the fatal battle, in dreams made vivid and distorted by the apothecary's potions.

The Danish fleet had put to shore in a cove a little up the coast. Scouts sent to spy on Fortinbras's forces reported only a feeble crew of men and horses, camped at the edge of a forest of green maples, around a fraying flag so faded by the sun you could no longer tell what color it had been.

The king rode ahead, with his two most trusted lieutenants at his left and right, and a small contingent of foot-soldiers following. The rest of the army he sent the long way around, behind the masking forest, to surround the camp and cut the rebels off from any inland reinforcements. This was an old strategic trick of his, to disguise the true strength of his forces with a weak front in the initial attack, then make a surprise showing from behind some natural blind.

They rode upon the camp to find it oddly deserted: the shells of empty tents, tended by scarecrows.

"They have abandoned their campaign and gone home," his lieutenant said laughing, dipping early into the hip-flask worn on his belt. Not until the hoofbeats behind were nearly upon him did the king even think to reach for his sword.

After that, they had no precious seconds to waste in thought; in battle every move must be automatic, practiced until it became instinct. But in the elongated moments of reflection afforded in his nightmares afterwards, he has developed a grudging respect for this son of Fortinbras. Only a man who had made his life's work the study of this particular military strategist would have known where to plot this ambush on the ambushers. Only a soldier who had followed the career of the King of Denmark even more closely than that of his own defeated father would have laid the trap as he had: a decoy camp, with the greatest part of his army scattered and concealed behind hills and coves of trees, to converge on their attackers. As Fortinbras, son of Fortinbras, charged down upon him, the king did not stop to analyze his emotion, but now he understands it: it was pride.

To think, a man would risk his life, his soldiers' lives, his country's reputation, the agreements of treaties, again and again and again, for a strip of land worth nothing but itself. All because he thought his father's pride lay buried there. Would he, Horwendil Hamlet, ever inspire such fanatical filial devotion? No, he decides, probably not. Hamlet, son of Hamlet, charged with the same, would make a complicated bloody philosophical mess of everything.

But this son of Fortinbras simply raises his arm to battle, and it is his father's arm. Without a moment's hesitation, he heaves the heavy vengeance of his father's spear down upon his father's murderer.

In his dream, the king is there again, turning his head to look at this magnificent young warrior upon him. Had he been wearing the beaver of his helmet down, the armor likely would have deflected the blow, at least in part. But he had worn it up, the better to savor his victory. And into this gap in the armor-plate, this narrow window of opportunity afforded by his overconfidence, does Fortinbras, son of Fortinbras, direct the fine point of his spear.

The tip slips in at an oblique angle between his helmet-strap and the fleshy part of his cheek, piercing the hollow of his ear so fiercely he is torn from his mount. He finds himself unseated from saddle to sky; from sky to mud, where his cry of rage and surprise is knocked out of him by the cold earth. Thus unreined, his terrified charger rears and bolts, leaving the king on no back but his own, surrounded by the enemy.

Forcing himself to his feet, he feels a jangling roar of pain and swoons forwards, clutching his hand to his ear. Blood runs down into his eyes, half-blinding him. A cacophony of terror assaults his eardrum: the crash of stormy seas. A high-pitched wail, like shrieking spirits, sirens through his head. Horsemen rise around him on every side, tall as trees. Their shadows block out the sun, punctuated all around by the bright glint of honed steel.

Then comes the nightmarish moment, the one he cannot forget. The one which festers and burns in him no matter how many potions he sucks down to numb the pain. Standing there, facing his death, the King of Denmark does the unthinkable: he begs for his life.

"A horse," his cracked lips mouth in agony. He turns to his left, to his right, but his lieutenants have abandoned him, and run away. Tears wash blood down his face as he cries out desperately: "My kingdom for a horse!"

One of the horsemen nudges his mount forwards at a walk, pushing the beaver of his helmet up to show his face. Fortinbras, son of Fortinbras, looks down upon the man who took his father's life.

"I'll take that trade," he says. Dismounting, he presents his own fine black stallion to the fallen king.

Rough hands are grabbing him then, rough voices jeering as Fortinbras's men hoist him up onto the horse. They take a length of rough rope, strapping him backwards into the saddle like a sack of something wet.

Then Fortinbras brings his face very close to the bruised and battered one tied to the horse's rump. "Remember," he says with a sneer. "I will be coming shortly, to collect on our bargain, witnessed here."

Then he slaps the stallion's rump, barking a Norwegian command, and the horse, obeying its master, gallops the king back to the sea.

*T*he king's wound festers. Physicians are summoned, medicines procured, but nothing can appease his suffering. The royal apothecary bids the maidens of the court to gather certain flowers from the fields, from which he distils a powerful tincture. Only three drops of this colorless liquid in the blighted ear eases his pain, bearing him away into dreams. After taking this cure, he must lie quite still for several hours, so he has his couch borne into the orchard, where he naps away his afternoons. He is ashamed of what he has become: a dull fat weed rooted in the waters of the Lethe.

●　　　●　　　●

*N*ever has learned to look before leaping, that boy. An unbroken Barbary: impetuous and green; foolhardy, brave. Lord Polonius smiles. Exactly like himself, at that age. "Remember your Homer, Laertes: 'tis a wise child heeds its own father.'"

This tempest finally comes to rest against the Lord Chamberlain's desk, the impact sending his scales askew and the glass globe of the lantern chattering alarmedly in its frame. "Knows, father."

"What's that?" Looking up from the legal documents framed in his spectacles, he sees Laertes is wearing that affectionately condescending expression he has been accustomed to adopting towards his father ever since he learned to grow a beard.

"The quote: 'My mother Penelope tells me I am Odysseus' son; but 'tis a wise child knows its own father.' Do you remember, how you used to sit with me and read the stories aloud, when I could not sleep?" From the way his eyebrows wrinkle up, he must believe the old man is getting absentminded in his dotage.

Unhooking his spectacles from his ears, Polonius lays them down upon a line writ small in the old Constitution. Then he reaches up his hand to pat his son upon the cheek, feeling the prickle of the sable beard. Already, it is beginning to show strands of silver among the black, like icicles, though he is not yet thirty. A tender memory returns to him, and he feels a cold wind sting his eyes.

"So tell me," he asks the young man, "are you yet wise?"

"I have all my teeth." Laertes bares a grin in proof. "But I cannot claim more than a schoolboy's wit until I have finished my degree. Why did you summon me from Paris, and with such urgent words I feared some catastrophe?"

"Would you have obeyed less dire summons?"

Laertes does not answer. He yet resents his father for insisting that he serve a full seven-year soldier's term before attending University, and now that he has finally achieved the freedom of the Sorbonne, contrives every excuse not to return for holidays. "My studies will suffer the longer I remain away from school."

"Study, then!" The Lord Chamberlain's is the finest private library in Elsinore—at least, while Prince Hamlet and his varied books of new philosophy remain away at school in Wittenberg. Polonius gestures to indicate the tall oak shelves lining the wall behind him, crammed with bound classics, well-saved from his own University days—everything in all the world, in other words, an educated man might wish to know. The look of horror this prospect arouses in the lad amuses him. "Is life so dull for you in Elsinore?"

"Of course not, Father," Laertes lies grudgingly. Though his feet have stopped their pacing, still one dances under him, and with his thumbnail, he traces the scroll of carved leaves wainscoting the table's edge. Polonius is glad to see by the mark in the crease of his thumb that, whatever his extracurricular occupation, he has kept up with his fencing, at least.

"I expect our homely entertainments here cannot compare to the taverns and gaming-halls of Paris—nor the brothels, neither." He smiles to see the boy coloring up. "Come, you need not look away—you can admit as much to me. You think I have always been an old man, but I was your age, once upon a time. Do you know, I even acted upon the stage, at University? I played..."

"...Caesar," Laertes finishes impatiently, still prickly with embarrassment. "I know. You were killed in the capitol. Brutus killed you."

"Ah," his father smiles sadly. "You have heard it all before?"

"Only every time the players come to Elsinore."

Thirty years now, and still can remember it with absolute clarity: the great hall all lit up with torches, and rapt pale faces of the fellows—some professors, too—all looking up at him as if he were an emperor. His own unfeigned astonishment as Brutus—a fellow-student with whom he had spent many a happy hour debating translations of Catullus—embraced him, roughly kissing his lips as he thrust the blunted dagger upwards into the dumbfounded flesh. Pressed chest to sweaty chest with the compact, muscular boy with only their bedsheets wrapped for togas between them, Polonius was glad he had only to gasp, "Et tu, Brute?" before the audacious blade split the bladder of blood secreted in his costume, and it burst.

He has told the tale, it is true—a thousand times or more. He has never told the tale, not to a soul.

Laertes will not be distracted from his purpose. "After all, it is nearly October already, and you know how soon the mountain roads become impassable with ice . . ."

"I know it." He can feel the ice coming in his bones, and worse every winter: an ache that starts subtle as hunger, but soon grows ravenous.

"Even now, it might take weeks to travel to Paris."

"Aye," Polonius agrees. "Or, indeed anywhere too far inland." The fur-lined robe feels as heavy on his shoulders as steel, and as susceptible to cold. Pushing back from the desk, he rises, ignoring the twinge of protestation from his joints. The radius of warmth before the fire helps a little; it beats back the most maddening pain, at least, which might drive a man to desperate acts. Rubbing his throbbing hands together, he glances at the mounted map of Denmark hung above the hearth, its edges dark with soot and grime. "And weeks more to return again, once the message had arrived."

"What do you mean? What message?" Laertes jumps up from his perch upon his father's desk and crosses to his side, folding his broad arms across his chest. "I am no longer a child, to be put off with riddles."

It is true: the man beside him is a mountain; Polonius has to crane his neck to look him in the face. Nodding, he motions his son to a pair of squat square armchairs set beside the fire, with a low table laid between for chess.

"You know King Hamlet has been unwell of late. Since returning from his last campaign, he passes nearly every afternoon asleep in his orchard." Suddenly afraid of eavesdroppers, Polonius peers through the squint in the door to ensure that the hallway is deserted. Then, shuffling the perimeter of the study, he pulls back each heavy woolen tapestry, checking the draughty dark corridor, wide enough to conceal a man, between the hangings and the damp stone wall.

"And I am sorry for it." Smirking at all this secrecy, Laertes toys with a carved ivory knight. "But what can my remaining here in Denmark do for him?"

"Not for him, my boy—for yourself!" Finally satisfied that they are alone, Polonius takes his seat, clasping his son's knee with a crooked talon. "For my father and my two lost brothers. For my own forgotten name. For your mother—may her poor, cracked soul find rest."

Laertes gives a start. Mother is never, never mentioned, not since she was sent away into the nunnery. His father could not have sobered him to his purpose more quickly had he invoked the Holy Virgin's name. Releasing the chess piece, he leans forward, suddenly intent.

"Of my life before I came to Elsinore, I have told you little."

"Only that you came here as an ambassador, after the war. The Polish territories, wasn't it?"

His father nods. *"It is true, I came from Poland. I was . . ."* He does not know what word to use: this language is all wrong, and offers only imperfect translations. *"I was a prince in Poland, actually."*

"Why, father—you never told me that!"

Polonius shakes his head, looking down into his empty hands. *"It was a small principality: a city. Not even a city. A town. Some scattered farms around. No one cared much about it, except as land to flatten in pursuit of something else."* Polonius shrugs. *"And I was never even meant to inherit the throne. Nothing of the sort. I was the youngest son, and the least inclined to politics. My elder brothers were educated in military strategy, foreign affairs, history, diplomacy—and fencing, for when those strategies all fail. In those other studies befitting a leader as well: rhetoric and psychology, the art of winning the voice of the people by feeding them promises.*

"I was called home from school when my father fell ill. He was moon-struck—his mind would come and go. He did not recognize his closest advisors, and mistrusted everything he was told. He was unable to govern as he had once done. Behind his back, my two brothers quarreled over the land, dividing and redividing his kingdom between themselves before they had inherited it. The church called for one to rule, my father's councilors supported another; and Denmark took advantage of the confusion to declare war."

Laertes nods in recognition. *"I have studied this—but in our history, King Hamlet was described as liberator of the Poles."*

Polonius shrugs. "He liberated many from their lives. My eldest brother rode out at the head of our defenses, and was killed in the very first battle. Then my second brother took his place leading our armies, and he, too, was killed.

"My father begged me not to join the fighting. In the army there was already talk of mutiny, widespread desertion. In some villages, no men were left alive between seventeen and seventy, and mothers wailed when they saw the flags of our armies approaching, knowing we would be leaving with their boys even of fourteen, fifteen, decked in the armor of the dead.

"But I rode out, cocksure, intending, as protagonist, to lead my men to certain victory. I fancied myself a hero, because I had played mighty Caesar on the stage." He chuckles, sadly. "Though, in truth, I have never been so very different from the way I am now. My only battlefields were paper ones. What appeared on the map to be a secure position—a mountain at our backs!—instead proved to be a valley surrounded by sloping hills. The site I had chosen for our camp was a dry streambed!" His mouth twists wryly, and he leaves a comedian's beat, before adding: "Well—dry until it rained. Then it froze."

"Dawn broke on a night without a wink of sleep among the men. It was a cloudless morning, bitter cold. Bitter beautiful, as well—a sheet of ice spread out as far as the eye could see. Every bleak barren tree limb was silvered with icicles, catching all the colors of the sun in dazzling array. We were surrounded by the largest diamond in the world."

Closing his eyes, he makes an airy noise, not quite a sigh, not quite a laugh. "We were also, as it turned out, surrounded by the enemy. I had no business putting us there. It was—" He shakes his head. His voice is so rough that it pains his throat to speak: "It was indefensible.

"They had the advantage of height on us, and the rising sun in our eyes. Our armor was by then all rusted stiff, and neither men nor horses could keep their footing. We could not feel the weapons in our hands, nor the hands that held them." He kneads his thumbs deep into his palms, as if to warm them were a thing impossible to dream. "Men died, and their blood froze solid on the ice. Horses died, and their blood and the sweat on their flanks and the white foam blowing out their nostrils all froze solid on the ice.

"I called a parley." He closes his eyes. "I sent up the white flags and hitched up a sled to carry me over the ice to where the king was waiting with his men. And for the rest of my life, however long, I will remember his face—every icicle in his sable beard—as he raised his beaver up, and with his sneer smote the final blow.

"'So, Polack,' he says, 'How much for your kingdom?' And then he begins to laugh, and all his lieutenants and signet-bearers and scribes begin to laugh."

"How did you answer?" Laertes is hardly breathing.

Polonius sighs. "I looked over the battlefield, at boys not half your age, in too-large armor, their last childish tears for their mothers and fathers gone solid still in their eyes. I thought of the frostbitten and wounded and hungry of my men who yet survived. I thought of my own fallen brothers, and my father dying in his bed at home. And I thought: what is a kingdom, anyway? Does the land know who is its king? Do its trees or fields, horses or cows? Do its chickens and ducks and cabbages? Do its people, even? Does it matter what name they cheer in parades when the trumpets sound and a suit of polished armor passes by?

"So I removed my helmet—for it was my only hat—and I said: 'It is yours, my liege, as I am yours and everything of mine is sworn unto your service.'

"So we rode together through the city, I at King Hamlet's side, shame burning through me mile after mile. And wherever we went, the people lowered their flags and fell silent, and we told them they were not Poles now but Danes. My father, seeing banners of the enemy's colors advancing on the capital, believed all his sons now dead, and with no more cause to absent himself from his last reward, took the dram of poison he kept locked in his private safe for just such an occasion."

"Oh, father!" Laertes stands and tries to take his hand; but Polonius is in another world and pays him no attention.

"Soon enough, we come to the gates of the castle. King Hamlet turns to me and says, 'So, Polack—How much for your castle, for lodgings for me and my men? How much for bread and ale and meat, to fill our bellysful?'

"And I bowed to him, quite deep, and said 'It is yours, my liege, as I am yours and everything of mine is pledged unto your service.'

"So the gates were thrown open to receive them. King Hamlet marched into the great hall and the blood of my brothers melted from his boots, staining the very carpets where they had first learned to crawl. His soldiers roamed the halls like wild beasts, pissing in the fireplace and spitting on the floors. And if some French arras or similar fine tapestry attracted their eye, they would tear it right off the wall, and take it for their own.

"All the livestock was slaughtered to feed them, all the grain gone to bake their bread. While the supper was prepared, all the wood went to boil their bathwater. After they washed, Lord Hamlet and his lieutenants dressed in my father's and my brothers' clothes—though they insulted and made fun of them most thoroughly, for our short breeches and wide collared cloaks were not the same fashions they were accustomed to in Denmark.

"The gong was sounded for supper, and Lord Hamlet took my place at the head of the dining table, and all his men were seated according to rank down its sides, left and right. The gong sounded again, and my wife entered, taking her customary seat at the foot. And when the king saw my fair young bride—for she was just the age your sister is now, and was indeed her copy as well as her namesake: as fair and slender, with the same white bosom..." Here he arrests himself in his description, seeing that Laertes has begun to blush. "Et cetera. His eyes grew wide, and he forgot his hunger for bread and ale. He spoke thus to her: 'What is your name, nymph?'

"She answered him honestly, for she had learned neither art nor artifice: 'Aphelia, my lord.' (It is the Greek for 'innocence.')

"But Hamlet has no other language but his mother-tongue, and he misheard. 'Come here, Ophelia.' The Greek for 'succor.'

"Then he turns to me—for I was standing at his right, to serve. 'So, Polack,' he says, 'How much for your wife?'

"I felt a lump like a walnut in my throat. You see, we had been handfasted from childhood, and respecting her tender age, I had not yet shared her bed myself. But I knelt on the stone floor before him and bowed my head, tears choking my voice as I said: 'She is yours, my liege, as I am yours and everything of mine is pledged unto your service.'

"He reached for his sword. I closed my eyes, certain the breath aching in my lungs would be my last. I felt the weight of the blade on my shoulder, the itch of its razor-edge just tickling my throat. Then he raised the sword over my head, and said: 'And you, Polack, are my Lord Chamberlain.'"

Rising from the chair with no small effort, the Lord Chamberlain retreats to the cabinet where he keeps his remedies, not realizing until he attempts to work the tiny brass key in the lock just how badly his cramped fingers are shaking. At last, he manages to pour a dram of aqua vitae from the stoppered bottle into the pewter medicine cup, downing the liquor without tasting it. "I never broke him of the habit of calling me that," he adds, "though he Latinized it after a year or two to Lord Polonius." Almost a laugh he gives, almost a sigh. "The original Polish joke."

For a long moment, Laertes says nothing; and when he speaks at last, his voice is low and colorless. "You sold my mother, for your position?"

"Sold!?" Polonius slams the cabinet shut, turning the lock with an audible click. "Of course not. Have you learned nothing of politics at school? A wise courtier never sells anything, my boy. She was a gift!"

"A gift!"

"I gave him the droit de seigneur—the feudal lord's ancient right to the wedding night." Returning to his desk, Polonius puts on his spectacles and reads aloud from one of the yellowed documents piled there: ". . . that the firstborn might be of royal seed."

Laertes sits, his head held in his hands, fingers clutching his thick sable hair until he recognizes it at last. "The firstborn? Then—I am a bastard?"

"But the king's bastard, my boy!" Polonius crows. "And everyone on the council knows it, too! Well, everyone except the queen, of course. But there is nothing she can do about it, if young Hamlet be delayed on the road after his father's death. The council doesn't want to elect him anyway—too many rumors." Smoothing his beard, he smiles proudly at this. The news his man Reynaldo had returned from Wittenberg had been well-circulated by his agents in the court. "Unless another blood relation to the king is found to make a claim, the throne is yours. The constitution says nothing of legitimacy." He taps his finger to the relevant paragraph, nearly dancing with the joy of sharing his heroic plan at last. "Can you not see? Your mother was my Trojan horse. And you, my dear, delicious boy—you shall be my Ulysses!"

But Laertes will not share in his delight. He sits before the fire, stupefied, for once perfectly motionless. "What of Ophelia? Is she . . . ?"

"Impossible to know." No, not impossible. Aphelia had known—he is certain of it—and the knowledge had cracked her mind wide open. But this small certainty only opens the mystery wider. He himself has turned the question over in his head for years. Had Aphelia taken her newborn daughter down to the river that morning to drown her because the child wasn't her husband's, or because she was?

Laertes hides his face between his palms, folded together as if in some prayer. "But she has confessed to me she loves young Hamlet. She swore me to secrecy with the news. And I—more wretched—I encouraged her! She must be told the truth!"

"And does the prince return her love?" The Lord Chamberlain's eyebrows twitch with interest. "Perhaps it were better that she never knew. If she and the prince were to marry . . ."

The young man's nostrils open wide. "It would be an incestuous union!"

"Possibly incestuous." Polonius hushes him, hearing footsteps nearing in the hall. His own voice lowers to a rough, guttural whisper. "Besides, in royal families such things are often overlooked. First cousins, for example . . ."

"They would be brother and sister, not cousins!"

The footsteps in the hallway slow. Polonius flies to him and clamps a hand over his lips until the passageway is clear again. "If my campaign fails, and young Hamlet inherits the crown, she may be my only chance to see my grandchild on the throne of Denmark."

"Your grandchild . . . ?" His mouth contorts with disgust. "But it wouldn't be yours, would it? No more than she is really your daughter, or I your son. You are nobody's father!" But when he sees the old man's face, he bites his lip as though to catch the words again and swallow them.

"Nobody's father?" Bowing his head, Polonius runs his thumbs across his eyelashes. "No—do not deny it. It is no more than the truth. Only, allow me to relate one tale. For my daughter's birthday last, I gave her a gift: a fine Venetian bowl filled with floating cut violets to keep beside her bed at night, so that her dreams might evermore be sweet. And I told her the water in this basin was a holy water, taken from a nearby blessed brook that possessed a certain natural magic, and the blossoms might never wilt, so long as she was virtuous and bound for Heaven. Since that day, every night as she has slept, I have tiptoed into her bedchamber with a handful of fresh violets gathered from the orchard, to replace those withered during the day, that she might wake each morning to an ever-living bouquet." He raises his head to the young man now kneeling at his feet. "Tell me—is this small deception wrong?"

"Of course not, father."

He turns away, pawing the air with his hand. "Do not call me that. I am nobody's father," he says. "You are right—I am only a foolish fond old man. And yet, I have loved my children, who are not my children."

"Of course we are your children," Laertes chides. "You named me for the Odyssey. Remember, your favorite scene? The one where the hero finally returns to Ithaca, and only his old, blind father recognizes his face, by the touch? It always made you weep. And then you would turn to me and ruffle my hair—and do you remember what you would always say?" He does a perfect imitation of the old man's voice. " 'You see, my boy, it is also a wise father…' "

Raising up his eyes, Polonius sees the tilt of his own father's head in Laertes's head, and knows it is the affect of his own as well. He hears his father's voice, answering: "It is also a wise father who knows his own child."

Taking his son's face into his hands, he kisses the smooth hot brow, anointing it with the salt tears still dampening his cheeks. "We shall discourage her infatuation. I will tell her Prince Hamlet is beyond her star; and you remind her of the inconstancy of young men's hearts. But grant me this boon: do not say anything of this matter to her. Allow me to die without having to endure that look in my daughter's eyes that I now do perceive in yours."

"There is no such look, Father," Laertes insists. "I swear, there is no change in my affections, nor in my duty to your lordship." He kisses his father's hand and gives a deep bow before departing.

After he has gone, the Lord Chamberlain sits for a long time at his desk, toying with his set of coin scales—not measuring out any currency, but only weighing down first one side, then the other, watching as they tilt and swing and come into a balance once again. He does his best for his children. He tries to give them good advice, even if he cannot always follow it himself. Moral rectitude he considers as a luxury item—one he knows he cannot afford for his own use, but still hopes to provide to future generations.

So: he might forbid his daughter to marry young Hamlet, and never allow the prince private access to her. And if their friendship grew too intimate, he might always intervene; his daughter would obey.

But what if he should die unexpectedly? He had seen it happen many times—a parent's will defied even before his body was in the grave. What if she and the prince were to elope in secret, before Laertes could reach her with the warning? He must take pains to ensure she understands the gravity of the matter, should he die before seeing her safely married off to someone else.

Dipping his pen into the ink, he addresses a letter to his daughter.

We know what we are, but not what we may be, he begins, then pauses, scratching at his snow-white beard. She might yet be his daughter, after all. His pate, though flaxen now with age, was fair even before. But she was so like her poor mother, it was impossible to tell she had been fathered at all. But it is a false steward, that steals his master's daughter to call his own, and so I must with heavy heart confess . . .

Continuing in this vein for no more than three or four pages, he breaks to her, as gently as possible, the circumstances of her parentage, warning her not to bestow upon young Hamlet any more attention than would be sisterly. Signing it "May God be at your table," he seals the letter and places it in his safe, marked with a note indicating that it is to be given to Ophelia in the event of his death.

Before he locks the safe, he feels in the back, past the stacks of coins and rolled parchments until he finds a little crystal vial, kept here as long as he can remember, against just such an occasion. He cradles it in his palm for a long moment before slipping it carefully into his purse. Then he rings the bell to summon his servant, Reynaldo.

The sleepy-eyed lad arrives late, and disheveled as usual. He has only one talent, and that is in remembering his instructions to the letter without understanding a whit of their intent. This alone makes him an exceedingly valuable servant, if occasionally maddening to instruct.

"Where is the king?" Polonius demands at once.

The simple boy blinks in confusion, murmuring a word in Spanish that Polonius does not understand. "Sleeping, my lord," he translates, letting slip a yawn.

"In bed?"

"In the orchard, my lord. But he has given word that no one is to disturb him there."

"Excellent," Polonius answers. He fetches his hooded cloak from its perch upon the wall; there is a chill of winter in the air. "For I have at hand a private matter, for his ear alone."

White Mountains and Ivory Towers

 After the midweek lecture, the boys discharged themselves from the hall, thundering through the wide oak doors before the noonday bells had finished tolling.

I gathered up my notes, and was taking up the rag to clean the slate when a gentle tapping interrupted me. Nobody ever knocked at the doors to the public lecture halls, so I dismissed the noise as my imagination.

A creak as the door inched open. "Master Horatio?" whispered a distantly familiar voice.

"Come in, come in," I urged, scanning the rows of seats for the satchel or penner, or slate sketched with caricature of myself that the timid student had forgotten.

But the gentleman who entered wore no scholar's gown. His suit alone could have granted favors. In his sword-belt, worn generously wide, a sturdy rapier swung from one hip, his dagger strapped to the other.

My stomach sank into the cold stone floor.

It is too late, I wanted to say. *Too late. I have already been punished beyond all reckoning. I have no heart left to cut out; your pound of flesh has already been taken.*

With uncharacteristic reticence, the Baron de Maricourt advanced into the hall. "The . . . schoolmaster in red said I might find you here," he offered, as if this detail did all to explain his unexpected visit.

But of course, there was no need to explain. What other reason might he have for seeking me out, but one? He had discovered everything, and come to take bloody revenge for the defilement of his wife and property. Worse, from the sound of things, he had already informed the dean of my sins.

"Are you alone?" he asked.

"Utterly." I wanted to jump in a piece out of my skin, but settled for breaking into a sweat. I was going to die. I was going to die, and I was going to lose my scholarship.

The baron cast a wary eye over the hieroglyphics of angles and signs still scrawled on the slate behind me —an academic obfuscation of a phenomenon anyone could crane his neck to see with his own eyes, barring cloudy weather.

"I would have summoned you to the house—but, you understand, this is a private matter." He cleared his throat again. "Ahem . . . er, yes, I think, a private matter."

I nodded. This was not precisely how I had imagined this scenario unfolding. For one thing, the baron had not yet raised his voice, much less his sword. This was all the more disconcerting, for it gave me hope that he might know nothing. In which case I should try to act as normal as possible. Unless he knew all, in which case a coy reply might spur him into a murderous rage.

Opening his purse, he removed a sheet of stationery, folded twice but yet unsealed.

"I need your services, to, ah—translate the letters for me into words. My eyes, you know. Usually, I would have Adriane to the task, but, er—"

I could not help my flesh; even at the sound of her name it rose, trumpeting its most triumphant point: she had been mine. I quickly moved to place the base of the lectern between the baron and myself.

"Can I trust you?" he demanded of me suddenly. Capon and onions on his breath, and ale; he was that close.

"My lord?"

"Your discretion. That you must never reveal what I am about to show you—or anything of our conversation here."

"Oh!" I gasped. "Why, of course. I swear I'll not speak a word of it to a soul. I swear by my . . . by my book." I rested my hand on the leather-bound journal, my book of poems. I had taken to carrying my lecture notes in it, enjoying the way its skin smacked down against the lectern, calling the class to order as effectively as the striking of a drum. It was not a Bible, but the baron would never have known the difference by my reverence.

He appeared mollified by this, and went on. "My wife Adriane has always been shrewish and stubborn. But now I have evidence to suggest some rogue has stolen in, and"—he cleared out his throat—"er . . . *done my office*."

His voice, a guttural basso growl, did not echo off the bare stone walls. I felt my own gut start to shudder to the same airless frequency.

"Know you his name?" I blurted out at a squeak.

But of course he did not—this was what he had come to me about. The baron set the letter on the lectern and edged it forwards with his fingertips.

"I believe this note is from the . . . ah . . . suspected. Adriane tried to hide it from me this morning, then became a good bit cross when I confronted her. But when she went out to the dressmaker's, I went upstairs, and there it was, on her little cherrywood table . . ."

I unfolded the pages, wondering if it would indeed be from Hamlet. My blood gave leap to recognize the familiar handwriting.

"This is not written by any man, my lord." In this, at least, I knew her more intimately even than her husband, for I could never mistake her hand. Firm in the downward strokes, faint in the finials, so that her capitals stood like tall towers capped in clouds, distant spires of castles in the air. "It is the writing of . . . of the lady herself." I could not speak her name without betraying myself. I wondered if I had admitted too much already.

"Well, hurry up, man—tell me what it says!"

Licking my cracked lips, I began to read:

Hail to my Roamed Heart,

"Aye, 'roamed' it has, away from its own right and proper home!" the baron scoffed. "Go on."

Love, forgive me for the cruel trick I played. Or else do not, and rail upon me every insult your wit can conjure to my injury; but come. Your words I love to hear, even your tirades against us (for, while you might revile one man or another individually, a woman, in your mind, is always representative of her entire sex).

Know I was never false of heart, though at times my tongue spoke something else than truth. There is only one I hate—

Here I was forced to turn the page. I found my hands shaking for fear that my own name would there appear, damned by her disdain.

—not you—but the other, my rival for your attentions, whom you loved so easily, and from whom I was forced to trick your heart bit by bit, by hook or crook.

"Aha! So he is married!" The baron paced while I read the lines. "That is a clue. They always have a wife tucked away somewhere in the country." So fixed was he on his view of his wife as innocent victim, he did not even seem to hear her plain confession.

Privately, I considered my own interpretation. Obviously the two she meant were Hamlet and myself, and our encounter in her bed had been a ruse to drive us two apart. Well, it had worked in that. If I had not lost Hamlet's love before, certainly my unkind abuse in the library had served the purpose.

I considered the problem. One of these men—the one for whom the letter was intended—she loved truly; while the other she despised, and had only pretended to adore. But which was which? Had Adriane tricked my attentions away from the prince? Or had she bargained Hamlet, verse by verse, from me?

As I read the next line, my blood flared up, and I wished I might know for certain that the letter had been meant for me.

Come to my bed tonight, after sundown, in the second dark. I will wait for you.

"Go on," the baron said impatiently. "What else?"

I shook my head. "That is all, my lord, aside from her signature."

"Nay, there is another bit there, under your thumb."

Reluctantly, I consented to read the postscript:

Think not of my husband, close as his watch may be over us. I have
the means already on my person to strike him deaf and dumb long
enough for our purposes. He suspects nothing of the truth, though I
arrange for my messages to be delivered right under his nose.

"Oho! So thinks she," sputtered the accused, his face gone crimson to the jowls. "Why—does she mean to drug me into swinish sleep with some foul limbeck?"

"It would seem so, my lord." Of course she already had the means—the same potion of siren tears she had used to seduce the prince. I wondered if her apothecary gave her a discount on it, she purchased in such volume.

"Well, I have caught her this time. Aye, and the fornicator as well. It is that scoundrel Will Swash-buckle—I am sure of it."

"Shake-spear," I corrected him. "Aye, but which one?" I covered this odd slip with, "I mean, what sort of man is he, this Shake-spear? A prince? A pauper?"

"A presumptuous jackdaw!" crowed the cuckold. "And I will make certain everyone knows it, as well."

"But how do you hope to catch him, if you do not know who he is?" I reasoned. "Where he lives, where he is from, with whom he associates?" I folded the letter up again, careful to match it back into the original creases. "Tell me—will the lady have missed this yet?"

"I think not." The baron frowned. "She is with the seamstress this afternoon, having all her winter gowns let out. I do not expect her home for another hour, at the least."

"Excellent." I passed the folded note back to him. "You must return this at once to her desk, removing from there all sign that anything has been disturbed. When she returns, give no sign through look nor word that you have any speck of doubt in her." On the other hand, this was just as like to rouse her suspicions. "Nor seem too solicitous, neither," I amended, "but behave in all ways as you normally would. She must not have any suspicion that her plan has been discovered until the messenger has been sent with the letter."

This would be the only way I could know whether the letter was meant for me, and thus if I had been the miserable stooge, damned by her hate, or the lover saved by her pardon with the aside: —*not you*—.

The baron nodded eagerly. "And should I track the messenger to see where he delivers it?"

"No, my lord!" I imagined that lifesaving "not you" split by the baron's bodkin. I would die happy, yes—but, still. "That is, he will likely have been advised to watch out for anything of the sort, and pretend ignorance if accused. It is vital that the letter be delivered to the one for whom it was intended, and that he keep the appointment tonight. Else you have no proof. Even a letter such as this does not prove guilt, but only opportunity." I dismissed it with a gesture. "It is worthless. It is not enough to convict a man, not without a name attached." I had read only a little law, in fact, but it was just enough to sway a man who had read none at all. "You must catch him in the act."

"In the . . . ? Good lord, you do not mean . . ."

I nodded, assuming a sagacity I did not possess. "Or at least in sufficient trespass on your property to force a confession from him. Else the law is not on your side to cry him out a sinner. Not without witness. I would not even bother to confront her, unless you can catch the man yourself. It would only alert her to your suspicions."

I would wait, then, to receive the letter, and stay well clear of her bed tonight. When the baron came to catch his prey in the trap, Adriane would play innocent, and the only proof, the letter itself, would be safe in my possession.

And if the letter did not arrive?

It would be a blow, indeed, to know I was hated by those whom I had loved most dearly. Still, I would at least have my revenge on the two who had betrayed me. Their affair would be ended, and Hamlet and Adriane both publicly humiliated.

"Tonight, then," the baron said. "Not too soon, I think. At cock's crow. That should give him sufficient time before sunrise to dress."

"To dress, my lord?"

"Of course, to dress! I would not have it said I slew a naked man." He was pacing out his plan before the board, as though delivering a lecture to the empty benches. "To dress, to drink a dram of ale—and of course to choose his weapon."

I blinked at him. "His weapon?"

"For the duel, of course! The Spanish swords, I think. They

are not so fashionable anymore as the rapiers, yet this might work to my advantage. A younger gentleman will be practiced in rapier and dagger, but perhaps not have the arm on him for the heavier instrument. Besides, the pair in my armory are engraved with a dedication from the archduke." He looked up, well cheered. "Ah, Master Horatio, I cannot thank you enough for your invaluable assistance in this. You will be my second, of course?"

I suddenly remembered the prince's most-feared prophecy, of dying in a duel at the age of thirty. I had poked fun at his superstitions; but now the forecast did not seem so farfetched.

"I would bring you ill luck," I stammered. "I cannot abide the sight of blood."

"Ah, a swooner." The baron nodded. "I suspected as much." He looked around at the empty benches, the cold ivory sunlight coming down through the narrow windowpanes in pillars. "No, I don't expect as you would ever see much blood in a place like this."

After he had gone, I returned to my room and forced myself to wait an hour by the slow crawl of my watch before beginning to anticipate the arrival of the letter. I did not even dare to go down to the dining hall in case I missed the messenger, but instead satisfied my stomach on a stale roll, pocketed the day before.

I mixed up some ink and tried for a while to write a sonnet about my situation; but I could hardly conjure up a plausible argument for stealing the mistress of my dearest friend when all my

writing heretofore had been all anguish at him for the same offense.

I kept arriving at the same conclusion: I had behaved no better
in this than he, and should forgive. But could this mercy then be
used to argue his forgiveness in return? Was love a chip that could
be traded, bargained, owed, demanded as a debt?

I wrote in this vein for a while, but in my heart, I knew that
love, like war, was not a null-sum game. A soldier might deliver
blows to his opponent equal to those suffered, but his injuries
were not by this erased, and both were left with scars.

The light changed color and began to fade, and still no messenger. I wrote until the words could no longer be discerned upon
the page, then lay on my bed and stared at the blank stone wall.

Perhaps the baron had altered his plan, preferring to subject
the letter to further analysis.

Or perhaps he had not been able to return it without arousing
Adriane's suspicions, and so she had put off the assignation with
her lover to another night.

But even as I invented these excuses, I knew the truth. Prince
Hamlet had received the call, and Prince Hamlet would accept
it. Prince Hamlet would be discovered to all, and Prince Hamlet
would die in a duel. And whatever satisfaction I had thought to
have in vengeance, I found a joyless, pyrrhic victory.

Ex Machina

I was dozing, long run out of hope, when the knock at last came at my door. Still half-conscious, and walking on needles, I leapt out of bed to receive Adriane's messenger.

But it was only a fellow from the college, coming to remind me of the gathering to observe the lunar eclipse through the new device: an innovation contrived by a local optician, after a theory proposed by that precocious Italian astronomer, Galilei.

At any other time, I would have been honored to be included in such a gathering, but at present I was hardly convivial. However, too dispirited to invent an excuse, I allowed myself to be cajoled into joining my colleagues at the observatory tower atop the Castle Church.

My ill spirits were little noted in this convocation, or else were counted among the many severe and peculiar reactions to the spying-glass. One scholar sat with his head in his hands, moaning about a life's-work of painstaking calculations and careful theories made at once obsolete. Some spoke together in hushed and reverent tones of New Worlds opened, Indias that were neither of West nor East. Many wept, including several silver-bearded emeritus astronomers (one of whom, peering through the narrow tube of the device, gave a cry and reached out his hand, like a babe, to try to touch the moon).

As the most junior present, I took the last turn on the astronomer's magical device. By then, the eclipse had nearly reached totality. Only a sliver of the moon remained; the rest was stained the color of old blood.

Alone in the observatory tower, the highest point of all the City, and given for a quarter of an hour the sudden power to examine anything I liked, I found myself training my aided eye not on the heavens, but upon the house of Denmark.

Above the embassy, I saw the prince's windows, dark and shuttered, near as if I had been standing beneath the willow in the yard. My heart raced, and I checked my watch, to the approval of the observing methodologists. Hamlet never went to bed this early. He must, therefore, be out. Still, this did not conclusively indicate that he had gone to her.

Raising the glass to my eye again, I sought out the baron's manor in the shadowy gardens of the gentlemen's estates that bordered 'round the City like a wreath. I could not see her window, but a tiny flicker of light twinkled there, too low to be a star.

It was too late already. And, if the prince was right and all our fates were preordained, it had always been too late. It was written in the stars; in this very eclipse of the most fluid and inconstant of heavenly creatures, the moon. Hamlet, Prince of Denmark, would be killed in a duel, and by poison as well: the venomous conspiracy of his sworn-truest friend.

But what was the point of this foretelling, unless such an augury might be defied? I had seen such tales played on the stage. True, the gods, in such instances, always punished those who interfered, in terrifying, pitiable ways. The history of literature as well as the literature of history suggested Fate could not be circumvented entirely, but only postponed, and such attempts inevitably led to tragedy.

Still, I thought, the hero always tried.

I found the prince's horse first, tethered to a chestnut tree just outside the baron's walls. Untying the Barbary, I tugged uselessly at the lead for a few frustrating minutes before remembering the bag of sugar.

At last the horse consented to be bribed and coaxed through the gap in the wall and into the courtyard, where with a series of frantic gestures, I directed the stallion to stand underneath the balcony.

The rope ladder was gone. The prince must have pulled it after him. I cursed. A fine time for him suddenly to have remembered caution! The candle-lantern in the window was melted half away, and inside I could see the orange glow of firelight.

"Halt!" I commanded the horse. "Stay! Oh, for heaven's sake, stand still." I reinforced this order with another sugar-lump, then scrambled to a stand atop the saddle. From this wobbly four-legged stool, I began to climb the wall freehand, clutching at woody rose canes for support. The thorns tore through my clothes and scratched my skin, and I clawed back at them, finding chinks and notches in the stone. A chunk of mortar crumbled under my insistent toe, rattling down the wall.

"Who's there?" A hoarse stage-whisper came down from the balcony.

I froze. In fact, I hardly had a choice; I was stuck halfway up the wall without sufficient toehold either to advance position or retreat, and hooked on brambles six different ways.

"A friend," I answered, in a position to be nobody's foe.

A hand reached down to grab me at the elbow; in a moment, I was hoist from the thorns, to a great protestation of tearing cloth. Catching my breath on the balcony, I discovered I was holding the prince's right arm.

"What—is it Horatio?" Hamlet was in his undershirt and breeches yet. The hammock-ladder lay in a haphazard pile at our feet. He must have only just arrived himself.

"Pieces of him." I surveyed my former best, now badly tattered, hose. My legs were scratched and stinging from the prick of thorns, though as far as I could tell, nothing was bleeding. "You must quit this place at once, my lord."

"Whatever is the matter?" Hamlet peered out into the courtyard, his towhead bare and visible as ever in the swiftly waxing moonlight as the eclipse passed over. "Is that my horse?"

But when I opened my mouth to explain about the baron's discovery, the duel planned at dawn, I found myself struck mute. I had been sworn to silence on the subject by Lord Maricourt. Absurd that I should feel loyalty now to one I had cuckolded so many times before. But my loyalties were more than to the baron—I had sworn on my book, which was as much as swearing by the prince's name. I would not—nay, I *could* not—break my word.

"I cannot be more plain, my lord," I said. "But you must trust me. Hear my advice, and refrain tonight." I began to uncoil the ladder, but the ropes were badly tangled.

Hamlet stood watching me, arms folded across his chest. "Now I see how goes the game. This is some trick, some bed-trick. You intend to take my place tonight and win your mistress back."

"Oh, my sweet lord—"

"Then you deny that you love Adriane?"

"I do deny it." But my flesh gave another answer for me. What a time for it to respond to the sound of her name! What could I call it but "love," the baseless thing that made my own most base thing rise and fall at this particular noise, this simple collection of syllables? I would always love her—assuming as a definition of "love" the swift demonstration of my sexual desire.

The prince chuckled in triumph. "Horatio, had you anything worth gambling, I'd invite you to play at cards. You are a terrible liar."

He started to the doorway, but I caught his arm and would not let him pass.

"Alas, 'tis true. I am of liars the most terrible. I have looked on truth askance and strangely—swore that foul was fair and fair despised. I vowed I would not praise your qualities to sell, for fear of being thought another hired sycophant. Then I gored these very thoughts and whored them out for cheap to serve another, though these memories of you were my most valuable possessions—aye, and my dearest, too.

"But all these lines were lies, my lord, that I ever wrote. Even those that said I could not love you any dearer. For when I began to write your praises, I thought you perfect, and so believed that my esteem, thus peaked, could only decline—for Time erodes all perfect things.

"But neither the king's decree, nor any of the million . . ." I at last drew breath, searching for the right word to describe all our mutual deceptions and infidelities, "*accidents* . . . that crept in twixt our vows have changed my love. True, I have been a fool, and of my own design. But though my actions seemed to qualify, know I was never false of heart." I begged him: "Hear my warning now."

For just a moment, Hamlet hesitated. "My heart has felt a prophecy of dread about this night."

"Then heed it, my lord, if you will not heed me."

I hung the ladder from its hooks and threw it over the wall; as twisted and knotty as it was, it was better than nothing.

"Then come with me," Hamlet pleaded.

Somewhere near the stables, I heard a dog begin to bark, then another. The baron's hounds.

"Spare the horse my weight," I told him. "But do not spare the spurs. Go now, and I will follow straightaway."

"Promise you will."

"I will, my lord."

"Swear it!"

"I will follow you." I rose my hand, though I had nothing to swear on but the prince's hand in mine. *"Hic et Ubique."*

At last, he leapt down to his waiting mount; then with a whistle, he was gone, leaving no trace but a neat black trail of hoofprints in the frost.

I started down the ladder after him. But as I turned, I caught sight of a dark figure silhouetted in the open door.

Of course she was there. I did not know how long she had been watching us, or what she managed to overhear. It made no difference. How could I have hoped for an entire conversation, even a single private thought in my own head? She would always be there, watching me, analyzing my every word for meanings, meant and unintentional. I wondered if she ever would ever uncover everything. Was it even possible?

She was naked despite the chill of winter in the air. In what must have been, I thought, a trick of light, her bare breasts looked enormous, watching me like round unblinking eyes. Pubic hair spread up her belly in a grinning mouth. I could not see her true face in this light.

"Aye, hurry away, before my husband catches you here," she said. "But do not go to the prince. Pursue your studies; take vows at a monastery; travel anywhere else in the world it pleases you to be. But to follow Denmark is to follow death."

I knew I should ignore her. "I have already taken vows," I said. "I am confined to him. He is my cloister. And what fear have I from death, who live already in Heaven: in his heart of hearts, in his most loving breast?"

She smiled, cruelly, but not without affection. "Do you hear the hounds baying?" she said. "It is already too late. My husband is a huntsman, and his dogs only raise such howl when they have caught the scent. They will follow Hamlet back to his front door." She shrugged, showing her hind-side as she turned. "True, they are bred to tracking venison—but a horse is not so different from a hart." She smiled at me over her shoulder. "Both are worthless until they have been broken."

At last, I understood: She had plotted all of this. She had enlisted me not to destroy Hamlet, but to destruct him, piece by piece, so she would know how he might be lured into her trap. Only someone who loved the prince with all his being could learn him well enough to satisfy her.

But in my love of the prince, there was an inherent contradiction. He valued me for my skepticism, the counsel of my rational mind, which might serve as a check to his own when it strayed too far to fancy. But I valued him with all in me that was irrational, illogical, devout. My loyalty to him depended on the willing suspension of all my good sense and sanity.

Suddenly, I knew what must be done—or undone—now. Quickly, I doffed my cap and began unfastening my belt, following her through the doors into her bedchamber.

"What are you doing?" Adriane hissed at me. For the first time, she sounded surprised. "Are you mad?" At least, this is what I thought she said; my heart was tick-tocking so loud I could not hear anything else above it, not even the voice of my own better judgment.

"If your husband catches a lover here, he will have no cause to call out his dogs after another. I will take the prince's place, and fight the duel."

I struggled out of my doublet and undershirt together, the former still half-buttoned. It was like peeling back a scab, shedding an itchy sunburn, so sharp was the cold air on my skin. Stepping out of my shoes, I slipped into the bed, awaiting my destiny.

I knew with certainty that I would lose this battle. This struck me no more personally than any other immutable fact. This was a fight fated to be lost, and fatally, by whoever took up arms. I would die. It was so, because it must be so. I had chosen it myself, and this made me feel a bit better about dying, somehow. Though not about the dull metallic clamor at the door: the noise of a lock protesting the assault of an insistent key.

•   •   •

Y ou?" The baron's face had gone violet with shock. "You?!?" He
rubbed his watery eyes. "Begging your pardon, lad, but I always
thought you were . . . ah . . . well . . . at home we had a bull . . ."
His voice wavered, then trailed off entirely into an uncertain clearing of the throat. "That is, you and that player fellow—the pale, ill-
humored one, who went around in frocks?—I always thought he
loved you." His tone to me was sorrowful, almost apologetic.

Had it been so obvious? Even an illiterate could read the language of the body and understand what a scholar had been unable
to uncover in months of study.

His shoulders slumped in disappointment. "I thought for sure
it would be that Shake-spear fellow. Was rather looking forward
to facing him, actually. I even heard it rumored he was some kind
of disguised prince. A great man—no offense intended."

His sword was still drawn and pointed at me, though in his
inattentive grasp, now aimed much lower than my heart. Not that
this was any better for my nerves.

Finally, Adriane donned her robe and intervened, setting her
hand upon his hilt, speaking in a low and soothing voice. "My lord
and husband, this poor bachelor has been conscripted, against his
will, to serve you with a priceless legacy."

"To serve me?"

Adriane nodded. "With an heir, my lord."

"An heir?" The baron and I spoke this together, for I was now
just as lost as the muddled cuckold.

The baron let fall his sword, not in a show of peace, but with the countenance more of a man bewildered out of his rage.

"Surely you of all men ever living understand—when the fruit of an orchard will not come true to seed, sometimes a graft is required from another tree." Taking her husband's arm, Adriane led him to sit at the bench before the virginals. "From fairest creatures we desire increase, a poet once wrote, and I have taken heed. I sought a man of rarest quality, who, because of some twist in his fate, would be unlikely ever to renounce his bachelorhood, and I enlisted him in collaboration to produce a child. He has stolen nothing of yours, and added to your holdings. This duty now completed, he may be discharged, with thanks."

Could this be just another lie? I wondered. But no—the moon tonight was full, as it must be, to be eclipsed. Her cycle, which then by my reckoning should also have been full, had been likewise eclipsed—and by my son?

"Of course," she continued, "for your reputation's sake, it would be wisest to keep the whole thing quiet, lest it be divulged that your heir is another man's bastard—and a common man's at that. A hired servant? They would make it out that you had purchased your title, and then purchased an heir to inherit it." Always she knew just which strings to pull.

"I would be made a laughingstock." He took a balled handkerchief from his sleeve and wiped his eyes. "And my son slandered with a bastard shame."

Adriane nodded, comforting him against her swollen breast.

Over his head, her eyebrows darted at me, advising me to take my clothes and run before he got over his shock and decided I was better off run through.

Slowly, afraid to call undue attention, I stepped into my breeches, pulling the doublet roughly over my head. But there was yet one question still unanswered. "But the child—is it . . ." I looked to the dark balcony, then back to her dark eyes. My lips mouthed soundlessly: *Hamlet's, or mine?*

Her face shone in the dying firelight: as pocked and flawed and perfect as the moon had been through the professors' scope. She looked on me with already nostalgic tenderness, as if treasuring the sight of my face for one last, fond moment before nodding: *Yes.*

Tales Told and Untold

He is no Dane. That much is clear enough. He is too slight, too dark, too unaccustomed to the sea. But from the way he stands aloft before dawn, clutching the rail, peering into the fog to catch a glimpse of the approaching shore, he looks for all the world like an anxious pilgrim returning home after long exile.

It was obvious from the sight of him that everything in the world he owned was in the satchel on his shoulder. The captain was surprised he'd offered up his watch before the schoolbook clutched under his arm. It was clearly worth more than the price of what he'd asked for: ordinary bunk and passage across the sound and up the coastline to the capital.

He was so desperate in his plea, the captain had accepted the trade, though he had no use for a portable clock. The ship kept sea-time and the sea kept its own time in tides. To have such a piece of work was like owning a beautifully drawn map to a coastless country, a book of poems written in a language he would never understand.

At eight bells (though the strange land-clock insists on chiming four) the mate relieves him for the morning watch, and the captain goes down to the bow deck to question the mysterious passenger. For all he knows, the man might be flying false colors—a spy, bearing in his scholar's skins a plot to bring down all the crowned heads of Denmark. He has caught wind of several of that sort crossing, of late: "students" traveling to and from the peninsula with unscholarly haste.

He has no sea-legs, of course. But this the captain does not hold against him. He would not admit it, but he himself is just as unsteady, when setting his feet on land. If one must be burdened with seasick passengers, he much prefers the ones who treat their illness aloft in the bracing air, to those who mewl and puke into their bunks like babes.

"Will it b-be m-much longer?"

The captain bristles a bit at the question; he is more used to compliments from passengers on his ship's speed across the sound. She draws less than two fathoms and can navigate the tiny bays and islands up the coast in half the time of a bloated galleon. Though she crews only a dozen fighting-men, the little pinnace can outrun any other pirate on the seas.

"An hour or so to anchor. Then we'll have to wait for the tides to turn." He would send the mate in the jolly-boat; no point in paying the port duty to put off a single passenger, especially one who was clearly in no position to remember favors. "Your first visit to Elsinore?"

"N-not a v-visit. I have c-come here to live."

The stranger, he notes, seems to suffer some sort of stutter—perhaps related to his palsy and unnatural bluish coloring.

The small craft travels swiftly through shoal waters. Doubled in the murky glass of the reflecting sound, the capitol soon emerges from a thumb-print on the sea, broad strokes suggesting wall and watchtower.

"A beautiful country, when the climate is fair," the captain allows. "On a clear day, you can see Sweden, across. Not in this fog."

"Is it . . . always . . . th-this c-cold?"

The captain stares at the traveler. "But sir, this is not yet even November!" he exclaims, genuinely taken aback. "Why, the wind does not even begin to cut its teeth before All Hallows' Eve!"

His salty laugh filled up the sails. Such a feckless dogsbody bore no threat to the crown, informer or not. It would be a miracle if he survived 'til spring.

⚘

Watching the castle draw near, I felt as though the sails were bearing me not towards the future, but away into some darker age. Hamlet had described his home as a prison, and indeed, there were few prisoners more heavily guarded than the royal house of Denmark. A tidal moat surrounded the castle grounds, setting it apart from the mainland on an island hill, the only escape into the sound. The hill appeared precarious; round as a beetle's back, it mushroomed out over its cliff-base, worn away by seawater.

Looking at the few windows and small dotting the fortress seat, I thought how gloomy the place must be inside, and how many terrible things might be imagined in the shadowy halls. Enough to make you willing to shed your own blood, just to see some color.

After escaping down Adriane's ladder in the dark, I had arrived at Hamlet's apartments to find every servant already awake and packing, the embassy in disarray. A harried housemaid informed me about the messenger arrived in the night from Denmark, a black band tied around his sleeve. The prince had departed at once, on horseback; no word left behind. The king, I supposed I should have to learn to say.

As the ship drew nearer, the endless creaking of the ropes and the sick slap and splash of the waves against the hull were joined by another sound, a terrible faraway moaning. Against the cliffs between the castle and the sea, the wind gave howl like a madhouse of mourners—a cry of tormented spirits, living or dead. Then, piercing the air, came a wail so plaintive and absurd it sounded more like the wounded hunted than the falconer: *Illo-ho-ho, hillo-ho-ho boy; come bird, come . . .*

At last I understood what I had done. This was no prison term of life. Hamlet had been condemned to Hades, and I had pledged to follow him into this underworld, even to the edge of doom, forevermore.

I bent over the rail and spilled black bile into the bile-black sea.

The graveyard was the oldest settled part of Elsinore, in an open stretch of rumpled ground between the seaport and the castle walls. At the bottom of the hill, the graves were mere dotted circles or long Viking-boats of charred stones, remnants of ancient crematory fires.

The ground rose rapidly, and soon I began to see these burial mounds replaced by rough-hewn stones with strange symbols cut into their faces. Many of these were overturned or cracked, with mosses sprung out their fissures or pushed up from underneath. There was no other sign of any living creature but the song of a blackbird, which in the eerie silence was peculiarly affecting.

As I neared the castle, my sense of scale was overwhelmed by the sheer size of the stone fortress. Massive ramparts towered above me, gun emplacements on a platform overlooking the sound. Cannons so large the blast from them would sound all the way to Norway.

The guard-house was unmanned, as was the platform. But a little ways away outside the gate, a man stained featureless with dirt was filling a gaping grave. As I neared, I could hear the man chattering to himself a bizarre and morbid monologue.

"There, that should keep you down," he said to the tenant of the grave, tamping down the cloddish dirt with the flat of the spade. "Knock, knock!" he shouted down to the corpse. "Naw, you cannot hear the likes of me, can you?" He laughed, obscenely. "Not even an I spoke Latin. Well, here's a good one, learnt me by a wise fool. Not wise enough to keep his head, acourse—there's none so clever as that, after the axe falls." With widely uncertain tune, he began to warble out a song with the refrain "*Nos habebit humus . . .*" all the while shoveling earth over his audience.

I recoiled from this callous display, but summoned the forces of reason to my side. Of course in his profession, the man had likely grown so accustomed to death, he had lost his sense of it—no more than the blacksmith felt the heat of the fire or the stable boy smelled horseshite. No more than I myself would feel the cold, soon enough, nor the sting of being ever left behind. I had to learn to be master to my passions, taking the blows and blessings of the prince with equal thanks. The king, I should say.

When the gravedigger saw me approaching, his face broke into a wide grin. His teeth were straight and strong and pearly white, all six of them.

"Are you a living man," he called out, "or a dead one?"

In all my studies of philosophy, I had never been posed this particular question. "Er . . . living, I think."

The gravedigger looked disappointed by this reply. Dismissing me with a swing of his arm, he returned to his work. "Master Bernardo of the Watch says if I see any more that's dead up and walking about, I'm to come and tell him right away. I stand to collect a jug of Rhenish for my trouble."

This seemed to me to be a self-perpetuating system, in which it was best not to interfere. "I have come from Wittenberg, to serve the crown," I offered. "I am a scholar."

I had decided this was a nicely nonspecific profession, for traveling. It sounded a better houseguest than "poet" (or, heaven forbid, "playwright")—quieter, less likely to drink up all his hosts' wine.

When the muddied man made no reply, I added: "I came to see the king's funeral."

"Well, you've missed his funeral." He loosed a shovel of earth into the grave, then looked up, brightening considerably. "You can see his wedding, though."

"Whose wedding?"

"Why, the king's!"

"But I thought . . . ?" I squinted at him, confused. "Oh, I see. You must mean the *new* king."

The servant merely shrugged, as much as to say a king was a king to him.

Well, this was news. Hamlet must have made far better time overland than predicted, to have arrived and been crowned already.

"And now he is to be married?" I could hardly believe the report. "When?"

"Why, for the rest of his life, sir—unless she goes first, acourse. Many a man enjoys a second bachelorhood, you know, and I've seen many a merry widow—though none ever before quite so quick about it as . . ."

"Yes, yes," I interrupted, before the man could develop his irrelevant tale any further, or break into song. "But when is the marriage to be performed?"

He scratched his head. "Why, they go before the priest tomorrow, sir."

"What, during mourning?" This was rather unusual—a wedding treading the heels of a death. Perhaps the prince—the new king, I should say—had inherited a tricky diplomatic situation, requiring a quick, politically expedient match.

"Aye, in the morning," the gravedigger agreed. "Luncheon banquet afterwards. Cold meats, I reckon—not many came to see the funeral, that was expected."

"And to whom is the king—the *new* king—to be married?"

"Why, to the queen, acourse!"

"Yes, of course," I said clench-jawed, my patience wearing thin. "The lady who marries the new *king* will be the new *queen*—but who is she now?"

The gravedigger looked puzzled by this line of reasoning. "The queen is the queen, sir," he explained, speaking as though I were a small child, and not a particularly bright one. "There's only just the one, you see."

"You do not mean he is to marry his own mother?"

But, of course, this was not *that* tragedy. His expression inquired after what sort of a place it might have been, that I had come from. "Certainly not, sir!" With a self-righteous nod, he staked his shovel down into the dirt. " 'Tis his sister he is marryin'."

I sighed. Clearly I was not going to get anywhere with this clown. "Perhaps you could show me where to find Master Bernardo?"

He looked unconvinced. "Er . . . beggin' yer pardon, sir . . ." His calloused fingers twitched toward my purse, "beggin' " something else.

Opening the calfskin pouch, I showed him that the weight in it was nothing but a stoppered inkhorn, a few split and fraying quills.

"I can give you something better," I offered. "A role."

"A loaf of bread?" he brightened.

"A part," I explained, "in the play I am to write."

He pawed at his scraggly chin, considering. "A play about a gravedigger . . . ?"

"Think of it—undying fame. Immortality."

The gravedigger shrugged; he would have had the bread. "Better'n nothing, I suppose."

Midnight. A platform before the castle. A night so dark you can hold a man's hand in yours and still not recognize his face. How true and sensible was the avouch of my own eyes, in such a state?

An apparition, they called it. Which is to say, the appearance of a thing, and not its self; which is to say an illusion, nothing more than fantasy. I would not let belief nor dread take hold of me.

But once we sat down on the icy stone to wait the hour, and Bernardo began to assail my ears with the tale, I found my eyes also strangely affected. They directed me to look to a certain star, burning so bright against the bottomless sky, until my eyes danced rings of green and indigo around it, and soon I began to believe I did see something illumined in that part of the heavens.

One of the Watch suggested it was the time of year when the walls between the worlds of men and ghosts are most permeable. Still, not until Bernardo suggested the spirit took the image of the dead king did I begin to reconcile the harrowing sight with a suit of armor I remembered, or a sneer.

I could not cross it, nor did the shade speak, though I charged it in Latin. I encouraged the guard to touch the shadow with his weapon, but the partizan passed right through it. Nor could we all agree where it was to be found. Here it was; then here; then it was gone. The illusion would not stay, no matter how I trained my eyes upon it.

I was trembling and pale, though not with cold, in the red-sky dawn. Fear and wonder raked their teeth through me. If I had only had with me the astronomers' spyglass, then I might be certain. But having seen the moon's face once with perfect clarity, how could I now trust the imperfect account of my unaided eye? I could not claim knowledge, only opinion.

It was not the king. The figure in the misted field was at most a thing like the king that's dead.

Most like.

Marcellus and Bernardo looked to me, awaiting my advice on whether to impart what we had seen tonight unto Hamlet. Upon my life, I knew his feverish imagination would hear speeches in the mist, though the spirit appear ever dumb to us. Neither love nor duty could compel me to acquaint him needlessly with a mote to trouble his mind's eye. The question hung before me. If I'd had a coin left to my name, I'd have tossed it.

"Let be," I decided at last. I gave a scientific rationale for it, involving dew in the high eastward hills resolving into mist under the mantle of the rising sun. " 'Tis nothing but illusion."

I only part believed it. But I would have only part believed it had I made the other choice.

❧

Gladdened by the unexpected arrival of his schoolfellow, Hamlet is persuaded at last to put off his mourning clothes. He yet grieves privately, but to humor his mother, he doffs his inky cloak and consents instead to suit himself in daylight blue.

When the queen sees the change wrought in her son's demeanor by the presence of one friend, she sends to Wittenberg for others, even engages a troupe of players he had sometimes mentioned in his letters. His uncle adopts him at once as his own son, and immediately grants the decree of succession the prince's own father had so long denied.

Because he is not out chasing spirits on the dawn of All Saint's Day, the prince is home to see a fair maid standing under his window. In his grief, he had forgotten the letters he had written to the Lord Chamberlain's daughter, the promises he had whispered once upon a time. She is clutching to her breast a bouquet of wildflowers. He calls down to her, and one by one, she names the flowers for him, hesitating when she comes to the long purples.

"I have heard these called dogs' cods by our crude shepherds," she admits, "but I do not know why."

For some reason, her blush provokes him. "Come up, and I will show you." He would shame and flatter her over and over, just to watch that excellent white bosom flush scarlet, then return again to its pristine condition. "Hoot like an owl at the door, and I will raise the latch to let you in."

She looks back over her shoulder. There is no one in the yard. "What if I am seen?"

"Scarf your shawl about your head," he bids. "They will say it was the baker's daughter." That enterprising wench sometimes earns a crumb or two of her own by paying evening visits to gentlemen in the court, and no guard nor servant ever questions her business.

So up she goes, undoes her clothes, and through a one-way door the maiden passes; Ophelia, wooden "O" upon which he lets play his destiny.

*T*he lovers endure such parental objections to marriage as have made for many a comedy; until at last Queen Gertrude intervenes, and with the punch line to a very old joke, discreetly explains to the affected parties why the betrothed can be no closer kin than cousins.

When his firstborn child is placed into Hamlet's hands, he is rendered speechless. An infant predisposed from every side to madness, melancholy, and ill-luck; there has never been a more perfect piece of work. What further answer could he seek, for any of his questions? A simple answer, to make a happy end.

But the only difference between Comedy and Tragedy is when the curtain falls. After the applause, Time keeps on its relentless march.

Polonius goes first, in bed; not a Caesar's death. A vial of odorless poison is clutched in his fist, and all his advice burnt to ashes in the fire. Ophelia mourns him, but it is not this loss but another that finally splits the fissures of her mind. An accident, an innocent reaching to grasp for his father's bare bodkin, then falling against it. The wound is hardly a scratch, but the toddling prince bleeds and bleeds as though his veins owed all the royal blood in

Elsinore. Ophelia never recovers from the child's death; she is sent away, to sing her lullabies under the care of ministering nuns.

Hamlet puts on his mourning clothes again. For how long does he grieve? Time has abandoned him. Each day drags like a fortnight. Music offers him no comfort, for then he is remembered of Ophelia's singing to the empty bundle of swaddling clothes.

Laertes turns his grief and fury against the enemy, re-enlists, and perishes on the blade of Fortinbras. The war with Norway never ends, despite periodic declarations of victory by one side or the other. The court falls into gloom.

Such unrelenting misery is tedious. After a month, two, four, Hamlet is so bored with grieving, he can scarcely remember any existence previous to it.

His mother comes to his bedroom, where he has closeted himself away. He thinks she has come to comfort him and turns his face to the wall, unwilling to receive her. But she does not comfort him. She sits at the foot of the bed and simply tells him, "All that lives must die."

Raising his head from his pillow, he understands her meaning: All that dies must live.

Gertrude lives, every moment up until the very last—her heart, the court physicians say, which was already weakened by a split. The king follows shortly after, drunken to distemper.

The Hamlet who inherits the throne is wiser if not so quick to wit as the cocksure prince who first returned from University. He understands more about people, and politics, and loss. He has learned the value of compromise. So there is something rotten in the state of Denmark. Something is rotten in every state: entropy; nature; matrimony; grace. Life is only possible amid continuous decay.

Rosencrantz and Guildenstern survive, though they drift apart after Rosencrantz inherits his title and returns to his father's estate. He marries a homily-spouting country wench who bullies and babies him as the biggest of their never-ending brood of fat-cheeked children. Guildenstern visits him at his country-house exactly once, returning to the City in less than a week. For a few years they meet to dine on occasion when Rosencrantz is in town, but soon no one would ever think to speak their names together.

Guildenstern remains at the Inns of Court, where he still trades in lies to keep up an existence of appearances. He falls seasonally in and out of favor, and is seen sometimes attending the theatre with a series of fair, foolish young men, each of whom he comes to loathe within a matter of weeks.

Hamlet grows old. Forty winters besiege his brow, which grows longer every spring, until it is as peaked and white as the Norwegian coast. His hose are too wide for his shrunk shank, and so he wears them rolled around his knees, as sagged as his old skin.

In the end, he sends away the physicians and courtiers and priests and will allow no one to tend him but Horatio. The unassuming scholar is still the only one whose judgment he trusts. His lords and gentlemen have turned away from him already, impatient for his death, jostling for position in support of their favored candidates for his replacement. Only one man has never left his side, and in his eyes he sees the whole world watching.

He frets to Horatio: how wounded is the name he leaves behind! He is parodied mercilessly by the younger courtiers. They mock him behind his back, as he once made fun of old Polonius, with his slippers and his spectacles. His well-reasoned advice is ignored, his philosophical soliloquies thought to be antique clichés, no more. They do not want to hear his tales of youth—how once, at University, he played upon the stage. They cannot believe he was ever young, ever beautiful.

But in Horatio's verses still he lives, forever young. Horatio brings the book to Hamlet's side. The king is half-blind with cataracts, and racked with a painful illness hanging all about his heart. But as Horatio reads, the image springs alive of Prince Hamlet, reborn in full and perfect form, perpetually straddling the cusp of manhood and impetuous youth.

Horatio is an old man now himself, though rather more cautiously kept than his master—and he spends out his labored breath to read the lines aloud. By force of will the poet has delayed his own quietus to render the life of his ever-living love in blank verse. From the evidence of his nightmares and the prince's scribbled thoughts, painstakingly deciphered through the various inconsistencies of spelling and of hand, Horatio has pieced together a tale of what might have been.

Into the common tragedy of ordinary life, he threads a purpose for all this suffering. In his fiction, Hamlet's losses are not inevitabilities, dealt at random by the fickle hand of Fate, but are embraced willingly, in pursuit of a nobler cause, as Horatio reports.

But, after the final page of the promptbook has been turned, the last act played upon his mind's eye, the old king is troubled still. Could he have ever been that hero Horatio saw in him? Given the chance to choose to be or not to be, would he have sacrificed his future to repay the sins of the past? Would he have placed such heed in the unproven prophecies of his soul, if he knew how much hung upon his choice? He needs another scene, a speech, a line explaining why. Only the most deranged of men, the most callow and cruel, could pursue his ideals so relentlessly. It would take a madman, he whispers, a lunatic.

Wouldn't it?

But he receives no answer. His duties at last discharged, Horatio has closed the book, and closed his eyes, and all the rest is silence.

*N*ah, you're turning it the wrong way, Captain. It's not winding, see? The little needles on the face just keep spinning around and round."

"I thought those were supposed to spin. Isn't that how the bloody thing works?"

"But not so fast, like." The mate takes up the watch from over his captain's shoulder. "See, this needle travels once around each hour, and the other one is like a dial, and makes one rotation in the morning and one afternoons. You need to twist it backwards to wind it."

"I just tried that," the captain huffs. "It gave a pip, and the dial spun back around, and I was right where I began this absurd chapter."

"Well, you've got it all out of joint," the mate says, shaking the timelesspiece. "It's going the wrong way around now, and I can't extract the key."

The captain throws up his hands, cursing young men and newfangled gadgetry.

"Well, ask the rum lubber you took it off, then, before he goes ashore at Elsinore," says Antonio to the captain. "Where is he, anyway?"

"Feeding the fishes." From his place at the helm, the captain gestures down to the foredeck, where Horatio is still bent double at rail, spilling out his guts into the deep.

*A*t that moment, I too was suffering from a crisis of emesis, though not seasickness. My rosebushes, poor dears, already bore the brunt of sibling rivalry nearly every morning. In competition with my swelling belly, they sent out new growth at an alarming rate. By springtime, they had begun to crawl into the windows of the rooms my husband had designated for the nursery, sending shoots breaking through shutter-hinges to let in the light.

Within a handful of years, they had clambered over and even through the roof, sealing the room in a ceiling of leaves, a trompe d'oeil brought to life. My husband worried about leaks, but on stormy dark nights the canopy of intertwining canes drinks up the rain, keeping foul weather from the tender heir as well as any thatch.

Already transgressing all expectations, the child had the audacity to be born female. Taking after all her fathers and none, she was the most-desired increase of all fairest creatures—beauty's rose, bred in a briar patch.

When she is old enough to speak and understand, I open a locked cupboard, taking out a book with a lambskin cover quilted in thread of gold.

"Your father's book," I call it, stroking at the yellowed suede, the same shade as my roses. A book pieced together from stolen scraps, bound in a forgotten suit of sabel.

Then the rosebuds snuggle down in their swaddling, and the blooms all turn their faces to the firelight. The actors, as I told you, are all spirits. Melted into air as mist, they will re-form and fall again as rain. They are huddled together, all compact in the infinite wings of the imagination's stage, still waiting for belief to give them life. And those with breath to hold, hold breath, all listening for the moment when the child says, "Tell me a story, Mama."

And this is the story she told.

Acknowledgments

I would like to thank my brilliant editor, Rakesh Satyal, and my agent, Mitchell Waters, both for daring to publish this novel so close to my heart, and for their astute critique and assistance in the preparation of the manuscript. The Institute for Humane Studies, the Arts Council England, and the Arch and Bruce Brown Foundation offered generous support through grants and awards.

I am extremely grateful to Andrew Motion, and to the many friends who read early (or late!) drafts and offered advice, encouragement, and sometimes a shoulder to cry on: Donald Currie, Linda Caprini, Steffen Silvis, Kathleen Worley, Theresa Patterson, Tahmima Anam, Joe Treasure, Jemiah Jefferson, Molly Bauckham, and Jon Kiparsky. Thanks also to my wonderfully supportive and loving family: Satisha Hermes-Smith, Arthur Smith, Jeremy Capps, and Oreo.